Praise for Anna Jacobs

'[Anna Jacobs' books have an] impressive grasp of human emotions'
The Sunday Times

'A powerful and absorbing saga – a fine example of family strife and struggle set in a bygone age'
Hartlepool Mail

'Anna Jacobs' books are deservedly popular. She is one of the best writers of Lancashire sagas around'
Historical Novels Review

'A compelling read'
Sun

'This is a rare thing, a pacy page-turner with a ripping plot and characters you care about . . . [Anna Jacobs is] especially big on resourceful, admirable women. Great stuff!'
Daily Mail

'Catherine Cookson fans will cheer!'
Peterborough Evening Telegraph

ANNA
JACOBS

One Perfect Family

Ellindale Saga Book Four

HODDER

First published in Great Britain in 2019 by Hodder & Stoughton
An Hachette UK company

This paperback edition published in 2019

4

A CIP catalogue record for this title is
available from the British Library

Paperback ISBN 978 1 473 67329 8
eBook ISBN 978 1 473 67328 1

Typeset in Plantin Light by Palimpsest Book Production Limited,
Falkirk, Stirlingshire

Printed and bound in Great Britain by Clays Ltd, Elcograf S.p.A.

Hodder & Stoughton policy is to use papers that are natural, renewable
and recyclable products and made from wood grown in sustainable forests.
The logging and manufacturing processes are expected to conform to
the environmental regulations of the country of origin.

Hodder & Stoughton Ltd
Carmelite House
50 Victoria Embankment
London EC4Y 0DZ

www.hodder.co.uk

Dear readers,

I hope you enjoy the fourth book in this series, which is set further up my imaginary Pennine valley from the town of Rivenshaw (also invented) in a tiny village I've called Ellindale. All the stories in this series are set during the first half of the 1930s. It was fascinating researching that era. Part of my research was to scan my memories for tales of my parents' teenage years.

I was going to focus more on Wilf in this book, but the minute I started to 'see' Crazy Tam, he took over the central role in the story. He is called that because he is so impulsive, especially when he sees an injustice happening. And that's how the story started – both in my head and on the page – Tam saving a child from being bullied. He also changed age from about sixty-five to fifty as I wrote. It's like that sometimes: characters leap into life.

Some authors plan their stories in great detail. I can't do that – I know because in my early days as a storyteller, I tried to plan one, only to discard the plot I'd worked so hard on after I'd written a couple of chapters. Why? Because better ideas popped into my head about what was going to happen. Where do these ideas come from? I have no idea. I was born with stories humming round my skull, even at the age of two, which is the earliest I remember making up stories about imaginary people.

Once I get going, the details of my stories often come to me during sleepless nights and it's like watching a movie. Even then I don't see a whole story, just the next few chapters.

I remember a lot of things about my childhood that took place a decade after this tale. There were some children, especially those who were different, who were mocked and treated shockingly by nasty people. Maybe that's why my father and sister got involved in social work and both made significant contributions, especially to the lives of children with intellectual disabilities.

My father became a Director of Social Services. He started the first youth club for such children in England, and I don't know who had more fun when they attended the weekly meetings, him or them. He hit world headlines in the '70s when he took over managing mental health services for a northern town and found several women who'd been locked up in mental asylums for fifty or sixty years – for having illegitimate babies. Of course, the babies had been taken away from them.

He got the women out of that place very quickly but some of them were too frail to be exposed to the media. A few of them had no family left, so he had them to tea every now and then. However, one of these women later got married – and my father was best man at her wedding!

I am very proud of my father. I'm just as proud of my sister, who ended up as headmistress of a special school for children with both physical and intellectual disabilities. She won a Lifetime Achievement award for her pioneering work in developing their social skills, both in and beyond her 'day job'.

So it's not surprising that I used an autistic girl as one of the main characters of this book, is it? There wasn't even a word for that behaviour pattern in the 1930s. See how Jinna blossoms when included in normal life by Tam!

And see how his impulsiveness provides him with the

family he'd always longed for as he helps two other children.

Enjoy your fourth visit to Ellindale!

Anna

NB. If you're interested in what England was really like in the 1930s, try reading J.B. Priestley's *English Journey*. He went round England and wrote about what he saw in a most entertaining manner, thus providing me with a great research resource and an enjoyable read. Thank you, Mr Priestley!

In Memoriam

This book is dedicated with much love to the memory of my last 'oldie'. My dear Auntie Connie (Constance Heyworth née Wild) died in March 2018 aged ninety-two. She was a second mother to my sister and me, and I took my first steps as a tiny child to walk into her arms. She was a delightful person, not an ounce of malice in her and could make friends with anyone she sat next to. We should all be remembered so lovingly!

Acknowledgements

My thanks to Helen Day and her wonderful collection of Ladybird books for supplying me with suitable reading material for small children in the 1930s.

I

Spring 1934

Tam stopped in a village on the outskirts of Wolverhampton. He'd visited Miss Parkins' house each spring for the past decade, ever since work became scarce in Lancashire. He preferred to go on the tramp, looking for jobs here and there, rather than apply for poor relief. He had a knack for finding work, too. Most of the time, anyway.

By this time he had one or two regulars like Miss Parkins, elderly ladies who wanted their gardens setting in order or needed odd jobs doing round the house and saved them up for him. He was handy at such tasks, if he said so himself.

But this year there was something wrong about the house. It looked – well, deserted. He hoped the old lady was all right. He'd found a lovely book in a second-hand shop to give to her, in return for all the books she'd given him over the years.

He opened the gate of the little semi-detached house and trundled his handcart round to the back door, as usual. As he raised his hand to knock, he saw a notice inside the glass window in the top half of the door: *Tam Crawford, please contact Mrs Brown next door.*

So he went round to see the neighbour, this time leaving his cart at the front.

Mrs Brown opened the door before he even got to it.

'I saw you coming, Tam. I told the lawyer you'd turn up about now. Wait there.'

She reappeared with an unsealed envelope. 'This is for you. It says you have to go and see Mr Eggleston as soon as you can.'

'Where's Miss Parkins?'

'Dead two months ago, just slipped away in her sleep, poor dear.'

'Aw, I'm sorry to hear that.'

'I'm sorry to lose a good neighbour. The house goes to her nephew and he's moving his family in soon, now that they've settled all the legal fussation.'

'Thank you.'

Since she didn't offer him a cup of tea, he walked back to the road, where he pulled the letter out and studied it. The lawyer had an address in the village, so no time like the present. At a guess, Miss Parkins might have left him some books. He hoped so. She'd taught him to enjoy reading and he couldn't do without books now.

Mr Eggleston kept him waiting for nearly an hour, but Tam didn't mind because they'd set out newspapers for clients to read.

When he was called through, the lawyer studied him before gesturing to a chair on the other side of his desk. 'Please sit down, Mr Crawford.'

He did so and waited.

'You'll have heard that Miss Parkins has died.'

'Yes. I was sorry.'

'She's left you a bequest.'

'That's kind of her.' He waited.

'It's three hundred pounds.'

Tam choked and it was a couple of minutes before he'd finished coughing and spluttering, and even longer before he'd managed to pull himself together. That was a fortune to a man like him.

The lawyer was smiling slightly. 'I'd guess this comes as a surprise.'

'Aye. A big surprise. That's a lot of money. Why would she do that?'

'She said she'd enjoyed your company for the past ten years, but felt you needed a fresh start in life. She hopes you'll spend the money on a house or shop, and settle down in Lancashire, instead of tramping all over the country. Oh, and she's left you all her books as well.'

Tam swallowed hard and murmured 'Mmm' to show he was still listening.

'She also wanted me to tell you she hopes you'll use some of the money to help people whenever you can. She respected you greatly for sharing what little you had with other people in need.'

He shrugged, feeling embarrassed. 'I do my bit when I can. People think it's daft of me, but there you are. I don't like to see children in trouble.'

'Nor do I, Mr Crawford, nor do I. Now, let's get down to practicalities. Do you have a bank account? We've been instructed to pay the money straight into a bank, you see. Miss Parkins was very emphatic about that. She said you were too kind sometimes and she didn't want you carrying money around in your pockets and frittering it away. She, um, also said people called you "Crazy Tam" with some reason. May I ask why?'

He shrugged. 'I've got a bit of a temper, especially when I see someone hurting a child. And also, I've been known to rush into things without thinking them through.'

He didn't want to dwell on that because he hadn't done anything impulsive for a while now. 'And, to answer your other question, I've got a little bit put by in the Yorkshire

Penny Bank.' Nothing like three hundred pounds, though!

'Good.' The lawyer stood up and shook his hand. 'Congratulations on your bequest. I hope you'll make good use of it. I'll get my clerk to attend to the paperwork and then he'll take you to the bank and make arrangements about giving you the books.'

And that was that.

When he came out of the bank Tam didn't know where to go. He'd counted on a couple of weeks staying at Miss Parkins' house in her garden shed, because it was still early spring and the nights could be quite cold.

He stopped dead as it hit him again. *Three hundred pounds!* It had taken him years of scrimping to save thirty pounds, and that would sound like a fortune to many people. Three hundred made him feel – unsettled, different. He'd better not tell people about his legacy. It was safer.

As he walked slowly along the street pushing his handcart, he passed a place selling used cars and as usual, he stopped to look at them. He'd learned to drive in the army during the war, like a lot of chaps, and had done odd jobs that involved driving over the years, so had kept his hand in.

He thought of how far he'd walked in the past month to get here and how he got tired more quickly these days. Well, he'd be fifty next birthday, wouldn't he? He'd just have a look at the cars, he decided. The ones here were nice, but too expensive for a chap like him.

A few minutes later he spotted a small Morris van round the back of the display area and went to have a look at it. It was several years old, of course, but vans like this were usually good runners.

A salesman came out of the building, studied him and hesitated.

Yes, Tam thought, look down your nose at me, why don't

you? I can't wear good clothes for tramping the roads. Just to put the chap in his place, he called out, 'How much is this van?'

Looking surprised, the man hurried over. 'Thirty pounds, sir.'

'You're kidding me. It's been in an accident. Look at the back of it, all battered those doors are.'

'But the motor is good and so is the rest of the bodywork. The van would be more expensive if there weren't a few little dents.'

'A few big dents, you mean.' Tam walked round it again. 'I'll give you twenty pounds for it.'

'*What?* Now who's kidding?' The salesman forced a laugh.

Tam shrugged and turned as if to walk away.

'Twenty-five pounds, then.'

'Twenty and not a penny more – as long as the engine is in good condition. I'd have to check that first.'

'I'd lose money on that.'

'No, you wouldn't. You can't have paid more than ten pounds for it with all those dents.'

They haggled for a while, then the salesman got the engine running and it did sound smooth. Tam asked if he could drive it round the block, so they both got in.

Eh, it was good to be driving again. And the man was right. It was a nice little runner. The brakes were good and the tyres still had plenty of wear in them. It was just the bodywork at the back that was a mess.

When they got back, Tam folded his arms across his chest and said firmly, 'Twenty pounds.'

'You'll bankrupt me.' The man stuck out one hand and they shook on it.

It wasn't till then that Tam realised what he had done. He'd turned into Crazy Tam again and done something on sheer impulse.

He could still say he'd changed his mind. Couldn't he?

He looked at the van. No, he wasn't going to change his mind. He reckoned he'd be able to make a living with it as a carrier of small loads. 'I'll have to go to the bank to get the money out. I hadn't planned to buy a van today.'

'It'll be waiting for you here. Though I'd rather you just told me if you've changed your mind.'

'I haven't changed my mind. Can I leave my handcart here? Will that convince you I want to buy it?'

The man brightened. 'Yes, sir. Of course you can. I'll keep my eye on it.' He gave directions to the nearest Yorkshire Penny Bank.

Tam strode off down the street and when he turned the corner he had to lean against the wall, because he felt all shuddery.

He'd promised himself not to do anything without serious thought.

Crazy Tam had struck again.

Well, this would probably work out all right, but it would be the last time he gave way to an impulse, the very last.

Definitely.

A week later a stallholder at the Rivenshaw weekly market nudged the woman at the next stall. 'Hey, look. Isn't that Crazy Tam?'

She looked round. 'So it is! Haven't seen him for ages, must be a couple of years or more since he's passed through. I thought he might have died somewhere on his travels.'

'Not him. He's a tough one, good for years yet.'

'He must be getting on though.'

Ozzy shrugged. 'Tam's the same age as me, nearly fifty. That's not old, not if you don't *feel* old.'

'I wonder where he's been this time.'

'Who knows? He told me once he just sets off without

knowing where he'll end up. I've never seen him driving a van before, though. He was pushing a handcart last time he came to Rivenshaw. I wonder if the van's his? How can he afford that?' Ozzy waved one hand to the man getting out of the shabby little vehicle.

Tam waved back and yelled, 'Be back soon.' He hung a scuffed leather satchel crosswise on his body and started to walk in the other direction. He'd only gone a few steps along the edge of Market Square when he stopped dead, staring into the yard at the side of the pub. He turned round and started running back to the stalls, looking furiously angry.

'Uh-oh! Watch out for storms,' the woman said. 'When he gets that look on his face, there's no telling what he'll do.'

Tam had hauled off the leather satchel as he ran and now flung it at Ozzy. 'Look after that for me, lad.' Then he ran back to the half-open gate, pausing for a moment to stare into the yard, keeping most of his body out of sight.

Ozzy said abruptly, 'It looks like he's found trouble. He goes mad if he sees someone getting hurt, even an animal.'

'Yes. He's a nice chap. But crazy.'

'He might need help. You keep an eye on the satchel and on my stall as well, Hetty lass. I bet it's that bunch of nasty youngsters who've started hanging around in that yard. They think no one's noticed the way they sneak in and out, but me an' some of the chaps are keeping an eye on them on market days. You can't be too careful when there's money changing hands.'

Tam peered into the yard again but still couldn't see exactly who the group of lads had cornered, only he knew what he'd heard. It must be someone smaller than them because he couldn't see who it was.

One of the lads was chanting, 'Dummy! Dummy! Cry for

your mummy.' That was what had caught his attention – that and a child's shrill cry of pain.

He still couldn't see the victim but he heard a whimper, so stayed where he was for a moment or two, trying to work out who was doing what. He didn't recognise the thin lad towering over the others in the group, but he seemed to be the ringleader.

The lad laughed and yelled, 'Who wants to poke the dummy next? Let's see who can make her cry the loudest!'

Raucous laughter followed.

As the lad grabbed the arm of the person hidden by the group and tugged her forward, Tam saw that it was a girl. Her clothes were torn and she was trying desperately to pull away. But her tormenter held her arms above her head while another lad jabbed her hard in the chest, making her cry out again.

'She can't talk but we can make her squeal.'

'My turn.'

As the next lad pulled back his hand for a jab, Tam erupted into the group of lads before they realised what was happening. Grabbing the one about to jab the lass with his hand, he hurled him sideways, sending him bouncing against the wall so hard he fell to the ground.

He turned to the leader, who was still holding her. 'Let go of her, you!'

The lad, who was taller than him, laughed. 'Who's going to make me? Not you, old man. If you—'

Tam took him by surprise, punching him on the side of the jaw and sending him staggering backwards. But the lad quickly regained his balance and shoved his victim forward into Tam, who had to grab her or she'd have fallen.

'You're wasting your time, old man. I'll find her again whenever I want to. See if I don't.'

As the bully turned to run away, Ozzy hurried into the

yard and moved forward to help Tam with the remaining lads. One of the two men who'd followed him shut the gate behind him with a thump.

The ringleader immediately changed direction, jumped on to a barrel and clambered over the high wall, disappearing from sight before anyone could catch hold of him.

The other two backed away from the men.

The girl was struggling now to get away from Tam, but he shushed her gently. 'It's all right, lass. It's all right. I won't let them hurt you again. Shh, now. Shh. Stand still.'

They'd called her 'Dummy' but as she looked up at him, he was sure there was intelligence shining in those bright blue eyes. She didn't speak but she must have understood what he'd said because she stopped struggling and stood stiffly beside him.

'That's a good lass,' he murmured. 'Stay near me till we've got rid of the other two lads who were hurting you.'

Keeping one arm lightly round her shoulders, he turned to ask them, 'What the hell did you think you were doing?'

'It was just a bit of fun. She's a dummy. Can't speak. No use to anyone.'

'And you think that's a reason to torment her?' He looked at Ozzy. 'Get rid of these louts before I forget myself. If I see them hurting anyone again, I'll knock them into the middle of next week.'

Ozzy clouted the one who'd poked the girl and shoved him towards the gate. 'Don't come anywhere near this yard again, either. I'm like my friend, can't stand bullying. If I see you hurting this lass or anyone else, I'll teach you what painful feels like, by hell I will.'

Both lads rushed for the gate, nearly falling through it in their eagerness to get away.

The girl was left standing beside Tam, stiff and wary but not moving away from him. He wondered for a moment why no one had come out of the pub to investigate the noise, but now wasn't the time to find out. If his baby daughter had lived, she'd have been about this age, he reckoned. Twelve or so. He sometimes wondered what his child would have been like if she'd grown up.

Eh, what was he thinking about that for? It had happened years ago. 'Anyone know who the lass is?'

Ozzy moved closer. 'I don't know her name but she lives out at Backshaw Moss with her mother. She comes to the market with Sarey Timmins every now and then, because the mother's not been well for a while. Kind woman, Sarey. It isn't easy to look after a dummy as she can't think or speak properly. Most folk wouldn't even try.'

Tam noticed the girl glare at Ozzy as he said that, so he continued to watch her. Once again, it seemed to him that she'd understood perfectly well what people had been saying. Was she unable to speak or didn't she want to?

'Can someone fetch Sarey?' he said. 'I don't want to take the poor lass out into the market till we can get her decent. Eh, what's the world coming to? Those young devils have even ripped her blouse and skirt.'

'I'll fetch Sarey.' One man ran off.

'They're a bad lot, them lads,' Ozzy said. 'The leader's Johnny Houghton's eldest. Like father, like son, eh? If they had a job to use up their energy, they'd not get into mischief so often. They tried to steal from my stall last week but we stall keepers not only keep our eyes open ourselves, we watch each other's stuff, so the lads didn't get away with it.'

'Them Houghtons have been causing trouble since I were a lad,' Tam said grimly.

'You're right there. I've no time for people like them, thieving and bullying because they're too lazy to work. I feel sorry for folk who steal food because they can't find work, and are hungry and desperate, but we're all doing it hard these days, and I can't help all the world, can I?'

'Better times are coming,' Tam said confidently. 'I've seen it down south.'

'Huh! I'll believe that when they arrive here in the valley.'

A woman came hurrying into the yard just then, her face lined and worn, her clothes shabby. 'Eh, Jinna, why did you wander off?'

She didn't wait for an answer, but said to Tam, 'The lass doesn't speak much but she talks to me a bit when she's not frightened. I bring her to market sometimes to give her poor mam a rest and she usually sits there good as gold, drawing. Only I couldn't find much paper for her today, and her pencil's worn down to a stub, so she wandered off.'

She looked at Tam again, frowning slightly. 'Jinna doesn't often go to strangers.'

He shrugged. 'I'm fond of children, most of 'em anyway. What's wrong with this one's mother?'

'She's not at all well.' Sarey glanced at Jinna and shook her head. 'I don't know what's going to happen to the poor creature when her mother, um, leaves us, but it won't be long before we find out.'

He took her point. 'That bad, is it?'

'Aye. It's a cruel world.'

'Where do they live?'

'Backshaw Moss, upper end. They've got a room in Mossy Row, same house as my friend Phyllis. That's how I know them.' She looked back towards the stalls. 'I see you've got yourself a van. You wouldn't have time to take Jinna home for me, would you, Tam? She's a bit restless today and I can't watch her all the time. I daren't miss the market. My family relies on what I can buy and sell here.'

He looked sideways and once again, it seemed to him that Jinna had understood every word spoken, because she was looking sad now. 'Aye. I'll take her home. I'm going up to Ellindale, so Backshaw Moss isn't far out of my way. But first we'll need to get her a new blouse and skirt. Look what they've done to her clothes! If I give you some money can you find her something at the second-hand clothes stall?' He held out a couple of coins.

She looked at him in surprise as she took them. 'That's kind of you. Yes, of course I can. I won't be long.'

As she left, the girl tried to follow her and Tam said gently, 'Stay here till she gets you some new clothes. That blouse is torn and so is your skirt, and they're too small for you anyway.'

She looked down at herself with the gaze of an innocent child, not a young woman aware of her own body.

It wasn't long before Sarey returned, carrying some clothes over one arm. 'I think these will fit her. Turn your backs, please, gentlemen.'

When the men were allowed to look again, Tam saw that Jinna was wearing the new clothes and stroking the blouse, which was a pretty shade of blue.

Sarey looked back towards the market. 'I really do have to go. There's someone waiting at my stall. Better come and get Jinna's drawings before you set off, Tam. She won't go back without them.'

He nodded and turned to Ozzy. 'Thanks for your help today, lad. I'll see you around.'

'Are you going to stay in the valley for a while this time or are you just passing through?'

'Depends. I won't stay in Rivenshaw because I'm not one for towns, but maybe I'll find somewhere to live further up the valley, in Ellindale. I like it up the top near the moors.'

He turned to Jinna. 'Come with me, lass. I'll give you a ride home in my van.'

She looked at Sarey, who said slowly and clearly, 'Go

home with Tam. In his van. Go home now. Get your drawings first.'

The girl nodded and followed her to the stall.

There, he thought. She does understand. Definitely.

2

Back at the market, Tam retrieved his satchel from Hetty, explained what he was doing and waited next to Sarey's stall while Jinna gathered up some crumpled pieces of paper that were obviously precious to her, trying in vain to smooth them out.

'She lives at Number Eight, Mossy Lane, think on,' Sarey called after him.

When he led the way across to the van, Jinna followed. He opened the door to the passenger seat but she hesitated, looking across at Sarey once again. The woman made a shooing motion with her hands.

'You'll have to show me which is your house,' he said once Jinna had got in.

She nodded.

He was, he admitted to himself, intrigued by this scrawny scrap of a girl. He'd met other folk who couldn't speak, but they were usually dim-witted with it. Unless he was very much mistaken, Jinna was just as clever as the next person.

So why didn't she speak?

Eh, kids were strange creatures and yet he wished he had a house full of them. He'd only had the one child – Pansy they'd called her – and she'd died when she was three. Measles was a terrible scourge for small children. His wife had simply faded away after that from grief and had died of a bad cold that had gone to her chest. Years ago, that had been. He'd have trouble even remembering Bertha's face if he hadn't kept his one photo of her and Pansy.

People had told him he should remarry. They meant well, but it had taken him time to get over such terrible losses and anyway, it'd been hard to find work that lasted, with jobs getting fewer and fewer all through the twenties. He couldn't have afforded to support another wife then and anyway, that's when he'd started travelling south to find work.

It had been a good decision. At first he'd gone hungry, but he'd gradually learned to sniff out temporary work nearly everywhere he went.

He hadn't sniffed out anywhere to settle permanently, though, because he always came back to the moors near which he'd grown up. He'd have stayed in Lancashire, or even across in Yorkshire, but the trouble was, work was mainly to be found in the south.

Things *were* changing, though, whatever Ozzy said. Tam had seen it with his own eyes. There were schemes being set up in some places to help the unemployed and since the government started giving out grants to encourage it, more house building was going on in the south.

Miss Parkins, the old lady he'd worked for every year for a week or two in spring, had let him sleep in her garden shed and fed him a meal in return for chatting to her in the evenings. Poor Miss Parkins! She'd been lonely, he reckoned. She used to be a teacher till she grew too old and had taught him all sorts of things.

One of them was that as far back as 1924 there had been an act of parliament to give grants to local councils to build houses, and quite a lot of towns had taken advantage of that. He'd been astonished to find that out. Why hadn't Rivenshaw Town Council done something to earn a grant, eh? He'd like to ask the mayor and councillors.

Then there had been another act of parliament four years

ago in 1930, Miss Parkins had said, giving local councils grants for slum clearance, on condition they rehoused the people who'd lived in the slums. There had only been a token attempt to do that in Rivenshaw, as far as he could tell.

Eh, they needed some people on the council with a bit of fire in their bellies, they did that.

He'd read a lot on his travels after Miss Parkins had started him off with the gift of a couple of books. He hadn't had much choice about *what* he read. It was just a question of what he could get hold of, so he'd read all sorts of books.

He didn't know where the years had gone, only that it was too late now for him to start a family, more's the pity. But not too late to do something with the money that the old lady had left him.

He was sorry Miss Parkins had gone. He'd miss her sharp insights into the world. He didn't intend to tell anyone about his windfall when he got back to Rivenshaw. It seemed a huge amount to him and would set him apart from any new friends he made.

Tam drove to the northern end of Rivenshaw and turned right off Reservoir Road, heading towards Birch End. The girl sat stiff and silent on the seat beside him and he realised suddenly that he'd been so lost in thought he hadn't even tried to chat to her.

His possessions rattled about in the back of the van. He'd packed them carefully when he started his journey home, had even pulled apart the handcart and put the pieces into the van. But however careful he was, something kept getting loose.

Good thing he had a lock on the back doors of his van because he wasn't happy to have to take it to Mossy Lane. The council should have got a grant to knock that narrow little street down years ago, yes, and the alleys behind it, because it was nothing but a slum and a breeding ground for thieves and worse. He was surprised the ramshackle buildings hadn't fallen down of their own accord.

Backshaw Moss was an outlier in the various districts that were counted as part of Rivenshaw. It lay closer to Birch End, really, but that was town boundaries for you. They rarely made sense. He supposed they'd grown higgledy-piggledy, based on some farmer selling land and it being grabbed as 'part of' an established area.

He didn't need to ask directions. He'd been born nearby, had lived here till he got married. Eh, what a long time ago that seemed now. He didn't feel any different in body from how he had in his youth, though he was a lot wiser in his head in his middle years. By hell, yes!

When he stopped the van, he told Jinna gently to get out and wait for him. He wanted to lock the doors of the vehicle carefully before leaving it.

Unfortunately she didn't wait for him. She ran into the house still clutching those dratted papers.

He finished locking the doors, slung his satchel across his body and followed her inside. Like most others round here, Number Eight was occupied by several families. A youngish man was standing at the front door watching what he was doing.

Tam stopped next to him. 'Which room does that lass live in?'

'Jinna? In the attic. Just her and her mother up there. Hey, wait!'

Tam turned.

'It's not safe to leave a loaded van here. People can see that it's full of stuff through the front window. I can keep an eye on it for sixpence.'

He should have thought of that extra precaution. 'I'll give you threepence. I'm not made of money.'

'All right.'

Tam studied the man's face, then nodded. He didn't have a shifty look. 'Thanks.'

He climbed two flights of stairs and found only one door at the top, half-open, so pushed it fully open and went inside.

Jinna was standing by the bed, gently shaking the woman lying on it and saying, 'Mam, wake up. Mam.'

Tam knew at a glance that it was no good doing that. The woman had died. He'd seen enough dead people to be sure of that.

He went across and laid one hand on Jinna's. 'Stop that, love. Your mam's dead.'

She turned to him, her eyes wide with sudden horror. She still didn't speak, but she shook her head a few times as if trying to deny it.

For a few moments he couldn't think what to do, then he decided he needed help, so went to the top of the stairs and yelled at the top of his voice, 'Someone come and help me.'

A woman called back. 'What's wrong?'

'There's a dead woman up here.'

He heard her exclaim in shock, then two sets of footsteps echoed up the stairwell. An older woman arrived first, presumably from the floor below, then a younger woman.

The older one came across to the bed and tut-tutted softly. 'Eh, the pity of it. And her only thirty. Sit on your chair, Jinna love. *Sit on your chair.*'

The girl did as she was told.

The newcomer closed the woman's staring eyes and covered her face with the ragged sheet, then turned to him. 'I'm Phyllis Gazwell. I've been Janet's neighbour for a few years. Eh, I didn't think she'd go yet. The poor thing's had a hard time of it lately.'

'Do we need to call a doctor?'

'I suppose we'll have to. You'll need a death certificate, won't you?'

'*I* will? Why would I need one?'

'Aren't you a relative?'

'No. I'm a complete stranger to them. I only brought Jinna home from the market to help Sarey out. There was trouble with some lads there, you see, bullying Jinna.'

'Oh, dear!' She went and yelled down the stairwell, 'Henty! Get yourself up here this minute.'

A lad came clattering upstairs. 'What, Mam?'

'Mrs Smith has died. We need Dr Fiske to come and see her. Go and tell him.'

The lad tried to peer past her and she shoved him back. 'Quick as you can, son.'

'Is this Dr Fiske new round here?' Tam asked. 'I haven't heard the name before.'

'Aye. He set up in Birch End late last year. Nice young chap. He'll come out on calls even for the likes of us, though he knows we can't pay him.' After a moment's thought, she added, 'Maybe we should send for someone from the council offices too. There aren't any relatives that I know of, so they'll have to do something about the lass.'

'They'll put her in the asylum,' the younger woman said with relish. 'And if you ask me, that's where a dummy like her belongs. I never feel comfortable when she's around, staring at everything like she never saw it before, and drawing stupid faces.'

'If you'd been kinder to her, she'd not have stared at you nor she wouldn't have drawn you looking like that.' Phyllis smiled. 'It was a cruel picture, but it was you all right. You look exactly like that when you're being nasty to someone.'

'Well! What a thing to say!'

'I speak as I see.'

Tam looked from one to the other in puzzlement. 'What have drawings to do with all this?'

'Haven't you seen that child's drawings?' Phyllis asked. 'If not, go and look at that pile of papers over there. You might as well. It'll be a while afore the doctor comes. She might not be good at speaking, but she's really good at drawing, that little lass is.'

He went across to the table and picked up the pile of papers. Immediately Jinna rushed across the room and snatched at them, but not before he'd seen the top one, a beautifully drawn image of the dead woman, sitting in a chair looking haggard beneath an attempt at a smile. It was as vivid as a photograph – and a good photograph at that.

'Can I please look at your drawings?' he asked gently.

Jinna only clasped them to her chest protectively.

'Please? I'll be very careful with them.'

'Let the man see them, Jinna love,' Phyllis said.

She frowned, then slowly held them out.

He put the papers on the table and leafed through the pile one by one, amazed at what he found. If he put them down crookedly, Jinna leaned over to adjust them, so he took more care and after that she left him to look at his own speed, though she still stood protectively nearby.

After a while, he turned to the neighbour. 'They're very good, like a proper artist's drawings. I'm Tam Crawford, by the way.'

She nodded, then looked across at the other neighbour, who was studying the meagre possessions on a shelf and still didn't bother to introduce herself. 'There's nothing anyone can do, so you might as well go back downstairs, Maddy Dawkins. You're only staying to see what you can pick up.'

'I've as much right to be here as you have.'

'Oh, have you? Well, Janet never let you come in here, did she? So I'll only be respecting her wishes if I throw you out.' She took a threatening step forward and the other woman retreated a couple of steps.

'Go on! Get out, I said!'

Another step and a brandished fist made the woman leave in a hurry.

'Sorry about that,' Phyllis said. 'But she'd pinch things if I left her on her own here.'

Tam waited till he had Jinna's attention again. 'Your drawings are beautiful, lass.'

She smiled shyly, the first time he had seen her smile.

Turning to Phyllis, who was watching him with a satisfied expression, as if she'd known how he'd react, he asked, 'Did Jinna really do these on her own?' They were exquisite, in spite of some of them being drawn on crumpled scraps of paper. He'd never met anyone who could draw so meticulously. And all this with a stub of a pencil and probably nothing to rub marks out with? It beggared belief.

'Aye. It's all she can do, really, draw pictures. Not that she needs looking after, no, she can see to herself and put a bite of food together too, if there's any around. But she would only talk to her mam – talk properly, I mean. She does say things to me now and then, but she won't speak at all to strangers or to folk as are unkind to her like that silly biddy downstairs. And the poor thing gets really upset if you change anything in this room. Everything has to be put just so, especially her chair and that old umbrella she found last year. Her mam trained her to stay on the chair when told and I think she feels safe there now.'

'Are you sure there are no relatives? I could go and fetch them, if you like.'

'Janet told me once or twice she hadn't got no family left now.' Phyllis sighed. '*I* can't do anything more to help the lass than I do now, Mr Crawford. I can barely feed myself, my husband and son, let alone take on providing for Jinna as well. And we're all living in the one room, so where would a lass that age sleep? You know how things are these days.' She looked at him pleadingly, shame on her face.

'Aye. I do know, missus. Terrible hard times, these are, here in the north.'

There were footsteps on the stairs and the lad came back. 'Mrs Fiske says the doctor will come soon as he can. And Dennis downstairs says he needs help to keep folk away from your van, mister, and could you pay me twopence to stay with him?'

Tam could have used this as an excuse to leave, and had even opened his mouth to say he'd better be going, only somehow he couldn't do it. Not till he'd seen that the poor lass was going to be looked after. 'All right. I'll pay you, but not till I come out to get my van.'

With a whoop, the lad clattered back down the stairs.

'You'll need to pay that money to me,' Mrs Gazwell told Tam. 'I'm the one as has to make the money stretch out to feed him. He could eat for two, my son could, if I had enough food for two, that is.'

'All right. I'll pay you.'

Tam was beginning to feel as if he'd strayed into a house of mirrors at a fairground, where everything kept changing around you. He stole a quick glance at Jinna, who was sitting on the chair again, not moving anything except her head as she watched them with utter concentration. She was holding the dark green umbrella, as if it comforted her.

Her gaze kept moving to whoever was speaking at the time. She definitely wasn't deaf, not even slightly, he decided. She was looking anxious, as if she understood that something was very wrong. But how much did she understand about her own position?

Eh, what a thing to happen to him, and on his first day back in the valley too. It'd upset him for weeks, thinking of this.

He really ought to leave them to it and carry on to his cousin's farm, but however much he reasoned that it wasn't his responsibility, he couldn't bring himself to abandon that poor child. Though what he could do about her was more than he could work out, apart from making sure no one bullied her or knocked her around again till she had found a new home.

He wasn't going to rush into anything. He'd done his dash at impulsive behaviour buying the van.

It seemed a long time till he heard a car draw up outside.

3

Douglas Fiske stopped his car outside the row of shabby houses, unfolded his legs from behind the steering wheel and eased himself out. They ought to make cars for tall men, he thought, as he had done many times before, but he'd probably not be able to afford one if they did.

He took his medical bag in with him and left the car unlocked. Well, the lock was broken. He knew it'd be safe, though, not because there was nothing in it worth stealing but because no one in this area wanted to stop the doctor visiting them if they were sick.

He noticed the lad who'd come for him standing in the street and waved to him as he went inside. He knew where to go, had visited the poor woman here before, so took the stairs two at a time. Since the door was open, he called, 'Doctor Fiske here,' and walked straight in.

He saw the neighbour he'd met here before. She was a good woman, the sort who helped her neighbours whenever she could. 'Mrs Gazwell, isn't it? Did you send for me?'

'Yes, doctor. We found Mrs Smith dead in her bed.'

He went straight across to uncover the dead woman's face, his heart sinking as he saw the girl who didn't speak sitting nearby. The dead woman had once come to ask his help with her daughter, because she was afraid of what might happen if she died and left the girl on her own. He hadn't been able to suggest anything.

When Mrs Smith fell ill, she'd asked in despair why her

daughter wasn't like other children. All he could tell her was that occasionally people were born that way, not fitting in, not behaving as others did, finding it hard to deal with other people. They weren't usually dangerous, fortunately. But no one knew why it happened and there was no cure. Some were of limited intelligence but he'd heard tell of some who had special skills, and he suspected the girl was one of the latter, given her beautiful drawings.

Mrs Smith had wept then, quietly and despairingly, and he'd had to bring in his wife to calm her.

The child was sitting to one side now, staring – she often stared so fixedly it upset people. What was her name? Ah yes, Jinna. He said hello to her and received only a wary stare in return, so turned to the remaining person, a man he didn't know.

'Are you a relative?'

'No. I brought Jinna home from the market today to help Sarey, who'd been looking after her, and we found the mother lying there dead.'

Douglas turned back to Mrs Gazwell. 'Do *you* know of any relatives, however distant?'

'I'm sorry, doctor. Janet told me there were none.'

He hated this sort of situation, absolutely hated it, but as his wife pointed out regularly, he couldn't take in all the waifs and strays in the world. 'We'd better contact the council then.'

'What can they do?' Phyllis asked.

'Not much. They'll have to put the girl in Barton House.'

The stranger scowled at him. 'What? But that's the lunatic asylum! Jinna's not stupid or dangerous, anyone can see that, just . . . a bit different.'

'Nonetheless, if there's no family to take her in, it's the only place there is. She can't be left to wander the streets. May I ask who you are, sir?'

'Tam Crawford.'

'Do you live round here?'

'I used to years ago and may do so again if things work out as I hope.'

'I see. Then you can't help any more here, so you should go on your way.' Some people stayed around when there was a death out of sheer nosiness, and Douglas didn't think it right.

Tam didn't leave, though, couldn't – not when he looked at Jinna's innocent face. He couldn't bear the thought of them putting that poor child in Barton House, which was a terrible place. You could hear the mad folk screaming in there sometimes when you walked past the gates. And she'd be forced to fit in with their regime. They didn't ill treat their patients these days, he'd grant them that, but everyone had to obey the rules.

They wouldn't let Jinna sit and draw, and that'd kill her, he just knew it. Well, it was a fellow feeling. It'd kill him to be shut away from the fresh air.

He didn't know he was going to say it till the words came out. 'I could look after the lass if there's no one else to do it.'

The doctor looked at him suspiciously. 'Why would you do that?'

'I had a daughter once. She died. So did my wife. It'd be a comfort in my old age to have Jinna living with me.'

'I was going to ask you what your wife thinks about that, but if you're a widower, you can't take the child.'

Tam suddenly realised why the doctor had said that and he didn't blame Fiske for being careful. Some men fancied young girls in the wrong way. Well, thank you very much, he wasn't one of those rotten sods. Only, if he said he had a wife, he'd have to produce her. Oh, hell, he'd better just say he'd changed his mind.

But the words wouldn't come out. Instead, one of his tales popped into his mind and before he could stop himself, he'd pushed himself deeper into trouble. 'I married again recently. My second wife will be happy to look after Jinna. She loves children.'

'Then you'd better bring your wife to see me. I shall need to approve you taking in a child who isn't a relative. Where do you live?'

'We've just come back to the north. We want to settle in the valley, in Ellindale, I hope. I've been on the tramp for a few years. You know how it is these days.'

'Yes. I know only too well. But I'm not releasing Jinna into the care of a man of your age, especially one who's been wandering round the country and hasn't got a permanent home. A girl that age, with Jinna's problems, not only needs a woman's care but a settled place to live.'

They were all staring at Tam now and words suddenly failed him. It was Phyllis who came to his aid. 'Tam will look after the child properly, doctor. He's a good man. And Jinna's really taken to him.'

'That's as maybe. It's a pity *you* can't take her in.'

'I wish I could, but we only just get by as it is. We couldn't feed another mouth.'

'Yes, I understand that but still—'

'Tam's going to let her draw, you see. You know what she's like about that, doctor. If she's allowed to do that, she'll be no trouble at all. *You* understand that; you've given her paper and pencils yourself.'

The doctor's expression softened a little. 'Yes. If she were more normal she could even become an artist and earn money for her work. She's good enough to do portraits and sell them. But I doubt she'll ever change how she deals with the world, so she'll need looking after. Um, do *you* know the second Mrs Crawford and where is she, anyway?'

Phyllis smiled brightly at him. 'Of course I know her. She's a cousin of mine. She's visiting some relatives in Bury, so we'll have to fetch her home early and introduce you. Then you'll see how respectable she is.'

His expression was still suspicious. 'Bring her to see me and my wife when she gets back, then. If we consider Mrs Crawford suitable we'll allow her to look after the girl. Will you look after Jinna till your cousin can get here, Mrs Gazwell? I can give you a shilling or two for her food.'

'Yes, doctor. And thank you for coming.'

'I'll let the paupers' burial officer know and give him the death certificate. I've been expecting this for a while, sadly.'

He pulled out his watch and let out an impatient grunt. 'I have to go. I've a difficult birth to attend.'

He paused at the door to say slowly and firmly, 'Remember, I'm duty bound as a doctor to see that orphans are properly cared for, and I'm also morally bound, which is far more important to me.'

'We'll go and fetch Mrs Crawford back this very afternoon, doctor,' Phyllis said. 'Tam has a van. He can drive us there.'

When Dr Fiske had driven off, she looked across at Tam. 'You haven't got a wife, have you?'

'No. Not now. I did have one who died. That bit was true.'

'Then why did you offer to look after Jinna and say you had a second wife?'

He shrugged. 'I don't know. I can't stand to see caged birds, let alone caged children, and I know what Barton House is like. It'd drive a lass like that mad.'

'I agree.' Phyllis waited to see what he'd say. Was he going to carry this through or run away? She couldn't help smiling. He'd been tugging his mass of curly hair into wild tangles as he spoke, as if trying to pull the solution to this problem out of his brain. Now he was trying in vain to smooth it down again.

After a few seconds of silence, during which she wondered if she dare suggest the idea she'd had, the one that made her speak out on Tam's behalf, she decided to risk it. He could only say no, after all, and *he* hadn't come up with any solutions, had he?

'You could ask someone to pretend to be your wife. It's the only way to keep Jinna out of that place.'

'*What?* Don't be silly. Who could I ask? What woman would do that anyway, pretend to be married to someone she's never met before to help a lass who behaves strangely? No one that I've ever met. What's more, if the woman is respectable she'll want me to marry her properly.'

'You're right. It'd be better to actually marry someone – unless you've got another wife tucked away somewhere.'

'Not me. I'm a widower and have been for years.'

'Well then, as it happens, I have a cousin who needs a husband as desperately as you need a wife. But she has a grandson depending on her so you'd have to take on the pair of them.' Phyllis waited but Tam only stared at her open-mouthed. He didn't turn and walk away, though, so she decided to take that as an encouraging sign.

'My cousin's daughter died last year and the husband ran off and left the child, the rotter. My cousin heard later that he'd died after a brawl, and serve him right. Then, to cap it all, *her* husband died suddenly. He was a nice chap, seemed healthy but just keeled over and died one day. So there was only her and her grandson left. Eh, poor Cara, she's had a hard time lately.'

'If she's your cousin, people round here will know she isn't my wife, so that's a daft thing to suggest.'

'She's not from round here. She's been living over near Bury.'

'Well then, I can't produce her today, can I?'

'You could if you wanted. You've got a van. You could drive

over there with me to meet her, see whether you get on with one another, and bring her back if you do.'

'Just like that? Find a wife and bring her back all in one afternoon? She'd have to be desperate to agree to it.'

'She *is* desperate. I just told you so. It's that or go into the poorhouse. An' I can't help her because we're barely scraping a living ourselves.'

'Let me get this straight – you're trying to marry *me* off to your cousin?'

'Yes. I've made a few matches in my time and I'm good at it.' She tapped the side of her forehead. 'I can tell when two people are right together and I'll know about you and Cara once I see you together.'

'Hmm.'

'It'd make me happy to solve Jinna's problem too. I'm fond of that poor lass. She's been kept shut in one room like a caged animal, her mother's that frightened of people hurting her. And other kids do pick on ones who're different, you must have seen it. But to keep her shut away like that, well, it upset me. That's why I took her to the shops with me sometimes. An' then when Sarey met her, she took her to the market, just every now and then. We might not have much money but we help one another when we can. So . . . what do you think?'

Tam stared at her angrily. 'I think I should just get into my van and drive away, never come back to Rivenshaw again. That would solve *my* part of this problem very easily indeed.'

'Why did you offer to look after the girl in the first place, then, if the thought of it upsets you?'

'How do I know? It just popped out.'

'Do things often pop out and land you in trouble?'

He shrugged. 'Occasionally. That's why they call me Crazy Tam. I felt sorry for her, didn't I? I don't even have a home to take her to. Not exactly. Not yet.'

'What does that mean?'

He shrugged. 'Someone told me about a chap taking an old railway carriage up to Ellindale to live in, and I've seen the same thing happen down south. They put old carriages at the seaside and rent them out for people to have cheap holidays in, only some people live in them all the time.'

'This isn't the seaside.'

'Well, I happen to know about a piece of land I could buy, and that's up in Ellindale as well. I was thinking of buying a caravan to put on it, not a railway carriage, because a caravan is already fitted out. I happen to know someone who has a caravan to sell, as well.'

'There you are, then. Sounds like you know enough to solve everyone's problems, including your own. I reckon that's a good idea, getting a caravan. Well done!'

She looked at his indignant expression and a chuckle escaped her, then another. She covered her mouth, shaking her head, seeming unable to stop laughing.

'What the hell are you laughing about, woman?'

'You're going to do it, aren't you? Look after Jinna and pretend to have a wife. You just don't want to admit it to me yet.'

Silence hung in the air between them, then he let out his breath in a whoosh. 'I must have lost my wits but yes, I'm *considering* it. For Jinna's sake, that's all. I feel sorry for her. I might not like your cousin, though, and if I don't, I'm *not* marrying her. There are limits to what I'll do, even to help that poor lass.'

'You'll like Cara. She's a hard worker and a sensible soul. She doesn't deserve to be put in the poorhouse. She was working and scraping by even after her husband died till her grandson fell ill. Ned would have died if she hadn't stayed home to look after him, but she lost her job because of it.'

'Ha! I've just thought of another problem. *He* will know I'm not his grandfather.'

'No, he won't. He's not even three yet. He's a friendly little lad, who'll go to anyone as is kind to him.' Phyllis chuckled again and gave Tam a mock punch in the arm. 'Aw, what's it going to hurt to come and meet my cousin? She's about your age, I'd guess. What are you, fifty or so?'

He shrugged. 'Nearly fifty.'

'Well, she's forty-five, if I remember correctly. And we're agreed about one thing: I won't have her made unhappy. If you don't like Cara or she doesn't like you, you can bring me and her back to Rivenshaw and then drive off in your van and forget all about it.'

'What'll we do with Jinna in the meantime?'

'She'll have to come with us. We can't leave her here on her own with a dead body. Someone from the council might take her away to that horrible place if we do. I wouldn't put it past that stupid female downstairs to report her to the council because she's a spiteful devil and she didn't get on with Janet. And that reminds me, I'd better tell my Henty to come up and guard what's left of Janet's things. They'll get stolen once the body's been taken away otherwise.'

Tam tugged at his hair again. 'I must have gone stark staring mad to do this. And I promised myself not to . . . ' His voice trailed away as he looked at Jinna. Another silence, then he spread his hands in a gesture of helplessness. 'All right, Phyllis. I'll come and meet your cousin. But *you* will have to persuade the lass to come with us. An' here's the twopence I promised your Henty.'

He went out to tell the lad keeping an eye on his van that he'd paid the twopence to his mam. Henty looked so disappointed, Tam slipped him a penny for himself.

Phyllis brought Jinna down to the van, seeming to know exactly how to coax her into it. Jinna was carrying her umbrella and something wrapped in a ragged cloth. When it crackled, Tam realised it was the drawings.

'How did you persuade her to come?'

'You have to tell her exactly what's happening, all in simple words, no ifs and buts, no pretending. She takes everything people say literally. If you said it was raining cats and dogs, she'd expect to see them tumbling out of the sky and look up. *She* couldn't tell a lie to save her life, bless her.'

They put the drawings in the back of the van but Jinna kept hold of the umbrella. He waited till both of them were settled beside him in the front, squashed into the passenger seat. 'When we get to Bury, you'll have to tell me where to go.'

Phyllis beamed at him. 'I'll do that. Eh, I shall enjoy a drive out. What a treat!'

He couldn't help smiling back. She was a nice woman and it was lovely to see how she managed the girl. He'd have to remember what she'd said if this worked out.

It was a big if. Perhaps this was all a dream – or a nightmare – and he'd wake up suddenly.

As if reading his mind, Phyllis said in a soothing tone, 'You'll like Cara, lad, you'll see. She's a nice woman and quite bonny for her age.'

'Ha!' He still wasn't sure he wanted it to work out.

4

Cara Pruin struggled to control herself, but in the end she couldn't help it. She sat down and had a good weep, muffling the sobs so as not to wake her grandson from his nap.

She'd sold everything she possessed except for what she stood up in and a few other clothes, their oldest, ragged garments. She'd tramped the streets in shoes with holes in their soles looking for work, but as soon as people found out she was bringing up her grandson, they said the job was taken.

She looked across the room at him. Darling Ned. The only one of her family left to love.

She'd not eaten for two days so that he could have something but now every last crumb had gone and he'd been crying this morning, saying his belly hurt, till he fell asleep. No, she couldn't put it off any longer, she'd have to go to the poorhouse and ask for help, which meant they'd put her inside.

It was called the Public Assistance Institution these days, she'd seen it on the sign outside, but it might just as well be called by its old name, 'poorhouse', because the local council ran it in much the same way. They should knock the horrible old building down.

If you were a widow of her age, there weren't any pensions or dole payments available, not that she'd been able to find. And if you lived in a slum, which was the only place where she could afford a room, there weren't any fancy charities nearby providing soup kitchens. She'd had to walk three miles to get that sort of help and she was too weak to do it regularly in return for a bowl of watery soup and a piece of stale bread, let alone she had a little grandson to take with her who was too heavy to carry that far.

Going to the poorhouse was the last resort for her and for most other people. They'd take Ned away from her, from what she'd heard, and put him in with the other children, then set her to work in the laundry or scrubbing floors. They might even let him be adopted by someone wanting a child, because he was a bonny little lad and usually very healthy.

But at least he'd still be alive, unlike her daughter, and that would have to comfort her.

She woke him up, got him washed and dressed – no one was ever going to say that she didn't keep him clean – and then she gave herself a few more minutes to sit and cuddle him, singing his favourite songs to distract him from being hungry. In the end she could put it off no longer and picked up the bundle with the last of their things in it.

Anything left in the room could stay there. She'd told her neighbour to take whatever she wanted.

It wasn't far but she was too weary to walk fast, what with a small child and a bundle to carry. When she got to the gates of the poorhouse, she trudged slowly past it – couldn't go in, just couldn't force herself.

It wasn't till she saw a ragged woman begging on the street corner that she stopped again, shuddering. She wasn't going to bring Ned up as a homeless beggar. So she turned round and began to walk back towards the poorhouse, feeling sick with dread.

Phyllis said to Tam, 'Turn left here and it's the third house on the right. Cara has a room at the back.'

'How do you get here to see her?'

'The carter comes to Bury once a month and I pay him threepence to take me with him. I have to sit in the back with whatever load he's carrying. I hide under a tarpaulin so his boss doesn't see me, but it's worth it.'

'You'd better go in first and talk to this Cara, then.'

'All right. You stay here, Jinna love. I'll be back in a few minutes. Stay here.'

As Phyllis walked round to the back, she grimaced at the foul smells and piles of rubbish. This district was worse than Backshaw Moss, and that was saying something. She knocked on the door and a woman immediately poked her head out of next door.

'If it's Cara you're after, she's gone.'

'What do you mean, gone?'

'Gone off to the poorhouse. She hadn't any food left for the lad and she couldn't get a job however hard she tried. Pity. I was going to look after him while she worked for a penny or two a day, but no one would take her on.'

'When did she leave?'

'About half an hour ago. She's walking slowly, but you'll probably be too late and they'll have locked her inside now.'

Phyllis ran out to the car. 'Cara's gone to the poorhouse. We might have time to catch up with her before she goes inside. Drive as fast as you can. That way!'

She directed him and Tam drove along as fast as was safe, stopping at a grim old building. It looked even worse than Barton House in Rivenshaw, as if it was scowling at the world. There had been no sign of a woman and child on the way here.

'Looks like we're too late.'

He wasn't sure whether he was relieved or sorry about that. He'd been curious to see Phyllis's cousin.

She glared at him. 'Oh no, we're not. I won't let us be too

late. I'm going to get her out again, if I have to knock the door down to do it.' She got out of the car and ran to the huge door, hammering on it before he could stop her.

Tam told Jinna to stay there and ran after her. He reached Phyllis as the door was opened by a grim-faced woman in black.

'This is the women's entrance,' she told him, barring the way with one arm across the doorway as if she expected him to try to push his way in.

Phyllis elbowed him to one side and confronted the woman. 'We've come to collect a relative, Cara Pruin. She's only just arrived, I think, and her coming here's a mistake. I've found her somewhere to go.'

'Oh, that one. She fainted.'

Tam didn't like the look of the woman but he was afraid Phyllis would shout and you rarely got anywhere by doing that. He tried to speak politely.

'I'm sorry to trouble you, ma'am, only Cara didn't know we'd found her a home. If we take her and her grandson away, that'll save the council the cost of feeding and housing two more paupers. Could we see her, please?'

'She's inside. You stay here, mister. I'll see if I'm allowed to bring her out to you.'

'The boy as well,' he said.

She looked at them both. 'This is respectable, isn't it?'

Phyllis looked at her angrily. 'Of course it is. I told you, she's a relative of mine, my cousin.'

'Well, *you* can come inside and see about your cousin but *he* can't come in by this door, even if he is a relative. The mayor himself would have to use the other door. We don't let women and men mix.'

Tam couldn't believe how scornfully she was speaking to them. 'I don't want to come in because I have my grand-daughter sitting in the van and I can't leave the child on her own. It's Phyllis who wants to come in and get Cara and the little boy out.'

'Hmm. Well, you both *look* respectable, I'll give you that, and if you've got a van, *you* can't be a pauper. Wait out here, mister.'

Phyllis followed her inside and the door shut behind the two women with a loud, echoing bang.

The place was like something out of the Charles Dickens books that Miss Parkins had lent him, Tam thought, with an involuntary shudder. But this was the 1930s, not the 1830s! They shouldn't still be locking people up in such grim places. It wasn't a crime to be hungry or too old to work, for heaven's sake.

He sighed. He was in it up to his neck now, wasn't he? What if he didn't like the looks of this Cara? How could he send a starving woman and her grandchild back into this horrible place? He wouldn't put a cat in here!

Eh, where would it all end, though? Was it only a few days ago he'd promised himself not to do anything else crazy?

Cara came to her senses slowly. She heard people talking nearby but it felt like such an effort to understand the words, she didn't even try to open her eyes. Then she heard Ned sobbing and forced herself to pay better attention to what was going on around her.

The first thing she saw was her cousin Phyllis arguing with a man dressed mainly in black. She had no idea who *he* was. How could Phyllis be here? Perhaps she was dreaming all this. But though Cara blinked her eyes a few times, it still looked like Phyllis and she knew she was awake again.

Thank goodness! Her cousin would help her sort things out, if anyone could.

She tried to sit up and Phyllis abandoned the conversation

to come across and help her. Ned immediately crawled on to her lap and burrowed his head against her.

Phyllis laid one hand on her shoulder. 'There you are, Cara love. Just take your time recovering then we'll get you both out of here.'

She scowled sideways at the man. 'And why anyone would want to *stop* them leaving is more than I can understand, mister-whoever-you-are.' She used the same argument as Tam had. 'You'd be saving the ratepayers money, after all.'

'Madam, this is an institution run by the local council and things must be done properly, according to the rules. This woman has now been entered in the admissions book and I can't—'

The woman who'd let Phyllis in said quietly, 'We haven't yet entered either of their names in the book, Mr Orling, because of the female pauper fainting on us.'

'Ah.' He turned to look down his nose at Phyllis. 'In that case, we can do as you wish and release her, but she may not come back here seeking help for another full week. I'll need a word with you first, if you please, Matron.'

As the two officials left the room, Phyllis had a strong urge to kick his plump backside to speed him on his way, but you couldn't afford even to speak sharply in these hard times; you had to pretend to be meek or you could wind up in trouble.

'Have they given you anything to eat?' she asked her cousin, who was looking as white as a sheet.

'No.'

'Mean devils. When did you last have something?'

'Two days ago.'

'Then as soon as we get outside we'll find a baker's and Mr Crawford can buy us some bread.'

'Who's Mr Crawford?'

'The man I've found for you to marry.'

Cara jerked bolt upright. '*What?*'

Footsteps sounded from the corridor and Phyllis said quickly, 'Shh. I'll explain later. He's your only chance to stay out of here. Remember that when you meet him. He needs a wife and you need a husband to support you. Do it for Ned, if you won't marry Tam for your own sake.'

'But what if I don't like him?'

'*I* like him very much or I wouldn't have brought him. He's a kind chap and not short of money.'

Cara couldn't work out what was going on because she still felt dizzy, but Ned was cuddled up to her, his little face tear-streaked and dirty, so she stopped trying to make sense of it and held him close, taking comfort from his warmth.

When he hid his head against her with a little yelp of fear as Matron came back into the room, she demanded fiercely, 'What have you done to upset him? Ned's not normally afraid of strangers.'

Matron looked scornfully at her and sniffed. 'He was crying because he wanted you and you'd fainted. I told him to be quiet and smacked his hand when he wouldn't do that. In my experience, it's best to teach a child to do as he's told *when* he's told, or he'll get into a lot of trouble as he grows older. But that's your business not mine now, thank goodness, so on your own head be it if you decide to go on spoiling the brat. Now, I can't waste any more time on you. This is the way out.'

'I want my bundle first.'

'We'll get it on the way out. It hasn't been touched. We always fumigate things before bringing them inside.'

'I've brought nothing with me that's dirty!' Cara protested.

Matron didn't say anything but her look said she didn't believe that.

'Stupid old witch!' Phyllis whispered and helped her cousin to stumble along the corridor, stopping at a small room to pick up the bundle.

All the time Ned held his grandmother's skirt tightly, shrinking as far away as he could when they got close to the matron.

Once they were outside, the door clanged shut behind them and a key grated in the lock.

Not even a word of farewell, Phyllis thought. What sort of people were these? Nasty folk, that's what.

Thank goodness Cara didn't have to stay there. Now all they had to worry about was whether Tam would like Cara enough to marry her.

The air outside was so fresh Cara couldn't resist stopping to breathe in deeply. Then she turned to her cousin. 'I'm that dizzy, I can't think straight. You'll have to tell me what you want me to do, love.'

'Oh, I will, don't worry.'

Cara watched Phyllis turn to the man standing waiting for them and heard her say, 'My cousin hasn't eaten for two days, Tam. You'll get no sense out of her till you've fed her. I'm sure you can afford to buy a loaf.'

Shame ran through Cara at that. She glanced at the man and since he was staring at her openly, she took a better look at him, too. A bit taller than her, a thick head of dark, wavy hair, only lightly frosted with grey, and eyes that did indeed seem kind. Was she really supposed to marry this stranger? And why did he need a wife so badly he'd take one out of the poorhouse?

What had her cousin done now?

She turned to ask Phyllis that, but everything whirled round her and went black.

*

Tam was just in time to catch Cara as her eyes rolled up and she started to fall. She was so thin she hardly weighed anything, but she was clean, thank goodness, and so was the little lad, who was crying lustily in Phyllis's arms and reaching out for his 'Nan-nan'.

Cleanliness had always been important to Tam, perhaps because he had an excellent sense of smell. Even when he'd only had access to streams as he tramped the countryside, he'd usually managed to wash himself most days and, when he could, he'd washed his clothes too.

Jinna brushed past him in response to Phyllis asking her to get out of the van and let the poor lady sit down in the front. Her clothes were rather dirty, though she seemed to have washed her body. When she lived with him, she'd have to learn to keep everything clean.

He froze for a moment. *Lived with him!* He hadn't decided about that yet. Why was he even thinking of taking on the care of a woman and two children?

People were right to call him Crazy Tam. And he was getting crazier. Buy a van one week, marry a stranger a few days after that. What would he get himself into next?

As he laid her gently in the passenger seat, he looked down at Phyllis's cousin. She was starting to come round again. Her hair was wavy and tied back with a piece of crumpled black ribbon, and her clothes must have been mended and darned a dozen times or more. The boy's clothes were in a similar condition: worn out, mere rags. Not enough to keep either of them warm on cool, early spring nights. Eh, it was a cruel world sometimes.

He turned to Phyllis, who was still holding the little boy in her arms.

'I think your cousin needs space to breathe and regain her senses. I'll have to rearrange the back of the van to make room for you three so she can sit in the front.' It only took him a couple of minutes, then he stepped back. 'Can you squeeze in there with Jinna and the lad, Phyllis?'

'Yes, of course we can. Give me Cara's bundle. And Tam—'

'What?'

'Thank you.'

'I haven't done anything yet,' he warned her but she just smiled at him so warmly, he couldn't help smiling reluctantly back.

Phyllis then turned to help the girl whose troubles had started all this.

He listened carefully to how she explained the situation to Jinna, using simple words and repeating them two or three times, until she saw the girl nod. And all the time Jinna was holding her bundle of drawings and the umbrella as if they were the most precious things on earth. Children were like that, he'd noticed. Seemed to feel safer with familiar toys or possessions to hold. The boy was holding a bit of reddish coloured rag in the same way.

Phyllis helped Jinna settle in before easing backwards into the narrow space herself and holding the lad against her. Ned kept pleading for his Nan-nan until he saw her sitting nearby in the front seat, then he held one hand out mutely towards her.

'Let your nan sleep,' Phyllis told him, then looked at Tam. 'Well, aren't you going to set off? Or have you changed your mind? Because if so, you'll still have to take us back to the valley. You heard what that man said: they're not allowed to go back into that place. As if anyone would want to!'

'I haven't made up my mind either way. How could I? I've not even spoken to her.'

He was *trying* to be sensible, only he couldn't persuade himself to turn this trio of needy people out into a harsh world without giving them a chance. He'd had some really good fortune recently, more than in his wildest dreams, and now felt he owed it to the kind fate that had looked after him to help other people in their turn.

Well, the kind fate had been a wise old woman, but it was what Miss Parkins had asked him to do, the lawyer said, help people. That seemed a fair exchange for the money.

He turned in the driving seat to look at the little boy, who was staring first at him then at his grandmother, wide-eyed and anxious. Tam smiled at Ned and at least the lad didn't cower away and hide his face. Those people must have treated him badly in the short time he'd been there because there were still traces of tears on his cheeks and a bright red mark on his hand and lower arm where that matron must have hit him hard.

Tam checked on Jinna, who was also staring from one person to the other, looking anxious. 'Are you all right there, lass? Can you sit there?'

She nodded, still clutching the drawings.

'You're a good man, Crazy Tam.' Phyllis let out a sudden chuckle. 'What's your surname again? Crawford? You're sure of that?'

'Of course I'm sure.'

'Good. Because I don't think my cousin Cara will want to be known as Mrs Crazy Tam.'

It came to him suddenly that he was acquiring not only responsibilities but a sort of family and that might not be all bad. 'Well, she'll not stop people calling me Crazy Tam. They always have done, because I do daft things sometimes on impulse. Only most of the things I do seem to work out all right in the end.' That thought made him feel better, because it was true. Maybe this would too.

Phyllis must have read his mind. 'What you've done today isn't daft, it's a kind, generous thing to do, and I'm sure you'll get your reward in heaven, Tam Crawford.'

'Hmm.' He realised how little he knew about this cousin of hers. 'Tell me about Cara. Is she a good housewife?'

'None better, given the chance. She's a good cook, too, when there's food available. And she used to sew a lot of patchwork when she was younger. Really pretty things, she used to make.'

He decided to warn her what her cousin would be facing. 'Um, I hope she won't mind living in a tent.' That did surprise her, he could see.

'A tent? Is that how you live, Tam?'

'Sometimes. We'll have to live in one for a while until I can get a home together. I'm buying a piece of land from a relative and putting a caravan on it, but we'll have to put up a tent on it till I can get the caravan I'm buying up there.'

He clamped his lips shut. He'd said 'we', shouldn't have done that. Not yet. Goodness, he didn't even know what Cara thought of this. She'd hardly even had a chance to look at him and still seemed a bit dizzy.

'As long as she has the lad, I'm sure Cara will cope with any sort of shelter that keeps the rain out. She hasn't had an easy life, you know. She won't expect luxuries.'

He wondered how they would go on in the old army tent he'd been using for the past few years, ever since he got the handcart. It was waterproof, the sort of tent that would last for years. They'd be a bit cramped in it, though. Cara might – well, she probably *would* despise what he had to offer.

He couldn't see how to get out of offering it now, though, and the trouble was, the more he thought of it, the less sure he was that he *wanted* to get out of it. Ned was a nice little lad and Jinna was like a flower that needed space and light to grow properly. As for himself, well, he'd been alone for a long time – too long.

He'd always wanted to have a family, had enjoyed having a wife, grieved for her when he lost her. Maybe even a makeshift family would be nice, given a bit of goodwill from everyone involved. People weren't meant to go through their lives alone.

Eh, but to let himself be rushed into it like this! That was the crazy thing.

5

Tam stopped at a baker's shop on the other side of Bury and got out of the van. 'I'll just see what they've got left over from today. We all need something to eat, don't we? I'm hungry, for sure. And I might as well get something for your family as well, Phyllis.'

'I'd be grateful.' But she looked a bit ashamed at the idea of taking help.

Tam looked away from her to Cara, whose hunger was written on her face, poor thing. His heart went out to her, as it did to all the people struggling to feed themselves and their families.

Inside the shop he fell lucky and was able to buy several broken loaves cheaply because it was nearing the end of the day. It seemed the baker's lad had dropped a tray of newly baked loaves from the second batch, smashing the corners of some.

He spotted some jars of jam for sale, so he bought one of those too. Well, dry bread wasn't a good way to eat a first meal together, was it?

Back at the van, he got out his bread board and knife from the box of cooking things and gave the little boy the first piece of crust, half-torn, half-sliced from the most battered loaf, with a smear of jam on it.

The child licked the jam off first and Phyllis shook her head at that but didn't tell him off.

To Jinna went the second piece but she didn't gobble it as

he'd expected. She examined it, then took a mouthful and chewed it carefully and slowly, seeming to be tasting every single crumb.

Only when the children had been served did he give a piece to Cara, who ate equally slowly and carefully.

'Just one slice each for now,' Phyllis murmured to him. 'They won't be used to eating much and more might make them sick, which would be a waste, eh? Oh, and we need to find some water. They'll be thirsty as well as hungry.'

So he went back into the shop and bought two bottles of dandelion and burdock, finding to his surprise that it had been made by a company called Spring Cottage Mineral Waters in Ellindale. That must be new since his last visit to the village at the top end of what he liked to think of as *his* valley.

He rummaged around in his box and found a couple of battered tin cups to pour it into so that Phyllis could help the little lad.

After a meal that seemed little more than a snack to him, he resisted the temptation to give himself another of the nice, crusty slices, because of Cara and the lad. Wrapping the bread in a clean cloth, he put everything away in the food box. Then he closed the van doors and set off again.

As they drove along, Cara turned her head sideways to look at him. 'Thank you.'

Her voice was low and pleasant on the ear. He could live with that voice. 'You're welcome. We need to feed you up a bit.'

Her voice was firmer than it had been. 'We need to talk before I take anything else from you.'

What did she mean by that? Was she going to refuse to marry him? That'd be a turn-up for the books.

He didn't ask her what she meant because her eyes had closed again. He wondered what she'd look like when she wasn't so gaunt. He didn't think she'd be ugly, because she had nice eyes, a straight nose and a neat chin.

Well, he'd often thought that ugliness came from inside people rather than from what their faces were like. Nastiness seemed to show itself clearly, and kindness too, especially in the eyes.

As they approached Rivenshaw, he asked Phyllis if she wanted to go straight to the doctor's.

'No. I think we should tidy everyone up first, because we want to look as respectable as we can. Maybe everyone could have a bit more to eat, too.'

'All right.'

But when he stopped outside her cousin's home, Cara said, 'Could you take the children inside for a few minutes, please, Phyllis? I'd like to talk to Mr Crawford in private.'

'You are going to be sensible?' Phyllis asked in a low voice, looking at her anxiously.

Cara didn't attempt to lower her voice. 'I don't know what sensible is, but I do want to talk to this man before I consider marrying him. Do you have any tea leaves?'

'A few.' She'd been hoarding them.

'Then put the kettle on. I haven't had a cup of tea for a week or more.'

'Take the rest of that loaf in with you, Phyllis,' Tam said. 'Those children will be hungry and ready for another slice. And take two of the other loaves for your own family.'

'Thank you. Don't take long, Cara. We still have to see the doctor and his wife.' She took the children inside, with Ned protesting once again that he wanted his nan and Jinna clutching her cloth-wrapped bundle of drawings and the umbrella.

As the others vanished from sight Tam waited for Cara to speak, because he didn't know what was on her mind, did he? He couldn't help noticing that she was clasping her hands together so tightly her knuckles were bone white. She stared down at them for so long without speaking that he began to worry and in the end, he said abruptly, 'No one's going to force you to marry me, you know.'

She looked up then. 'I'm worried that someone is forcing *you* to marry me.'

'Sort of.'

'What does that mean?'

'It's that young lass, Jinna. She has no one else now her mother's dead. They'll lock her away in the asylum if I don't look after her, because she isn't like other people. Only they won't let me look after her unless I have a wife. The lass *can* speak, though I've only heard her say a few words, but she doesn't speak often, Phyllis says, and only to people she knows.'

He paused, trying to be clear about his feelings. 'You can see she's not stupid from the way she follows a conversation, and she can draw – well, I've never seen drawings as good as hers, never in my whole life. She draws any time she can get hold of paper and a pencil, Phyllis says.'

'That still doesn't explain why *you* want to take her on, a man of your age, if you're not related.'

He heard the suspicion in her voice and said sharply, 'Not for any bad reason like those you're wondering about. I offered on impulse, all right? I do things like that occasionally, if I see something that upsets me. But when I thought about looking after her, it seemed a good idea. I had a child once, you see, but Pansy died when she was three. Then my wife died too. So I've no one left who's close to me. I always wanted to have children.'

'Why Jinna, though? She's not like other children.'

'It's *because* she needs me more than others do. The council will lock her away in a place like that one we found you in today if I don't look after her, and it'll kill her, I know it here.' He thumped his chest several times to emphasise the point. 'I can't stand to see children suffer, or animals.'

'Oh. I see. That's . . . kind. But marriage is such a big step!'

It slipped out. 'I've been feeling a bit lonely lately.'

Her voice was almost a whisper. 'Me too. I was very happy with my husband.'

'I was happy with my wife.'

Cara nodded as if accepting that. 'Still, marriage is a big step, living and sleeping together. We're complete strangers.'

'Look, we don't need to get wed till we know one another better. Nor I won't touch you in that way at first, if you don't want me to. Is that what's worrying you? We can live like brother and sister till we get to know one another. But you must promise to look after Jinna properly and . . . and to talk to me. I like chatting. And I'll look after your Ned in return. He's a bonny little lad. It'll be a pleasure.'

'Phyllis says you're a kind man.'

'Am I? I'm an impulsive one, I know that. I hope it won't upset you too much if they, um, call me Crazy Tam. I only do crazy things when I get angry at cruelty or unkindness, not all the time. But I'm a good provider and I have a bit of money saved.'

She continued to study him, then said softly as if speaking to herself, 'I'm tempted, I really am. But how do I know whether it's the right thing to do or not? Marrying for nothing but desperation seems . . . well, wrong.'

'Eh, you've got me there, Cara. If it's any help, I don't think a person can ever know for certain whether they're making the right choice until they've lived together for a while. You just have to do your best as you go along. And I promise I'll do that.'

'Mmm.'

'But we're managing to talk, though we hardly know one another, and that's a good sign.'

Her face brightened. 'Yes. It is. Where would we live, Tam?'

So he explained his plans all over again and her face brightened still further.

'We'd live up in Ellindale, near the moors? *Ellindale?* That's my favourite place of all.'

'Is it? Well, it's mine, too. I've got a second cousin there who said he'd sell me a bit of land. But we'll be living on it in a tent to start off with. I've got an old army tent and it's a good one, even if it is faded and stained. It's waterproof as long as you don't touch the canvas when it's raining, and with the summer coming on, we'd be all right for a while in it. Do you know Ellindale well?'

'Not as well as I'd like to. I've been up there several times and walked across the moors. It was so lovely I dream about it still.' She swallowed hard. 'You promise you won't touch me in that way till we're comfortable together.'

'Not if you don't want me to.'

'Most men wouldn't agree to that. Don't you like women?'

She was certainly blunt.

'I haven't bothered about that sort of thing since my wife died. I've been on the tramp, and that can be hard. I haven't had the chance to get to know any woman well and I don't think I could, um, do it with a complete stranger.'

'No. Me, neither. How would we make a living?'

'I've just bought the van, as I told you. I thought I'd spread the word that I can carry or deliver stuff, or take people somewhere like a taxi does, but cheaper. I'm rather good at finding ways to turn a penny or two.'

'And I'm good at making one penny do the work of two.'

As silence fell again, he thought she'd fallen asleep, but no, she was staring down at her hands again and the sight of those white knuckles still upset him.

As if she felt him staring at her, she straightened her shoulders and looked him in the eyes. 'I'll do it then.'

'Marry me, you mean?'

'Yes.'

And to his huge surprise, he found that he was not only glad of that but delighted.

'You're smiling, Tam.'

'Well, I'm pleased about it.'

'You might regret it. You hardly know me and I've a temper on me at times.'

'If we set our minds to it, I think we'll manage to rub along together. I like children and we'll have two to raise.'

At last she gave a real smile and it was like the sun coming out from behind storm clouds. 'Two children. How wonderful. I loved raising my daughter. Times weren't as hard then.'

'Hard times or not, you won't any of you go hungry,' he promised. 'I'll make sure of that. Now, let's go inside and see if there's a cup of tea ready. I'm parched.' And he needed a rest from all this emotional talk. Cara's dilemma tugged his heart every which way.

Henty was waiting for them in the hall. 'I can keep an eye on your van again, mister.'

'Aye. Twopence all right?'

The lad sighed and glanced at his mother.

'He won't need to give you any money, son, because he's bought our tea,' Phyllis said sharply.

The lad sighed but didn't protest.

'Thank you, Henty.' Tam gestured to the stairs. 'Ladies first.'

He watched Cara follow Phyllis, climbing up them one by one. He was amazed that she made it without help, she moved so wearily. How long had she been short of food, poor lass?

Phyllis gestured to them to come into the room her family shared. It was immaculately tidy.

'This is my husband, Don. Have they taken Janet's body away from upstairs, love?'

Don nodded.

'You and Ned can sleep there tonight, Cara, as long as you don't mind having Jinna with you.'

'Why should I mind?'

'There aren't any proper beds, so you'll have to sleep on the floor, but I saw some blankets in Tam's van and maybe he'll lend you one or two?'

'Of course I will,' he said at once.

Phyllis nodded. 'Good. I know Janet paid the rent till the end of the week.'

'That female from downstairs sneaked up again and tried to steal things, even while Janet's body was still lying there. But we stopped her.'

'There! You can't get lower than that, can you? Any road, that stuff belongs to Jinna now, so when you leave tomorrow, you should take everything with you. There isn't much but every bit helps, doesn't it? We should have gone and got the stuff from your room before we left Bury, Cara. It was stupid of me not to think of that.'

Cara flushed. 'You'd not have found much. I'd sold nearly everything I had. Most of my things are in that bundle.' Tears welled in her eyes at the shame of that and she changed the subject quickly. 'Where are you going to sleep tonight, Tam?'

'I'll find somewhere out of town to park the van, like I did last night, and bed down in the back of it.'

'Oh. But you'll need your blankets then.'

'I've got three, one for me, one for you and one for your grandson.' Since there was no clock on the mantelpiece, he pulled out a battered old pocket watch that someone had given him in return for a week's work and checked the time on that. 'Now, don't you think we'd better go and see that doctor and his wife? We don't want them coming after Phyllis for not sorting things out decently for Jinna.'

'Oh. Yes.' Cara heaved herself wearily to her feet.

'We can go in my van, easier on young Ned that way. I'll carry him downstairs, shall I?'

'Thank you. What are we going to tell them about Ned?'

Phyllis's voice was brisk. 'The truth, that he's your grandson and your daughter died, so you're caring for him. That's why you were in Bury, looking after her. We don't need to say anything about exactly *when* this happened.'

'Good idea. Let's go and get it over with.' Tam held out his arms, feeling pleased that Ned came to him quite happily, and led the way downstairs.

It was good to be with people again. He'd spent far too much time alone in the past few years. Maybe this would all work out.

When they knocked on the side door at the doctor's house, the one that led to the surgery, it was opened by a young maid. 'The doctor's closed now, unless it's an emergency, and he's having his tea.'

Phyllis took charge. 'He asked us to come round this evening and we won't keep him long. Could you please tell him Mrs Gazwell has brought Mrs Crawford to see him. We'll wait till he's finished his meal.'

'Oh, er, you'd better come in if he *asked* you to see him tonight.' The maid switched on the electric light in the waiting room and they sat down on the old bench provided for patients' comfort.

They didn't have long to wait. Dr Fiske came in with his wife, who looked to be a brisk sort of woman. She was younger and much shorter than him. The two of them paused in the doorway to study the group of people openly.

Tam waited for the doctor to take charge, but it was Mrs Fiske who asked the questions. And it was Cara she spoke to mainly, asking about the children, with a couple of questions for Phyllis as well.

Very sensible answers Cara gave, too. He liked that about her. He could never have married a fool.

It didn't take Mrs Fiske long to make up her mind, it seemed. She turned to her husband. 'I think everything seems to be in order. I've met Mrs Gazwell before and trust her. Just one or two questions for you, Mr Crawford, then we're finished. Are you going to settle in the valley?'

'I hope so. I have a cousin up in Ellindale.'

'How shall you make a living?'

'I've saved up and bought that van you can see outside. I'm going to set up as a carrier, and do a few other things as well. I always manage.'

'A man of enterprise,' the doctor said.

Tam shrugged, not sure whether this was meant sarcastically or not.

The doctor was now studying Cara. 'Your wife has obviously not been eating well. How did that happen?'

'I didn't tell him how bad things were,' Cara said quickly. 'I went to take charge of my grandson after my daughter died. Tam was working down south and things were worse in Bury than I'd expected. Me and Ned have been going a bit short, but now Tam's back, we'll be all right.'

'Quite the philanthropist,' the doctor said.

'No. Just a practical chap who likes children,' Tam contradicted. 'I'm no do-gooder.'

'What is it but doing good to take in Jinna?'

Tam was going to contradict him until Phyllis nudged him. He snapped his mouth shut before it got him into trouble again.

'I shall tell the council that a relative I approve of has taken charge of Jinna,' Dr Fiske said. 'It'll save a lot of complications. See that you don't let me down, Mr Crawford. I'll be keeping an eye on what you're doing.'

Mrs Fiske took her husband's arm. 'Well, now that it's all settled, we'll get back to our meal.'

The maid showed them out and switched off the light, leaving them standing together in the darkness.

Tam gave way to a small impulse. 'The smell of the doctor's dinner made me hungry. Is there still a fish and chip shop in Rivenshaw?'

It was Phyllis who answered him. 'Yes.'

'Good. I'm going to buy us all some fish and chips. We'll get a better night's sleep on full bellies. Tomorrow we'll go up to Ellindale and speak to my cousin Peter about that piece of land he promised to sell me.'

He felt very tired now and it was a relief to leave the others and find himself somewhere quiet to park the van. He'd slept in it overnight yesterday and found it a damn sight comfier than lying under a hedge.

Eh, it was going to be a busy day tomorrow.

He'd expected to lie awake worrying, but found himself sliding towards sleep almost immediately.

6

Todd Selby was driving up to Spring Cottage to visit Leah when he noticed a battered black van parked in a lane to one side of the main road. Since he was in the car repairs and sales business, and had friends in Ellindale, he knew most of the vehicles up this end of the valley by sight. He didn't recognise this one, though.

He braked, wondering if it had broken down and the driver needed help, but he couldn't see anyone nearby. Maybe the driver had left it and walked home. He continued up the hill, glad not to feel obliged to help. He didn't want to get dirty when he was on his way up to see Leah.

He'd spent the whole of yesterday repairing an older vehicle for a new customer. The engine had been the devil to sort out after years of neglect, and how it'd kept going until recently, he couldn't think. And then the customer had looked unhappy at a repair bill of just under four pounds, which included a couple of new parts and an oil change.

Although Todd was making an adequate living repairing and selling cars, it wasn't a generous living and the trouble was Leah did have money. She wasn't rich, but she was much better off than him. Her late husband had left her a house and land up near the moors in Ellindale, as well as the business she'd started, Spring Cottage Mineral Waters, a small fizzy drinks factory.

His heart lifted as he approached her home, the last house in the village. He'd promised to check her delivery vehicle yesterday and had arranged to come up early to look at it before it left for its day's rounds. It was misfiring apparently, usually an easy thing to fix.

He'd met Leah when he first came to Rivenshaw, because she was the sister-in-law of his partner Charlie Willcox. He'd fallen in love with her almost at first sight, which was stupid when she was married, but these things happened. She and Jonah had seemed happy enough together, more friends than lovers, he'd often thought. But he'd liked her husband too, so that was that.

Sadly Jonah's lungs had been damaged in the Great War and although he'd lived for fourteen years after it ended, he'd taken a turn for the worse last year and died suddenly.

Todd should have been able to start courting Leah after a few months had passed, because that's how things were done, but life always seemed to hand you a complication or two. The one that had stopped him in his tracks this time was Leah finding out she was carrying Jonah's posthumous child.

She'd had the child in September, a healthy little boy, and after that Todd had started finding ways to be with her, making it clear why. She'd welcomed his company, had feelings for him, you could always tell. Not that there was much they could do together in winter, especially with a baby in tow. There had been a few sedate strolls in the park with little Jonty in a fancy Silver Cross pram, and occasionally they'd both been invited for tea at Charlie's house on a Sunday.

With the finer weather they would be able to meet more often without scandalising people, but there was still a lot to think about before he asked her to name the day. It wasn't the child who was the obstacle to them marrying quite quickly; it was Todd's own pride. He still hadn't come to terms with the idea of marrying a woman so much better off than himself.

His heart did a happy little skip as he turned into the big

yard and saw her standing at the factory door, her dark hair blowing in the breeze, her face lifted to the rosy dawn light over the Pennines. She hadn't seen him yet so he stopped just short of the gateway for the sheer pleasure of watching her. She was a quiet, peaceful sort of person and that showed in her whole stance.

As Leah came out of the factory, she paused for a moment to breathe the fresh air deeply. A chill breeze was blowing fitfully, but it looked as if it was going to be a fine day.

She'd left her baby son in the house with Ginny and nipped across to the factory to check that all was set for the day's work, something she did every morning. He'd been sitting in his high chair, chewing at a crust of bread, safe under the watchful eye of her housekeeper and friend, who started work early, as they all did.

The child had been called after his father but somehow the 'Jonah' had turned into Jonty. Leah employed a daily girl to keep an eye on him and help Ginny in the house. And since the factory was only across the yard, she could go across to see him several times a day.

She worked hard, not so much because she needed the money the factory made, but because the people in the village desperately needed the jobs it provided. That had been one of her main reasons for starting the fizzy drinks business in the first place.

Hearing a car, she glanced towards the village, smiling when she saw Todd's van turn into her yard. Her delivery driver would have seen it pass and would probably walk up from the village to join them now, but she hoped she'd have some time on her own with Todd before Peter arrived.

She looked at it thoughtfully as it came to a halt. She'd been expecting Todd to propose for a few weeks now, and he hadn't. Why not? They got on so well. There was only one reason she could think of: her money. Perhaps Todd needed encouragement to persuade him that it didn't matter.

On that thought she started walking across the yard and as he got out of his car, she took the initiative and greeted him with a hug.

He stared at her in surprise for a few seconds, then hugged her back. 'What did I do to deserve this? Not that I'm complaining.'

'I felt like hugging you. My sister thinks she's too old for hugs and kisses now she's at grammar school, and Jonty's too young to hug me back properly, so I have to depend on you for that.'

'I'm at your service, always.'

When he kissed her, she returned the kiss willingly.

'Oh, Leah, I think we—'

They heard footsteps on the gravelled road that led from the village only to Spring Cottage and the old barn in which the factory and youth hostel were housed.

He glanced over his shoulder, muttered 'Oh, hell!' and stepped away from the embrace.

Peter Cotman, her driver, came to join them and, after a quick nod of greeting, began to explain to Todd exactly how the delivery van had been misbehaving.

Shooting a rueful smile at Todd, Leah turned towards the house. 'Come and have a cup of tea before you leave.'

By the time Todd joined her half an hour later, having adjusted the van and taught Peter a couple of things about maintaining it, her sister Rosa had come down for breakfast and Ginny was finishing cooking it.

As he accepted a cup of tea, Todd turned to Leah's sister. 'I can give you a lift into Rivenshaw, if you like, Rosa.'

'Thank you, but I like to see my friend Evelyn before school. We always sit together on the bus.' She accepted a hearty breakfast from Ginny and concentrated on it, propping a book up on the sugar bowl to read as she ate.

Leah rolled her eyes at that, but didn't stop her reading as most grown-ups would have done. Rosa was a highly intelligent lass who wanted to become a doctor and she read more books in a month than most folk read in a year.

By that time Betty, the young maid mainly employed to look after Jonty, had washed and dressed the baby and brought him to sit with his mother while she got her own breakfast, hearty meals being a much-valued part of the girl's job.

Holding her son, Leah walked with Todd to the door. 'Come and have tea with me later. Rosa's having tea at her friend's house after school and I'll make sure we're not interrupted.'

'I'd love to but I can't today. I have to go and see a man who wants to sell his car. Look, how about you come to the cinema with me tomorrow? They're showing *The Good Companions* again and you said how much you'd enjoyed it. Rosa will keep an eye on Jonty, surely?'

'I did enjoy it. I know it's a silly story, but I loved the singing and dancing, and most of all, the happy feeling it left me with.'

'I'll come and fetch you.'

'No, I can perfectly well drive myself down to Rivenshaw. That'll cause less talk.'

He couldn't help feeling bitter at the care she always took to give folk no cause to gossip about them. 'We can't have people talking, can we?'

'I have my sister, my son and my business to think of, Todd. It's hard enough being a woman in charge. There are men, and even women, who would love to find something to blacken my name.'

He closed his eyes for a moment, angry at himself for speaking sarcastically to her. 'Sorry if I sounded sharp. I get rather . . . well, *frustrated* about trying to court you. You're such a busy person, and so important to the people of Ellindale.'

'I get frustrated about it too. So we'll go to the cinema tomorrow and hold hands in the darkness, eh? Then you can walk me to my car and stand chatting for a while, if it's not raining.' She took a deep breath and added, 'Perhaps we should, um, start making some long-term plans?'

He stood very still as the meaning behind these words sank in. 'Perhaps we should. Very long term.'

Her smile was glorious. He let himself give her another quick hug, and who cared if the other women saw it from inside the house? After a final kiss on her soft cheek, he drove off down the valley.

At the other side of the middle village, Birch End, he slowed down again. The black van was still there and this time its bonnet was up and a man was bent over it. Definitely something wrong. Oh well. It didn't matter if he got his hands dirty helping someone now.

He stopped by the side of the main road at a place where it was wider and went to see if he could help the stranger.

Leah's words were still echoing in his mind. Why on earth was he even hesitating to ask her to marry him? Because he was a fool, that's why.

Tam saw a man coming towards him, so stood up from investigating the van's engine.

'I don't think we've met before. I'm Todd Selby.'

'Tam Crawford. I used to live round here, but I've been working in the south for a few years and I've just come back.'

'I'm a newcomer to Rivenshaw, only been here for a couple of years. How long will you be visiting the valley for this time?'

'I've come back permanently, I hope. I'm intending to get

married and settle down here.' He pulled out his watch and sighed. 'I was supposed to pick up my fiancée and her family at eight o'clock in Backshaw Moss. They'll be wondering what's happened to me.'

'Did you find someone nearby to take you in for the night?'

'No, I slept in the van. Saves a few pennies, sleeping rough. Do you know anything about car engines?'

Todd chuckled. 'I ought to. I'm a motor mechanic. I have a repair workshop in Rivenshaw and I sell second-hand cars too. Let's see if I can help you. What's the problem exactly?'

Tam looked at him in relief. 'Blessed if I know. It was going all right yesterday but this morning I couldn't get it to start.'

'Has the van done this before?'

'I've only owned it for a few days. I bought it in the Midlands. It seemed in good order and I got it cheap because the bodywork needs attention.'

Todd bent over the engine, pleasantly surprised by what he found. 'It doesn't look in bad condition, unlike some of the cars I get asked to repair.'

'That's what I thought when I bought it. I'm not a mechanic, but I know enough about motors to hear whether they're running smoothly or not.'

Todd checked out various things and found a similar problem to Leah's delivery van, a simple blocked carburettor. That seemed to happen to people quite often. He was able to get it unblocked and the man let out a groan of relief.

'How much do I owe you?'

'Nothing. Didn't take long or cost me anything.'

'That's very kind of you.' As Todd looked down at his hands and grimaced, Tam passed him a dirty rag. 'Here, wipe your hands on this. It'll get the worst off.'

'Thanks. You're welcome to come back to my place to wash your hands properly and have a cup of tea if you've time.'

Tam studied the watch, which was even more battered than the van. 'I'd love to but I'm late and they'll be worried.'

Todd had taken to his companion, so he said, 'Well, another time, then. Drop in if you're nearby. I'm just off the main square. Willcox and Selby Motors. I live there at my business. The place will be tidy but it's rather dilapidated.'

Tam grinned. 'Not as bad as our place will be. We'll be sleeping in a tent tonight if things go as I hope. I'm supposed to be buying a piece of land further up the valley from my cousin and then I'll get a caravan taken up there to live in for the time being.'

'There are a lot of people doing that these days. One chap took a railway carriage up to Ellindale only last year. The whole village turned out to help him.'

'Yes, I heard about that. Good idea. I'm going to set up as a carrier, in case you hear of anyone wanting such services on a small scale.' He flourished one hand towards the van.

'Let me have your exact address once you settle and I'll bear you in mind. If you're moving to Ellindale, they'll take phone messages for you at the village store and charge you only a penny for a lad to take the message to you. And they'll let you make phone calls from there for twopence.'

'That's very decent of you. And them.'

'We try to look after one another in the valley.'

'Not so much in Backshaw Moss, where I grew up.'

'Ah. Terrible state the place is in. There's talk of the council doing something about it – if they can only agree what. Anyway, I hope things go well for you all.'

Tam held out his hand. 'Thanks for your help, Mr Selby. I'm really grateful.'

Cara came out to greet Tam when he arrived in Mossy Row. She was looking worried but brightened up when he explained what had delayed him.

'Have you got Jinna's things ready?'

'Yes. And if we can't fit all of her furniture and other things in your van, Phyllis will look after them till we have somewhere to live.'

'How did you get on with the lass?'

'Very well. She's no trouble if you explain slowly and carefully. But Phyllis is worried she'll be upset at leaving her home, says the poor lass doesn't like change. We think we've explained it to her, but you can never quite tell how she'll behave in a new situation, Phyllis says.'

'We've no choice but to move her.'

They gathered together all Jinna's mother's furniture and cooking equipment and Tam frowned at it. 'Do we need all this? Most of it's rubbish.'

'Every piece will help if we're setting up home,' Cara said. 'You never know. Even if you pull it to pieces and use it for a fence or firewood.'

As they loaded the things into the van, Jinna grew more and more distressed. They tried to explain to her that because she was leaving, they had to take all her possessions with them, but she kept shaking her head.

In the end, they put her drawings into the van and she was persuaded to get in as well. She sat next to little Ned, looking anxious and clutching the old umbrella close to her chest.

'She loves that umbrella,' Phyllis whispered. 'Whatever you do, don't try to take it away from her, or her drawings.'

The furnishings made it a tight fit for Cara and the two children to squeeze into the van. She took the passenger seat, holding her bundle of possessions, and the youngsters squeezed into a space Tam had made right behind her.

It was having Ned beside her that seemed to settle Jinna most, because he was such a sunny-natured child, he automatically expected everyone to be friendly.

When he took Jinna's hand and smiled up at her, she looked down at it, then sideways at him.

He bobbed up again to plonk a kiss on her cheek. 'Kiss me back!' he ordered, pointing to his own cheek.

Cara held her breath. Would Jinna do that?

'Kiss!' he said more loudly.

The girl leaned forward and gave him a quick kiss, then he nestled against her trustingly.

Cara let her breath out in a long, slow sigh of relief. Perhaps Ned would be the key to helping Jinna settle down with them. It wasn't going to be easy.

Tam drove slowly up the valley, stopping a couple of times at places where there was a clear view to let the others look out across the moors. Each time he pointed out places he'd actually been to. He told them how he'd loved clambering up to the higher parts when he was a lad. Once, Cara pointed to a path she'd walked along.

They guessed it was Jinna's first view of the moors from close by from the way she stared. She was silent, as usual, but it seemed to him that she was listening carefully to what he said and looking at the places as he pointed them out. Once, he saw her hands twitch as if she longed to hold a pencil and draw the scene they were looking at, and he made a mental vow to get her some better paper and a new pencil.

Just before they got to Ellindale, he stopped to look round in puzzlement because there had been changes to the road at the bend and that made him unsure of the next part.

'Is something wrong?' Cara asked.

'It's hard to get my bearings. It's been a while since I've been up here. The road's different along that edge. I think that wall's new. And that railway carriage is standing at this side now. Eh, it's quite big, isn't it? How on earth did they get it up here?'

'It's as big as a house,' she said. 'Bigger than any place I've lived in, for sure.'

He didn't start driving again because he was trying to work it all out. 'I thought I'd remembered clearly where the piece of land was that my cousin Peter wanted to sell, even though I've only seen it once.'

He frowned and tried to bring the picture of it into his mind, but somehow the pieces wouldn't fit together. 'I thought it was on this side of the village. Maybe it's that bit of land just before you get to the railway carriage. Eh, how could I have forgotten? Anyway, there's the lane that leads to Peter's farm. Let's go and find him. He's lucky to have inherited a farm, isn't he, even a small one like this? Skeggs Hill Farm, they call it. That means a bearded man in Norse.'

'Strange name for a farm. Perhaps the original owner had a beard.'

'I suppose so. I envy Peter. No one can throw him out of his home. He's about the same age as me but his dad died when he was twenty so he had to take over. His mother didn't make old bones, either. Gruelling hard work, it is, scratching a living from the land up here. The Kerkham side of the family rarely live to a ripe old age anyway. Us Crawfords usually do much better.'

They drove along the badly rutted track that was only a little wider than the van and drew up at the small, tumbledown farmhouse, which was flanked by a few sagging wooden sheds.

As they stopped a man came out from behind one of the sheds, looking beyond weary. He used his rake like a walking stick to support himself as he came across to the van.

'Were you wanting to buy some eggs?' Then he bent and peered at the driver more closely. 'Tam? Is that you?'

'Yes. Bad pennies always turn up again, don't they?'

'I thought you must be dead. We haven't heard from you for years.'

'It's only four years since I was last here.'

Peter eased his back and sighed, and to Tam's mind, he looked years older than he should have done, and not at all well.

'I've been all over the south working. I got one job that lasted several months. I kept meaning to write but you know how it is. I'm better at talking than writing.'

'How long are you back for this time?'

'I've come to stay. I want to buy that plot of land you offered me last time.'

Peter gaped at him, then looked sideways. 'Eh, I'm sorry, but I sold it to Harry last year and he's living there now in the railway carriage. Surely you noticed that?'

Tam could hardly draw air into his lungs, he was so shocked.

Peter was looking upset too. 'We were that short of money, I *had* to sell it.'

Tam stared out of the window at the nearby railway carriage. Its brass fittings had been polished and its windows sparkled. And oh, he wished it didn't exist.

What the hell was he going to do now?

7

Cara sat watching the two men through the windscreen of the van. She could tell there was something badly wrong from the expression on Tam's face, so she opened the door on her side to hear better. She was in time to discover what had upset Tam and her heart sank. But then she saw how upset he was and that mattered more. He'd gone pale and hadn't moved since Peter told him the news.

'Stay there, Jinna! Stay there, Ned.' She slipped out of the van and hurried across to Tam. If she could do nothing else, she could offer him comfort and support.

A woman came out of the farmhouse and hurried across to Tam's cousin, ignoring the visitors. 'Are you all right, love?'

'Yes.' He leaned on her, looking as if he was too tired to stand upright. It seemed to Cara that he had gone even paler than Tam. He seemed much older, though she knew the two cousins were about the same age. He didn't say anything but left his wife to carry on the conversation.

'I overheard what you were saying, Tam. Such a shame you didn't come back sooner! It'd have been nice to have relatives nearby, not that Harry Makepeace and his wife are anything but good neighbours, but still, blood is thicker than water, isn't it?'

Tam still seemed lost for words, so Cara said, 'Yes. It'd have been nice. But perhaps we can find another piece of land for sale nearby.'

'I haven't heard of any, but if you ask at the shop, Lily can spread the word. Everyone from the village is in and out of there regularly.'

Peter said, 'I suppose you could pitch the tent on my land, just for a few days. There are one or two flat bits at the bottom end. But there's only our spring up this end for you to get water from, so you'll have to carry it in a bucket.'

Cara was surprised that his offer was so grudging. Surely he could be more helpful than that? His wife kept watching him anxiously, but she didn't say anything more. She didn't even offer them a cup of tea. She too looked deep down tired, but not nearly as bad as Peter.

Perhaps he'd been ill and they were short of money. Yes, that might be it. This didn't look like good farm land, though what did she know about it? Only what she'd read or seen on the newsreels on the few rare occasions she'd been able to afford a visit to the cinema.

When his cousin volunteered no other suggestions, Tam said curtly, 'We'll go and ask at the shop before we decide anything. They may know of somewhere we can put up our tent for more than a few days. We'll have to come back here if we can't find anywhere for tonight, but we'll try not to trouble you.'

Hilda Kerkham looked shamefaced, but then her husband swayed and she had to support him more carefully. She didn't even turn back to them, but helped him towards the house.

The door shut with a bang as if she'd pushed it with her foot.

'What's going on there?' Tam wondered aloud.

'He looks really ill to me.'

'Aye. He used to be a big man, but he seems to have shrunk since I last saw him. Anyway, let's get on. We need to find somewhere to sleep tonight.'

*

Cara and Tam returned to the van and he drove back slowly to the main road, but stopped there and switched off the engine.

'Are you all right?' she asked. 'Or is something wrong with the van?'

'Nothing the matter with it. It's me that's gone wrong. I've mucked it up, Cara, and I don't know what to do to put it right. Eh, what must you think of me? I'm a right fool, I am, building a dream on what me and Peter said four years ago. I just rushed in as usual when I got the idea, expecting the land still to be here, because land can't move away, can it?'

'We'll work something out.'

He looked at her so apologetically, she felt her heart twist with pity for him, but he'd continued speaking before she could think of anything to make him feel better.

'There's you, Jinna and Ned, all depending on me now. And I thought, I really thought, this time I was going to have a family and be able to make a real home for us all, a home no one could ever take away from us if I'd bought the land.'

'You've still got a family. They can't take that away from you.'

He clutched her hand suddenly. 'Have I? You won't leave me, will you? I'll try not to make any more bad mistakes.'

'Ah, who doesn't make mistakes in this life? I've made a few, that's certain. Look, I've nowhere else to go, Tam, and even if I did have anywhere else, I'd not desert you, not when you've been so good to me and Ned. Yes, and you've been good to Jinna as well. You've got a kind heart and that counts for a lot with me.'

She'd never seen anything like the look in his eyes as what she'd said sank in. It was as if they came to life again, brightening by the second.

He grasped her hand. 'Did you mean that? Did you really,

truly mean it? You'll stick by me, even though I've made a
mess of it all, even though you hardly know me?'

'I'd not have said it else.'

He let out his breath in a big whoosh. 'Then somehow or
other, I'll find a way to give you a proper home, lass.'

'No, *we* will find a way. You're not alone now, Tam. Perhaps
I can find a job, cleaning or doing laundry or whatever, and
we can rent a single room for the time being. There are always
rooms to let in Backshaw Moss. We'll just have to squeeze
in together till we get our new lives sorted out.'

He made a sort of growl in his throat. 'I'm not going back
there, whatever happens. I left Backshaw Moss when I was
fifteen and swore I'd never live there again. It pulls you down,
that place does, pulls you right down and sucks the hope out
of you.'

'Then we'll find somewhere else to rent a room.'

'I don't know what I ever did to deserve a woman like you,
Cara.' He quickly wiped away a tear. 'Just . . . just give me
a minute or two to pull myself together.'

'This'll be a good time to let Ned have a wee, then. No
one will see us if he goes behind the van.'

He watched her coax her grandson out and walk round to
the back of the van. What a grand woman she was. No
complaints, no blame, just there to help in any way she could.

He looked across at Jinna and saw she was watching him
with her usual intent stare. 'Are you all right, lass?'

She stared for a moment longer, then nodded, and this
response seemed like another step in the right direction.

'Good.'

He heard Cara talking to Ned in a low voice. It occurred
to him that he hadn't heard even the slightest hint of shrill-
ness in her tone, in spite of the mess he'd made of things.
She had a lovely voice, low and calm.

'We'll be all right,' he said aloud. He didn't know what

he'd do, but for once he had a bit of money behind him and he had the start of a family.

It suddenly came to him that they were like a patchwork quilt, him and his new family, the sort his auntie used to make. The pieces of material were all separate and different when she started sewing them, but by the time she'd finished each quilt, the pieces all fitted together beautifully.

It'd be hard to work something out, harder than he'd thought when he asked Cara to marry him, but there had to be a way to make a home and a new life for them. And when they were quiet and private somewhere tonight he'd tell her about the money. That'd cheer her up.

She'd stood by him thinking he had nothing much left, and that meant so much to him.

Cara lifted Ned back into the van and he settled down next to Jinna, who was still clutching the umbrella, holding it upright in front of her with both hands. As Cara watched, her grandson reached out for Jinna's nearest hand and tugged at it. In spite of all their troubles, he was such a friendly little soul; her little sunshine, she sometimes called him.

She watched Jinna look down at their joined hands in surprise but he gave the girl one of his lovely smiles and said, 'Jinna an' Ned.' She seemed to consider that, head on one side, before she gave him a faint smile in return. Best of all, she didn't try to pull her hand away.

As Tam had said, Jinna understood perfectly well what was going on, she wasn't stupid, just . . . different, as if she was standing apart, not knowing how to join in. It occurred to Cara that the girl needed *teaching* how to behave with people. Could you do that? Well, you could try, couldn't you?

She looked at Tam, who was staring straight ahead, still looking upset. She could have wept for disappointment herself, but what good would that do?

As she stretched to ease her back from bending over with Ned, a woman came through the gateway of the railway carriage and strolled up the road, carrying a bowl. Cara said, 'Good morning' instinctively, out of politeness.

The woman stopped, giving her a warm smile. 'Have you been buying some eggs from the farm? I hope there are some left.'

'No. My, um, husband is a cousin of Mr Kerkham. We just called in to see them.'

'Nice to meet you. I'm their nearest neighbour, Nina Makepeace.' She pointed to the train carriage. 'We live there.'

'Yes. So we were told.'

'Is something wrong?'

Cara couldn't hold back completely. 'Tam was hoping to buy that piece of land. He'd talked about it with his cousin a while back, even set the price. We were going to live on it.'

'Oh, dear. You must be upset.'

Cara nodded, trying to stay calm. What had happened wasn't this woman's fault, after all. 'These things happen.'

The woman started walking again, then stopped and looked back. 'If you need somewhere to stay for a night or two, Leah might let you stay at the youth hostel. I used to work there as matron and I know the season for walkers hasn't started properly yet. They only charge a shilling a night per person, including breakfast.'

'Youth hostel? I've read about them. I didn't know there was one round here. It's a while since I've visited Ellindale.'

'It's in the old barn next to Spring Cottage, at the top of the village. There's a fizzy drinks factory at this end of the barn and the youth hostel is at the other.'

'Thank you.' Cara remembered walking up to that end of the village the few times she'd come here but couldn't remember the details. Maybe they'd have a piece of land next to the youth hostel where Tam could pitch the tent for a while. It wouldn't hurt to ask.

She got back into the van. 'The woman who just walked up to your cousin's said we should ask if we can stay at the youth hostel for the night, because it hasn't opened for hikers yet. But it's a shilling a night per person, though that's including breakfast, and that'd soon mount up. So I wondered if they'd have a piece of land where we could pitch the tent, just for a few nights. It'd give us a breather and time to think what to do next.'

'I can't see the owner letting us pitch a tent and stay.'

'Why ever not? We're perfectly respectable. It's worth a try, Tam. I don't think your cousin wants us to stay on his land.'

'No. Nor do I.' After another silence, he shrugged. 'I suppose we could try. It's not far to go, after all, just the other side of the village. And I can afford the money for a few nights.'

'Are you sure?'

'Yes. I'll explain about that later.'

When Leah was getting a breath of fresh air, she saw a battered van chug up the slope from the village, stop for a moment at the gateway of Spring Cottage, then drive into the big yard between the house and the factory. It came to rest outside the youth hostel end. A man got out, then a woman with a small child. Last of all was a girl of about ten or twelve.

She went across to see what they wanted. You didn't often get families coming here. It was usually people wanting to buy bottles of fizzy drinks or hikers wanting to stay at the youth hostel. The sky had started to cloud over and she shivered. It looked as if it was going to rain soon.

'Can I help you? I'm Leah Willcox and I own Spring Cottage and the fizzy drinks factory.'

The man gave a quick glance at the sky before replying. 'My family and I are looking for somewhere to stay for the night and the lady who lives in the railway carriage at the other side of the village suggested we ask you if we could stay at the youth hostel for a night or two.'

She studied them before replying. If Nina had sent them, then her friend must consider them respectable and Nina was a shrewd woman. 'The hostel isn't ready for visitors yet, but if you don't mind putting up with that and making up your own beds and cups of tea, I'd be happy to let you stay. It's a shilling a night each and that includes breakfast. But I'd not charge for the little boy.'

The two adults exchanged nods, looking relieved.

'That's very kind of you, Mrs Willcox.' He looked at her for a moment, in case she wasn't married, but she didn't correct the way he'd addressed her. 'We can easily do the beds ourselves, and anything else that's needed. I'm Tam and this is my wife Cara, her grandson Ned and Jinna. We've just adopted her.'

Leah looked at them again. 'I think I've seen her at the market. She sits drawing behind one of the stalls, if I remember rightly.' A strange girl, people said, who couldn't speak, but she didn't look simple-minded to Leah.

'Yes. Jinna used to go to the market with a neighbour, but her mother's just died so she's come to live with us now. She draws beautifully. I've never seen anyone catch a likeness as cleverly.'

'Well, you can either pay for your lodging or if you'll clean through the place from top to bottom, I'll let you all stay for two nights free, breakfast included. It was cleaned thoroughly before it closed for winter but it's dusty and needs freshening up and clean sheets putting on all the bunks.'

It was a generous offer, she knew, but they looked as if life had battered them. And heaven knew, it'd cost her almost nothing to help them. Besides, she really did need the place cleaning.

The woman beamed at her. 'I'm happy to do that for you, Mrs Willcox. I'm a good worker.'

'We'll both muck in,' Tam said at once. 'My wife's been ill and I don't want her doing any heavy work for a while yet. I'm not ashamed to do anything, whether it's considered women's work or men's, if it's an honest way to earn a penny. Thank you very much, Mrs Willcox. We're grateful.'

'That's excellent. I shall have to hire a matron soon so that I can open up for the summer but in the meantime there will only be your family staying there.'

'I read about youth hostels in a magazine someone gave me,' Tam said. 'They're a new thing, aren't they?'

'Yes. They're meant to let ordinary young people have holidays in the countryside cheaply. We only opened this hostel two years ago. Let me show you round.'

Cara turned to see Jinna standing by the van, looking round as if checking for enemies.

'I don't think that girl's been in many other places apart from her home,' Tam whispered to the two women. 'Her mother kept her away from other people, you see, Mrs Willcox.'

'Poor thing.'

He went across to Jinna. 'Come and look at the rest of the youth hostel, lass.'

She looked at him doubtfully.

'There's nothing to hurt you here. We're going to stay here tonight.'

She looked round again, then turned back to him.

'We'll go and see the men's dormitory first,' Leah said.

'Come on, Jinna,' Tam urged as the girl still didn't move.

It was Ned who solved the problem once again by taking Jinna's free hand. 'Come an' see.'

At last the girl moved forward.

Thank goodness for that little lad, Tam thought.

Mrs Willcox took them to see the day area on the ground floor, the men's dormitory beyond it, then the women's dormitory, which was upstairs. 'We lock this door at night to keep the men and women separate. The matron of the hostel has her own two rooms off the day area and shares the women's bathroom.'

Tam noticed a sign saying 'Baths 6d extra' and wondered how often guests took advantage of that.

As they came back into the day area, Leah said thoughtfully, 'Perhaps you should use the matron's rooms. The children could sleep in the living area. We have some spare mattresses you can use.'

'Good idea,' Cara said quickly. 'That way we can get the dormitories cleaned and we'll only have the matron's rooms to tidy when we leave.'

'We're looking to buy a small piece of land,' Tam said. 'Like my cousin Peter sold to Mr and Mrs Makepeace last year. They paid five pounds for it, I believe.'

'I haven't heard of anything else for sale, but I'll certainly spread the word. I'll go and fetch you some tea and milk from the house, and I've got a spare loaf you can have for breakfast.'

And then they were alone in the matron's area.

As it started raining, Tam grinned and said, 'Talk about in the nick of time.'

8

Cara stared at Tam, then had to sit down suddenly at the small table. Her hands were shaking as she pressed them to her cheeks. 'I can't believe how lucky we've been to find this place.'

'Perhaps our luck has turned.' Tam went to sit next to her, putting an arm tentatively round her shoulders. He liked to touch and hug people, but they didn't always like him doing it, even though it was well meant. 'We've been very lucky indeed, considering. We're even paying our way. We'll be all right here, I'm sure.'

'Yes. She's nice, isn't she? Mrs Willcox, I mean.'

'Yes. But she's nobody's fool if she owns that fizzy drinks business next door as well as this place.'

'How wonderful it must be to have your own home and business.'

'That's one of my dreams, Cara, but having a family comes first. I may be too old to have children of my own, but I'm not too old to bring up children who need homes. We'll make a life for ourselves and those two children one way or the other, I promise you, and that will include having a proper home, maybe even one with an inside bathroom.' He hesitated, then said in a rush, 'I won't let you down. Just give me time.'

She gave him a tired smile. 'I don't need a palace, you know, Tam, though an indoor bathroom would be wonderful one day. If I just have somewhere clean and decent for the children, I'll be fine.' She hesitated. 'I hate lying to Mrs Willcox about us being married, though.'

'So do I. I don't like lying to anyone and I usually manage not to. Maybe I should tell her the truth about us.'

'Or I will, if an opportunity comes up.'

He nodded and changed the subject. 'One thing: as soon as we have a place to live in permanently, we'll book a wedding at the registry office. You have to be a resident in the area for that. It'll keep the whole thing quieter than a church wedding. Unless you're set on being married in church, that is?'

'No.' Her voice was sharper than he'd ever heard it. 'The curate in Bury didn't even try to help me and Ned when we were in trouble, not even one penny from the poor box. He said we should pray for guidance, and told me the poorhouse was set up for people like me. So I'm not going back to church until I find one where the minister cares about everyone, not just the rich people.'

'I feel a bit that way too. Um, there's something else I need to tell you.'

'Oh?' She looked at him as if bracing herself for more bad news.

'It's good news.' He saw her relax a little. 'I have a bit of money put by, over fifty pounds actually.' He couldn't say the full amount, even to her; he felt safer keeping what seemed to him like a fortune secret from everyone.

Cara gaped at him, mouth open.

'I inherited some money recently from a lady I used to work for every year in the south, and I had a bit saved of my own as well. That's how I bought the van. So you see, there's enough for us to live on for a good while even if I don't earn another penny, and we can afford to buy you and the children a few more clothes, too.'

He turned to look at Jinna as he spoke and saw that she'd

gone to stand near the front entrance and was alternately looking out at the van, then back at them, as if trying to keep an eye on everything. She'd stayed close to them as they were shown round the youth hostel. And bless her, she was still clutching that dratted umbrella, even indoors.

He lowered his voice. 'You know what, Cara? I think Jinna doesn't know what to do in new places because she hasn't been to many. We should try telling her every detail of what to do each time we go somewhere new.' He went across to the girl. 'Come inside and sit down with us, love.'

But Jinna didn't move, only turned towards the van, looking anxious.

He suddenly realised why. She'd be wanting to get her drawings from the van. They and the umbrella were the two links to her old life and it would probably make her feel better to have them nearby. 'We're going to stay here for a day or two, Jinna. We'll be sleeping here tonight and tomorrow night. Your things will be safe in the van.'

'You and me and Ned will sleep in the room over there.' Cara pointed to it.

Jinna looked round the kitchen and living area with that intent stare as if learning everything about them by heart, then she moved a couple of steps forward to look through the bedroom door.

Cara went closer to Tam and whispered, 'I should have asked you first. It's all right if Jinna, Ned and I sleep in the bedroom, isn't it, Tam? Once you and I get wed, we can . . . um, change our sleeping arrangements.'

'Fine by me, lass.'

She held out one hand to the girl. 'Come and look inside the bedroom properly, Jinna.' Again she repeated, 'You and Ned and I will be sleeping here. Come with me.'

As Jinna took the hand that was offered and went with Cara into the other room, Tam felt relief run through him.

It seemed to him, it really did, that Jinna was learning to trust them. Would she start to speak to them? Phyllis had told him the girl had spoken to her mother all the time. He'd only heard her speak once, when trying to rouse her dead mother, but her voice had sounded normal enough.

He watched through the open door as Cara put her arm round Jinna's shoulders and saw how the girl stiffened as if she didn't like this. Cara must have noticed too, because she moved away again.

Eh, that lass was like a puzzle. Maybe there was a way to knock down the invisible walls that seemed to surround her, and help her get on better with people. If so, he'd find it. He was good at unravelling puzzles.

'This is the bedroom,' Cara explained again. She sat down on the bed and found it very comfortable. She patted the mattress next to her. 'Come and sit down.'

Jinna studied the bed but didn't move. Then, just as Cara was about to repeat her request, the girl came to sit beside her, a short distance away, still holding tight to the umbrella. But it showed she'd understood, didn't it? Cara thought.

With a laugh Ned hurled himself on to the bed between them and she only just stopped her grandson putting his dirty shoes on the bedspread. She kept hold of his hand. 'Don't dirty the bed with your feet, love.'

After a moment or two sitting there and letting Jinna study the room, she said, 'Let's go and have a proper look round the kitchen now.'

But once they left the bedroom, the girl stopped and looked towards the front door again.

Tam made a gesture with one hand to stop Cara speaking, so she let him take over. 'I think she's too worried about her drawings to take things in properly.' He raised his voice a little. 'Jinna, love.'

She turned towards him.

'The rain's eased off. Come out to the van now, Jinna. We'll get your drawings and clothes. We can bring them in here. They'll be safe here.'

The girl moved towards the door at once.

'Me too. Me too.' Ned followed the others outside, leaping up and down for the sheer joy of it, holding his mouth open to catch the raindrops.

Cara watched them go. She'd never met a person like Jinna. She didn't like to see anyone so on their own, which that poor lass was, even when in the company of others. Knowing what some people could be like, Cara intended to make sure they understood that Jinna wasn't stupid, just . . . different.

Would people from Ellindale give the girl a chance if they knew more about her? She did hope so. To her mind, the mother had done the wrong thing by keeping Jinna away from other folk and stopping her speaking to them.

Could she and Tam undo some of the damage?

Tam wasn't the only one who'd longed for a proper family again.

Once he'd brought the second and final load of personal possessions into the youth hostel, Tam went back to the door to study the sky. The rain had stopped but he could still sense the dampness in the air. It was definitely going to rain again.

Mrs Willcox came out of the house at the other side of the yard with a canvas bag and a jug of liquid, which she was struggling not to spill as the heavy bag swung to and fro. He went across to help her.

'Sorry to keep you waiting for your cups of tea, Mr Crawford, but I had to take a phone call.'

'That's all right. We were just bringing our things in for the night.'

He hesitated because his conscience was still giving him

trouble. Since Cara felt the same about lying to this kind woman, he took the risk. 'I think we'd better tell you how things stand between me and Cara, because you might wonder at how thin and ragged she looks.'

'I did rather.'

'I only met her yesterday. Her cousin introduced us, said we could help one another. Me and Cara aren't married yet but we're going to be. She needs a husband to look after her and her grandson, while I need someone to help me look after Jinna. We've got on well, right from the start, so we're both happy with the arrangement. And, um, just so you know, Cara will be sleeping with the children till we do marry.'

To his relief, Mrs Willcox didn't look at all upset. 'Thank you for telling me that. I'm sure those children will be glad of a proper family, so it sounds like a good idea for you two to marry.'

'I'll enjoy having a family. I really like kids.'

'So do I. We must introduce your Ned to my Jonty tomorrow. Little ones seem to enjoy each other's company, even when there's a difference in ages.'

'Ned loves meeting people. He's a happy little soul. At the moment we need to go and buy some proper food because Cara and Ned have been going short and need feeding up. Will there be somewhere open on a Sunday?'

'Knock on the back door of the village shop. I'll phone Lily and tell her your situation. She'll let you buy a few groceries to put you on.'

'I hope you won't mind if we go shopping before we start on your cleaning.'

'Not at all. You need food first and foremost. And I'm glad you told me about your situation. I did wonder about how thin your fiancée was, because you aren't, and you didn't seem like the kind of man to keep his family short of food. But neither of you seemed the kind of people who'd try to cheat me or anyone else either, so I waited to learn more about you.'

He let out a relieved sigh. 'That's all right, then. Um, there's another thing you may be able to help me with. I need to buy a few clothes for them as well as food. Do you know of a good place to get decent second-hand things in Rivenshaw?'

'That's easy. My brother-in-law has two pawnshops in Rivenshaw and the one Vi runs for him has a whole floor of better quality clothes upstairs. You can leave your car in the street where Todd's business is, and the pawnshop is just round the corner. It won't be open till tomorrow, of course, but I'll phone Vi first thing in the morning and let her know you're coming.'

In the youth hostel she put the food and milk down, smiled at Cara and left them alone.

Tam took a deep breath and confessed what he'd done.

Cara went bright red. 'What must she think of me!'

'Nothing bad. I told her you'd be sleeping with the children till we could get wed. And then I asked her where we could buy you some new clothes.'

'I'd be glad of one or two things, but we'd better not spend much money till we see how it all works out,' Cara protested.

'We'll only be buying second-hand things. That won't cost too much. It wouldn't look good for me if I'm trying to start a business and have a wife going round in threadbare clothes. Mrs Willcox has told me where to buy them.'

The stubborn look was still there on her face, so he added, 'If you won't come and help me choose some clothes tomorrow, I'll go and buy them for you on my own. Only, we need things for Jinna and Ned as well, so it'd be better if you did come.'

Cara flung her arms round him suddenly and gave him a quick, shy hug.

'Does that mean you'll come?' he said into her ear, keeping tight hold of her.

'Yes. And I'm grateful.'

As they moved apart, he indicated the food Mrs Willcox had brought them. 'Let's eat something before we go to the village shop. I'm famished even if you aren't.'

'I'm ravenous.'

When they turned round, they saw Jinna standing watching them with a puzzled expression. She was still holding that stupid umbrella in one hand but she was clutching Ned's hand on the other side.

It brought a lump into Tam's throat to see the two children standing close together. It was as if they really were brother and sister.

As they walked down to the village shop, Tam said, 'No stinting, now. They say an army marches on its stomach and I think it's the same for working people. They need decent food if they're to work hard.'

Cara smiled sadly. 'I'll take my lead from you and cook whatever you prefer to eat.'

'Nay, lass, you'll have to sort that out. I've only ever fed me as I travelled round, so I won't know what four of us will need. But I'll say it again: *no stinting*. Those children need good food if they're to grow up strong and healthy.'

Her voice was husky. 'You're a good man.'

As they were walking round to the rear of the shop, Tam said abruptly, 'I don't think we should call you my wife. If we're going to live in the valley, we should start off as we mean to go, by being honest. I shall call you my fiancée, like Mrs Willcox did, if that's all right with you.'

'I'll do whatever you think best. I don't know whether I'm coming or going at the moment, everything's happened so fast.'

He grinned. 'That happens with me sometimes. Don't worry. I'll look after you.'

Inside the shop Tam had to take over a couple of times and insist on buying other items. That put a smile on the young shopkeeper's face and made Cara take deep breaths and put her hand across her mouth in an attempt to keep her feelings hidden.

It was a good thing they had a couple of clean sacking shopping bags with them as well as the only basket Tam owned. The shopping filled all three of them by the time they'd finished, and Jinna and Ned were both happily munching apples that Tam had bought.

'We should have come in the van,' he said.

'It's not far and only one of the bags is heavy.'

He took it out of her hands, and another bag too. 'I'll carry them. You're looking tired now.'

'Tired but happy.'

He was happy too.

Before they drove into Rivenshaw the next day, Cara tried to make Jinna and Ned as tidy as possible, but their clothes were as threadbare as her own and Ned had almost grown out of the things he was wearing.

Tam knew his way around the town centre, because it hadn't changed much, and followed the directions to the shop, which had a sign saying *Willcox For Value* above its window. It was a pawnshop but had a side entrance for those pledging goods, and a separate, much smarter entrance at the front for those seeking to buy 'superior second-hand goods and quality used clothing'.

The side entrance had a queue waiting to pawn clothes after the weekend, but the front entrance had no one waiting, nor were there any other customers inside the shop.

The lady behind the counter studied them. 'You must be

Tam Crawford. Mrs Willcox phoned to say she'd recommended you to bring your family here.'

'And you must be Vi. She spoke very highly of you.'

'That's nice to know. Now, who exactly needs clothes?'

He waved one hand at Cara. 'My fiancée, her grandson and our adopted daughter.'

Vi studied the girl. 'I've seen the lass at the market. Isn't she the one who draws pictures of people? I didn't know she was related to you.'

He avoided that pitfall by saying only, 'Her mother died, so we're adopting her.'

'I was going to slip out next market day and ask her to draw a picture of my two nephews. It'd make a nice present for my sister. It's her birthday in a couple of months, you see. Would she do that if I brought them along, do you think? If it's good enough, I'd pay her for it and provide some good paper and pencils for her to do it on.'

Tam gaped for a moment, then said, 'I'm sure Jinna would love to draw your nephews.'

'We'll give it a go, then.'

He cleared his throat. 'Um, what would be fair payment for that, do you think? If the drawing's good enough, I mean, though I bet it will be.'

'I'd pay five shillings for a sketch of the two of them, if it's good, and I'll get it framed at my own cost. I could bring the lads to the market or else up to Ellindale.'

He let out a long slow breath. 'We need to find somewhere to live first. We're camping out at the youth hostel at the moment.'

'Are you looking for rooms or a house to rent?'

'I was going to buy a plot of land and put a caravan on it till I could afford a house, only the plot I saw last time had been sold and a railway carriage put on it.'

'I know the one you mean. Getting that carriage up the

hill was so exciting. Half the town turned out to help or watch.'

'If you hear of any other similar plot of land for sale, please let me know.'

'I'll do that. Now, about these clothes, we keep them upstairs.' She beckoned to a young man standing at the rear of the shop. 'Take charge here, Colin.'

An hour later they left the shop carrying several parcels because Tam had insisted on Cara buying a couple of changes of outer clothes and a good coat and hat, not to mention some underclothes. And very smart she looked too now. She scrubbed up nicely, as the saying went.

Jinna had watched Cara try on clothes and choose some, so when it was her turn, she let the two women help her, only insisting that the umbrella be nearby at all times. In the end they gave it to Ned to hold, which kept him quiet playing with the folds of material and seemed to satisfy its owner that it was safe.

As they were leaving the shops, Cara stared at the girl, who looked so different in the new clothes. When the children walked ahead, she whispered to Tam, 'Did you ask Phyllis how old Jinna is?'

'No. I thought she was quite young, about eleven or twelve, but now I'm thinking she's maybe fourteen or so, because she's, you know – ' He waved his hands in a curving gesture and added, ' – got her figure. So she's not going to be a tall woman. She's probably old enough to leave school.'

'Has she ever been to school, do you think?'

'I shouldn't think so. We'll have to ask Phyllis. I'd call there on the way home but I think it'd confuse Jinna to go back to the house where she used to live, so I'll go another time on my own or speak to Phyllis at the market next week.'

It took a while for them to get back to the car because some of the people they encountered stopped to greet Tam and ask how long he was staying this time. He introduced Cara each time, but let Jinna stand to one side. People must have recognised the girl because they didn't even give her a second glance, let alone try to speak to her.

When they got back to Ellindale, Cara didn't get out of the car immediately. 'Thank you, Tam. I've never had such nice clothes in my whole life before.'

'You look nice in them.'

She could feel herself flushing. She found Tam so easy to be with and so generous, she didn't regret agreeing to marry him, not at all. Her first husband hadn't been nearly as easy to deal with, though he'd been a decent enough fellow who didn't thump her as some men did. She couldn't imagine Tam thumping anyone or she'd not have agreed to marry him.

It was lovely to feel safe, safer than she had for a long time, as well as happier with something to look forward to. And though she'd have married Tam without the money, whatever people said, it did make a difference to your peace of mind to have something to fall back on. Just imagine having so much saved!

Tam also made a difference to how she felt simply by being himself, because he seemed to have a happy nature, a bit like Ned. His smiles and cheerful conversation made her and other people around him feel more cheerful, even in times like these. She'd watched some of the women he chatted to today lose their downcast look.

She sneaked another glance at herself in wonder as he opened the van door for her. These clothes might be second-hand but she did think they flattered her. They'd look even better when she'd regained the weight she'd lost. Would he notice that, too? She'd had a nice figure once.

Then the first drops of another shower fell and Tam

exclaimed, 'Hurry up, everyone!' They all ran into the youth hostel.

Cara was amused to see that Jinna made no attempt to put up the umbrella, just continued to clutch it.

9

That same day Finn Carlisle finished reading his morning newspaper, sat frowning at it for a moment, then walked round the ground floor of Heythorpe House looking for his wife. He found Beth in the kitchen, chatting to the servants about meals for the coming week, and waited for her to finish before asking, 'Do you fancy a stroll, love? I know the sky's clouding over but I think the rain will hold off for a while yet and there's something I want to look at.'

'Fine. Where are we going? If we're going across the moors, I'll have to change into my boots.'

As if he'd take a wife who was carrying his first child across such rough ground! 'No need for that. I want to look at that big room behind the pub, the one where the village children come to get their free glasses of milk every day. I'd like your opinion about an idea I've had.'

'I'd love to get some fresh air before the rain sets in.'

They donned warm outdoor clothes, because spring hadn't shown much sign of warmth yet, and left the house. At the road he stopped, as he usually did, to look up the hill towards Spring Cottage and then down into the village itself. He gestured back at their own home. 'I still find it amazing that this big house belongs to me – to us both now – and that we can spend our married life in such a beautiful place.'

'I know, love. It is a beautiful house. But much as I love it, I'm even more happy to have married the lovely man who owns it.'

'And you're far more important to me than any house could ever be.'

For a moment they both stopped talking to exchange loving smiles, then she added, 'And the way you play with my Daisy and Kit is wonderful.'

'They're fun to be with. They're *my* children now as well.'

'I'm glad you're not a grasping sort of man, Finn. I read somewhere that only people who aren't greedy for money should be allowed to become wealthy, then they'll use their money wisely. Look how much good you've done with your inheritance already.'

'All I've done is help a few people here and there.' He began walking down the hill into the village itself, feeling embarrassed as always when someone praised him.

'What's the idea you want to talk to me about, Finn?'

'Setting up a job club. We've already talked about doing that so that the people who're out of work can learn new skills. And I intend to make sure they get a free meal each time they attend. You can't learn new things if your stomach is growling with hunger. I read in today's newspaper about a new club that's been started up near Oldham and it made me realise I'd let the idea slip.'

'Half the village will be there if you offer them free food.'

'I shall limit membership to people who're desperate for a job, not their dependants. I can't afford to feed everyone in the village. *You* might think I'm wealthy but I only have a modestly comfortable income by any other standards. Anyway, never mind that. We were talking about the job club. It's very important to give those who're out of work somewhere to go and something worthwhile to do. They get so bored and downhearted just hanging round.'

'You're right there. What exactly would they do at the club?'

'The clubs I've read about offer classes in reading, writing and arithmetic. People need a better education these days and quite a few of our village folk can't read or write well, because they missed a lot of school when they were children to help their families, especially the girls. We could also provide sewing classes and woodwork.'

Beth stopped walking to scowl at him.

'What's the matter? Why are you looking at me like that?'

'People always offer sewing classes for the women and woodwork for the men. Which one of those do you think might lead to a job?'

'But women will usually get married sooner or later, and anyway, they don't become carpenters. It's the men who need to support a family, and for that they need practical skills.'

'As long as I can remember people have been saying that, but look at what it's been like for widows who lost their husbands during the Great War. Who's supported them for the past fifteen years? No one, that's who. They've had to support themselves. And look how many women couldn't find husbands after the war because there simply weren't enough single men left to go round, so they've always had to support themselves, too.'

'I know, but—'

'And only a couple of years ago, I was in desperate straits myself when my selfish pig of a first husband ran off with another woman. It was me who had to support our two kids then.'

He hadn't meant to upset her, so he said in calming tones, 'Yes, I do realise that, love. But still, you can't deny that *most* wage earners are men.'

'They're only the wage earner when they first marry. Both men and women can be killed by an illness or an accident, as quickly as that.' She snapped her fingers.

'Darling, there are—'

She set her hands on her hips and looked at him challengingly. 'Queen Victoria isn't on the throne now; we're a third of the way through the twentieth century and we've got King George on the throne, the second king since Victoria. Things have to change. When they're widowed, women still won't be able to earn enough money to support their families because employers pay women only half what they pay men.'

'Yes, but—'

'And the other side of that is that men who lose their wives don't know how to run a house, so they rush round searching for a wife. They're like little children who need looking after. If it were up to me, I'd make everyone learn to do everything at home and at work.'

She looked so adorable when her eyes sparkled with anger that he couldn't resist grabbing her and giving her a quick hug. 'You'd have made a fiery suffragette in the old days, my love. But I doubt many men would agree to learn about housework, even if you paid them to.'

'I know. Lucky them! I certainly never enjoyed scrubbing floors. But I still think they *ought* to learn. As for suffragettes, votes for women don't put bread on the table, so I'd not have got involved with that lot, even though it's only fair for women to be able to vote like the men, as they do nowadays. It's jobs that matter most to men and women both, when it comes to providing for a family, Finn, jobs!'

'You're right, only there isn't a lot of work to be found at the moment, especially in the north.'

'I know that. I read your newspapers because I like to learn about the wider world and when we visited your relatives down south it made me realise that times are already changing and work is changing too. I think your club should help people get ready for the jobs there will be in better times, new jobs like making motor cars or repairing electrical goods for the home. Women and men both.'

He had opened his mouth to protest that she was tilting at the moon, then shut it again. She was right, really. You

ought to aim high and try to achieve more than your parents'
generation had. One of his favourite poets had said it best.
He'd never forgotten the lines in one of Browning's poems:

> *Ah, but a man's reach should exceed his grasp*
> *Or what's a heaven for?*

'You don't have to convince me, Beth.'

'I know. I just get so angry sometimes at what women have
to put up with.'

He took her hand again and they carried on walking,
swinging their clasped hands to and fro like a pair of children.
'I'm definitely going to need your advice, to keep my ideas
modern. If we try to do more for the women in our job club,
what sort of classes could we offer them?'

'How about typewriting? Doing accounts. Bookkeeping.
Lots of women work in offices these days. And teach them
dressmaking skills, not for in the home but for work outside.
How to work in a shop, which needs good arithmetic. Even
how to drive cars and vans.'

'You're such a "modern woman" at heart.'

'Just because I'm happy in my marriage to you and have
another sort of future ahead of me,' she patted her swelling
stomach, 'doesn't mean I've stopped using my brain. Or ever
will, I hope.'

'No. I love your bright shiny mind, which tosses jewels of
ideas at me regularly. Right then, love. Let's bear all that in
mind. But we can't do anything about our job club until we
find a place where we can run classes. And that's what I want
to do today.'

They arrived at The Shepherd's Rest and went in by the
main door. Izzy poked her head out of the back to see who
it was. When Finn explained what he wanted, she gestured

towards the rear of the pub. 'You know where the big room is. Go and see if it suits.' She vanished into the back again without waiting for an answer.

Beth grabbed his arm to stop him moving. 'I haven't finished my list of classes. We could teach *both* men and women how to start up a little business, like a café or a workshop. That'd need them to understand simple accounts, know about finding wholesalers, be acquainted with the relevant trading laws, and how to work out whether something would be profitable, all sorts of things – even if they're only going to cater for hikers and holidaymakers part-time in the summer. People can usually be shown better ways to do things.'

She kept hold of his arm, so he waited, surprised at how many ideas she was tossing out. She might not have been formally educated, but she was a clever woman. He loved that. It made his life more interesting.

'And while we're at it, we could get some of the people from the village together to work out how to attract more visitors to Ellindale. We get a few people coming up the valley in cars and then going for short walks in the finer weather, which the older folk say didn't happen much before the war. We could provide a place for them to leave their cars, make more paths across the moors – easy ones as well as harder ones – paths that lead people to places with beautiful views. We could put signposts up and seats here and there. That'd give visitors something to come here for. And they'll all want cups of tea and refreshments.'

'Is that all?'

She let go of his arm. 'For the moment. I haven't had time to think about details, but I could think about it and make a list, if you like.'

'Do that.'

He looked at her proudly. She'd surprised him today. Given

the chance, Beth had blossomed, astonishing him with the breadth of her interests and how quickly she picked up new ideas. He hoped this coming child would be as clever as its mother.

He opened the door of the big room and they stood in the entrance studying it and assessing its suitability for this new use, after which they walked slowly across it to the little scullery at the far end and looked at that, not that there was much to look at.

'What do you think of using this place for the job club?' he said at last.

She frowned. 'It'd be fine, but it's not always free, is it? What would we do about the children's free milk morning and afternoon? Or what if someone wants to hire the room for a wedding party and Don and Izzie need to get it ready? People from Birch End come up the valley to Ellindale for that every now and then because it's cheaper here.'

'You don't think Izzy could have the milk given out in the pub instead?'

'No. Definitely not. That would mess the place up and anyway, kids don't belong inside pubs, which always smell of booze.'

'Hmm.' He went across to look out of a window at the side of the room and she joined him.

'Why are you looking at Hillam House, Finn? That's not suitable for a job club, surely? It looks as if it's ready to sink into the ground the next time a storm hits it. People from the village stay away from it in case it caves in on them – and half of them think it's haunted. Even the kids don't try to break into it to play.'

'It never has blown down though, has it? Even the slates are still all there on the roof.'

'Are you really thinking of using that for your job club?'

'It might be all right.'

'You'd have to get the owner to do some work on it, but I suppose it'd be worth it if you pay him rent. Who does it belong to? No one in the village seems to know.'

He gave her a rueful smile. 'It belongs to me. I told you when we married that I owned one or two cottages in the village and you didn't ask which, so I thought you weren't interested.'

'I didn't want to sound mercenary. I wasn't as confident about your love as I am now. Or about my new life.'

'No one could ever think you mercenary. You say what you mean and I like that. Anyway, this is one of the places I own. I gather it was acquired by one of my ancestors in payment for a debt and they kept quiet about it, letting the former owner stay on till he died. Or so the lawyer thinks. It was before his time.'

'It looks very old.'

'When I inherited Heythorpe, the lawyer told me the house wasn't safe because it was so old and I should just knock it down. I've kept meaning to knock it down so that no one gets hurt if it gets damaged in a storm, only I've been so busy with other things, I haven't got round to it. Anyway, it didn't seem urgent.'

She shook her head in amazement. 'You own that building and you never said. What's it like inside?'

He shrugged. 'I don't know. Don keeps an eye on the old house for me. He said he'd tell me if there was any storm damage.'

'I've seen him chase away tramps if he sees them hanging about near it. I just thought he was looking after the village. That man can certainly keep a secret.'

'I asked him not to tell people. I was a bit embarrassed when I inherited so much, with most other people having trouble putting bread on the table.'

She looked at him fondly. 'You're a softie, you are. Let's

go and have a look inside it, then. Is it really haunted, do you think?'

'I don't know. Are you afraid of ghosts?'

She chuckled. 'Not when it's broad daylight and I have my own hero to protect me. But I'd not want to go there on my own at midnight, I must admit. Maybe Hillam House can be made safe. It might be just right for our job club. Wilf Pollard would be the man to ask.'

'Good idea. Is he home at the moment? He's been going off for a couple of days at a time, doing jobs for that man from the railways who helped deliver Harry Makepeace's carriage up to Rivenshaw.'

'Only one way to find out, my dear Mr Carlisle. Let's go and see if Wilf's at home today.' She linked her arm in her husband's.

'We can kill two birds with one stone. I've been meaning to ask him to come and do a few little jobs on Heythorpe House as well. The place is so old-fashioned and he seems able to turn his hand to anything practical.'

'That's a good idea, too.'

They were lucky. Wilf answered the door to them himself. He looked tired but greeted them with his usual cheerful smile.

'Would this be a convenient time to speak to you?' Finn asked.

'Of course. You'll excuse me if I yawn, though. I was late getting home, had a devil of a job to finish. If Mr Oakham hadn't told one of his men to drive me to the station, I'd have had to spend the night in the waiting room. As it was I just caught the last train, but I had to walk up to Ellindale from Rivenshaw. Didn't get to bed till well after midnight.'

'Where were you working this time?'

'Over in Rochdale. If I could afford a motorcycle, it'd be a lot easier to go here and there for Oakham's jobs and I could do more of them. Eh, I should be glad of what work I do get, shouldn't I, and never mind having to travel about so much, and I *am* glad of it, of course I am! But I can't help wishing there was more work round here because I miss the children. Anyway, that's enough about me. Come in and Enid will make us all a nice cup of tea.'

'Thanks but not just now. What we really want is to show you something and pick your brain about it. Might even lead to some work closer to home but I'm not promising anything yet.' Finn explained about the old house that was half hidden behind the pub.

Wilf looked across the green at it. 'Who doesn't know the old Hillam place? It sits there as if it's keeping watch over the village. I've never been inside it, though, nor do I know anyone who has, come to think of it. I shall enjoy this. Do you have a door key? If I remember rightly it's a big, old-fashioned lock and you don't look like you're carrying one of those huge iron keys.'

'The key's kept above the coalhouse door, on the lintel.'

Wilf rolled his eyes. 'So that anyone who wants a night's shelter can find it and get inside.'

Finn shrugged. 'If someone is so desperate for shelter, they're welcome to use the place, but for some reason, no one has ever broken in.'

They walked across to the house and stopped at the front to study it closely, even though they knew it by sight.

'What was it used for originally?' Wilf asked.

'Hanged if I know. Old farmhouse, perhaps. Though it doesn't look quite right for that.'

'Hillam means "settlement on a bank or hill" according to the book about the origins of names at home,' Beth said.

'Is there anything you don't know?' Finn asked.

'I remember everything I've read, but that leaves a lot still to find out about the world.'

'Why were you looking at origins of names?'

'I wanted to look up the name of our house and then I read on. I met a few names I recognised.'

And she never forgot anything she'd read. She was truly amazing. 'And Heythorpe means?'

'Hey means an enclosure made of brushwood and Thorpe is an old Norse word for village.'

The two men studied the house again.

'Norse again, eh? I don't think it's that old. That piece of land could have been used as a safe place looking down the valley, I suppose,' Finn said doubtfully.

Wilf moved to study the stonework. 'Well, the building may be old, but it doesn't look as if it's ready to fall down. I don't think it was a poor man's house; it's too big and well built. Shall I go and fetch the key for you?' He hurried round towards the back of the house without waiting for an answer.

Finn turned to Beth. 'It'd be better if you waited outside, love. We don't want to risk anything, do we?'

'I'll wait here till we're sure it's safe, but then I'm coming in. I'm too nosey to stay out here, and why should you two have all the fun?'

Wilf came back with two keys and handed them to Finn with a little mock bow. 'The bigger one's probably the back door on the lower level of the building.'

Finn gestured to the front door. 'Let's go in this way. The lawyer's notes said it was only fit to knock down, but one of the reasons I didn't do that was if I knocked it down, the stones might have been pinched. Do you want to go first, Wilf? You'll have a better idea than me if it's safe. But watch how you go. I don't want you getting hurt.'

Wilf walked to and fro across the front of the house. 'You were right. If you'd knocked it down, the stones would have been taken, one here, one there, because they're nicely dressed. As it is, the house hasn't been damaged in any way that I can see and actually,' he went to squint along the side from the front corner, 'the walls don't look to be sagging or bowing out.'

He patted it as if it was a pet dog. 'Sometimes you'd think old houses were deliberately hiding themselves from the world and putting people off going inside. I've slept in a few when I was out on the tramp looking for jobs, and in some of them I felt comfortable, while others gave me an uneasy feeling. I left one of them in the middle of the night, because I kept hearing noises in the room where I was trying to sleep and yet no one else was there but me. I'm not a fanciful man but that made my hair stand on end.' Wilf shuddered at the memory.

He examined the stonework round the front door, his fingers gently tracing the outlines of the row of bigger stones arranged in a pattern. 'Beautifully put together, these are. Will you let us in, old house? We mean you no harm.'

Finn opened his mouth to protest at this superstitious way of talking to the house, then something made him keep quiet. He didn't know why but he too felt it was the right thing to do.

The lock was stiff and the door moved inwards only a short distance before sticking. Wilf looked at the hinges, poking them with his fingertips. 'Old and a bit rusty. I don't think this front door's been opened for a good long time. Not since my grandfather's day, from what I've heard. People have always used the rear entrance, so I'd guess that door needs attending to as well. It'll only take me a minute to nip home and fetch my oilcan. Soon have the hinges working properly again. Eh, these must be three hundred years old at least. People knew how to make things to last in those days, didn't they?'

Finn looked at him in shock. 'Do you really think the house is that old?'

'Must be if the hinges are, don't you think? I've stayed with Dan Oakham a couple of times when we were out on jobs. He owns an old house, says he can't abide modern ones, and he's got a barn next to it that's even older, where me and another chap slept sometimes. Grand old place, that is. It has hinges very similar to these and Dan seemed sure they were that old. He'd know about that if anyone would.'

Wilf hurried across the village green to his home and was back in less than five minutes holding a battered oilcan the size of a teacup, with a long, thin spout. He carefully dripped oil on the hinges, gave it time to trickle in, then wiggled the door to and fro.

It groaned a protest but opened wide enough for them to squeeze inside, so Wilf dripped some more oil on the hinges. 'We'll let it soak into the rust while we look round.' He put the oilcan down and gestured to Finn to lead the way.

'I'm coming too,' Beth insisted.

'Give me a couple of minutes to check the inside,' Wilf said.

She stood just outside the front door, arms crossed, foot tapping, impatience in every line of her body.

10

Wilf moved forward, feet crunching on dust and fragments of plaster and other debris. He gestured to Finn to stay where he was, examined the nearest door frame, then thumped it, finding it solidly in place. He walked quickly along the corridor to the rear of the house, touching and thumping, then came back to join the others.

'Why did the lawyer say this place was in a tumbledown state, Finn? I reckon it's good for another hundred years. I bet he never even came inside.'

'Mustn't have done. You can come in now, Beth love.'

She joined them, beaming at her two companions. 'Isn't this exciting?'

Wilf barred the way for a moment. 'Let me go right into each room first. I might notice something you'd miss, like the floor giving a bit under you because the joists are rotting.'

'All right. It's bigger than it looks from the outside, isn't it?'

They followed Wilf into a big echoing room on the right with a window looking out on the village green and then into a smaller room on the left. The plaster on the inner walls was patchy and crumbling in parts and the wood of the window frames and doors looked faded where it had caught the sun through the windows.

At the far end of the hall were other rooms on either side and two sets of stairs, one leading downwards, the other up.

In every room Wilf stood and sniffed. 'There's no smell

of damp.' He looked towards the stairs leading down. 'They took advantage of the slope to build an extra level below. I've seen it from outside and always wondered what it was like but there are wooden shutters on the inside of the windows. Let's see what's down there first.'

He led the way down the stairs into a kitchen, dimly lit through gaps in the shutters. Finn opened them and light flooded in to show how huge the room was. At one end stood a large table, as dusty as the rest of the house.

Beth walked along one side wall, which had several doors in it, opening them fully. 'Scullery, storerooms and laundry. Look at that copper boiler. Isn't it huge? It's green with age but it'd look lovely if it was polished.'

Finn stayed in the centre of the room, turning slowly round on the spot. 'This place is far bigger than I'd expected.'

'That's because the rear part is hidden from the road, so you never see the whole house. I definitely haven't seen any sign of damp or dry rot.' Wilf moved to and fro, checking the walls and window frames.

He was surprised to see Beth's initial excitement fade from her face to be replaced by sadness.

'Poor old house. No one's loved it for decades. What happy times this kitchen must have seen, though. We'll bring people back here again, see if we don't.'

Finn was about to move across to his wife but Wilf set one hand on his arm and touched a finger to his lips.

She moved around the lower floor as if she'd forgotten her companions, running one hand over the kitchen windowsill, murmuring that they must put pots of herbs here again, then turning to say that they'd bring in benches and chairs to set round the table, like in the old days.

Then she jerked and turned to her husband as if suddenly coming back to the present. 'Sorry. Did you say something?'

'No, love. You were talking aloud, speaking to the house.'

'Oh, dear. I thought I was just thinking about it. You get a feeling when you go into an empty house, don't you? As if it's been happy or sad, as if it welcomes people or not. I think this place welcomes people and has been lonely without them.'

She turned to Wilf. 'If you can set the house to rights again, and make sure the kitchen range is still working, this big room will be just the place for us to run a job club. Can we go and see the upstairs now?'

'Of course we can. The stairs are probably as sturdy as the rest of the place, but again, let me go up and down them first to check that they won't give way under us.'

They went back to the entrance hall and Wilf studied the stairs as he went up to the top floor. They were made of old dark wood with plenty of scuff marks on the treads, which had slight hollows in the middle from centuries of use. Though the banisters were plain, a good craftsman must have made them, fashioning the joints to fit perfectly and using well-seasoned wood that hadn't warped in all these years.

From the top he called down, 'They're all sound.'

Finn gestured to Beth to go before him, and noticed how she reached out to stroke the dusty banister rail as she went up. He followed her, letting his own hand caress the smooth old wood. He'd bet generations of children had slid down that banister rail. He grinned and decided that one day he'd come here on his own and have a go at it.

Once upstairs he saw Beth touch something in each room, the mantelpiece, a windowsill, the door handle.

'My grandma was like that,' Wilf whispered to Finn at one stage. 'She could sense things others couldn't.'

'I'm not sure I like that thought.'

'It's a gift, like any other, Finn lad. It's how you use it that makes the difference.'

There was another floor up yet another flight of stairs and

there they found some bedrooms, one with furniture piled around it – heavy, old-fashioned pieces.

'Look at this!' Beth pounced on something. 'It's a cradle.'

She started to drag a heavy wooden object out from behind a big wooden chest and Finn grabbed her to prevent her from picking it up.

Wilf got it out, setting it on a rickety table and watching as she used her handkerchief as a duster.

'It's going to be beautiful, just what our baby will need for the first few weeks, Finn love. Eh, I had to put my other two kids to sleep in drawers when they were tiny, because I couldn't afford a cradle. We'll clean and polish this one and our sons will lie snugly in it.'

She always said 'our sons' and seemed so certain that was what their children would be, Finn thought. He wouldn't mind a daughter as well, one with her mother's lively ways and clever mind.

'I'll go over the cradle for you and polish it properly,' Wilf offered. 'This wood is oak.'

'Look at the carving round the edges. It's only a narrow line of leaves but they've been carefully shaped to add a touch of beauty to an everyday object.' Beth gave the cradle one last stroke and stepped back, smiling at him. 'Thank you, Wilf.'

They went downstairs again, and the other two went home, leaving Wilf to go through the place in more detail. He watched them walk away, arm in arm, their love for one another showing so clearly.

It'd be a real pleasure to help Beth. When she'd lived in the village, everyone had seen her cope bravely with hard times after her husband ran off. Neil had never come back and no one had missed him, not even her, he was sure. The fellow had been a lazy good-for-nothing and hadn't deserved a pretty, hard-working woman like her.

And now Beth had remarried, finding a good man this time. She didn't flaunt her second husband's wealth or look down her nose at her old friends and neighbours, either.

That was how people should be with one another. If he ever made good money, he'd not think himself above his fellow men.

He smiled on that thought. When had he ever made good money? He'd been getting through these hard times by the skin of his teeth, going off on the tramp, carving little figures from bits of wood he scavenged and getting a friend to sell them at the market in Rivenshaw. He'd always managed to keep himself and his wife fed and pay the rent without going on the dole. It had been a struggle, though.

But a man could dream of a better life, couldn't he? It was all that kept you going sometimes, dreaming of happier times when you were soaking wet on a cold rainy day, tramping the countryside without finding work.

As Finn and Beth walked home, arms linked, he said, 'I thought you wanted a brand new cradle for our child.'

'I did until I saw that old one. Think of the babies who've slept in it. It felt as if they'd left happy dreams there.' She saw him frown and said quietly, 'I think people do leave traces behind as they pass through this world. They make houses seem happy or unhappy. You can sense it the minute you walk into a place.'

'Some houses do seem more . . . welcoming, I suppose you'd call it, but I don't think I can sense that as strongly as you do. You certainly seemed to like that old house.'

'I did. I wonder why it was abandoned. Are you sure the lawyers said it was falling down?'

'You can check the records at home, Beth. I still have all my correspondence with them. In the list of what I inherited it states very clearly that Hillam House is old and dilapidated, not worth restoring. I don't even know when my family acquired that house.'

'We liked the feel of it when we went inside, yet people from the village have kept away from it for as long as I can remember. I wonder why. You wouldn't know about it, being an outsider, but us kids used to dare one another to touch the front door knocker.'

'And did *you* do that?'

'Once or twice. It didn't frighten me but my mam told me off for going near it. I'll check your family records and find out what I can. I love looking through old papers and seeing how people lived. That account book I found last week in the library has recipes in the back. Good ones, too.'

She yawned as she was speaking and he smiled. 'Go and have a nap. It's that time of day.'

'I wasn't like this when I was carrying the other two. All I had was morning sickness for a few weeks. This time I've hardly been sick at all, but I feel sleepy by the end of the morning and have to have a short nap.'

'Well, there's nothing stopping you from doing that, is there? I might go back to the house and make a few plans with Wilf.'

She was yawning again, so he left her to it.

Wilf decided to start at the top of the house and walked round the top floor again, checking the walls more thoroughly and then sorting through the jumble of furniture to get some idea of what there was.

He heard the front door open and footsteps on the stairs, and turned as Finn came up to join him.

'Beth's having a nap. How's it going here?'

'I've checked this floor and it's just about watertight, even after all these years. There's been a small leak in one place. Soon fix that. Um, if you want me to, that is, Finn?'

'Yes. In fact if you want the job of going through the whole house and setting it to rights, it's yours. I'll pay you at whatever rate you think fair to work fast, maybe hire someone to help you. I want to get this place ready to use as quickly as we can.'

'Happy to do that.'

'And after it's finished, I'd like you to go through Heythorpe House. I want to bring it up to date. We could put in another bathroom for the servants, for one thing, and make better arrangements in the kitchen and laundry, put in a gas stove, for instance, now that we have gas out here in Ellindale. Oh, and it needs a new sink in the scullery – there's only an old sandstone slopstone there at the moment. And you can do anything else Beth and the other women think would improve matters.'

Wilf couldn't stop himself from beaming. 'That'll take a few weeks.'

'Yes. Is that all right?'

'Definitely. It's what I've been praying for, work that'll let me stay at home with Enid and the kids.'

He and Enid had tried for kids for years but never succeeded. Now, he loved their two adopted children as dearly as if they were his own. Their mother was dead and their father in prison for a long time. Ronnie and Peggy had settled in quickly, responding to kind but firm treatment after the cruelty and neglect of their actual parents. They were blossoming like flowers in spring and so was Enid now she had children to love.

He realised Finn had asked him something and was waiting for an answer. 'Sorry. What was that again?'

'Will Dan Oakham mind you working for me in the coming weeks? Obviously this won't be a permanent job, and I'd not like you to lose other chances.'

'Dan won't mind. He has a few men he calls in when he

needs them and he shares the work out among us. There isn't any work at all with him half the time, because we're not permanent at the railways, we just get the overflow work, so to speak. It's a good thing my friend can sell the occasional carving of mine at the market. That makes a big difference.'

'That's settled, then.'

The two men shook hands on the bargain, then Finn started to discuss the practicalities of setting up the house for the job club. 'Beth's looking forward to seeing about furniture for this place once it's ready, but I'd be grateful if you could organise some men to help with the fetching and carrying from our house.'

'We can bring some stuff down from the top floor.'

'The spare furniture from the attics at Heythorpe is old-fashioned and some of it needs mending, but perhaps you can deal with that? You're good with wood. There ought to be enough for our purposes.'

'I heard Crazy Tam is back and he's got a van. Perhaps we can hire him to transport it. He's staying in the youth hostel at Spring Cottage.'

'Good idea.'

'I'll go through the furniture in both places and see which pieces are usable,' Wilf promised.

'Right then. The sooner you can get this place fixed up, the better. If you need to hire help to do it quickly, find someone.'

'Don't you want me to check that with you first?'

'No need. I trust you completely and you'll know people's worth as workers better than I do, since you grew up in Ellindale. All I ask is that you try to hire people from the village, if possible.'

'I will. I'll go home and get my measure and some paper, then start making notes on what I find. I could come round to your place this evening to show you. Is that quick enough?'

He didn't want to miss a day's pay and was already working out what it would be fair to charge. How strange to have an employer who was also a friend.

'That'll be fine. I'll go home now and start working out what activities to offer in the job club. I think Rivenshaw's town council offers grants to help such projects, so I'll get in touch with them as well.'

When Finn had gone, Wilf ran home, burst into the kitchen and picked Enid up, swinging her round and round till she shouted at him to put her down.

'Whatever's got into you, Wilf Pollard?'

'I've just landed a job in Ellindale for a few weeks, perhaps longer.'

She cheered and plonked kisses all over his face. 'That's wonderful, just wonderful. What will you be doing?'

He explained and she stared at him in amazement.

'Do you know how to do all those jobs, love?'

He moved his hands in the air as if outlining something. 'If I don't know now, I'll figure it out when I see what's needed. The only thing I'm not sure about is putting in electricity, but I can ask Harry Makepeace about that. I know he's working full-time for Mr Willcox in his electrical shop, but he'll be happy to help me figure out what's needed – and Mr Willcox will encourage him to do that if Flynn agrees to buy the things he'll need, like kettles, from Willcox's shop in Rivenshaw.'

'Harry's settled in well in the village, hasn't he?'

'Him and Nina both.'

'He's got the inside of that railway carriage really comfortable now, good as a house, it is. Nina showed me round it the other day after I ran into her at the shop. She says Cathie's keeping really well these days, no breathless attacks. The child hasn't looked back since her dad brought her to live in the clean air up here. Eh, it'd be lovely to own your own home like they do, wouldn't it?'

He stared at her wistful face. He felt just the same. Suddenly determination filled him. 'One day we'll have a place of our own, too. Things are going to improve in Lancashire like they have in the south, I can smell it in the air.'

'Get on with you. You've always been a dreamer.'

'Wait and see. I got us through the worst times without going on the dole, didn't I? And I'm getting more jobs these days, so what's dreaming got to do with that?'

'I still think hard about every penny I spend. But we've got children now and that makes me happy. They're much more important than money. I can't tell you how much I love Peggy and Ronnie.'

'You don't have to tell me. I see it every day.'

He saw tears well in her eyes and had to hold her close for a few moments till the emotions had subsided. Only he knew how upset she'd been that she'd never quickened with a child of her own body.

He had to blow his nose good and hard to get rid of the tears in his own eyes. 'Right then, I need to get to work.'

She patted his cheek and stepped back. 'So do I. What a good news day this is.'

But he couldn't resist another quick hug before he sorted out what tools he needed to take to Hillam House.

11

Leah put the phone down, grabbed her coat and crammed a hat on anyhow. Snatching her handbag from the sideboard, she called, 'Ginny, I have to go out and I don't know when I'll be back. That was the grammar school. Rosa's been taken ill.'

She was already at the door by then and didn't stop to explain further. Well, she didn't know much else to tell them, did she, only that she had to get to her sister as fast as she could.

She drove down the valley road more quickly than usual, but fortunately most people were either at work or about their business, so the roads were almost clear.

When she got to the school, she abandoned the car in front of the main entrance and rushed inside.

A woman standing behind the counter looked up.

'I'm Mrs Willcox. I got a message that my sister Rosa was ill.'

'It was me calling. You didn't let me finish before you put the phone down. They've taken her to the cottage hospital.'

'*What?* What's wrong?'

'I couldn't say. Matron sent for an ambulance and your sister was carried out on a stretcher.'

Leah's stomach lurched with terror. People didn't call an ambulance for nothing. She turned and ran back to her car, driving as quickly as she could to the south side of town, where the cottage hospital was situated.

Once again, she abandoned her car near the door and ran inside the main building.

The woman behind this reception counter couldn't explain anything either. Speaking soothingly, she showed Leah into a cubicle. 'Please wait here while I fetch someone who can tell you more about your sister.'

The minutes ticked by slowly and Leah jerked to her feet every time she heard someone walking past. It seemed an eternity until footsteps stopped outside her cubicle. A nurse slid the curtain aside and said, 'Mrs Willcox? Please come with me.'

'Is my sister all right?'

'Matron will explain.'

Leah followed the nurse, so anxious she could hardly breathe.

Splendid in a starched, winged cap and gleaming white apron over a navy blue tailored dress, Matron stood up to greet her but stayed behind the desk. 'Ah, Mrs Willcox. Please sit down.'

As soon as Leah had done that the matron said in the tone of voice of someone talking to a stupid child, 'There is no need to worry, Mrs Willcox. Your sister is going to be all right.'

Leah sagged in her chair, then the words sank in. '*Going to be* all right? What happened? No one will tell me what was wrong. Rosa was a bit pale this morning and didn't eat much breakfast, but she didn't seem *ill*. She hates to miss school.'

'Your sister collapsed with acute appendicitis, so she must have been in considerable pain this morning. If the school matron hadn't been quick to realise what it was likely to be, the girl might have been in real trouble. As it is, they got her to hospital quickly and since she'd thrown up her breakfast, the doctor was able to operate at once. Rosa is recovering in the operating theatre at the moment. She's too old for the children's ward and will be taken to the women's ward once she's fully conscious.'

'Can I see her?'

'Not until she's settled in her bed. This is a small hospital and you'd be in the way if you went into the recovery room.'

'Rosa's never been ill before. I can't believe I didn't notice something.'

'Girls of that age can be very secretive about their bodies. Now, is there someone we could send for to be with you? Your husband, perhaps?'

'I'm a widow and I'm my sister's sole guardian.' She wondered briefly whether to send for her brother-in-law, but though she had no doubt Charlie would come, he wasn't the sort of person to make you feel calmer.

Then she thought of Todd. She had no doubt he'd come and he was a sensible man. 'My fiancé, Todd Selby. He'd be a comfort to me and a help if I needed something.'

'Good. You'll be better if you have someone with you.' She made a tutting sound and added, 'My dear, don't look so frantic. We have a very good doctor and he was quick to operate. Everything's going to be all right.'

'If I could just *see* Rosa.'

'Soon. Now, I'm going to send you to our inner waiting room till your sister is settled and fully awake again, which may take half an hour or more. In the meantime, is your fiancé on the telephone? Oh, good. Give Mrs Broughton at Reception his number and she'll put a call through to him.'

A few minutes later Mrs Broughton handed her the telephone. 'Here you are, Mrs Willcox. Please be quick because other people may need to speak to someone at the hospital.'

Leah couldn't stop her voice quavering as she said his name. 'Todd? It's me.'

'What's wrong?'

'Rosa's just had an emergency operation to remove her appendix. I'm waiting at the hospital to see her now. Could you—' she still couldn't keep her voice steady. 'Could you come here and stay with me?'

'I'll be there in five minutes at most.'

'Drive carefully. I don't want two people I love brought in here on stretchers.'

'I'll drive very carefully, my darling.'

She couldn't bear to sit still and the room was so small she began pacing up and down the entrance hall. But Mrs Broughton came across to ask her to stay in the waiting room because she was upsetting other visitors by looking so anxious, so she stood looking out of the window, tapping her fingers on the windowsill.

The minutes passed slowly and there was no sign of Todd, no word about Rosa. What was keeping him?

After their second night at the youth hostel Tam finished his breakfast and looked sadly at Cara. 'I think I'd better go and see Mrs Willcox. She only said we could stay for a couple of nights so we may have to leave here today.'

She nodded. They'd discussed this the previous evening before she joined the children to sleep in the bedroom. Neither of them wanted to be a nuisance to someone who had been so kind to them.

'I lay awake last night, racking my brain, but I couldn't think what to do about finding a place of our own.'

'There must be rooms or even a house to rent somewhere in the valley, Tam. Unless you want to go to some other town?'

'I told you: I definitely don't. I came back here to stay, and that's what I'm going to do, whatever it takes, as long as it's all right with you. I know I've got some money, but I don't want to spend a penny of it if I don't have to till we know what we're getting into.'

'I agree.'

He stood up. 'No time like the present. I'll nip across to the house and speak to Mrs Willcox.'

After he'd gone, Cara turned to Jinna. 'Can you help me with the dishes, please?'

Jinna nodded and started clearing the table, stacking the dishes in the exact same way Cara had shown her the first time they washed up after moving in.

Cara ran some hot water from the gas geyser over the sink and began the washing up. What a treat it was to be able to get hot water immediately! She'd always had to boil a kettle or a panful till now. 'Here. You dry the dishes for me.' She kept an eye on the girl, but once Jinna had been shown how to do something, she seemed to remember it. Indeed, she seemed to think it was the only way to do a task from then on and looked bewildered if they tried to do it slightly differently.

'It'd be easier if you started speaking to us. Can't you try?' She glanced sideways.

Jinna stopped work, frowning and opening her mouth then closing it again.

'At least tell me why you don't speak to us. Tam heard you speak to your mother, so we know you *can* speak.'

The girl put her arms round her chest as if protecting herself, then said in a whisper, 'Mum said to keep quiet, always keep quiet. Always.'

Rejoicing that she'd managed to get a reply out of Jinna, Cara tried to carry on casually, 'Why did she tell you that, do you know?'

The silence dragged on, but she waited, desperate to find out and help this girl who seemed trapped behind invisible walls, so she waited.

'People get mad at me,' Jinna said slowly.

'Why?'

'I say the wrong things. They get mad.'

'I wouldn't get mad at you, whatever you said.'

Jinna was still looking anxious, so Cara began washing the other dishes to give her more pots to wipe. 'Tam wouldn't get mad at you, either. He doesn't get mad at people.'

'He got mad at those boys who were hurting me.'

'That was different. They were being unkind to you. It's wrong to be unkind.'

Jinna frowned as if she was thinking about what had been said, so Cara finished washing the dishes, then began to set the rest of the kitchen to rights. If they were leaving, everything had to be left as they'd found it, or she'd not feel right.

She and Tam had cleaned the rest of the youth hostel in payment for staying, and done a good job of it, too, if she said so herself. It seemed strange to have a man doing housework, but he seemed to know what he was doing.

She had a sudden idea. 'Jinna, why don't you try speaking to us? Just to me and Tam and Ned at first. Like you did to your mum. We're your family now. We won't get mad at you.'

Another of those frowns, another of those silences, then a nod.

Relief ran through Cara in a happy tide. That was the key for all of them, she was sure: family. Everyone needed people they could rely on.

Oh, how she had longed to be part of a proper family again when she was left on her own with her grandson! She had been so lucky to find Tam. She smiled and mentally corrected herself: *lucky that Phyllis had found Tam for her.*

She owed her cousin a lot for that.

When Tam went outside, Mrs Willcox's car wasn't parked under its shelter as usual. Surely she hadn't gone out already? Had she just nipped to the shop? Only one way to find out.

He walked across the yard to the house and knocked on the door of Spring Cottage. It was opened by Ginny.

'Could I speak to Mrs Willcox, please?'

'She went out. Didn't you hear the car leave?'

'No. The kitchen's at the other side of the hostel. Do you know when she'll be back?'

'I'm afraid I don't. The school phoned to say her sister was ill so she rushed off. Who knows when she'll be back? She might have to take Rosa to see the doctor.'

Dismay ran through him and collected in a heavy lump in his chest. 'She said she'd let us stay for a couple of days but—'

There was a sudden screech from inside the house and someone called to Ginny to come quickly because Jonty had spilled his milk all over everything.

'I'm sure you'll leave the place tidy. I have to go. That lass hasn't the sense she was born with in an emergency.'

He was left staring at a closed door.

When he got back, he saw Cara's face fall and knew his disappointment must have shown on his face.

'She won't let us stay?'

'She's not there. The school called. Her sister is ill. Ginny said she was sure we'd leave the place tidy, so Mrs Willcox can't have been expecting us to stay. Then Ginny got called away by that young maid screeching for help.'

'What are we going to do?'

'We can't stay where we're not wanted. We'll have to look for somewhere to rent. We'll drive round all the streets in Rivenshaw, look in the corner shops for notices, look in the newspaper at the library. And if we can't find anywhere by late afternoon, we'll have to come back and ask to camp on my cousin's land till we do find somewhere to rent.'

'Oh, dear. It was obvious your cousin didn't want us.'

'I know. But we've not got any choice and I'm sure Peter

won't turn us away. I *am* his cousin, after all. I know there are always rooms to let in Backshaw Moss, but I'm not going there. The drains are so bad it makes people ill. I had a brother once who died because of them. Everything about that place is bad. There are folk living there as'd steal your last crust, an' they'd try to bully Jinna. As for my van, I'd be feared to leave it parked in the street overnight, I would that.'

'Not many people have cars or vans there anyway, from what Phyllis has said.'

'No. Or anything else much, either. The houses there are good for nothing but knocking down. Look, Cara, I've got some money. If the worst comes to the worst and my cousin won't let us stay, we'll find lodgings for the time being. But only if we absolutely have to.'

She took a deep breath and nodded. 'That's what we'll do, then.'

'I'm sorry to have got us into such a mess.'

That brought a faint smile to her lips. 'I was in a far worse mess when you rescued me from that place, Tam. We'll manage somehow.'

'Ah, you're a grand lass.'

'And you're a lovely chap.'

They spent the morning driving round Rivenshaw, looking for a house to rent. There was nothing in the newspaper, nothing in the adverts on cards at corner shops, either.

After buying something to eat and using the public conveniences near the park, Tam looked sadly at Cara. 'It'll take time to put up the tent, so we'd better go and see my cousin Peter and arrange to camp there for a few days.'

'Then what?'

'We keep on looking for a building plot *or* a house to rent. We're not penniless. There must be other farmers selling off bits and pieces of land to help them through the hard times. I've come across it several times when I was on the tramp.'

Like him, she was reluctant to dip into their savings, he could tell. Money was so hard to come by, you had to watch what you did with every farthing.

Todd ran into the hospital and explained to the woman at the reception desk that he was looking for Mrs Willcox. 'I'm her fiancé.'

'Good thing you came. She's panicking and getting in people's way, coming out every five minutes to ask about her sister.'

He was surprised at the woman's grumpy tone. 'Where is she?'

'In the special waiting room at the back.' She pointed. 'And try not to make a noise.'

Todd went in and found Leah standing looking out of the window. She spun round rapidly at the sound of the door opening, her face twisted with anxiety. He held out his arms and she rushed into them, gulping and trying not to cry.

Once she'd calmed down a little, he asked, 'What exactly is going on?'

'Rosa collapsed at school and she's had to have her appendix out. Only they won't let me see her, not even a glimpse. I have to wait till she's recovered from the anaesthetic and been taken to the ward. I've looked after her since she was little, Todd. If I could just *see* her, be sure she's recovering. Why won't they let me? Something must have gone wrong.'

'No, they'd fetch you quickly if something was wrong. They're always like this in hospitals. You have to do as they tell you. Rules and regulations about everything. Don't ask questions. Don't make a noise. They're worse than the army!'

She gave him a watery smile. 'I know I'm being silly, but she's so precious to me.'

'I know. Come and sit down, love, eh?'

He kept hold of her hand as they sat on two hard wooden chairs next to one another. He patted their linked hands from time to time with his free hand but she didn't seem to notice. She didn't try to let go of him, though.

'I'm glad you sent for me, Leah. It made me feel wanted.'

'I knew you'd come, knew I'd feel better with you by my side.'

Suddenly all his fears about asking her to marry him seemed foolish. Life twisted and turned, and you had to grab happiness whenever you could. 'Everything would be easier for both of us if we were married, Leah love. I don't know why we're waiting. Do you?'

'I've been waiting for you to ask me. I wasn't sure whether you were quite ready to take the plunge yet.'

'I was worried because you have more money than me.'

She stared at him. 'I thought that was stopping you. I don't care about that. Jonah had a lot more money than me but it didn't stop us living happily together.'

'No. I've been silly, and I'm going to stop that right now.' He grabbed hold of her other hand. 'This isn't a very romantic place for a proposal, but darling Leah, will you please marry me, and as soon as possible, because I can't bear to wait any longer?'

'I don't want to wait, either. Of course I'll marry you.'

He raised each of her hands to his lips in turn, kissing them gently. 'You've made me a very happy man. Rosa can be our bridesmaid and Charlie can give you away. I think we have to give a month's notice that we're getting married.'

The door opened and a nurse came in. 'You can see your sister now, Mrs Willcox. This way.'

Todd moved forward with her.

The nurse frowned at him. 'We don't want too many people in the ward at this time of day. It's not visiting hours yet.'

'My fiancée is upset. I'd like to come with her. We want to tell Rosa that we've just named the day.'

For a moment the nurse's stern expression softened and with a little shrug, she said, 'Very well. But only for ten minutes. She needs to rest.'

Rosa was lying in a hard, narrow bed, face pale, eyes closed. When she heard footsteps she opened her eyes. 'Leah.'

Her sister bent over to kiss her. 'How are you, love?'

'My head's all dopey and my stomach hurts.'

'In future, tell me if you feel ill or have a pain.'

'I didn't want to miss my lessons. I thought it'd go away. It has before.'

'You're top of the class. It won't hurt to miss one or two lessons.'

'But I *like* learning things. Will you ask Evelyn to get me the homework?'

'Yes. But not for a day or two. I'll go and buy you a book to read in the meantime.'

'Thank you.' She looked beyond her sister, seeming to notice Todd for the first time. 'Hello, Mr Selby.'

Leah took his hand. 'Todd and I have just agreed to get married as soon as we can, so I'm going to need a bridesmaid. Another reason for you to get better quickly.'

Rosa rolled her eyes. 'About time too. Everyone in the valley knows you're going to get married.'

They both gaped at her.

'They do?'

'Yes. You look all soppy when you're together.' She wriggled down in bed. 'So I'd better start calling you Todd, hadn't I, if you're going to be my brother-in-law?' Another wriggle, a wince and her eyes closed.

'We'll leave you to sleep,' Leah said softly.

'Mmm.'

The nurse on duty said brightly, 'You can come again during visiting hours, from four to six in the afternoon.'

When they got back to the entrance, Todd said, 'What do you want to do till we're allowed back?'

'Buy Rosa a book then go home.'

'Why don't you go via my business and I'll make you a cup of tea? You look exhausted.'

'You're sure you can spare the time?'

'Very sure. I can always spare time for you.'

12

Leah got into her car and followed Todd to Willcox and Selby Motors. As she drew up outside she saw Mr Crawford walking away from the front of the premises towards the van, looking down-spirited. His fiancée was sitting in the passenger seat of the van, also looking unhappy, and the two children appeared to be squashed in the back of the van among the family's possessions.

Only then did Leah remember she'd been going to tell them today that it was all right for them to stay on a few days longer at the youth hostel. Oh, no! They must have thought they had to leave. Guilt shot through her.

He hadn't noticed her, so she flung the car door open and yelled, 'Mr Crawford! Stop! Stop!'

He turned round and waited for her to hurry along the footpath to him. 'Hello, Mrs Willcox. We tried to thank you but you'd left for the hospital. How is your sister?'

'She's recovering nicely. She had acute appendicitis and had to have her appendix out suddenly.'

Todd drove into the yard, got out of his car and came over to join them, putting an arm round her shoulders as if he knew instinctively she was still feeling upset. 'How are things, Mr Crawford?'

Tam hesitated. 'Um. Well, not so good, Mr Selby. We've been looking for a house to rent, but the only places are rooms in Backshaw Moss and I'm not having my family stay there. It's a filthy place, really bad drains.' He looked at Ned, and added, 'Little kids get sick and die there. Um—'

Leah guessed what he was going to ask and spoke first. 'I'd intended to speak to you this morning about an idea I've had but I forgot everything when I had to rush to the hospital to see my sister. I'm so sorry.'

'Nay. Your sister comes first. Family is so important.' Once again, his eyes went to the two children in the van.

A sudden gust of wind whirled past, dragging at their clothes and sucking the warmth from their bodies. When she shivered, Todd said, 'Let's go inside my house to talk. The weather's gone back to winter again this afternoon. You all look as if you'd welcome a cup of tea.'

'Thanks, Mr Selby. We'd love one.' Tam went back to help his family out of the van.

Once they were inside, Todd gestured with one hand at the rather bare room. 'I'm just camping out here, as you can see. Most of the house isn't even furnished. Sorry about this untidiness. I'll put the kettle on. Leah, please sit in my chair. It's rather shabby but it's comfortable. Would you like to sit over here, Mr Crawford, Mrs—?'

'Pruin.' Cara put one arm round Jinna's shoulder. 'And this is—'

'I know Jinna by sight. How is the drawing going, lass?'

She stared at him, not speaking, but her lips twitched into an almost-smile for a second or two.

Cara spoke for her. 'Jinna's doing some lovely pictures for us.' She patted a chair. 'Sit down here, love, next to Ned.'

Leah watched them. The girl was still looking stiff and wary. Mr Crawford had certainly taken on a difficult task, making a family out of this group. 'I was wondering if you'd like to spend another night or two at the youth hostel?' She was pleased to see Tam's face brighten immediately into that slightly crooked smile that was so peculiarly his own.

'Are you sure that'd be all right, Mrs Willcox? We don't

want to inconvenience you, what with your sister being ill and all.'

'I'm sure. Are you still intending to settle permanently in the valley?'

'Oh, yes. I'd like to live as close to the moors as I can and Cara doesn't mind where she lives as long as she has a decent home, eh lass?' He smiled at his fiancée as he continued, 'Ellindale has always been my favourite place, but there wasn't much work in the valley when I was younger, and when my wife died I went on the tramp. I just kept wandering round, coming back to visit whenever I could afford it, even though I've no close relatives left here now apart from the Kerkhams, and they're not really close.'

'They're not very, um, very sociable people, though perfectly polite to everyone, of course.'

'No. They've always kept themselves to themselves. I shan't be dependent on them for company, though, because I shall soon make friends here again once I start up in business as a carrier with my van. I've always been good at finding ways to earn a shilling or two. But I can't do anything properly till I find somewhere permanent for us to live.'

Frustration bubbled up and he exclaimed, 'Worst of all, Cara and I can't even book a wedding till we have a permanent address in the valley.'

Leah decided to put a vague idea she'd had yesterday into action. 'You know, if you don't mind continuing to squeeze the four of you into the matron's living quarters, I could offer Mrs Pruin a job temporarily till you do find your own place to live. I've not been able to find anyone suitable to act as matron there and I'm sure you could cope with looking after the hikers, Mrs Pruin. It's mainly housekeeping stuff: beds and clean bedding – which goes to the laundry in Rivenshaw – simple breakfasts, with the occasional evening meal.'

She could see the answer before she heard the response

as Cara's face brightened, making her look younger suddenly.

'I'd enjoy that. I like making people comfortable.'

Todd was still looking thoughtful. 'I'll ask around about houses to rent or plots of land to buy, and get my partner Charlie to do the same. He knows more people than anyone else in Rivenshaw does, if you ask me. Someone must have a piece of land for sale. Five pounds, wasn't it, that Mr Makepeace paid for his plot?'

'Yes. I have the money and once that's settled, I know how to get hold of a caravan to live in till I can afford to build a proper house.'

Jinna tugged at Cara's arm, leaned forward and whispered, 'Ned needs to go to the lav.'

Their host looked at Jinna in surprise when she spoke.

Cara realised her grandson was jigging about uncomfortably. 'I wonder if Ned could use your lavatory, Mr Selby?'

'Of course. It's out at the back, through that door and across the yard. I'll show you.'

'Will you take him, Jinna?' Cara asked. 'You can go yourself at the same time.'

With a nod, the girl stood up, and Todd showed the two children where to go.

'I didn't know Jinna could speak,' Leah whispered.

Keeping her voice low, Cara said, 'Her mother told her not to speak to people, and kept her mostly shut away from them. I don't know why she thought that necessary. The girl seems perfectly sensible to me. But she's not used to dealing with the world, so we're hoping to help her understand what to do and say in everyday life. She's agreed that she'll speak to me and Tam, and we'll see how she goes with that, then we can maybe persuade her to speak to others.'

Leah shook her head sadly. 'People can be cruel, especially children, when someone's a bit different. But still, it was

strange to keep her shut up at home and tell her not to speak
to people. What on earth was the mother thinking of?'

'I've wondered that myself.'

'Well, if I can help in any way, just let me know.'

'You're very kind.'

'People have been kind to me. I like to pass it on.'

Jinna came back, hesitating in the doorway until Tam beckoned her across, then sitting stiffly upright on the edge of
the chair beside his. When Ned came to stand next to her
and leaned against her, she relaxed a little and put her arm
round him in just the same way Tam put an arm round any
of them who was close.

Once they'd finished their drinks, Tam stood up. 'We'd
better get going. We need to buy some meat for tonight as
well as settling in again in the hostel.'

'We'll work out the details of how to run the youth hostel
tomorrow, if that's all right,' Leah said. 'I have to go home
and get some clothes and books to take to the hospital for
Rosa. Once she wakes up properly, she'll want something to
do while she's in there. That girl's brain isn't idle for a single
moment unless she's asleep. Jonah used to tease her that she
probably thinks up mathematical problems to solve even in
her dreams!'

After Tam and his makeshift family had left, Leah leaned
back in the old armchair. 'I'm so tired. I'll rest for a few more
minutes, then get off home.'

'Have a little nap,' Todd suggested. 'You aren't allowed
back in the hospital till four o'clock, after all.'

'No, I'm not, am I? I'll just close my eyes for a few minutes,
then.'

Still as a statue he watched her, listening to her breathing
slow down and deepen into sleep. He left her and went
out into his workshop with a happy smile, thinking how

wonderful it would be when they were together every day.

It was over an hour before she came out to join him and her cheeks were distinctly rosier.

'Do you feel better now, Leah love?'

'Yes, thanks. But I really do have to go home. Ginny will be wondering what's happened to me. Thank you for coming to the hospital. I needed you.'

'My pleasure. Before you leave, let's agree on a date for our wedding and book it as soon as possible. I've been waiting such a long time for you. I don't want to wait any longer.'

'I know. But we couldn't do anything till after I'd had Jonah's baby.'

'I fell in love with you a long time before that – the first time I saw you, in fact. Only you were married to Jonah and I knew you'd never betray him. Nor would I go after a married woman. The problem was, I couldn't think of courting any other woman after I'd met you, my darling. So how about tomorrow, before you visit Rosa, we sort out a date and call at the registry office in Rivenshaw to set up our wedding.'

Her smile was wonderful to see. 'Yes, let's do that. But not a fancy wedding, eh? Just ourselves and those closest to us.'

He took her hand and raised it to his lips. 'Your wish is my command.'

As they walked out to her car, he was wishing she could stay longer or he could go with her. Unfortunately he still had some repairs to finish for a client. It'd been a strange sort of day but it had ended well. Better than well.

He was so happy at the thought of setting a date for his wedding that he wanted to make the whole world happy too. It was good that they'd run into Tam and his family and been able to help them.

He hoped the four of them would find somewhere permanent to live in the valley. Surely someone would have a small piece of land to sell? Five pounds for a small, useless piece of earth seemed to be the going price in Lancashire in these hard times when few people had even one pound to spare.

Whistling cheerfully, he went back to work, smiling every time he thought of marrying Leah – which was quite often.

'It feels like coming home,' Cara said as they chugged up the last slope before Ellindale. 'Don't forget to stop at the shop. I need to buy something to put with the meat for a stew.'

'I hadn't forgotten.'

'And we need to do something about how you sleep. You can't be comfortable on the floor.'

'I'm comfortable enough. At least we're all together.'

'Well, I think you deserve better than a hard floor. We could bring in a mattress from the men's dormitory and put it on the floor for you.'

'Good idea. But I'd rather sleep on a bare floor with you three nearby than on a soft feather bed miles away.'

He said such nice things, she thought as she turned to the girl. 'Jinna, love. Stay here and keep Ned with you in the van.'

'We'll stay here.' Jinna watched her anxiously as if checking whether what she'd said was all right.

'That's right. Good girl.'

'Stay here,' Ned echoed at the top of his voice. 'Stay here! Stay here!' Then he began singing a nursery rhyme.

One day, Cara decided, I'll teach that girl to shout and sing, too. She's far too quiet for a young 'un. No wonder she's so obsessed with drawing. She's probably never had any friends of her own age or been allowed to run about outside. I wonder if she even went to school? Can she read and write? Now wasn't the time to ask her, but she'd wait for a quiet moment and find out.

'Our lass spoke to you a few times today,' Tam commented as they walked towards the shop.

He was calling Jinna 'our lass' already, Cara thought. She'd already learned that was Tam's way. He dived straight into everything, even making a family. She kept that thought to herself in case he thought she was criticising him. She wasn't. It was a nice way to behave. Honest and open. Better by far than lying to folk, keeping things secret and sneaking around.

Aloud she said only, 'Jinna said her mother told her not to speak to other people because they used to get angry with her when she did.'

'Angry? Why would they do that?'

She shrugged. 'My guess is she blurted out whatever she thought and offended them. Some people can be far too blunt-spoken and perhaps she's one. There was a lad in my class at school like that. The teacher shouted at him so often, he stopped talking. He was just the same when he grew up, saying exactly what he thought, not to hurt people but because he couldn't seem to do anything else.'

'I've met people like that, too. Some folk call them tactless; others say they're honest.'

'Well, if Jinna's mother was timid, she might have been afraid of upsetting people. We'll no doubt find out if my guess is right, but—'

' – *we* won't get angry with her,' he finished off.

In the shop, they found Frankie Kerkham with a shopping list in his hand and the young shopkeeper putting items into his shopping basket. A bowl of eggs stood next to it on the counter.

'Morning,' Tam said to them both. 'Not at school today, lad?'

'No. Dad's not well, so Mum needs me to help with the animals. An' I brought the eggs in.'

'What's wrong with your dad?'

Frankie shrugged. 'He gets to feeling weak, so he has to lie down.'

That seemed a strange sort of illness, Cara thought. 'What does the doctor say it is?'

'Dad doesn't like doctors. An' anyway, it costs money to see one.'

'There's a new young doctor in Birch End who'll see folk for nothing if they're broke.'

'Mum won't ask for charity. She says she'd rather die first.'

Lily interrupted. 'That's everything on your list, Frankie. It comes to three and sixpence, with the egg money taken off.'

The lad fumbled through some coins and blushed bright red. 'You'll have to take something back. I haven't got that much money.'

The shopkeeper hesitated.

'Tell me what the difference is. I'll pay it this time,' Tam offered.

'Mam won't like that.' But Frankie looked longingly at the tin of corned beef Lily had removed from the basket after she'd added up the coins he was holding out.

'Well, you don't need to tell her then, do you? Go on. Give him the corned beef back, Miss Pendle.' Tam turned back to the boy. 'Tell your dad I'll pop in to see him tomorrow.'

'Dad doesn't want people coming to the house and staring at him.'

'Staring at him? What's to stare at?'

'He's gone that thin, Mam says he's like a skellington, except for here, where he's gone fat.' The lad patted his belly, then hesitated and said, 'Thanks for helping us, Mr Crawford. If you don't mind, I won't tell Mam about you buying us the corned beef, though. We've been a bit short lately.'

'I'm your dad's cousin, so I'm family, and family should help one another. You ought to call me Cousin Tam.'

'All right. Cousin Tam. I've never met anyone called Tam before. Is it short for something?'

'Aye. Short for Thomas but my dad was called Thomas, so I got shortened to Tam, because we had a neighbour called Tommy.'

'Tam's a nicer name.'

After Frankie had gone, the shopkeeper shook her head sadly. 'Mr Kerkham's been ill for a while now, though he tries to hide it, but you could see him getting worse. That lad is having to work hard on the farm and he's missed a lot of schooling because of it.'

Tam didn't like the sound of that. The Kerkhams were, after all, relatives. 'I'll find out what's going on and if he needs to see a doctor, I could drive him down to the one in Birch End. Now, we need to buy quite a few things because Mrs Willcox says we can stay on at the youth hostel and Cara can work as matron.'

'Welcome to Ellindale, then. I hope you'll all be happy here.'

Once they'd bought the groceries, he hesitated, then looked out of the window at Jinna, sitting so patiently in the car. 'Have you got any paper – you know, a pad or an exercise book? My daughter likes to draw. And she'll need a pencil too.'

The shopkeeper followed his gaze and looked out of the window at the van. 'Isn't that the girl who sits with Sarey at market sometimes? How can she be your daughter?'

'Her mother's just died and—'

'She's a distant relative of mine,' Cara put in quickly. 'So we're adopting her after we get married. We're fond of her already so we're treating her as a daughter.'

'Oh, that's nice. Congratulations. And if you're going to

be the matron at the hostel, I'll be seeing you often over the summer. Mrs Willcox buys food for the people staying there from me, you see. She's done a lot for this village, starting up the fizzy drinks factory after she married Jonah Willcox, and encouraging hikers. That all brings me extra customers.'

'And now she's going to marry Mr Selby. He seems a nice chap.'

'Yes. Good luck to them both. I'd rather stay single, personally, though. I really like running the shop, even though it's hard work.'

As they came out of the shop Tam grinned at Cara. 'Quick thinking, love. It'll be all round the valley within a couple of days about Jinna. And just let anyone else call her a dummy, like those lads did. I'll make sure they regret it, by hell I will.'

Once they got to the van, he pulled the pad out of the canvas shopping bag and gave it to Jinna. 'This is for you, love. Paper to draw on. And I've got you a new pencil, too.' He pulled it out of his jacket pocket.

She stared at him, mouth open, then took the pad and lifted the cover, stroking the paper gently and then ruffling the pages, her eyes alight with joy.

Her words were perfectly clear this time. 'Thank you, Tam.'

The happy light stayed in her eyes all evening long and the pad got its first drawing after tea, a portrait of Ned that was so lifelike, Cara was astounded.

'Why, that's lovely! It's as good as a photo. When we get our own home, I'll get a frame and we'll hang it on the wall if that's all right with you?'

The girl nodded and smiled at her. She didn't do another drawing that night or make any alterations to that one. Well, it didn't need anything else doing to it, was perfect as it was.

'I should have bought her a rubber too, only she doesn't

really need one because she doesn't make mistakes, does she?' Tam said when the children had gone to bed, and he and Cara were sitting chatting.

'No. She's got a real talent there. I hadn't realised how good she was. No wonder Vi at the pawnshop said she'd pay to have a drawing of her nephews done.'

'I'm thinking Jinna could earn money doing that at the markets. What do you think, Cara? She'll need to have a way to earn a living on her own one day, after all.'

'Will the council let her do that?'

'I'll find out once we're married and settled in. Only if she wants to, of course. I'd not force her.'

'Poor Jinna. She hasn't had much of a life so far, has she?'

'No. It brought tears to my eyes to see her happiness at having that pad. Ah, Tam, you're a good man, you are.'

He blushed and she chuckled as she got up. He might be good with words, but he wasn't good at accepting compliments. She was gradually getting to know things like that about him.

She thought he liked her as much as she liked him. You could tell, somehow. You felt comfortable with some people right from the start.

She was a lucky woman.

Her eyes went to Jinna and Ned. She was fond of the girl, too, and it was lovely how Jinna and Ned got on so well.

Everything had changed for the better in just a few days. It was like a miracle.

Tam sat there on his own for a while longer before he began to get ready for bed. As Cara had suggested, he'd brought a mattress in from the men's dormitory, pushed the chairs back and put it on the floor to sleep on, which was a definite improvement on bare boards.

In fact, he felt a lot better about everything. It had been

a memorable day, going from worry about where to live to happiness at finding a place for a while. And in Ellindale, too. He hoped things would go smoothly at the youth hostel. The four of them needed time to settle in together as a family.

But though they had somewhere to stay for the moment, what they really needed still was a proper home, so that he and Cara could get married and make a normal happy life for Jinna and Ned. Children needed to feel safe and settled.

And then he sat bolt upright in the dark room as it occurred to him that if they were staying here for a while, he and Cara could book their wedding immediately, which would be one problem solved. Would she agree to it?

He flung the covers back, intending to knock on the bedroom door and ask her about it right now, then common sense told him not to wake her up and he snuggled down again. She'd been tired out after their busy day and it could wait until morning. She was still recovering her health after not eating properly for quite a while, if he was any judge. Well, from now on he could make sure that didn't happen to her.

He was looking forward to marrying her, though he wasn't sure exactly what happened at a registry office wedding, because he'd never attended one. He definitely didn't want to get married in church. Well, he didn't know any of the current ministers in the valley's various churches and chapels, so how would he know which one to choose?

He was still thinking about Cara when he fell asleep, a smile on his face.

13

The next day dawned bright and clear and as soon as he'd finished his breakfast, Wilf took his tools across to the old house. Propping the front door open to let some fresh air into the musty interior, he went downstairs to the kitchen and opened the back door as well to get a through draught.

As he was doing this, Simeon Waide, the oldest resident of Ellindale, came hobbling across to find out what was going on. Although he was itching to get on with things, Wilf waited for him, knowing the old man had little to fill his time with these days except chats with other people from the village.

He spent a few minutes telling Simeon what he was going to do, then gently sent him on his way. It was still cold, but Simeon was well wrapped up and there was a bench in a sheltered, sunny spot at one side of the village green that he'd made into his own special place.

Wilf watched him shuffle slowly off to sit there and tell anyone who passed what was happening at the old house. The old chap would have plenty of interruptions by nosey parkers during the day.

Whistling tunelessly, Wilf took the stairs two at a time. He'd decided to attack the rooms one by one, beginning with the top floor.

It took him most of the morning to sort through the bits and pieces that had been dumped in the biggest room up there. He set some aside for mending and re-using, and took others outside and across the green to his own home to chop up for firewood. He passed a few broken pieces on to a couple of elderly neighbours for the same purpose.

His next task was to get rid of the dust and debris in the attic. He collected buckets of rubbish, including various small and unrecognisable lumps and plaster that had fallen off the walls. As he dumped them outside he was interrupted several times, because there was always someone else who wanted to know what was going on.

Occasionally a man would ask if there was any chance of work. The desperate need on their faces always upset him, but he'd promised some casual work to one young man already and there was nothing else needed. He told them he'd bear them in mind. What else could he say?

He stopped for something to eat around noon when Enid brought him across a sandwich and a pot of tea. He didn't want to leave the old house unwatched in case someone nipped in the back way to scavenge.

The young chap he'd been wondering about offering work to hadn't been around this morning. Probably had to go down into Rivenshaw to sign on for his dole. He'd give him till mid-afternoon, then offer the job to someone else.

Even as he was thinking that, someone knocked on the back door frame.

Wilf studied Ricky Blair through the open door. Thinner than he should be, as were many folk. Would he still have the muscle power to put in a full day's work? Only one way to find out.

When Ricky looked pleadingly at him, Wilf said straight out, 'It's what I told you: I can give you a couple of days' work if you're a hard grafter.'

It brought a lump to his throat to see the look of hope blossom on the young chap's face as his words sank in.

'I'll do anything, Mr Pollard, anything at all.'

He looked at Ricky in surprise. He was going up in the world if people were going to call him 'Mr Pollard'.

'Good. We'll say six shillings a day, starting as soon as it's fully light, and three shillings for this afternoon, if you want to start straight away.'

'I do, I do! Thank you. You won't regret it.'

'No. I don't think I will. How's your mother?'

'She's improving all the time. She'll be even better when she hears about this.'

'You haven't asked what you'll be doing here.'

'I'll do whatever is needed, Mr Pollard.'

Wilf thought about it for a moment, but didn't correct him about the 'Mr'. Most folk of Wilf's age in the village were on first name terms but if he was going to be managing two jobs for Mr Carlisle – and the one on Heythorpe House would be quite a big one – he'd have to show that he was in charge. Becoming 'Mr Pollard' to other people instead of 'Wilf' was one obvious way to do it, though it'd feel strange.

Ricky was still waiting patiently so he pulled his thoughts back to the matter in hand. 'Right then, it's clearing out today. Come inside and I'll give you a quick tour.'

He distinctly heard Ricky's stomach rumble, so he stopped and waved one hand at the remains of his own dinner, half of the sandwich and the last of the pot of tea. The latter was lukewarm and stewed, but no one who was hungry and longing for a drink of something other than water would complain about that. 'Do you want to eat the sandwich first? I've had enough and it seems a shame to waste it.'

Ricky looked him straight in the eyes, clearly understanding that this was a kindness, but unable to refuse it. 'Yes, please. Thank you very much.'

'Get it down you while I squeeze another cup of tea out of the pot.' Wilf was still hungry, but he'd had breakfast and would be having another meal at teatime, which Ricky might not, so he'd manage without.

By the end of the afternoon, the top two levels of the house had been swept clear and the debris was all neatly piled in the backyard.

Wilf nodded to his helper, who was looking exhausted, and slipped him a half a crown and a shilling. 'You did well.'

Ricky flushed. 'I haven't got any change, Mr Pollard.'

'You worked harder than I'd expected, so keep the extra sixpence.'

Tears welled in the young man's eyes. 'Thank you. What time do we start tomorrow?'

'Seven o'clock will suit me if you don't mind getting up then. I'm an early riser, can't stay in bed once it gets light.'

'I'll be here.'

Ricky walked away looking a different man from the hunched, miserable young fellow who'd knocked on the back door earlier.

It didn't take much to lift their spirits, Wilf thought. Or his own. Eh, he was hungry now, though.

'You great soft lump!' Enid said when he pinched a piece of crust and told her about the sandwich. 'Why didn't you come home for another one?'

'It'd have hurt his pride. It's easier to take something not wanted than to deprive a man of his dinner.'

She kissed him on both cheeks, setting the two children giggling. They were getting used to displays of affection between their adopted parents now, he thought with a smile, but the first few times he and Enid had cuddled one another openly, they'd stared open-mouthed.

The poor things had had a miserable start to their lives with parents who both neglected them, and a father who thumped anyone near him when he got angry. Wilf loved to see them decently fed and clothed, and playing happily.

He doubted he'd ever be rich in money, but he and Enid could make their family rich in love.

Finn drove down into Rivenshaw to speak to someone from the council about the possibility of a financial grant for setting up and running a job club. He'd heard that someone had started a club to the south of Rivenshaw and been given money to help with it, so why not in Ellindale?

He was directed to Miss Westing, a weary-looking older woman in a cubby hole of an office with a wall that was half window from waist height upwards, cutting her off from the corridor.

She offered him a chair and closed the door, for all that was worth when they were on view to anyone passing.

'If you can just give me a minute, I'll finish labelling this file.'

It was only a minute, too, then she asked his business, listened carefully and, when he stopped speaking, agreed that yes, there might be funds available if the project was shown to be worthwhile.

Since she didn't volunteer any further information, he had to drag what he needed to know out of her question by question. 'What do you mean by "worthwhile"?'

'If it's considered likely to give the men useful skills.'

'What sort of skills would those be, exactly?'

Miss Westing sighed as if this was all too much trouble. 'Any skills that may help them get jobs.'

'There are very few jobs available in the valley, whatever skills men have. I had thought that one of the main purposes of a job club would be to give them somewhere to go, some-thing to *do*.'

'Well, the council won't pay for them to sit around; they must be engaged in useful activities. Any skills they learn must be suitable for such jobs as *might* become available in the future, so you'll need to offer them *practical* classes.'

He felt they were going round in circles but didn't allow himself to follow her example and sigh. Instead, he asked, 'You only spoke about men? What about women?'

'Married women are not allowed to be involved. They'll only take men's jobs.'

He glanced down at her left hand, which had no ring on it, then back at the sour expression on her face. 'What about single women?'

'Classes for them are occasionally allowed.'

'*Allowed?* What do you mean by that?'

'If the council allocates money, then of course it must supervise how that money is spent. Men are obviously going to be the breadwinners for their families so any job club would be for their benefit.'

He didn't attempt to do any more arguing. She was behaving more like a tame parrot than a thinking human being.

'Do you have any information I could take away and read, Miss Westing, so that I can understand all the details?'

'You haven't told me anything specific about your project yet.'

'I own an old house up in Ellindale that's not been occupied for many years. I thought it could be used to house the job club, and of course I'd not charge rent for that. The people who come could learn carpentry, and improve their reading, writing and arithmetic skills, even do some simple accounting, perhaps, in case they find a way to start a small business.'

She pursed her lips and frowned as if considering this, so he waited.

'You would not in future change your mind and seek to charge rent, Mr Carlisle?'

'No, definitely not. I have no need of the rent money.'

Jealousy flickered on her face for a few seconds, there was no mistaking it. Then she studied him for so long and with such an assessing expression on her face that he felt as if she was working out the cost of each item of clothing he was wearing.

Before they could continue their conversation, a man passing in the corridor looked through the window, stopped and opened the door without knocking. 'Mr Carlisle, isn't it?'

'Yes. Um, do I know you?' The man looked vaguely familiar but Finn couldn't place him.

'We did meet once. I'm Harvey Rixom, the elected councillor for your village.'

Finn didn't remember them meeting but the name was familiar and he'd heard nothing complimentary about the man, so he merely inclined his head and waited.

'I keep hearing about you and your many kindnesses to your poorer neighbours. Very laudable. I hope our Miss Westing is being helpful today.'

Finn was tempted to say she wasn't, but she had grown stiffer than ever at the interruption and the visitor hadn't even greeted her, so it wouldn't do to be as rude to her as this man had been. After one quick glance in her direction, Rixom had ignored her and focused on Finn. Talk about appalling manners!

'Miss Westing is going through a few things with me, yes.'

'Anything I can do to help?'

If he'd ever seen an insincere smile, this fellow was wearing one, Finn thought. It didn't reach his eyes and barely curved his thin lips. 'Not at the moment, thank you. We're just getting started.'

The man stood there, eyes narrowed as if trying to assess

exactly what Finn meant, then as Finn half-turned back towards Miss Westing, he said, 'Goodbye for now, then, Mr Carlisle.' He carried on down the corridor, not attempting to close the office door behind him.

Finn got up and closed it. 'Not very polite to leave the door wide open when you leave, is it and why didn't he knock before he came in? Now, where were we, Miss Westing?'

Was it his imagination or did she seem a trifle friendlier from then on? She still seemed to find it hard to relax, but she began volunteering information. He'd guess from her lack of facial expression when Rixom joined them that she didn't like the man, either, but didn't dare let it show.

He left with some papers that must have been copied on a Gestetner machine and stapled carelessly together. Whoever had done it hadn't been able to produce good copies. The wax master sheet must have been used too many times. Surely the council could do better than this limp set of instructions for those trying to help residents who were out of work?

Or perhaps they didn't want to help; perhaps they had other uses for council funds.

After his experience this morning Finn wasn't at all sure it'd be worth the bother of trying to get a grant for his job club – not if it brought the council poking its nose in, dictating what to do and keeping women out of it. Which would mean him meeting the whole cost of running it.

Well, there were worse ways of spending his money and he could spare it.

He stood still for a moment or two, raising his face to the sunshine and smiling as he thought of what his wife would say about this.

He was quite sure she would be furious at the way women were specifically excluded by the council's rules. In fact, Beth would probably fizz with anger and indignation, then help him find some way to get round unfair rules like that.

It was a good thing he and every member of his household didn't live extravagantly. They'd all been short of money at various times in their lives and none of them, himself included, could have been wasteful, however much money was coming in. That was just wrong.

He got into his car and set off across the town centre. It was when he was driving past Todd's workshop that an idea occurred to him and he braked at the sight of a neat little Ford motor car standing by the side of the road. *Cars!* The numbers of them in use were increasing every year. He'd read in the newspaper that there were expected to be three million of them by the end of the decade. Just imagine that! Why, even when you drove in the depths of the country you'd see another vehicle every minute or two.

If some of the men who came to the job club could learn more about cars, either how to repair them or how to drive them, maybe that would be a useful practical skill for various jobs that might become available?

Finn had read articles saying that many families would have a car of their own when times grew better, not just rich folk. Some people scoffed at that idea but Ford motor cars like this one had already shown the way to cheap motoring. Such a pity the company had moved its factory from Manchester to Dagenham – and taken the jobs with it, away from the north.

He looked round as another car passed by. There was still work available repairing and selling cars, as Todd had shown. Maybe that was the way to go.

Finn left his car at the side of the road and went in to speak to Todd about his idea.

His friend listened carefully and was all in favour of teaching the club members more about motor vehicles. He didn't need persuading to let men come down to his workshop for a basic lesson or two about engines and tools.

'Could you teach them to drive cars as well?' Finn asked. 'We'd pay you.'

Todd held up his hand in a refusal. 'Not me. Doesn't matter how much you paid, I wouldn't do it. It can be a hair-raising task sitting next to someone who's learning to drive and you need the patience of an angel with some folk.'

'Who could teach them to drive, then? Who does that in Rivenshaw?'

The two men looked at one another as the same idea occurred to them both.

'Since old Mr Eustace retired, there isn't anyone giving driving lessons, not just in Rivenshaw but in the whole valley,' Todd said. 'Most people get a friend or relative to sit with them in the car and practise till they more or less know how a car works. But some just get in and drive, which is why there are so many accidents.'

He shook his head at that thought. 'Thank goodness the government is going to make driving tests compulsory from next year. That should help. And they're starting to let people take the test voluntarily this year, so there may be work for someone straight away – only how are your club members going to learn how to give driving lessons, let alone afford a car to teach people in?'

'Hmm.' Finn had read about that too, but hadn't thought about giving driving lessons as a job opportunity until now, just repairing vehicles. 'Perhaps we could persuade Mr Eustace to come out of retirement for a day or two a week to show some of our men how to teach driving, the ones who acted as drivers during the war. We could even set up a driving school in Rivenshaw ourselves. I'd buy them a car – second-hand, but in good condition.'

'I'd help you find one and I'd keep it well maintained for you as my contribution.'

They grinned at one another and shook hands.

'And maybe, if one of them is a good driver already, he can get one of the new jobs there will be teaching people about the driving tests.'

'Not a word to anyone,' Finn said. 'Except Leah and Beth, of course. We can't leave them out. It's just the sort of thing your Leah will want to get involved in, only she's like my Beth: she'll insist that women must have a chance to learn new skills as well as men.'

'Leah told me that Jonah would have wanted her to use some of the money she inherited from him to help other people find jobs. As she's helped a few already by setting up her fizzy drinks factory. She's a wonderful woman.'

Finn nodded. He felt the same about Beth. 'I dare say there will be some women who won't want a male driving instructor, so it all fits to train one or two women as well.'

'I doubt the men will like women being involved.'

'They'll just have to lump it. Anyway, *they* won't be in charge of setting the scheme up: I will. And if they don't want to work with women, no one's forcing them to join *my* club.'

'And the council? What are you going to do about them? They'll not allow such a thing if they're making the rules. A lot of arrangements in our valley are made by men who think they're still living in the nineteenth century.'

'I'll give the council the chance to get involved in my job club, Todd, because if they do help to fund it, that'll make my money go further. I don't have unlimited funds, after all. But they're not telling me who is allowed to join, because I don't think they know themselves how these job clubs work best. You're right. There are a lot of old fuddy-duddies running things, either working there or elected as councillors, people who haven't moved with the times, or who are too timid to speak out against men like Rixom. And there are some councillors who are outright villains.'

'I agree.'

'And speaking of Rixom, I'll admit to you that I can't stand the fellow, Todd. He walked straight into Miss Westing's office today without even knocking. Yet he's rarely available to help if a poor person in Ellindale has a problem, though he's all over those with money.'

'Ha! I can't stand Rixom either. He came here to see me soon after I set up in business and not because he wanted to buy a car. He didn't say anything I could lay a complaint about, but it was clear that he was available to help if I needed council support – for a consideration. And he's not even the representative for this ward so he must be in cahoots with someone else to come to see me here with such an offer.'

'He'll be working with more than one other person, if he has the power to get things through council.' Finn made a disgusted sound in his throat. He hated cheats.

Todd studied him, head on one side. 'You know what? *You* should stand as a councillor, Finn. There are some local elections coming up quite soon.'

'Me? I've no experience of that sort of thing, and I don't want to have, either.'

'All the better. You'd act fairly. At least think about standing. You'd easily get elected because you're well liked in the valley. Think how good it would be to see Rixom toppled from the Ellindale ward and some of the jiggery-pokery stopped at least.'

Finn grimaced and shook his head again. There was no way on earth he'd get involved in such matters. Apart from the fact that political manoeuvring wasn't the sort of thing he'd enjoy being involved in, he hated public speaking, did it badly. Anyway, he'd have enough on his plate with this job club, not to mention the other small projects he was involved in, such as the coming modernisation of his creaky old house.

Besides, council meetings and other business would take

him away from Beth and her children. He enjoyed spending time with them, hadn't realised what fun small children could be. He couldn't wait for his own child to be born. More than one in the coming years, if he was lucky.

Beth was, as she'd told him, fit and well, her body coping easily with pregnancy. No, he didn't want to do anything that would take him away from her regularly.

A few minutes after Mr Carlisle had left, Councillor Rixom returned to Miss Westing's office, once again entering without knocking. He closed the door and sat down without waiting to be asked.

'What did Carlisle want?'

Helen stared at him. 'It was private business.'

'I'm an elected councillor. What goes on in my area *is* my business.' When she still didn't speak, he leaned forward. 'I have influential friends in the town hall, as you found out once before. Do you value your job here?' He paused, smiling, and added slowly, *'What did Carlisle want?'*

'To ask about grants for setting up job clubs.'

Rixom frowned. 'Where would he be intending to do that?'

After another hesitation, she said, 'In Hillam House, which is near the centre of Ellindale.'

'I know the house you mean, but I was told it wasn't fit to be inhabited.'

'I wouldn't know, but he says he can sort that out.'

'How?'

'I don't know the details. He hasn't put in an application yet. I've only just given him the forms.'

'Let me know when he puts the forms in and I'll check them for you. I probably know more about property in Ellindale than you do.'

He didn't wait for an answer, taking her agreement for granted.

Tears filled Miss Westing's eyes as he walked off down the corridor. She got up and closed the door, leaning against it for a moment or two as she fumbled for her handkerchief and dabbed her eyes, hoping no one would pass by till she'd calmed down.

It didn't do to cross Mr Rixom if you wanted to keep your job, and she was the sole support of her widowed mother.

But oh, it wasn't fair! She didn't want to betray anyone, let alone Mr Carlisle, who was a really nice man, as polite to her as if she were a queen.

As she sat down again, determination grew in her. She'd keep an eye on what Mr Rixom was doing. There had to be a way she could warn Mr Carlisle if she found anything out, and she'd find it. She knew a lot about the lower levels of town hall employees, people like her who only wanted to earn an honest living.

They saw more than certain folk realised.

But there must be no sign of where the warning came from if she discovered what was being planned.

Who did she know up in Ellindale? She'd have to ask her mother if they had any distant relatives or family friends there. Her mother knew everybody in Ellindale and Birch End because she'd lived in the valley all her life. Helen told her about the goings-on at work and she too felt angry at the cheating that went on.

Surely there must be someone they could trust?

But first, Helen would have to keep her eyes open and get proof of what was being planned.

Dare she do that?

She thought of the way Rixom had walked into her office without even knocking and nodded. Yes, she did dare.

Harvey Rixom went straight to the other end of the town hall to visit Brian Gratton, a very useful man who had a fairly senior administrative position there. It didn't occur to him to hide what he was doing. Several of the 'less important workers' watched in silence as he passed by. It felt good to be respected.

Harvey tapped on Gratton's door and was greeted with a gesture to come in.

'Fetch Mr Rixom a cup of tea, Mary,' Gratton added.

She hurried out and Harvey sat down, not bothering with chit-chat. 'It seems that Hillam House is about to be renovated and used. Why the hell didn't you check it properly and put in a requirement for it to be demolished, on the grounds of public safety, as I suggested a while back?'

'I did have it checked, but the building was in a perfectly sound condition. There was nothing to be done. And since the new owner hasn't been near it, I didn't think it was urgent.'

'You should have told me what you found. I'd have made sure its condition deteriorated rapidly, as old houses often do.'

Silence.

'We'd better do something about that now. What do you suggest, Gratton?'

'There's a limit to what I can do here. *I* don't have the power to stop him.'

Harvey scowled at him. 'Look into it. There must be some old ordinance or other you can apply to it. And don't take too long about it.'

'But I—'

'Do as I say. You'll be well rewarded.' Rixom got up and left the office.

14

Tam checked with Mrs Willcox that it'd be all right if they left the youth hostel unattended and they got ready to drive into Rivenshaw mid-morning to book their wedding at the registry office. It was located somewhere in the town hall, apparently.

He'd asked Cara if she knew what happened when you got married there, but she had no more idea than he did.

He looked at the children with pride as they got into the van. Cara had done wonders with them, dressing them in their new clothes and even tying a blue ribbon in Jinna's dark, straight hair. The girl would have looked quite pretty if she hadn't had that solemn staring look that made her seem . . . well, admit it, different from other girls. He'd never seen anyone, adult or child, who looked to be concentrating so hard. Was that because the wider world was so new to her or was it simply her nature?

His future wife was looking rather nice too, because Cara had got up early that morning to wash her hair and had tied it back into a sort of bun. Only this 'bun' was made up of curls, not hair scrunched together in a lump. It didn't matter that her hair had a fair few silver threads in it, he liked the effect and told her so, smiling when colour rose in her cheeks.

As they were setting off they saw Hilda Kerkham walking down from the village. When she saw their car, she stopped and waved to ask them to stop.

She didn't wait for him to speak but rushed into speech. 'Could I ask a favour, please, Mr Crawford?'

'Cousin Tam,' he corrected.

'Cousin Tam, then. I want to send this letter to my brother, and it's rather urgent, only I haven't got a stamp and Lily at the shop has run out. I don't have any change at the moment but I'll give you the penny when I get my next lot of egg money.'

Her look of barely concealed shame as she said this made Tam wonder if she didn't even have a penny left to buy a stamp. Had the money young Frankie spent in the shop been her last few coins? It seemed likely. Sadly, she wouldn't be alone in having an empty purse in times like these.

'I've got some stamps in my wallet, so I'll put one on the letter for you and post it in Rivenshaw. And you don't need to pay me back, for heaven's sake. What's a penny between cousins?'

Her voice was barely more than a whisper and she didn't meet his eyes. 'Thank you.' She passed the letter to him and he handed it to Cara to hold, then said goodbye and set off driving again.

Cara echoed his thoughts. 'I don't think she has even a penny left. And there's a sign in the village shop saying "No credit" so I bet that's why she couldn't get a stamp.'

'Just what I was thinking. I'll have to keep an eye on her and Peter. I can't have my cousins starving to death just down the road, now can I, not to mention that nice lad of theirs?'

'Why haven't they gone on the dole like others? You don't get much but it's enough to keep you alive.'

'I don't think they're entitled to it because they own a farm.' He frowned, then shook his head. 'I don't know the rules properly, because I've always managed to earn enough to keep going, but I have some vague idea that's the rule. I'd better check on them when we come back.'

'You'd be best doing that on your own, without me and the children, and I'll have to be at the youth hostel in case any hikers turn up, so you can go down to the farm after you've dropped us back home.'

She turned to see Jinna staring at the envelope she was holding and held it out. 'Do you want to look after this for me, love? Once we've got a stamp for it, we'll let Ned post it. He'll enjoy putting it in the pillar box.'

'I'll be careful.' Jinna took it from her, letting Ned look at the writing on the front as if he could read it, but not letting him take hold of it.

'What do the words say?' she asked after a while.

Cara tried to speak casually but she was shocked. 'Can't you read them?'

'I know a few words. I know what my name looks like. I can draw other words, too, but I don't know what they say.'

'It's good to know words. This is what it says on the envelope.' Cara read out the address. Here was the opportunity to find out more, she decided. 'Didn't you go to school, Jinna?'

'No. The attendance man came to see us, but Mam talked to him and said afterwards they didn't want me.'

It was the longest speech Jinna had made so far. 'Did she say why?'

'Because I didn't talk when he asked me questions.'

'Why not?'

'Mam told me to keep quiet when he was there or she'd smack me.'

That was ridiculous, Cara thought. The more she heard about the woman, the angrier she felt.

Jinna answered her unspoken question. 'Mam couldn't read either. She said reading and writing were too hard for people like us.'

Cara exchanged shocked glances with Tam, then turned

back and said casually, 'I know an easy way to learn how to read. I'll teach you, if you like.'

She saw Jinna start to shake her head, so added quickly, 'It's not hard so I'll teach Ned at the same time. It's fun to learn my way. Perhaps your mother didn't know about the easy way.'

Jinna looked at her in surprise, then frowned as if trying to think this over. After that she stopped protesting at the idea.

The girl didn't say anything else as they drove into Rivenshaw but she continued to stare at all they passed, turning her head sometimes to look back at something that interested her. It was as if she was hungry to see and learn about new things.

It was a wonder Jinna had turned out so well, after being a near prisoner for most of her life. She seemed to have a pleasant nature. Look how kind she was to Ned. But Cara was going to teach her to read and get her to a good standard too. She'd enjoy doing that. And everyone should be able to read and write.

Tam would agree, she was sure. She looked sideways at him. Ah, she was so lucky to have met him. She'd make sure he never regretted marrying her.

They found their way to the registry office, which had its own entrance at one side of the town hall. Tam tried to stand back and let Cara pass him, as was polite, but she gave him a gentle push.

'You go in first. I don't know the way.'

'I've never been to the registry office before so I don't know the way either, but I've eyes in my head and a tongue in my mouth, haven't I?' He led the way in, surprised by her nervousness. Ned had once again reached out for Jinna's hand and was sucking the thumb of his free hand.

Tam felt like the Pied Piper today.

He stopped to read the signs on a wall panel just inside the door, then followed the arrow next to the words 'Register Office' along a short corridor to a door bearing the same sign with 'Enter' beneath it. 'Aha! Here it is.'

He opened the door and again stood back to let Cara go first, which she did. But she waited for him to go up to the counter first. There was no sign of anyone so he rang the little brass hand bell set at one end with a card in front of it saying 'Ring For Attention'.

A young man with a pimply face peered out of a door behind the counter. 'Won't be a minute, sir.'

When he joined them, Tam didn't waste time. 'Me and my fiancée want to get married.'

'Oh, good. We haven't had a wedding booked yet this week. I do enjoy weddings.' He got out a large, leather-bound ledger. 'I have to ask you a few questions before we can book it. First, are you residents of Rivenshaw or the valley right up to Ellindale, because that's the only area we cover?'

'We are now. I was born here and I've come back to settle.'

'You have to have lived here for at least seven days.'

'Oh.'

'Perhaps your fiancée has been here longer?' He looked at Cara.

'No. We've, um, just got jobs up in Ellindale.'

He pushed the paper aside. 'Then I'm afraid you'll have to come back when you've been here for a full week.'

Tam grimaced at Cara, then turned back to the young man. 'We can do that, but first can we make sure there aren't any other rules to stop us getting wed?'

'Of course, sir. Your details have to be written in the Marriage Notice Book,' he tapped the ledger, 'and made available for people to look at for three weeks, in case there's a problem. You can book your wedding for any time during the three months after that.'

'Oh, dear!' Cara looked so disappointed Tam put his arm round her shoulders.

'Is there no way of getting married sooner, only we've got the children to consider and we want to set up a home *together*. Cara is responsible for her grandson and we're both adopting Jinna, who is a distant relative.'

The young man studied them. 'You're neither of you married to someone else?'

Cara drew herself up. 'Certainly not. I'm a widow.'

'My wife died many years ago,' Tam said.

'Sorry. No offence meant but I do have to check. You could apply for a Superintendent Registrar's Licence, then you're allowed to get married seven days after you register, though not in an Anglican church or chapel. Only, that would cost you three pounds.'

Tam's head was spinning by now. Stupid rules and regulations. Who invented them? Whoever it might have been was a twallop, to use one of his father's favourite insults. But it wasn't this young chap's fault. He was just doing his job.

'We don't belong to any church here and we want to give the children a home quickly, but three pounds is a lot of money, so I reckon we'll come back after seven days and wait the three weeks after that. What do you think, love?' He looked at Cara and she nodded agreement.

Tam turned back with another question. 'We want to get married here, not in a church. How do we arrange that?'

'Come back after you've been in the town for seven days and we can sort it all out then. It's not hard. I just have to book you in for a ceremony. But it has to be held in the morning.' The young man handed over a printed sheet of paper. 'It's all written down here.'

'Thank you.'

They left the registry office and outside Tam stopped. 'Sorry about that, Cara lass.'

'It's not your fault. And it'd be stupid to waste three pounds just to save three weeks before we marry because we'd still have to wait a week after registering.'

'You're sure you don't mind?'

'Certain. I can't bear to waste money. I'm disappointed, though. I didn't think it'd take so long. I'd expected it to be simpler and easier than a church wedding. Let's go straight home, eh, Tam? I've had enough for today. We'll come back next week. It's not long to wait, after all, just under four weeks in all. That'll soon pass.'

But as they passed a small bookshop on one corner just before they got to the van, she stopped and looked at him hesitantly. 'Maybe they sell books I could use to teach the children to read? I'm sure Jinna will pick it up quickly. Could we afford to buy one or two, do you think?'

He didn't hesitate. 'We certainly could. Learning to read is very important for everyone. *And* we'll all join the library as well next time we're in town.'

It was chilly in the bookshop, as if the owner couldn't afford the expense of heating it, and the shelves could have done with a good dusting, Cara thought.

A man peered out from a back room, saw them and came into the shop.

'Good morning. Can I help you with anything or do you just want to browse?'

'We're looking for some books to teach my grandson to read,' Cara said.

His face brightened. 'Children's books are in this corner, but I wonder . . . You see, I also sell second-hand books and you could buy far more of them for the same cost as for a couple of new books, plus I don't have all that many books in the new section that are suitable for beginners, so I might have to order them for you, but I have some second-hand ones.' He waited, head on one side, like a little bald bird.

'Good idea!' Tam said at once.

Cara looked at the dusty shelves. 'As long as the books aren't dirty.'

'Oh, dear me, no. I'd not accept dirty books. There may be a few marks of reasonable *wear* on them, but I never buy second-hand books from dirty people.' He leaned forward and added in a lower tone, 'They smell bad, you see.'

'All right. We'll look at them.' She grabbed Ned's hand just as he was about to pull a book off a shelf. 'Don't touch.' She looked at Jinna and added, 'We don't touch books unless we're going to buy them.'

The girl nodded.

'My name's Twomer,' the man said and waited expectantly.

'Tam Crawford and this is my fiancée, Mrs Pruin.'

'Pleased to meet you both.'

Mr Twomer led the way into the back room and lifted a box of books from a shelf to a small table at one side. 'Younger children's books are in this one, twopence each. You won't do better than that anywhere.'

'Which are the best ones to teach reading?'

He pulled them out and shuffled through them as if he knew every book personally. 'How many do you want?'

She looked at Tam.

'Two shillings' worth.'

Mr Twomer looked instantly happier . 'I can see you appreciate the value of buying books for children.'

Muttering and sorting books into piles, he emptied the box. 'There you are. Those two piles are suitable for younger children to learn on.'

She and Tam sorted through the books, asking Mr Twomer's help and showing them to the children. Jinna touched one or two of the covers, which were brightly coloured, and as she seemed to approve of the illustrations, they put those on a pile of books to buy.

After one quick glance at each book, Ned preferred to flip the pages gently from one end to the other.

When they'd finished making their choice, Mr Twomer added two more books to the piles. These were more worn than the others.

'There are more than twelve there,' Cara said.

He shrugged. 'Call the two extra ones a bonus, since it's in a good cause. No charge. They're very worn, so won't sell easily.'

'That's kind of you.'

'I like to see children learning to enjoy reading. Anyway, it's self-interest on my part because if they do, you'll probably come back to buy more for them.'

'We will definitely be coming back. Thank you.' Tam sorted through the coins in his pocket and handed over two sixpences and a shilling.

Cara gave the four top books to Jinna. 'Will you carry these back to the car for me, please?'

Ned looked at her eagerly, so she gave him one book, which he clutched tightly to his chest. 'Don't drop it, now.'

When they were sitting in the van, Jinna asked, 'Can I look inside the books?'

'That's what they're for. Just be careful not to tear the pages.'

Jinna opened one book slowly and carefully. Ned leaned against her, watching as she turned the pages slowly. Both of them seemed to be studying the pictures.

'I think that was an excellent idea,' Tam whispered to Cara.

Her voice was choked with emotion as she replied. 'I feel rich, being able to buy books for my grandson.'

'It's not as good as being able to arrange our wedding, but still a good thing to have done with our day. Food for their brains is nearly as important as food for their bodies.'

Tam had a quick cup of tea and sandwich at the youth hostel, then walked down the hill to visit his cousin and find out if Peter needed help. He wouldn't rest easy till he made sure the family was all right.

From the end of the track he saw the son shovelling muck out of the hen house and frowned. Why was that lad not at school again?

When Frankie saw him, he set down his spade and waited.

'Good morning, Mr Crawford.'

'I'm your Cousin Tam, remember.'

'Sorry. Cousin Tam, then.'

'Is your dad around?'

'He's having a lie down.'

'So you're doing the work and I'd bet you've not been to school for a while, eh?'

A shrug was his only answer.

'I'll speak to your mam, then.'

'She says to tell anyone who comes poking their nose in that she's busy.'

'And is she busy?'

Frankie hesitated, flushing and looking embarrassed.

Tam spoke more gently. 'Tell me what's going on, lad. I can see that something's wrong.'

Tears welled in the boy's eyes. 'Dad's been really bad lately. He's coughed up a lot of blood an' he can't even get to the lav without help.'

Oh, hell! Tam thought. *It's even worse than I'd thought.* He patted Frankie's shoulder as he argued with himself about whether to interfere or not. He was trying not to dive into things now that he had three other people depending on him,

only . . . well, he couldn't leave his cousin and family to
starve, could he? No, he just couldn't.

'I'll pop in and ask her if I can help.'

'No one can help now.' Frankie wiped his eyes and nose
on his sleeve. 'I hear them talking at night. They think they're
keeping quiet but I've got good hearing. Dad's going to die
soon and then what'll we do? He keeps telling her he's not
going to die yet and he's feeling a bit better, but he's that
thin and weak, he can hardly stand up, so anyone can see
it's a lie. She cries when she thinks no one's around. I see
how red her eyes are sometimes in the morning.'

Tam lost the argument with his sensible self. 'Right, then,
I'm going in to see your parents. You stay here. I'll tell them
you tried to stop me going in.'

Frankie made no attempt whatsoever to bar his way.

There was silence inside the house and although Tam made
a noise shutting the door, no one called out to ask who had
come in. That gave him time to have a quick look round.
Eh, it was a poor place. Clean, though, you had to give
poor Hilda that. People said things like you could have
eaten your dinner off the floor, but he reckoned you really
could have done that here, except for the part near the
entrance.

There was no sign of food, though, no fire in the old-
fashioned range, nothing on the shelves in the small pantry
except a half-full packet of salt and a small bowl with two
eggs in it.

He heard someone moving and called out, 'Anyone at
home?'

The sound stopped, then he heard footsteps moving
towards the kitchen and Hilda came in to join him.

Her voice was sharp. 'What are *you* doing in our house?'

'I've come to see how my cousin is.'

'Peter's all right. You can't see him now, though. He's asleep.'

Tam looked at her. 'He's bad, isn't he?'

She swallowed hard and had opened her mouth to speak when a voice called faintly from the back room.

'Hilda!'

She whispered, 'Please, Cousin Tam, go away and leave us to manage.'

'But you're not managing, are you?'

There was the sound of something metallic falling and she ran back to where she'd come from.

Tam followed, to see her picking up a tin cup from the floor by the bed. It must have held water, because the floor was wet.

The man lying there seemed to have got thinner in the few days since Tam had last seen him. He was like a living skeleton now.

He stared at Tam, closed his eyes for a minute, then said in a husky whisper of a voice, 'Come in.'

Tam moved forward. 'I'm sorry to see you like this, Peter.'

'Aye. Can't fight the devil in my belly for much longer, and I've tried, heaven knows I've tried.' He paused for a moment, struggling for breath, then looked at his wife.

Tam found it touching to see the love that shone between those two, even now. 'Don't blame your lad,' he told them as the silence continued. 'He tried to stop me coming into the house.'

'He's a good 'un, our Frankie is.'

'I can see that. Look, I'll go and get you some food from the shop. It'll keep you going a bit longer if you eat something light and nourishing.' He doubted that, but you had to speak as if death was still some way off. He'd done that in a ditch once with a complete stranger, who'd died at dawn still holding his hand.

He told himself to concentrate but his companions didn't seem to have noticed his lapse of concentration. 'Can you give me a list of what to get, Hilda, or do you want to come to the shop with me?'

'Just a loaf and a quarter pound of butter will do us. We still have eggs.' Her voice was harsh as she added, 'If there's a stale loaf that's cheaper, buy that. And I'm only taking your charity because there's nothing else we can do and I c-can't—' She broke off and struggled for control for a moment. 'Can't bear to see that boy so hungry. Heaven knows we've tried everything we could. That land we sold to Harry Makepeace was a godsend. Helped us through the winter, that money did.'

He knew they'd not want the doctor brought in, but he was going to do it, even if it meant dipping into his own savings. First, though, they needed food. 'I'll go and fetch you something to eat, then.'

Peter laughed hoarsely. 'Wasted on me and I'm not hungry anyway, but it's not just the lad. My Hilda needs to eat as well.'

When Tam went back into the kitchen, he nearly bumped into Frankie, who was so close to the door he must have been eavesdropping. 'You heard?'

'Yes.'

'Come up to the shop with me then, and you can carry the food back.' He beckoned the lad outside before adding in a near whisper, 'After that I'll drive down to Birch End to fetch Dr Fiske. He'll come and from what I hear, he won't ask for payment from those who can't afford it.'

'There's nothing he can do, though, is there, Mr – Cousin Tam? So what's the point?'

'He can't do much for your father, but it'll make the formalities easier on your mother . . . afterwards, you know.

If a doctor's seen your father recently he can give your mother a death certificate and that saves a lot of fussing around.' He paused, then asked gently, 'How are *you* managing, lad?'

'I'm doing my best but I can't keep up with everything as I should.' Frankie gestured round at the little farm.

'Just do the best you can and we'll concentrate on making things easier for your father before we think about the farm. Except for the chickens, of course. You'll have to keep them fed. I'd better buy you some chicken food. Do they sell it at the shop?' At Frankie's nod, he said, 'We'll take this one step at a time, eh?'

They walked up to the shop together. As they got near, the boy quickly smeared away a tear with his sleeve. Tam pretended not to notice.

After they'd bought some food, he sent the lad home with it and went up the slope to the youth hostel to tell Cara what was going on and get the van.

Eh, what next? he wondered as he walked back to the youth hostel. You solved one problem and another popped its head over the wall before you could say Jack Sprat.

But he couldn't leave his cousins to cope on their own. He just couldn't do it.

When was he going to get time to court Cara properly as she deserved? He'd have liked to bring her little presents and spoil her a bit.

15

Cara listened to Tam's explanation of what he'd found at the farm and agreed with his decision to help his cousin's family.

'I'm sorry, lass. This'll take some of our money.'

'Of course it will. But what sort of person lets a relative starve?'

When he hugged her, it went on for a long time because she hugged him back, nestling against him like a bird come home to roost.

'It really upset me to see him like that,' he confessed in a low voice as he pulled away and wiped the tears from his cheeks. 'I'm sorry to be such a softie.'

'I'd rather marry a softie than a man who thumped me.'

Her voice was so bitter he grabbed her arms and held her in front of him. 'Did your husband do that?'

She shook her head. 'No, but towards the end, it got to him, being out of work, and I was afraid he might.'

'I'd never hit you. Or anyone.'

'I know.'

'How can you be sure?'

She smiled, then, a lovely smile that lit up her face. 'Because you're Tam, Crazy Tam, a man who helps people, even a dumb lass he's never met before when he sees her being bullied by some nasty lads. A man who comes to find a woman in trouble because they can help one another. A man who has time to listen to Ned, who buys Jinna a pad to draw on, and who feels he has to look after his cousins. That's how I know you won't hurt me.'

He felt a bit embarrassed by what she'd said. 'I just . . . do my best.'

'Your best shows what a kind, decent chap you are. And I'm glad we're going to get wed. I won't be lonely any more. Nor will you.'

He had to blow his nose good and hard then, he was so touched by what she'd said. How did she understand the loneliness of being on the tramp week after week? Oh, you met people, plenty of them, but none of them really cared about you – or you about them. And most you only saw briefly, except for a few you met in places you visited every year.

After he'd put his handkerchief away, she patted his arm. 'Go and fetch the doctor now, Tam. There are a couple of young chaps booked in at the hostel for tonight so I have to stay here because they want to buy their tea. But I can manage just fine, so take as long as you need.'

When he'd gone, Cara turned to see Jinna watching her.

'I like Tam too,' the girl said and went back to playing with Ned without waiting for an answer.

It was as if she didn't know to expect an answer, Cara thought. Aloud she said, 'I'm a lucky woman. Very lucky. We're all lucky to have Tam.'

And she too had to blow her nose a couple of times before she could carry on working, because she didn't think Jinna would understand that you could weep for sheer joy.

Tam drove down to Birch End, going steadily because he was upset and didn't want to cause an accident.

The doctor wasn't holding a surgery that afternoon, so Tam rang the bell outside the waiting room at the side of the house.

Mrs Fiske answered it. 'If it's not important, I'd be obliged if you'd come back later. My husband has had a hard morning, he's tired and he's only just sat down to eat his dinner.'

'I'm sorry to disturb him, but I think my cousin is near death and seems to be in a lot of pain.'

Her sigh seemed to involve her whole body. 'You've been here before. Aren't you the man who's adopted that young girl, the one who draws so well?'

'Yes, Mrs Fiske. We're all living at Mrs Willcox's youth hostel in Ellindale and my cousin lives in the village.'

'Well, you seem like a sensible man who wouldn't come down here without good reason. What exactly is wrong with him and is he a patient of my husband's?'

'He's called Peter Kerkham and he has a small farm in Ellindale. I reckon the problem could be either a growth or TB from what I've seen in other people. He should have come to see Dr Fiske before now, but he couldn't afford to pay and was too proud to take charity.'

'Do you think my husband can perform a miracle if your cousin's really bad?'

'No. But I think your husband coming to see him will set Peter's wife's mind at rest. She'll know that no one could have done anything to help her husband and that will comfort her later. She's very upset and is holding it all inside herself.'

'If it's TB, my husband will have to check the rest of the family and notify the authorities, so it's important to find out.' The doctor's wife shook her head and made a soft tutting sound. 'Oh, very well. Come in and wait for him to finish eating his main course. I'll keep his pudding till later.'

Tam sat quietly in the waiting room, glad of a few minutes' rest. Dr Fiske wasn't the only one who was tired. Tam felt as if he'd been running round the district for days. How long was it since he'd met Cara? Less than a week. Eh, what a lot of changes had happened in that short time! And now there were these extra problems and it looked like he was the only family member around to deal with them.

Footsteps heralded the arrival of the young doctor, who questioned him and agreed that Hilda Kerkham might feel better if a doctor was brought in. 'You're sure this man's near to dying?'

'I'm afraid so. I've seen a few men die over the past few years. You can't mistake that look.'

'No. I've seen it all too often lately as well. Is your cousin religious? Do you need to fetch a minister to speak to him as well?'

'Eh, I don't know. He and I have never been close and I've been on the tramp for years, only just come back. But I couldn't see him and his family starve to death, now could I? So I poked my nose in. If I'm any judge, he's in a lot of pain and trying to hide how much from his wife. Maybe you could give him something to ease it.'

'We'll see. Tell me where he lives.'

'Skeggs Hill Farm. It's a small place on the left side of the road just before you get into Ellindale. I'll wait for you where you turn off. If you look outside now you'll see my van and be able to recognise it.'

He gestured outside to show his vehicle and the doctor came to peer from the doorway and nod.

Once he got to the farm, the doctor didn't spend long examining Peter, then he took some packets of powder out of his medical bag and gave them to Hilda. 'One of these morning and evening will help with your husband's pain.'

'Thank you.' Peter's voice was barely audible, as if he could hardly summon up the energy to speak.

In the living room, the doctor studied Hilda. 'You and the

lad look as if you've been going short of food. I'll tell the ladies at the soup kitchen to send you something. No, don't protest! That's what they're there for. They're good women who're helping a lot of people. There's always someone coming up the valley who'll drop some off for you but we can't tell you when to expect it.'

She stared at him numbly, then nodded, not protesting about taking charity now, Tam noted.

As the doctor closed up his bag, she asked in a hoarse whisper, 'How long does he have?'

'You can never tell exactly, but a few days at most, I'm afraid.'

She clapped one hand over her mouth, rocking to and fro, her eyes going in the direction of the bedroom as she tried to hide her distress from her husband. Frankie moved to put his arms round her, making shushing noises.

For the moment they both seemed unaware of the other people in the room.

'Shouldn't your son be at school?' the doctor asked when she calmed down a little.

'I can't manage without him.' She sank down on the nearest chair as if she hadn't the strength to stand up any longer.

'I'll give you a note to say that, then, in case they send the attendance officer round.' He pulled a pad and a fountain pen out of his bag and wrote the note immediately. After flapping it to let the ink dry, he gave it to her. 'The attendance officer and headmaster will accept this.'

'Thank you.'

Tam saw the doctor out, then came back. 'Anything else I can do for you, Hilda?'

She shook her head. 'Thank you, no.'

'Is there someone from your side of the family who could come and stay with you?'

She hesitated, then shook her head.

He was surprised that she hadn't mentioned her brother. 'Well, me and Cara are up at the youth hostel if you need us suddenly. It won't take Frankie long to run up and fetch us. Any time, day or night. I'll pop in to see you morning and evening.'

She gave him a tired smile and leaned her head against the chair back, closing her eyes.

It made you thankful for what you had, he thought as he got in his van and set off back to the youth hostel. Deeply thankful.

On the way back Tam passed the old house Wilf was working on. Three men were standing outside chatting, looking as if they were waiting for something. What was going on there? Another time he'd have stopped to find out but for the moment all he wanted was to get back to Cara and the quiet comfort of her soft voice.

On the other side of the village he passed the entrance to Heythorpe House just before he got to Spring Cottage and to his surprise there were three men waiting there as well.

He slowed down a little. Something was definitely going on. No, better not stop. He'd been away longer than he'd expected and Cara might need his help if there were several hikers settling in.

She looked up as he went into their quarters. 'How are they?'

'Bad. I had to fetch the doctor and *he* reckons Peter only has a few days to live.'

'Oh, no! How terrible! And I can't offer to help because we now have four men and two women staying tonight. The prospect of fine weather must have brought them out hiking.'

'Lucky them to be able to afford a holiday.'

'Well, the women are maids and their employers have gone

away so paid for them to come hiking. I expect that's cheaper than leaving them in the house.'

'They've fallen lucky with the weather.'

'The men are on short time and said the minister at their church gave them the money to pay for their stay here, so they could go out walking for a day or two. Wasn't that kind of him? I know it's only a shilling a night and a bit of food money for the daytime, but not everyone would think of it. I wish they'd had youth hostels when I was young. I never got away, just got married at eighteen, as you did in those days.'

'Aye.' He looked across at Jinna, who was scrubbing some potatoes. She didn't look up, concentrating hard on what she was doing as always. 'I see you've got a helper.'

'Yes. Jinna's a big help to me. She's a hard worker once you show her how to do a job.'

'Where's young Ned?'

Cara chuckled. 'Under the table, fast asleep. One minute he's running round shouting his head off, next there's silence and he's found somewhere to lie down. That boy could sleep on the top of a pole once he tires himself out.'

Finn looked out of the window of his sitting room and saw that a few men had gathered near the entrance to his property. Were they coming to ask him for something? He stood watching and they seemed to be having a heated discussion.

Beth came to join him, threading her arm in his and gesturing towards the group.

'What's going on, love?'

'I haven't the faintest idea.'

'Well, they've been there for at least quarter of an hour, so they must want something from you. I'm surprised you didn't see them sooner.'

He looked at her guiltily. 'I fell asleep over the newspaper.'

As she laughed at him, the curve of her stomach pressed against him and he laid one hand on it for a moment, longing to meet his child. It moved gently inside her and joy filled him.

'Now you're awake, why don't we go out and ask them what they're doing, Finn?'

'I was hoping to spend some time with you.'

She reached up to caress his cheek. 'Later, my darling. Do you want me to come with you?'

'Why not? They aren't rioting, don't even look angry, just excited. But they must want something.'

He opened the front door and they strolled up the drive to the gateway. By the time they got there, the men had fallen silent and turned to watch them.

'Can I help you?' Finn asked.

The men remained silent for a moment or two longer, then someone nudged Horry Bensill forward and he whipped off his cap. 'Begging your pardon, Mr Carlisle, but is it true?'

'Is what true?' Surely they hadn't found out what he was planning already?

'That you're starting a job club.'

'I'm *thinking* of starting one, yes.'

'Is that why Wilf is clearing up the old house?'

'Yes. It's about time I did something with it.'

'My cousin went to a job club down to the south of Rivenshaw. He told me it saved his sanity last winter, an' kept him warm too. He learned all sorts of things, useful or not, and in the end the curate who was running it helped him write off for a job an' gave him a reference. When he got the offer of the job down south, the curate even gave him the train fare. So off he went to make cars in Coventry. He sends money home regular and his family is going to move down there next month.'

Another man stepped forward. 'Would your job club be held in the old house, then?'

'Yes. There's plenty of room inside.'

The man frowned. 'My wife says it's haunted. She won't go near it. Wilf says he hasn't seen any ghosts while he's been working there, only a lot of spiders crawling around the corners. They probably chased away the ghosts.'

There was a laugh at that.

'When will the club be starting, sir?'

'As soon as I can get the house ready and set up some activities.'

'We could help you get the place ready, Mr Carlisle. No need to pay us. It'd be good to have something to do.'

They all nodded at him, looking so eager, even for unpaid work, that it broke his heart.

'Well, we'll have to ask Wilf to organise something. He's good at that. I was thinking of distempering the inside. The walls are a mess and so are the floors, and a coat or two of white would make the whole place brighter.'

'We could do that for you.'

Finn made up his mind. 'Wilf is in charge of setting the house to rights. Go and see him, tell him I sent you to help.'

'He could organise the king, that one could!'

'I'm also going to need a small committee to help me plan the job club. Who wants to be part of that?'

All five men indicated Bensill again.

Finn smiled at the man's look of near panic. 'Looks like you're elected, Bensill.'

'I've never been on a committee before. I wouldn't know what to do.'

'Then that can be the first thing you learn. It's not hard.'

Bensill took a deep breath. 'All right. I'll do it. The sooner we can get the club going, the better. There's no *meaning* to our lives without work, Mr Carlisle. How soon do you think we can start the club itself?'

'We can open it during the daytime next week as long as the distemper's dry. Some of you can help carry furniture across to it from my house. Again, though, it'll be up to Wilf how that's done.'

'That young chap as is working with him is calling him *Mr Pollard* now.'

There was silence for a few moments, then one man shrugged. 'Why not? We'll give him credit for being in charge. He's a clever chap, Wilf, I mean *Mr Pollard*, is. You have to grant him that.'

'I can't promise you there will be proper classes yet, but it'll give you somewhere to go and I'll provide something simple to eat at midday.'

The men looked at him warily.

'How much will that cost?' one of them asked.

'Nothing. It's all part of the club. Bensill, will you pick another man and a woman to be on the committee with you? I want to start discussions about it tomorrow.'

'Why do you need a woman?'

Beth stepped forward. 'Because this job club is going to be for women as well as men.'

There was utter silence for a few seconds, then a man at the back said, 'But women don't need jobs like men do. They're not the *breadwinners*.'

Her voice was sharp. 'Oh, aren't they? Single women and widows don't have anyone to look after them; they have to support themselves. So that makes them breadwinners to my mind. And married women don't have enough to manage on when there's no money coming in, so they have to find ways of earning a few pennies here and there. Those without small children will be glad to learn anything they can. I know about that from my life with my first husband, because he wasn't a good provider. I'm going to be on the committee and I want another woman there with me as well because I'll not be able to attend for a while when the baby comes.' She laid one hand on her stomach.

They looked at her uneasily, then one man said, 'Well, my sister's sharp as a tack – too sharp at times – and she can't get a job either. I could ask her if she's interested. I bet she'll snap your hand off about it.'

'You do that,' Beth said.

Finn took over again. 'Right. We'll hold our first meeting of the committee at ten o'clock tomorrow morning here at Heythorpe House.'

Bensill gave him a beaming smile. 'Thank you, Mr Carlisle. We'll be there.'

Finn watched them walk away. They waited till they were out of hearing to start talking and by then a couple of men were clearly arguing. One was the chap who'd protested about women taking part. He hoped they'd get used to that. He didn't want any hassles. People had to pull together in times like these, men and women both.

'How did I get myself into this?' he murmured.

Beth gave him a quick hug. 'Because you can't bear to see how unhappy they are, or how cold they get walking around all day.'

'Are we doing the right thing to help them, though?'

'Who knows? We're doing *something*, though, not just leaving them to fret and fester. The council is supposed to be setting up more schemes to help them and the government gives them money for it, but they're a lazy lot at the town hall and they haven't got nearly as much done as they could have. Some of them are worse than lazy; they're on the fiddle. But even though people know about it, what can they do without proof?'

She paused to stare at him, head tilted to one side. 'You

know what? *You* should stand for council, Finn. You'd get things done.'

He groaned. 'Not you as well.'

'What do you mean by that?'

'Todd said the same thing, but I'm not interested. I have enough on my plate with what I'm doing.'

'My mam always used to say that if you wanted something doing, you should ask a busy person. Finn, darling, you'd be just the man to stir them up at the council.'

'No.'

'But—'

'*No*, I said.'

She fell silent but the trouble was, she still had *that look* on her face. His only hope was that she'd be too busy helping him set up the job club to have time to coax him into doing anything else. If he could just hold out till the baby came, he might be able to avoid standing for council because she'd have her hands full for a while. Well, everyone told him she would.

Who knew with Beth? She was a law unto herself. Did more than two other women.

He looked sideways and caught her staring at him as if she'd never seen him before. He couldn't hold back another groan. 'When I said no, Beth, I really, really meant it. I'm *not* going to stand for the town council.'

'Tell me why not. You're starting a job club, after all.'

'I'm not good at public speaking, if you must know. I hate it.' He hesitated, then told her the truth. 'I used to stutter as a child. I grew out of it mostly, but speaking in public brings it on again, and I sound like a fool.'

'Oh. I didn't know.'

'I don't tell many people about it.' It was his turn to get an idea. 'Why don't *you* stand for election? You'd make a far better councillor than me anyway.'

'Ha! *I* know I could do it, but people round here wouldn't elect a woman, especially one who's grown up poor, and even if they accidentally did, none of the other councillors would listen to her. But they would listen to a man, especially one like you, who's well thought of. No, it definitely has to be you who stands. Nobody ever died of speaking in public.'

'Beth, I—'

She moved away. 'We'll leave it for the moment and talk about it another day. I have to go and speak to Mrs Jarratt about baking something for the committee to eat tomorrow morning.'

She didn't mention the council again that day but he caught her looking at him speculatively several times.

He watched her too, afraid she'd overdo things. But she'd been right when she said she carried babies easily. She seemed almost as full of energy as usual, apart from the occasional desperate need to have a short nap. It made him chuckle to see how she fought against sleeping in the daytime. He'd caught her fast asleep only yesterday at her desk, head snuggled down on some accounts she was checking.

As the day passed he thought a lot about what he could do for the men and women who joined the job club. It was important, a responsibility that came, somehow, with his unexpected inheritance of Heythorpe House from a distant relative a couple of years ago.

Such a pity that new Special Areas Act wasn't going to include Lancashire when they used it to try to attract light industry to depressed areas. Why on earth had the government left Lancashire out? Why places like Glasgow and Liverpool, but not his home county? There seemed to him to be an equally great need for jobs here in Lancashire.

The local council hadn't done much about clearing slums and building new houses in Rivenshaw and the valley, either, and there were grants for that. Some other nearby town councils had done a lot. Shame on the Rivenshaw one.

But he wasn't the man to change that. He doubted one man could make a difference to what was going on anyway, even if he did get elected. Which he wouldn't if they once heard him stuttering and umming.

So he was *not* going to stand for council, whatever anyone else said or did.

16

On the Saturday morning Cara served a simple breakfast to the hikers, all of whom wanted to leave early so that they could walk across the tops to the next youth hostel. It would be a fairly long walk because their destination was just outside Todmorden, but two of them said they'd been that way before and could guide the others, and you could always catch a bus for the last stretch if you felt too tired to walk all the way.

One added cheerfully, 'I'd rather save my pennies and walk, though. Feet are free and my dad repairs my shoes for me.'

After they'd gone, Tam insisted Cara sit down and eat breakfast with the family before she started clearing up the living area of the hostel. It'd be the first time she'd had to change the pillowcases and sheets, the latter being simple bag-like affairs of hard-wearing cotton twill, which would be sent to the laundry in Rivenshaw after each use.

When they'd finished eating, he braced himself to visit the farm, using the van in case Hilda needed him to go down the valley for something or, horrible thought, fetch the doctor again. He left it on the main road because he didn't want to bump it along the uneven farm lane too often. That narrow strip of land desperately needed levelling.

There was no sign of anyone but when he knocked on the door, Frankie opened it and said, 'She says to tell you we're fine.' He looked quickly over his shoulder into the house, which made Tam guess that Hilda was nearby listening in. She must still want to keep visitors away.

Tam didn't believe for one moment that they were doing fine, so whispered, 'Let me past, lad. Your mam needs help, even though she won't admit it.'

Frankie hesitated, then took a step backwards.

Hilda was standing by the inner door. 'Nice of you to call, but we're all right, thank you, Cousin Tam.'

'I called to see how Peter is.'

She pressed her lips together in a tight, pale line for a moment, then said in a scrape of a voice, 'How do you think?'

'Did he have a bad night?'

It was Frankie who spoke. 'Yes, he did, even though he took the powder the doctor left. Mam was up with him every time I woke.'

Tam looked back across at Hilda. 'Why don't I sit with him for a while and you have a bit of a rest, love? I can spare the time.'

She scowled at him and he thought she was going to refuse, then a big yawn took her by surprise and her shoulders sagged wearily.

'Well, perhaps for an hour or so. You won't go until I get up again, will you? I don't like to leave Frankie on his own with his father.'

So Tam found himself sitting by the bedside of a dying man, not for the first time. Even since yesterday there were changes and Peter looked almost transparent, as if he were literally fading away. Eh, life was such a chancy business. There was a Latin phrase that Miss Parkins had taught him: *Carpe diem.* Seize the moment, she said it meant. He'd never forgotten it because it made such good sense. It was similar to what his grandpa used to say: *Never put off till tomorrow what you can do today* and the old man had always added, *because there might not be a tomorrow.* Both of them were good rules for living.

Peter opened his eyes, looking round as if searching for something. Or someone.

Tam could guess who and leaned forward. 'Your Hilda's having a rest. Is there anything I can get you, lad?'

'Drink of water.'

A jug and the tin mug were standing beside the bed, so Tam poured some water and helped his cousin hold the mug.

'I'm not hungry, but I do get thirsty. We have such sweet water here on the farm. It never tastes half as good anywhere else. That's why they set up the fizzy drinks factory at Spring Cottage, you know, because of our lovely clean water.'

When his cousin closed his eyes, Tam thought Peter had gone to sleep again, but he opened them and stared pleadingly.

'Will you . . . promise me something, Tam?'

'If I can.'

'When I've gone, will you help Hilda and Frankie?'

'Yes, of course I will. If she'll let me, that is. She's a proud woman.'

'You'll have to find a way to make her accept help. You allus were a clever chap. You'll manage it.'

Tam wasn't so sure. Hilda was a strong-willed woman.

Another pause, then, 'She'll want to move away from here. She's not bred to farming, doesn't love it up here either, so she'll want to sell the farm. She'll need help to do that. The farm won't be worth much, not now, but they ought to get *something* for it to give them a fresh start.'

'I'll help them if I can.'

'*Promise* me.' With a huge effort he held out one trembling hand and beckoned with his fingers for Tam to shake on the bargain.

What could he do but agree to help Hilda and her son? 'I promise.'

A long sigh and a nod was the only answer he got.

Peter's fingers weren't very warm and when Tam let go, the hand dropped limply on to the bed. 'Just lie quietly, Peter, unless you want something. Your Hilda needs a rest, so we'll let her sleep for a while longer, eh?'

He didn't even know whether his cousin had heard this last remark because Peter's eyes had closed and he was breathing those slow, dragging breaths that Tam had heard before in very sick people.

Definitely not long to go now, poor chap.

When he heard Hilda's voice in the kitchen a couple of hours later, Tam checked Peter, who was still dozing, and went to join her.

'Did you get a nap, love?'

'Yes. I fell asleep as soon as I lay down. Thanks for that, Tam. I needed it. Where's Frankie?'

'Working outside. He's a good lad.'

Her voice grew sharper. 'Too good to be stuck on this useless muck heap of a farm. It's not good enough land to make a decent living from, and it's not big enough, either. It's always been a struggle, even when Peter was young and strong. I was strong, too, in those days. I'm not now.'

'Peter said you'd want to sell the farm.'

'Let him think that. I've tried once, when he first fell ill, and all I got offered was ten pounds. *Ten miserable pounds!* The house alone should be worth more than that.' She scowled round. 'If I have to, I'll walk away and leave it to rot rather than be cheated. I have to get my boy away from here, give him a decent chance in life.'

'It's your choice. Now, if you'll be all right, I'll go home and see if Cara needs my help with the hostel.'

'I'll be fine. Two ladies from a church drove up and left us a meal. Thanks again, Tam.'

As he walked slowly out, excitement began running through him, but he didn't let on about that to Hilda. What she'd said had given him an idea, though for once he'd managed to control himself and not rush in feet first. But she was right. The house *was* worth more than ten pounds. He'd have to pay ten pounds to get a small caravan, a shabby old one, too. Why not pay the same amount and get a whole house?

He stopped at the beginning of the lane to stare round the farmyard. There were outhouses too. And the house had an upstairs. He hadn't even seen that but from the number of windows there must be at least three bedrooms.

Eh, what was he thinking? Peter was still alive, so there was no doing anything at the moment. But later, after the inevitable happened, if she still wanted to sell the farm – well, Tam could offer her more than ten pounds and still come out the winner.

For once he was going to think hard about this and not rush in. But he might discuss it with Cara. She had a good head on her shoulders. Would she think him mad even to consider offering for Skeggs Hill Farm? Would she want to live there?

Who knew?

But he was only *considering* it, not offering to buy it. Wasn't he?

The idea was on his mind all afternoon, so of course the first thing he said when he and Cara were alone that night after tea was, 'I've been thinking . . . '

'I could see that. You were only half with us tonight. Out with it.'

'When Peter dies, Hilda is going to sell the farm. I was wondering whether to buy it.'

She gaped at him, mouth open, then closed her mouth with a snap and frowned at him.

The silence dragged on till he couldn't bear it a second longer. 'Well, go on. Tell me what you think, lass.'

'We neither of us know anything about farming.'

'I wasn't going to *farm* it. Only, I think I could get it for about twenty pounds. It's only a small holding and the land's poor, so it's not worth as much as you might think. She's only been offered ten pounds, but I think twenty or even twenty-five might be closer to a fair price.'

Cara continued to frown, so he rushed on, 'It'll cost me ten pounds to buy a small caravan and there are four of us now. There's a whole house at the farm already. Several bedrooms. It could be made really nice.'

'Oh.'

'What does that mean?'

'It means: I don't know what to think, Tam.'

'Don't you reckon it's worth considering, even?'

She spread her hands helplessly. 'I've never had ten pounds in my purse at one time in my whole life, let alone thought about the price of *buying* a house. As for me being married to a man who owns one, I'd as soon have expected to fly to the moon.'

'Well, think it over now and we'll talk about it again tomorrow.'

She continued to stare at him, then nodded slowly and said in a near whisper, 'It'd be grand, though, wouldn't it? Having a house of our own, I mean.'

'Yes. Wonderful.'

He'd been going to offer to make them cups of cocoa, but she went out to clean the women's lavatory and washbasin. When she got back, she paused to say, 'If you're sure we can afford it, do it. Goodnight, Tam love.' Then she passed him and vanished into the bedroom.

He wished she were sleeping with him, not the children.

There was nothing left for him to do but go to bed. Once there he had difficulty getting to sleep. As he tossed and turned he decided they were right to call him Crazy Tam. He was daft, he was – daft as a brush! Fancy blurting out a thing like that so baldly. It was probably stupid for a man like him to think about buying Skeggs Hill Farm. No one on his side of the family had ever owned a house, let alone a piece of land as well. What if his carrier business wasn't successful?

He'd tell Cara to forget about it tomorrow.

No, he wouldn't. He'd tell her to think about it again, even more carefully. And he would think about it too. Well, they did need a home of their own, didn't they?

Eventually he fell asleep and had the most vivid dream of his whole life. It seemed as if he was living at the farm, standing on his very own doorstep staring out across the moors, breathing in the wonderful fresh air and feeling at peace with the world. He felt so good that after he woke up, he couldn't give up that dream. Just couldn't abandon it.

Did Cara mean what she'd said? Would she really be happy to live there? Beggars couldn't be choosers, but he wasn't a beggar.

Was he right and it would be a wonderful place to live? Or was he thinking of doing something even crazier than usual? It'd be bleak up there in the winter. Though you'd still have the views.

But even dwelling on the possible problems didn't dampen down his longing for a place to settle. And she'd said it'd be fine.

On the Sunday morning Tam woke early but there was no sound from the bedroom where Cara and the children were sleeping. Eventually he grew fed up of staring into space while his thoughts whirled about his head like mad butterflies, so he got up and dressed, standing his mattress on its end against the wall.

Even after he'd lit the kitchen range and made a pot of tea there was no sound from the bedroom. No, wait! Was that something? Yes, surely it was. He waited impatiently and was relieved when Cara came to join him in the kitchen.

'The children?' he whispered.

She mimed sleeping and went to use the women's bathroom without a word.

When she came back she stared at him so hard he felt apprehensive. Was she still all right about buying the farm? He didn't know her well enough to tell.

'There's tea in the pot.'

He watched her get a cup, worrying that he hadn't told her the truth about how much money he'd inherited, which meant he could easily afford to buy the farm. Only now didn't feel like the right time to confess to that. It might make her think he was in the habit of lying.

And also, he had to admit that although the money he'd been left was very comforting it was also a bit embarrassing to have so much when for most of his life he'd been scrabbling for every penny. Most of the people he knew were still struggling to put food in their children's bellies – and not always succeeding.

Cara came straight to the point, even before she got herself a cup of tea. 'I had no right to suggest you should or shouldn't buy the farm yesterday. It's your money, your decision.'

'I'm still only thinking about it, actually, but—'

'But what, Tam?'

'I'd really like to live here in Ellindale and look out across the moors. And if we bought the farm, we'd never have to

worry about paying rent again. But if you don't like it up
here—'

'I do like it. Only, it's a farm as well as a house. What
would we *do* with all that land? Not to mention the animals?
I don't even know how to look after hens, let alone sheep.
Do you?'

'No, I don't know. I hadn't got that far. Well, only to think
I'd sell the sheep to another farmer and see if we could learn
how to keep hens.' He went to stand next to her as she
checked the fire and put on another piece of wood.

'I'm glad we didn't have hikers last night. We need to talk.
Let's sit down for a while.'

She came to sit beside him and it was so cosy they just
sat and enjoyed the restful feeling, didn't say much at all.

That was something else he liked about her: she could
keep comfortably silent.

As the weather was fine, they took the children for a walk
that afternoon and though Jinna seemed scared of the open
spaces at first, having Ned beside her again seemed to make
her feel safe.

Tam talked to both children from time to time, pointing
out little animals and insects. That made Jinna stop and
stare at whatever it was and he wondered what she was
thinking. Was she remembering the creatures to draw them
one day?

When they got back to the hostel, Cara had the idea of
telling the children a story, making it up as she went along.

Ned was used to stories, but Jinna sat open-mouthed and
had to be told several times that this wasn't real, it was just
pretend.

She muttered 'Just pretend' a few times but seemed to be
enjoying it – or was it being part of a group that she was
enjoying? He couldn't tell.

But he smiled as he watched them, enjoying himself. It was good to have some time to relax and get to know one another. They were beginning to feel like a proper family.

He wasn't surprised when the children grew tired early and Cara sent them to bed.

'I see she took that dratted umbrella to bed with her,' Tam commented when she came back to sit with him.

'It makes her feel safe. So does Ned.'

'He's a grand little chap.'

'Isn't he?'

After a few moments he dared to ask Cara if she'd thought any more about Skeggs Hill Farm.

'I haven't thought about much else,' she admitted. 'Only I don't know what to say.' She gave him a rueful smile. 'Which isn't like me. I usually know my own mind.'

'We've had so many changes in the past few days, we're all bound to feel a bit uncertain. But it's going well, don't you think, the family side of things, I mean?'

She smiled at him. 'Really well.'

'Tomorrow we should go down to Rivenshaw to buy some fresh fruit and vegetables and find a butcher. We'll buy what we can from the village shop, of course, but Lily doesn't sell everything we need, especially greengroceries. Have you made a list of what we need? I have a couple of things to add to it.'

She nodded and went to find a scrap of paper and hand it to him.

'This isn't enough. You're still too thin and need to build up your strength, and we've got two growing children to think about.'

'Can we afford more food? We don't want to use up your savings if we're thinking of buying a house and you haven't been able to start working with the van yet.'

'We have rent-free housing for the time being, thanks to Mrs Willcox and you. So you're making a good contribution to the family.'

She beamed at him for that.

'Look. I've more than enough money to feed us for a whole year without earning any more. We're well placed compared to other folk.'

He waited while she finished her cup of tea and poured another one, frowning down at it, then asking in a low voice, 'Would it really be possible for us to buy the farm, Tam? Do you have enough money for that without leaving us short?'

'Yes, I do. Well, it would be possible if Hilda let us have it at a reasonable price and all she's been offered until now is an unreasonably low price, so I don't see why she wouldn't snap up my offer. Only we can hardly discuss that with her until after Peter's buried, can we?'

'No.' She sighed happily. 'I can hardly take it in. One week I'm in the poorhouse, lowest of the low, the next I'm engaged to marry you and I'm eating properly again. Then to top everything, you're talking about buying a house of our own. Who wouldn't want to do that?'

He let out the breath he'd been holding and waited for her to continue.

'I'm not used to being lucky, Tam. You'll have to give me time to get used to it. Since I met you, well, I keep thinking I'm dreaming, things have been so much better.'

'If you're dreaming, then I am too. Don't forget I was only left this money just before I met you by a kind old lady I used to do jobs for every year, so my life's been turned upside down, too. You're not *regretting* meeting me, are you, lass?'

He was teasing, sort of, but he held his breath again as he waited for that important answer. He felt he was dreaming to have met such a nice woman at his time of life.

Her smile was honey-warm. 'I'm definitely not regretting anything. Even if you didn't have the money to fall back on, I'd still like to make a new life with you. We get on well, you and I, don't we? We haven't had a single cross word in all the time we've been together.'

'I think we get on very well indeed.'

For a moment they smiled at one another like two love-struck youngsters, then he forced himself to be practical. 'Let's plan tomorrow, then. We'll go shopping in Rivenshaw but I'd better go and check on Peter first. I might mention my idea of buying the farm to Hilda, if it seems a good time to do that, or I might not. Have to play that by ear.'

'We'll have to book our wedding while we're in Rivenshaw, don't forget.'

'Eh, yes. I was even forgetting about booking our wedding in the excitement about the house.'

He was trying not to let that excitement overcome his common sense, but it was there, jiggling about in his chest, telling him that changes were going to happen, maybe the best things that had ever happened to him in his whole life. The thought of buying a house was exciting, yes, but it was the family part of things that excited him most: Cara and the children. Not alone any longer. Married. Already the three of them were far more important than the money.

Thank you, Miss Parkins! he said mentally, as he had been doing all week.

For all he was nearly fifty, he'd only had a real family life for a short time since he turned sixteen, what with the war and then his first wife dying, then having to go on the tramp to find work. He hadn't realised how desperately he wanted to settle down till he met Cara and with her, little Ned. And Jinna. He mustn't forget Jinna. It had all happened because of her, really.

If he were a child, he'd be dancing round the room. As it

was he lay back on his makeshift bed and waved his arms around like a madman. A family *and* a home! Who could ask for more than that? It'd be perfect, absolutely perfect. He thumped the mattress a few times to emphasise that, then fell soundly asleep.

After an early breakfast on the Monday Tam walked down to the farm on his own, hoping not to hear bad news. Frankie was mucking out the pigsty and waved to him as he passed. The poor lad looked subdued and sad. Well, you would, wouldn't you, if your father was dying?

Hilda came to the door, looking weary.

'Morning. You don't look as if you got much sleep.'

'I did better than the night before, thanks.' She tried to smile and failed. 'I'll be all right, Tam.'

'You're a brave woman.'

Tears welled in her eyes but didn't fall, though she had to take a deep breath and pause before continuing. 'What choice do I have?'

'None. But don't forget you've got me now if you need help.'

'I'm grateful. You're a good man.'

He didn't know what to say to that, so changed the subject. 'We're going to the shops in Rivenshaw soon, just for a few things Lily doesn't sell at the village shop. I'll get Cara to sort you out some food. What do you need, apart from bread, which we can order from Lily?'

'I'm fine, thanks. Just a bit of something for the boy to eat.'

'No. For you *and* the boy – and for Peter too, if he can still eat.'

'All right. Get whatever is cheap, doesn't matter. We're not fussy. We have eggs and I can let you have a couple in return, if you like.'

He knew she couldn't really spare them but she was trying not to be too beholden. 'I'll tell Cara. She'll be glad of them.'

'Bye, then.' Hilda closed the door so quickly, he suspected she hadn't been able to hold back the tears any longer.

He went to collect the others and they got ready for their outing. They drove down from the youth hostel to the shop together to order the bread, then they drove on down the hill.

Jinna was sitting in the back with Ned, still clutching that damned umbrella. He was sick of the sight of it. She might not join in the talking but she was listening intently.

He had a sudden idea. 'Let's buy some humbugs and have a little reading party tonight,' he said suddenly. 'Yes, and we'll have a bottle of ginger beer, too.'

'Should we be so extravagant?' Cara looked worried.

'Yes. I want to make reading a special treat for the children. You'll like that, won't you, Jinna?'

'What's ginger beer?' the girl asked.

He'd noticed before that she often fixed on one part of what he said and tried hard to understand it, thus losing the rest of the meaning. He was getting to understand her a little better. She was like someone in a strange land where she didn't understand the language the people spoke, except for the odd word here and there. He'd met Frenchies during the war and had only understood snatches of their conversation and it seemed to be the same for her all the time.

Well, if her mother had mostly kept her in that one room, she'd not have talked to many people or seen many new places, would she?

Ah! She'd folded her arms across her chest and was tapping her left forearm with her right hand, on and on, as if it comforted her. He'd seen her do that a few times, too, when she was in new surroundings.

'Ginger beer is a special drink, Jinna. It's fizzy, full of little bubbles and they tickle your tongue when you drink it. That feels nice as well as tasting nice. They make it at Mrs Willcox's factory next to the youth hostel and put it in bottles to sell to people. We'll buy a bottle from the village shop on our way back when we pick up our bread.'

'Oh.' He saw her mouth the words *ginger beer* and waited for a moment before asking, 'Do you like humbugs?'

She frowned, then shook her head. 'They smell funny.'

He'd half-expected her to ask what they were as well. 'Where did you smell them?'

'The sweet stall at the market.'

Cara joined in. 'I like pear drops better than humbugs. Let's get those. We'll let you smell them before we buy any, Jinna. You'll like them, I'm sure.'

'Pear drops,' she repeated.

'Pear drops,' Ned shouted at the top of his voice. 'Pear, pear, pear!'

He calmed down when they reached Rivenshaw.

Tam noticed Jinna go very quiet and still as they got out of the van, standing close to Ned. She always went quiet in situations where she wasn't certain what to do. Eh, that poor lass had so much to get used to. How would they ever get her through it?

But at least she was speaking now when the family were alone together. And asking questions. He must remember to tell her that it was good to ask questions when you didn't know about something.

In fact he'd do it now. 'Jinna love, it's good to ask questions when you don't understand something. You keep doing it as we walk round the town.'

She looked at him in that long, thoughtful way she had, then nodded slowly.

He was determined to do whatever was necessary to get

her more used to the world around her. And he wanted to take that worried frown from her face. A child shouldn't look so deeply worried.

And she was his child now!

17

On the Monday morning Finn had an early breakfast, then walked down the hill to the old house. If truth be told, he was feeling a little nervous about the start of the job club.

When he went inside, he was delighted to see that Wilf and his various helpers had done a good job of clearing up the interior, and so quickly too. The place was not only looking better but feeling better as well. Strange how this house seemed to show its feelings. He smiled ruefully; or else your own imagination did that. No, his wife said the same about the house: she seemed quite sure it had feelings.

Oh, he was being silly! He should just get on with the day's activities.

The basic arrangements for the day had been easy to plan. Beth and Mary Jarratt were going to provide some food for the midday meal, but he'd already bought some broken biscuits, tea and sugar at the shop. Lily had promised to send across some milk for the tea once the farmer had delivered it.

It was what the club members were to do this first day that still had to be worked out. He tried to comfort himself with the thought that even having somewhere to go would be an improvement on their long days spent mooching around, trying to fill the hours. You couldn't hunt for jobs when there were none going, after all.

Wilf was already waiting for him at the house, with a young

chap standing to one side looking expectant. It took Finn a few seconds to remember his name.

'Morning, Ricky. How are things?'

'Going a bit better, Mr Carlisle, thanks to Mr Pollard. He's offered me some more work on your house as well as here. You can be sure I'll do my best.'

Mr Pollard, not Wilf, Finn thought. Had he inadvertently pulled Wilf a step higher on the social ladder? There were such subtleties to these things. He hoped it wouldn't set any backs up to have Wilf in charge, but who better?

'Ricky's a hard worker and a quick learner,' Wilf said in his quiet way.

Finn gestured round the interior. 'You must both have worked hard. This place is looking better than I'd expected.'

Both of them beamed at that compliment.

'What time do you think people will come?'

'I sent out word not to come till nine o'clock,' Wilf said. 'It's not as if we have any proper lessons set up yet, or anything much for them to do, really. With your approval, I'm going to get some of them to clear up outside the back today, and I had a word with Lily.' He looked at Finn as if uncertain whether to continue.

'Go on.'

'She told me the other day that she can't keep up with her back garden, she works such long hours at her shop. So I suggested getting a couple of our lads to tidy it up for her in return for a good hearty meal. She offered to slip them a shilling each as well if they could get it ready for the spring planting. I told her to do that secretly and not mention it to me again.'

Finn knew why. The men would lose some of their week's dole money if it were known they'd been paid, and not just one day's worth if the benefits assessor applied some of the rules he could apply. People in that position could be unfair and harsh sometimes. They were fortunate in the valley that their current local man wasn't too much of a stickler – well, he wasn't as long as people were polite to him.

'Lily doesn't know much about gardening, nor do I, but maybe someone who comes today will and then I'll put him in charge of the gardening and call it a practical lesson.'

Finn looked at him in surprise at this initiative, but that was Wilf for you, always coming up with little suggestions once he'd assessed a new situation. What did they call a man who could do so many things? A polymath, was it? Or was that only someone who could learn about many different subjects? Wilf's skills lay in practical matters not book learning, but his instinctive insight seemed to cover a variety of trades.

'That's a good idea, Wilf. If it goes well, I could spread the word that we can supply garden teams and we'll say they're learning new skills – well, actually, it *will* be new skills for some of the men. I'd better speak to the benefits assessor about how to do it first.' He pulled out a little notebook he was using to remind himself of tasks to be done.

'There are so many different means tests they can apply, I get confused,' Wilf said.

'So do I. We don't want to do anything that will reduce the men's welfare payments.'

He put the notebook away in his inner jacket pocket. There were far too many details to pay attention to, and it was a good thing Wilf was so capable that he could be left to get on with the physical work while Beth and Finn both kept an eye on the paperwork and regulations. Finn still hadn't discussed with him how much it would be fair to pay him for doing this job. He'd do that later.

There was a tap on the back door.

'I'm a bit early,' the man said apologetically, twisting his cap round and round in his lumpy, work-worn hands, 'only that latest babby of ours won't stop skriking. He has the lungs of an adult when he's upset, that one does. I don't know how my Jane stands the noise all day every day.'

Finn smiled at Wilf. They both knew that this was probably an excuse to get here before the others.

'Come in.'

Wilf gestured to the tea urn. 'Are you any good at making cups of tea, Jim?'

'Aye. When I have the tea leaves to make it from. Why?'

'Everyone who comes here is going to have jobs to do. Maybe you'd like to take charge of making the tea?'

Jim's face brightened. 'I heard we'd be getting summat to eat and drink.'

'Yes. As long as you lot make it and clear up afterwards. We're sharing all the jobs here, including the cleaning.'

'I'm your man, whatever you need doing, Mr Pollard.'

Finn watched in admiration as Wilf found small responsibilities for each man who arrived, sometimes shared. When it came to housework, some of the men protested that they didn't know how to do that, but he only shrugged and told them the women would teach them how to do everything properly. 'We've got the use of this house from Mr Carlisle, but we must keep it clean ourselves.'

A couple of men muttered to one another at the idea of women telling men what to do, but when the women arrived, in a group as if for self-protection, no one was anything but polite to them.

Finn didn't address everyone until they'd all had a cup of good strong tea and got a couple of biscuits in their belly, followed by a refill of weaker, second-brewing tea. He tried to explain what they were planning to do.

'You mean we can have *real* lessons here, not just things to fill time – not that I mind filling time?' one man asked. 'Learn to drive, even?'

'Yes.'

'That'll be grand. I've allus fancied driving a motor car.'

'I want to start by making a list of your names and as we do that, you can tell me whether you can drive or not, and whether you have any other special skills.'

A scrawny man of about Finn's own age admitted that he'd been a full-time driver in the Great War and Finn was delighted.

'Good man. We thought we could get Mr Eustace to teach those of you who are already experienced drivers how to teach others to drive.' He paused to add emphatically, 'Especially those who have a lot of patience. If Mr Selby can lay his hands on a good, second-hand car, I'll buy it and set up a driving school in Rivenshaw. We'll see if we can build it up into full-time jobs for a couple of you, teaching others to drive. It's a useful skill and going to get more useful in the future, I'm sure.'

There were gasps and happy-sounding murmurs.

One of the women nudged another, who went bright pink. 'Please, Mr Carlisle, Ethel here was a driver during the war as well. She's a widow now but her kids are old enough to leave on their own and she needs a job just like a man does because she's the breadwinner.'

He smiled at Ethel. 'What sort of vehicles did you drive?'

Her voice was rather faint at first, shaking with nervousness – he could relate to that, by heck he could – but he encouraged her with nods and murmurs, and she settled down as she went on.

'We women drove ambulances at first. That's how I learned. And later on I drove big trucks to deliver supplies from factories to various barracks and camps around Lancashire and Yorkshire. I drove cars too, sometimes, big ones for the officers.'

'Sounds like you've had a lot of driving experience, Ethel.'

'Yes, but I'm out of practice.'

'That's what the job club is for, to give you practice and prepare you for jobs as times get better.' He saw some hostility on one or two men's faces and added, 'I bet there will be ladies who prefer a woman driving instructor to a man. We don't want rival driving schools setting up for women and pinching our pupils.'

The same men nodded reluctantly, so he continued, 'Mr Selby is willing to give introductory lessons to a few of you about car repairs, to see if you'd like to learn more. He can't be a full-time teacher, because he has a business to run, but he can give you a start and show you what's involved to find out if you've got a capacity for that sort of work. Not everyone does. No shame in that.'

He looked round, feeling a bit worried at how silent they were. Had he said something else that upset them, apart from talking about women learning to drive as well as men?

Then someone at the back said, 'Me, I'd like any kind of work.'

The others were still silent. As he scanned their faces, he saw that a few of the dozen or so men were swallowing hard, while others had overbright eyes, and Ethel was openly mopping tears away while her friend patted her back.

That made him feel rather emotional himself. He hadn't realised how hard it would be for them to cope with hope after all this time without it. He hoped his job club would be a help. It wouldn't be his fault if it wasn't.

That same Monday, Leah drove down to Rivenshaw and left her car at Todd's place, then they walked across town together to transact a very important piece of business.

'Charlie will throw a fit about me arranging for such a simple wedding,' Leah said. 'You know what he's like for putting on a show.'

'He won't fuss too much because he still hasn't got a lot of money to spare these days. Most people don't realise how far he over-extended himself when he bought the electrical goods shop, but you and I do, eh? He's only now starting to get a decent profit from it, thanks to Harry Makepeace. I must say that chap is a wizard at repairing things.'

'I read in the paper that sales of electrical goods are increasing all the time, especially in parts of the country where there's plenty of work, so things ought to continue improving for Charlie. He's been lucky on the whole, and he's created quite a few jobs in Rivenshaw, so he doesn't deserve to go under. '

'He's not the only one who's seeing an improvement. More cars are being sold, too, mostly in the south but even here in the north,' Todd said cheerfully. 'I sold another one this weekend.'

'Oh, good.' She stopped to remove a stone from her shoe, balancing awkwardly until he knelt down to help her remove the shoe and put it on again.

'Proposing to you, is he?' a lad called out from across the road.

'Already done that,' Todd yelled back.

She could feel her cheeks getting warm.

'You're blushing,' he teased, holding out his arm for her as they started walking again.

'Well, people don't usually call out to me about that sort of thing.'

He stopped walking again to give her a very loving look. 'I'd like to shout out to the whole world that we're going to get married, Leah.'

She was glad they were nearly at the registry office because much as she loved him, she was a quiet sort of person, not used to parading her emotions in public.

They went inside and paid their shilling to be listed in the Marriage Notice Book for the coming week. At the same time they booked their wedding for the first day they could.

'Done!' Todd said as they left. 'You look happy, my darling.'

'I'm very happy. My marriage to Jonah was an arrangement between two friends who found it convenient to marry. I grew fond of him but what I feel for you is far stronger.'

'Good. Let's see if we can light a fire that will burn between us for the rest of our lives.'

They stood gazing at one another in the dingy corridor until someone walked briskly past, then Todd plonked a quick kiss on her cheek and they moved on hand in hand.

As they were walking out of the town hall, they met Tam and Cara coming in, followed by Jinna, who was clutching little Ned's hand. It wasn't clear whether the girl was looking after him or he was looking after her.

'Hello, Mrs Willcox,' Cara said.

'Good morning. Or is it afternoon?' Tam said.

Todd stopped to grin at the other couple. 'Not quite afternoon yet. Are you on the same errand as us? We've just booked our wedding.'

Leah elbowed him in the side but he paid no attention.

'Have you really?' Tam asked. 'Well, what a coincidence! I wish you all the best, I do indeed. And you're right: me and Cara are here on exactly the same errand.'

Both men were beaming as if they were kings of the castle. Irrepressible was the word that occurred to Leah to describe them both. She exchanged resigned glances with Cara. Both of them would rather keep things quiet, but they had a fat chance of doing that with men like these.

Leah tugged Todd's arm. 'Come on. We have a lot to do today.'

They said their goodbyes and moved on.

'We'd better call on Charlie and his wife now and tell them,' Leah said. 'He'll be home for his midday meal still. And mind, we're not going to let him arrange anything fancy, whatever he says or does. I want a few friends to share the day with us, and that's it.'

Once Tam and Cara had gone through all the formalities for arranging their coming marriage, they left the town hall and went shopping.

Jinna was looking anxious again, her eyes darting here and there as always happened when she went to new places, especially ones where she felt threatened.

Tam nudged Cara. 'Keep an eye on her. She's probably worried about those lads. I wonder how long they've been tormenting her for.'

'It isn't market day, Jinna,' Cara said. 'I don't think those horrible boys will be in town today.'

Jinna stopped to look at where the market was usually held, and then turned round on the spot, as if checking everywhere before walking on with them.

To Tam's surprise, when they met Harvey Rixom, he stopped to ask them how things were going up in Ellindale. That immediately made Tam suspicious. He'd only once spoken to Rixom and that hadn't been a cordial exchange. He was surprised the fellow even recognised him, let alone remembered his name.

'I heard your cousin was on his death bed, Mr Crawford.'

Tam shrugged. 'He's not a well man, but he's not dead yet.'

'I must call and see if his wife needs anything.'

'No point. I'm looking after them.'

'Well, as the councillor for that ward, I do like to keep my eye on those in need.' Rixom looked at Jinna, who immediately shrank closer to Cara. 'I must say it's very charitable of you to take on the dummy.'

Tam stiffened and realised suddenly that he'd clenched his hand into a fist. He unclenched it before he spoke. '*Do not* call my adopted daughter that! She can speak perfectly well when she wants to, only she's very choosy about who she talks to. And she's so good at drawing that people are offering her money to do portraits of their loved ones, so she's not stupid, either. There aren't many people who can find ways of earning good money in these hard times.'

Rixom gaped at him, then looked at Jinna in puzzlement. 'Paid for her drawings?'

'Yes.'

'Well, I hope it's not a fluke.'

'Definitely not. She's a very clever girl, my Jinna is. Now, we must get on. We have a lot to do.' Tam turned to Cara and offered her his arm again, not bothering to take his leave of Rixom.

'I don't like that man,' she said in a low voice once they were out of earshot. 'I wouldn't trust him as far as I could throw him, and I wouldn't pick him up in the first place.'

He laughed. 'I've never heard that twist on the old saying.'

'It's what my gran used to say.'

'I like it and I agree with you about him. What I don't understand is why he wants to visit Hilda. He's not famous for his charitable acts. Oh, forget about Rixom. We've better things to attend to. I don't want anything to do with the man.'

Rixom went on into another part of the town hall to visit Brian Gratton and catch up on the latest news about the old house.

'You've let them start renovating the place! I thought we'd agreed to stop that and keep people away from it.'

'I couldn't do anything, Mr Rixom. That Carlisle chap has started a job club and he hasn't needed a grant.'

'I thought you said you'd be able to stop him using the place!'

'I thought I could. Only it's his house and his money that's involved. I sent one of my men up there to have a look at it and since it turns out the house is structurally sound, even if it is old-fashioned, none of the council ordinances apply. I'd have to have very good reason to stop Mr Carlisle using it or the mayor would throw a fit. I was going to tell you before the next council meeting.'

'You should have let me know at once.'

'I, um, didn't know it was urgent.'

'It will be urgent if they use their job club to renovate the old house completely and then sell it for a fat profit instead of having a cheap old ruin to sell for what they could get. There's a decent amount of land attached.' He stood frowning and after a moment exclaimed, 'Damn that fellow! Who'd have thought *he* would have inherited Heythorpe House?'

He'd been all set to buy Hillam House off Finn's cousin, the previous owner, who hadn't any idea of the real worth of the place when Rixom had sounded him out on one of his rare visits to the village.

The woman who'd been walking past outside, and stopped when she heard the conversation through a partly open window, hurried on again, frowning.

She knew more secrets than people realised but this one upset her more than usual, because she saw the men queuing to sign on for the dole each week. Sometimes the queue stretched nearly to the window of her office.

It was so unfair for that greedy man to try to stop some of them getting their spirits lifted by a job club.

Oh, she wished she wasn't so helpless!

*

When he left Gratton, Rixom went over to the Records Office and took down a book of old building regulations that were no longer applied but hadn't been repealed. It was an unofficial volume, used by the clerks to settle the occasional dispute. In theory these regulations were waiting to be repealed, but no one had got round to it.

He had looked through it idly years ago while waiting to see the mayor. Within a few minutes he had found the entry he vaguely remembered and was studying it carefully. Yes! His memory hadn't let him down. This regulation about 'satisfactory and safe' (unspecified) heating, cooking and sanitary facilities in 'habitable dwellings' would fit the bill nicely.

If he played his cards right, he and his friends would make a nice profit from this little project.

He had another piece of information to search out while he was here. Now that Peter Kerkham was near death it would be good to be prepared. He smiled as he found what he wanted.

It had been extremely helpful to have such a good memory for details; it had helped him get started on his quest to join the elite folk of the valley.

18

Leah clutched Todd's arm as they walked up the garden path to her brother-in-law's front door.

'Here we go. Charlie's car is there, so I guessed correctly and he's still at home.'

Todd looked down at her white-knuckled grip on his arm in surprise. 'I didn't think you'd be this nervous.'

'Charlie was very close to Jonah. It was he who arranged for us to marry. He'll be hurt that I'm marrying again, whenever I do it, and I really don't want to be at odds with him, because he's been kind to me in many ways. He's also a showman, as you must have realised, so that's another reason he won't like us having a quiet wedding. He'd want to use it to invite useful business acquaintances.'

Marion's maid opened the front door just then and smiled at them. 'Please come in, Mrs Willcox, Mr Selby. I'll just let *my* Mrs Willcox know you've called.'

For once, Leah couldn't smile at the ongoing joke about names between her and the maid.

Marion came out of the morning room at the front of the house.

'I saw you coming. How lovely to see you. Do come in.'

Leah hesitated. 'I hope this isn't an inconvenient time, but I hoped to catch you and Charlie at the same time to tell you our news.'

He came running down the stairs just then and stopped beside his wife.

'I think we can guess the news.'

'Not all of it,' Leah said quietly.

'Let's go and listen in comfort, then.' Marion led the way into the small family sitting room.

When they were seated, Leah told them straight out, 'Todd and I have just booked our wedding and we wanted you to be the first to know.'

'But you aren't even engaged yet,' Marion protested.

Charlie frowned at them and to Leah's intense annoyance, he stole a quick glance at her stomach.

Before she could say anything else, Todd surprised her. 'We're going to look at rings this afternoon, engagement *and* wedding rings. We don't want to wait to get married, so we're doing the deed very soon.'

'How soon?' Charlie demanded.

'In four weeks.'

Marion exchanged shocked looks with her husband, then turned back to Leah. 'But that won't give us time to plan a wedding properly.'

'If by that you mean an elaborate wedding reception, I don't want one of those. I'm not a fancy sort of person and the only guests I want at my wedding are close friends and relatives.'

'No, no! You can't do this in a shabby way!' Charlie protested. 'As my brother's widow and the owner of Cottage Springs Mineral Waters, you have a position in the valley to maintain. And besides, we need to show everyone that Marion and I approve – which we do, I assure you. You'll cause talk by doing the thing so quickly.' He patted his stomach suggestively.

There he went again, Leah thought angrily.

Todd reached for her hand. 'Let them talk, Charlie. They'll soon be proved wrong about that.'

'Even so—' Charlie began.

Marion cut him short. 'It's not our decision to make, dear.' She turned back to Leah. 'I've seen how you two look at one another so I was expecting some sort of announcement. I wish you a happy life together.'

'Well, I'll put on a reception for you, at least,' Charlie said. 'We can—'

It was Leah's turn to interrupt. 'If you don't mind, we'd rather arrange that ourselves. We'll probably hold it at Spring Cottage or in the big back room of The Shepherd's Rest in Ellindale, so that some of our guests won't be overawed by a fancy meal at a Rivenshaw hotel.'

Charlie stared at her. 'Some of your guests won't be *overawed*? Who are you talking about?'

'Ginny and some other people from Ellindale.'

'You don't invite servants to a wedding!'

'I do when they've become good friends.' Leah looked pleadingly at Marion, who was usually far more tactful than Charlie, hoping she'd intercede again.

'It's their wedding, Charlie. Stop trying to butt in.' Marion turned back to Leah. 'We'll be very happy to attend. Which church is it at?'

'We're getting married at the registry office, with only you two and Rosa present at the actual ceremony – well, I hope you'll be there and that *you* will do us the honour of being our second witness, Charlie. My sister must be the first one, of course. Marion, if we could have three witnesses, I'd ask you too.'

Silence followed, then Charlie turned to look at his wife.

'We'd love to attend,' Marion said at once. 'And Charlie will be happy to be your witness – unless he takes a huff and backs out, in which case I'll do it.'

Charlie had been going to speak but snapped his mouth closed at this and Marion took over again. 'Todd, I hope you know what a treasure you're getting in Leah.'

'Yes, I do. I've loved her since the first time we met, but I could see how happy she was with Jonah, so I could do nothing about it then.'

'I should think not!'

Todd was tired of biting back his annoyance at his friend and business partner's attitude. 'Oh, get down off your high horse, Charlie! This is our lives we're talking about, not a business deal.'

He waited a minute but when Charlie didn't respond, he stood up. 'I have to get back to work, so we'll leave you now. We wanted to tell you before we tell any outsiders. We'll let you know the details of the day once we've sorted them out.'

'We're the first to know?' Charlie asked.

'Of course you are, except for Rosa.'

That seemed to mollify him and he gave Leah a hug. 'I hope you'll be happy, however you tie the knot!'

'I think I will be, and Todd already loves your nephew.'

'We all do. He's a lively little fellow, isn't he? Jonah would have been so proud of him.'

There was a moment's silence, then they all pushed aside their sadness at losing Jonah and carried on with their day.

Todd didn't start the car immediately but turned to Leah. 'You expected Charlie to react like that, didn't you?'

'I'm afraid so. He'll calm down now he knows we told them first and Marion will help us deal with him. I do hate being at odds with people, especially ones I'm fond of.'

'He'd better watch how he deals with you in future, though. I'm not having him behave so suspiciously towards you. Patting his stomach indeed!'

She chuckled. 'Towards the end, you and he were like two cocks about to battle over their hens.'

'Were we really?' He grinned at her.

'Yes. And what's the betting that Marion is telling him off for it at this very moment?'

'No betting. She rules him with a rod of iron, though at times he does things without consulting her, like when he bought that run-down electrical goods shop.'

'She loves him dearly, but I sometimes think she's the one with the better business brain in that marriage. Her own business may be small but she's become very popular with people who still have money to pay her to design their business and personal stationery, and other things. She loves doing it.'

Leah paused as something occurred to her. 'I wonder if Marion would help Jinna, teach her more about other art materials perhaps. That girl is very talented with a pencil. I wonder how she'd be with paints. I want her to do a sketch of my Jonty as soon as Tam and his family get settled somewhere.'

Todd leaned across the front of the car to kiss her cheek. 'You'll have to ask Marion next time you see her.'

As they set off, he added, 'You may be quiet, but you can stand up for yourself.'

'I've had to look after myself for years and I'm not afraid to do it, but I don't like arguments so I try to avoid them.'

'I hope you'll let me stand beside you from now on if there are any problems.'

'Of course I will. And I'll stand beside you, too.'

'That's my girl!' There was such strength in Leah. He admired her as well as loving her. 'Anyway, let's go and find a ring!'

The man behind the counter of the jeweller's straightened up as they went into his shop, clearly delighted to see a customer.

'We'd like to buy an engagement ring for my fiancée,' Todd said. 'And a wedding ring to go with it.'

'Certainly, sir.' He pulled out a tray of sparkling diamond rings from the locked cabinet, but Leah didn't like any of them enough to want to wear it every day. She'd never owned a diamond and somehow these didn't tempt her, however much they sparkled. They looked too cold.

Then another tray of rings under the glass-topped counter caught her eye and she bent over it to point. 'What about that one?'

'It's a second-hand ring, madam, though of a very good quality.'

'What does that matter? It's so pretty.'

'Don't you want a diamond?' Todd asked.

'I didn't know what I wanted till I saw that one. I've always loved amethysts.'

She held out her left hand and the jeweller slipped it on her ring finger. 'There! It fits perfectly.'

Todd studied it, then raised her hand to his lips and kissed it. 'I like it too. We'll take it.'

She caught sight of the price. 'Are you sure?'

'Of course I am.'

'Do you want to wear it now?' the jeweller asked with a smile, as if he already knew the answer.

'Oh, yes, please.'

'Let me take the price tag off for you, then.'

That was quickly done and he put the ring down on a small pad. 'Better leave it off till we've sorted out a wedding ring for you.'

'Just a simple one,' Leah said.

Another tray of rings was brought out.

One ring immediately caught her eye. Plain except that it had little stars stamped in it at intervals.

The jeweller brought it out and she tried it on. 'It must be my lucky day, because this fits too. I love it.' She turned to Todd, holding her left hand out.

He took her hand and studied the ring. 'Perfect. It goes really well with that engagement ring.'

She went over to the window to stand admiring the rings in a beam of sunlight. 'I love the purple and gold together.'

'So do I.'

Todd paid for the rings and then she had to take off the wedding ring and put it into a little box, which he slipped into his inside jacket pocket.

'That was surprisingly easy,' he said as they left the shop.

'Why should it not be?'

He stopped walking to study her. 'I don't know. But it seems to me that you make everything as easy as it can be. No fuss about which ring. No hankering after things you can't have. I'm a very lucky man to have won your love.'

'We're both lucky that we met. But it won't be luck that makes our marriage happy; it'll be love and working at fitting together.'

'I think you must have been born wise, Leah.'

'What a lovely compliment.'

'Wouldn't you rather I talked about your beautiful eyes and gleaming hair?'

'Definitely not. I'll grow old and my hair will turn grey, but if it's up to me, our love will only grow brighter – and stronger.'

19

When Tam and his family got home, a lad from the village was waiting for them outside the hostel. 'Miss Pendle at the shop says you're needed at Skeggs Hill Farm, Mr Crawford.'

'Thank you.' Tam slipped him a penny, then turned to Cara. 'I'd better go and see what's happened straight away. Can you manage all right?'

'Of course I can. And we can guess why you're needed, can't we? I shan't expect you back till you've done whatever's necessary.'

He got back into the van and bumped down the rough road that led through the village, then on to the even rougher lane. Cara was right. There was only one thing it could be to make proud Hilda Kerkham ask for help.

From inside the house he could hear the sound of weeping, which confirmed that Peter must have died. He knocked on the door but didn't wait to be invited in.

There was no one in the kitchen and the sobbing was coming from the bedroom, so he called out, 'It's Tam here.'

There were footsteps and the boy came hurrying out into the kitchen. 'Oh, Cousin Tam, thank goodness you're here! Dad died this morning and Mam won't stop crying.'

'She loved him.' Tam could see that Frankie had been crying as well, so he pulled the boy into his arms and gave him a hug. Eh, that lad was so thin, it felt as if he would break into pieces if treated too roughly.

When Frankie drew away, Tam fumbled for his handkerchief to offer it, but the boy had already pulled a clean rag out of his pocket and was using that to mop his eyes.

'Let's go and see your mam now. She'll need comforting.'

'I tried to hug her but she pushed me away.'

'She won't be thinking straight. Won't be for a while, I reckon, so don't let anything she does upset you.'

Tam went into the bedroom, where a still figure was lying on the bed. There was no mistaking that Peter was dead. 'I'm here, Hilda. What can I do to help?'

She turned towards him, still keeping hold of the dead man's hand. Without hesitation, Tam went to her, putting one arm round her shoulders and trying to move her gently away from the bed. But she wasn't having it and flung herself back on her husband's body, wailing and sobbing.

Tam let her cry for a moment or two, then tried again. 'You have to let him go, love. Your son needs you too.'

She froze for a moment, then his words seemed to sink in and she stood slowly up. 'Yes.'

'And there will be arrangements to make. Maybe I can help you with those.'

Her voice was bitter. 'All I have to do is contact the parish church in Birch End so that they can arrange a pauper's funeral for him in a mass grave.'

'Ah. Yes.'

'Well, I may not be able to afford a proper funeral for my Peter, but I'm the one who's going to lay him out, and I'll do it properly. I can at least do that for him.'

'You mustn't start till the doctor's seen him.' He turned to the boy still waiting by the door. 'Frankie, can you go to the shop and ask them to phone Dr Fiske and tell him your father's died?'

'Yes.' Looking relieved, the boy ran out at once.

Tam kept his arm round Hilda's shoulders. 'Let's put the kettle on now. You need something to brace you.'

She let him guide her towards the kitchen, stopping in the bedroom doorway to look over her shoulder. When Tam moved forward and started to put the kettle on, she took over and he stepped back, letting her make the pot of tea.

When it was ready, he gestured to the table. 'Let's sit down, eh?'

As she was pouring the tea into a cup, Frankie came back in. 'Miss Pendle phoned the doctor. He'll be up within the hour. She says no charge.'

He held out a paper-wrapped parcel. 'She sent us a loaf as well, with her condolences.'

Hilda's voice was dull. 'Kind of her.'

She made no attempt to take it, so Tam gestured to the lad to put it in the bread bin at the other end of the table. 'Cup of tea, lad?'

'Yes, please.'

Tam silently pointed to a chair next to his mother, but Frankie came to sit beside him instead and truth to tell, it didn't seem as if Hilda even noticed what her son was doing because she was staring into space, her eyes unfocused.

Once Hilda had finished her cup of tea, Tam poured her another one and she nodded her head in thanks. But she went back to staring blindly across the room, still making no attempt to discuss the situation.

This would be the right time to tell her about what her husband had asked of him, he decided. It'd give her something else to think about.

'Hilda love, can you listen to me for a minute or two?'

As she turned her head towards him, he went on, 'I made your Peter a promise the other day. It seemed to give him peace of mind and he knew I'd keep my word. I promised him I'd make sure you and the boy were all right.'

Her voice was suddenly sharp. 'I'll not be all right till I bury my husband and leave this godforsaken place.' She sagged in her chair. 'But I can't do that till I sell the farm, can I?'

'That's the other thing we need to talk about. I'd like to buy the farm from you.'

Both his companions gaped at him.

'But you're not a farmer!' she protested.

'I don't want to *farm* it. I want a house to live in, a house of my own. I was going to talk to Peter before he died about buying yours – afterwards, you know – but he went so quickly, I'll need to talk to you about it instead. Will you sell it to me?'

'Oh dear! I can't. I've already offered it to my brother. It was in the letter you posted for me. James can easily afford it and if I'm forced to sell it for ten pounds, it might as well be to him.'

'Ten? I was going to offer you twenty-five.'

She repeated his words in a shocked whisper, but didn't seem able to say anything else.

He wasn't going to try to force a woman who'd just lost her husband to think about money and bargaining. It'd be wrong. But oh dear, he wished he'd spoken earlier.

'Tam, I—' She broke off as there was the sound of a car outside.

Frankie rushed to the window. 'It's the doctor.'

'Let him in.' She brushed away more tears and stood up as Frankie opened the front door.

'This way, Dr Fiske.'

When the doctor came back into the kitchen from the bedroom a short time later, Hilda stayed with her husband's body.

'Cup of tea?' Tam asked him.

'Can she spare it?'

'Yes. I'm keeping her supplied.'

'Strange how it comforts people,' the doctor said as he sat clasping his cup for the warmth. 'It's a stimulant, really.'

'It helps get folk through hard times.' Tam looked towards the bedroom again, but there was no sign of Hilda joining them. 'Has she said anything about the funeral?'

'Only that it'll have to be a pauper's burial. I do hate to see those.'

Tam didn't even think as he said it. 'Do you know anyone who does really cheap funerals? You know, without a fancy coffin or hearse. She's upset about having a pauper's burial.'

The doctor looked at him. 'Are you thinking of paying for it?'

Tam nodded, miserably aware that he was diving into something yet again, only Hilda had been so upset about Peter not having a grave of his own, he couldn't bear it. What would Cara say to him spending that much money on someone they hardly knew, though?

'There's a chap I know who does cheap funerals for people able to scrape a few pounds together. It'll only be a simple pine coffin, mind, and taken to the church and cemetery in a little van instead of a proper hearse. A group of us have put some money towards the cost of the graves. Can you afford five pounds for the funeral?'

'Yes.'

'You're sure?'

'Aye. He was my cousin, you know, doctor.'

'Ah. I was forgetting that. Shall I let the undertaker know?'

'We'll have to ask Hilda first. Can you wait a minute or two longer?'

'If you don't mind me having another cup of tea. I've been rushing round today. I'd welcome a rest.'

So Tam went into the bedroom, where Hilda was lovingly preparing her husband's body for burial. No tears now, just a white, grim face, gentle touches and utter concentration.

'Hilda, love, the doctor says he knows someone who'll do a funeral for five pounds. I can afford to pay that and—'

She turned towards him, froze for a moment, then flung herself into his arms. 'Oh, Tam, Tam, thank you! You're a good friend, you are, the very best. Can you really afford to do that?'

'Aye.' He waited, expecting her to weep all over him, but she didn't. She stood back, her head held high now.

'I can't tell you how much that means to me, and would have meant to Peter.'

'That's all right, then. I'll tell the doctor and he'll send whoever it is to see you.'

'I know who it is. He's called Owen Jeavons. But I didn't even have one penny left in my purse, so I had no hope, no hope at all, of a proper burial. Oh, Tam, thank you!'

You'd think he'd given her the moon, Tam thought.

He would have liked to go on discussing her selling him the farm, but she turned back to tend her husband. Surely, after the funeral, she'd reconsider his offer? If her brother was only going to give her a measly ten pounds for the farm, it wasn't fair, and Tam's offer was fair, given that it was a small farm with very poor land.

But who knew how grieving would take her? Would she be thinking sensibly? Or would the blood ties to a brother be more important? It was possible the man might be giving her and Frankie a home as well.

He went back into the kitchen and found the doctor preparing to leave.

'Well?'

'She's happy for us to use this undertaker. It meant a lot to her.'

'It always does. It comforts them greatly to have a respectable burial and a grave to visit. Just one thing more: the death certificate is on the table. She must register the death at the town hall, and it'd be best to get it over with soon. I'll send Owen Jeavons up to discuss the funeral with her. He'll probably come at once. He keeps a stock of coffins. I don't think he's had any funerals for a couple of days.'

After the doctor left, Tam was wondering whether to go home and tell Cara what had happened when Hilda came back into the kitchen.

'I need to get in touch with my brother and let him know about Peter. James is on the phone at his shop.'

She looked at Tam pleadingly, 'I don't want to leave Peter. I shan't have him for much longer. Could you phone my brother for me, please, from the shop? I'll get him to reimburse you for the call.'

She flushed and looked uncomfortable as she added, 'I don't think James will pay anything towards the funeral, though. He's rather, um, tight-fisted.'

'Well, Peter was my cousin, so I'll not be hounding you to repay me. Had we better wait to phone your brother till this Jeavons chap comes and sets a time for the funeral, though, do you think?'

'Oh, yes. Yes, of course.' She sat down and rubbed her forehead. 'I'm not thinking clearly, I'm afraid.'

'I'm not surprised on such a sad day. I'll stay with you if you'll let Frankie go up to the youth hostel and tell Cara what's happened.'

'It'll do him good to get out.'

'Have you any food in the house?'

'There's the loaf Lily at the shop sent.'

'I'll make sure we get you some more bits and pieces.'

'Thank you.'

But he doubted she'd eat much, or notice what she was putting into her mouth.

Owen Jeavons turned up just as Tam was thinking of going home for his evening meal and calling in at the shop on the way with Frankie to get food for them.

Jeavons was like a caricature of an undertaker, being tall and thin, dressed in rusty black, wearing a rather battered top hat with weepers on it. The piece of black ribbon flapped about behind him as he walked and it was a good thing, Tam thought, that the weepers were the only trappings of his trade. Eh, they did look silly and old-fashioned.

The man had arrived in a battered van and offered to take the body away and lay it out, but Hilda shook her head.

'I've done that already. I knew what to do. And I want to keep him here with me tonight.'

He looked at her and Tam thought there was genuine sympathy in his gaze.

'I brought a coffin with me. May I see your husband? Then I'll bring it in and help you lift him into it.'

She nodded and led the way into the bedroom.

Tam left them to do what was necessary and waited with Frankie.

'It's horrible,' the boy said suddenly.

'What is?'

'Dying and all the fuss you have to go through.'

'Did your father have a bad time of it?'

'No. He just sighed and he was gone. I've never seen anyone die before. It's Mam who's having a bad time of it, and she's still got the funeral to get through tomorrow. And what will she do afterwards? How will we live? I can't do everything on the farm and they'll make me go back to school now Dad's dead.'

'I should think her brother will help her out. You'll probably go and live with him.'

Frankie stared at him in horror. 'If she tries to make me live with my uncle, I'll run away. I mean it. I'm not letting him beat me like he beats his own children. I've been doing a man's work lately an' I don't feel much like a child any more.'

Tam was shocked at this revelation. 'You've done well, better than most lads would, that's for sure. But you'll have to do what your mam decides, live where she says.'

'She told me she's going to sell the farm.'

For all his claims to be grown up, tears showed in his eyes. 'I don't want to leave here, Cousin Tam. I like farming and I don't like being shut up indoors. An' I like living in Ellindale, too.'

'We can't always have what we want, lad.'

'Oh, I know that. Who doesn't? But even though I'm still a lad, I don't have to put up with unkindness and cruelty, an' I won't, either, whatever anyone says.'

'I'm sure your uncle won't hurt you.'

'Ha! You've never met him. His family are all terrified of him. He thumped me when me and Mam went to visit him.'

Hilda brought the undertaker back into the kitchen just then, so Frankie stopped talking. She'd arranged to hold the funeral in the late afternoon of the next day and to ride to the cemetery in the undertaker's van with her husband's body.

'Frankie can ride down to Rivenshaw with us, if you like,' Tam offered, 'as long as he doesn't mind sitting in the back with Jinna and Ned. We can bring him back afterwards as well.'

'You're all coming to the funeral?'

'Of course we are. Now, I've got to go home. Write down your brother's phone number and I'll call at the shop on the

way and let him know what's happened. Frankie can come
with me and bring some food back for you both.'

'Thank you, Tam.'

The phone call went through easily and Tam explained to
James Boales about his brother-in-law dying.

Frankie stood beside him, listening.

There was silence for a few seconds, then a thin, rather
high voice said, 'Couldn't have happened at a more inconvenient time, but I suppose I'll have to attend the funeral.
I'm not bringing my family with me though. I need to leave
my wife here to tend the shop and the children need their
schooling.'

'Did you receive your sister's letter?'

'Yes. A begging letter. What do I want to buy a farm for,
and why should I pay her good money for a worthless piece
of land? She won't need money anyway. I'll be putting a roof
over her head – hers and her son's. None of my family is
going into the poorhouse, or whatever they call that place
now. I'll put the money the farm brings me towards her keep.
I don't want to be out of pocket. Tell me the time again, and
where the funeral is being held.'

Tam gathered his patience together and went through it
all once more.

'So it's not going to be a pauper's funeral?'

'No. I've put up the money for it, since Peter is – *was* –
my cousin.'

'Well, that's a relief. I'll meet you at the church, then afterwards I can drive Hilda back to the farm and see what she
has that's worth selling before she moves in with us.'

Tam felt anger sear through him at this heartless conversation, and was sorry that poor Frankie had to hear it. But
he could do nothing to help Hilda with her future life. It was
her choice to go to her brother.

As he turned to go home, he stopped and said abruptly. 'I'll just come back and have another word with your mother, Frankie.'

He'd give her one last chance to sell the farm to him instead.

Hilda was sitting by the kitchen table, not seeming to have moved since Tam and Frankie went to the shop.

She looked up listlessly, her whole body seeming to be drooping. 'Did you get through to my brother?'

'Yes. He's coming to the funeral tomorrow. Just him.'

'Why not his wife?'

'He says she'll be needed in the shop.'

She looked at him in dismay. 'But my Peter is *family*! They should be showing respect by all of them attending. They should have closed the shop for a bereavement, or got someone else in to serve.'

Tam didn't know what to say, so kept quiet.

'Did James – did he mention the farm?'

'Um—'

While he was still fumbling for words, she filled in for him. 'He said he didn't want to buy it, didn't he?'

'No, no. I think he's going to sell it for you. He says the money he gets can go towards your keep.'

'He always was mean.'

'Look, I just want to say that I'd still like to buy the farm and I'll still pay you twenty-five pounds for it. Remember that if you change your mind.'

'I couldn't go against James. He has a temper and I need him to put a roof over my head and Frankie's too. Frankie won't be allowed to leave school for another two years when he'll be fourteen. I'm sure James will let us live with him, if only because he would hate to have a sister and nephew in the poorhouse.'

Tam made a murmuring sound but she seemed to be talking aloud to reassure herself rather than telling him anything.

'My brother will see that Frankie gets work when he leaves school, too, I know he will. That's the main reason why I'm going to him, however hard he is to live with. He's done quite well for himself, knows a lot of business people in Oldham, so he'll be sure to find a job for my son when the time comes.'

'And what will he do for you, Hilda?'

'Set me to work, I expect. Well, I wouldn't expect to sit around idle. I never have and I never will. I don't really care what happens to me, Mr Crawford. I just don't care any more. It's my son who matters now.'

What could he say to that? He certainly couldn't find her son a job. But he wasn't paying his money to the man he'd spoken to. He hadn't even met James Boales, but after only one phone conversation, he already detested the mean-spirited sod.

So he told her where he stood, 'There's just one thing. My offer to buy your farm is for you only. If the money is going to your brother, I'll withdraw my offer.'

'He'll find someone else to sell to. I'm sorry. I have to think about Frankie's future. You see so many lads who can't find a job.'

Tam left it at that and went home. It had been a long, hard day. It should have been a happy one, with him and Cara booking their wedding – eh, had that only been this morning? – but Peter's death had spoiled that.

Cara would have good reason to be angry with him for being out so long, leaving her to deal with any hikers and the two children. He was expecting recriminations or huffiness at least when he got back, because it was nearly bedtime now.

Instead she greeted him with one of her warm smiles. 'I

fed the children and put them to bed. They're both asleep already. Are you hungry, Tam?'

He had to stop and think about that, there was so much churning around in his head.

'I'd forgotten about food. Let's sit and chat for a few minutes while I calm down, then I'll eat. You won't believe what Hilda's brother said about her situation. It's really upset me.'

He explained, ending, 'If she goes to live with him, she'll have a miserable life. Utterly miserable. And so will poor Frankie.'

'He's a nice lad, a hard worker.'

'Yes. But it's not my place to try to stop her. Pity she wouldn't sell to me. I'd have liked to live on the edge of the moors.'

Cara got him some food, and he found she'd waited to have hers with him. It was very pleasant to sit and chat quietly as they ate, and for a while afterwards. She was a lovely, peaceful sort of woman.

Thinking about that made him say it to her. 'I enjoy chatting with you. You're good company, Cara.' He couldn't help smiling at her reaction. 'You're blushing.'

'I'm not used to compliments.'

'I don't give empty ones. I meant what I said.'

'Well, you're good company too, Tam.'

'You don't mind about the five pounds for the burial?'

'No, of course not. He's your cousin.'

So he risked pulling her into his arms and kissing her. And very satisfactory it was, too.

He was still smiling as he said goodnight. Snuggling down on the narrow mattress, he kept thinking what a nice woman she was, how lucky he was to have found her.

It'd be hard living in such crowded quarters with the children underfoot once they were married. They had to find somewhere else to go. Eh, it was such a pity he hadn't been able to buy the farm. It'd have made a lovely home and there was room for his van, room for the children to play outside as well.

But there you were. Life had given him Cara and two children to raise. It was more than he'd expected at his age.

He'd have really liked to live in Ellindale, though.

20

On the Tuesday morning, one of the two men working on the back garden of the old house nudged his companion. 'Is that who I think it is?'

His friend looked round and scowled. 'Rixom! I hate that sod. Calls himself a councillor, but he's not done anything for Ellindale. All he's interested in is himself.'

'Why is he standing over there looking at this house, do you think?'

'Perhaps he wants to buy it. I was told he'd bought a few places here and there, mostly in Backshaw Moss. He rents them out but he won't do any maintenance so they're nearly falling down.'

'I heard about him buying a couple of places there and in Birch End, but not about him buying anything up here.'

'You must have been ill when he bought that cottage Mrs Jarratt and Dilys used to live in. Good thing they've got themselves live-in jobs with Mr Carlisle, eh, or he'd be turning them out and doubling the rent money. The farmer's relatives left when Rixom bought it for that very reason.'

'Hey up! He's looking this way. Don't let him see you watching him, keep on digging. It doesn't do to get on the wrong side of him.'

The two men began turning over the soil again, picking out the bigger stones and chucking them on to a pile at the side, stealing sideways glances at Rixom.

'Damn me! He's coming across here now. Nip inside and

warn Mr Carlisle to lock the door against him, or he'll start poking his nose in and finding something to complain about to the council. That's how he got that cottage from the farmer, said it was unfit for human habitation and needed pulling down. Only he didn't pull it down; he put people in it, didn't he? Said they were only temporary. He thinks folk don't know about his tricks. Ha! As if you can keep anything secret round here.'

But Eddie wasn't listening. He'd cast his spade to one side and run into the house.

Finn swung round as hobnail boots clattered in through the back door, and Eddie burst in, slamming the door shut behind him and leaning against it.

'That Rixom chap is coming to call and he never does anything that won't benefit himself, so Mikey thought we should warn you, Mr Carlisle, not to let him inside. He'll find something to complain about, say this place isn't fit for habitation and next thing you know, you'll have the council on your back to demolish it an' he'll be collecting rent from *temporary* tenants.'

'Is he that bad?'

'Worse. Damned liar, he is, about all sorts of things. Him an' a few others on the council. Never believe a word he says.'

'I'll come outside then, meet him on neutral territory.'

'Beg pardon, sir, but don't be so certain about that, even. There are things the council can say about the outside of houses too.'

Finn was amazed at how emphatic Eddie was about Rixom being here for no good reason. He followed the other man out and heard Rixom berating Mikey about not putting his back into his work. What business was it of Rixom's how these men worked anyway? He wasn't employing them.

He marched across to the patch of partially dug earth, stopping between Rixom and Mikey.

'Can I help you?'

'Just coming to see how you're going here, me being the councillor for Ellindale.'

'Things are going well, thank you, but I'd rather you left it to me to deal with the members of my job club about how they work.'

Thanks to Eddie's warning, he was watching Rixom more closely than he hoped showed, and saw the fellow's mouth tighten into a narrow line for a moment or two, as if unhappy about what he'd said. Well, too bad.

'Perhaps we could go inside, Mr Carlisle, and talk privately?'

'No privacy there. I've got people doing work all over the interior.'

'Does the benefits man know what's going on here?'

'Might I ask what business that is of yours?'

'I like to keep an eye on my constituents, see they don't get into trouble – and make sure that they do what's expected of them if someone takes an interest, as you have done. The rules are there for very good reasons. It's kind of you to do this, I'm sure, but I gather you've not gone through the council with this job club of yours and that can lead to trouble.'

'Can it, indeed?'

The two club members had abandoned all pretence of digging and were resting on their spades, listening.

Rixom looked round. 'Mr Carlisle, will you—'

Since the fellow wasn't going away, Finn said curtly, 'Perhaps we could move away to the other side of the house if you want to talk about something private?'

'Yes, good idea.' Rixom tried to keep his voice friendly, aware that he'd not made a good start with Carlisle today.

Only it had irked him greatly to see them putting the old house to rights when he had counted on being able to buy a run-down old place cheaply. Then, when times were better, he'd be able to build at least four dwellings on this piece of ground.

Before many years had passed, he intended to become rich, and it'd be by his own astuteness, not because some stupid old relative left him a big house as they had this chap. He took a deep breath and told himself to go gently.

'Now, Carlisle, I wonder if this house meets all the required building standards. It's very old and we mustn't put these poor chaps' safety at risk. I'd be willing to go through the interior with you and tell you whether it's safe or not. I have considerable experience in building and renovating dwellings.'

'Why would you want to do that?'

'Well, because I'm your local councillor. You know that.'

'I'll bear it in mind if I have need of your help. But as it is, I think we're making a very good start on the job club. The house was soundly built in the first place and is still in a good condition, however old it is. So I shan't need to trouble you for help.'

'You may find it to your *advantage* to trouble me.' Rixom managed to keep a pleasant smile on his face but he could hear the acid undertone in his own voice. Well, he had only to see Carlisle to feel envious of the fellow's undeserved luck and large house full of servants.

'Let's leave it at that, eh?' Finn turned away and walked across to join the two men, completely ignoring Rixom.

As the unwelcome visitor walked past them to get back to the road, a shovelful of damp earth suddenly hit the back of his lower trousers. He swung round. 'What the—'

'Eh, sorry Mr Rixom,' one man said. 'My shovel slipped.'

Rixom studied his face. He'd remember this man. Oh, yes. And make him regret that rudeness.

But as the other man dug up a shovelful of earth and drew his elbow back to toss it, a scowl on his face, Rixom hastily hurried out of reach. He wouldn't put it past these uncouth fellows to chuck more earth at him.

At the main road he stopped to stare back at the three men, who were laughing about something. Him having dirt thrown over his clean trousers, probably. How dare they!

He never forgot an insult. Never. As they would find out.

He glared down at his trousers. He'd have to go home and change now, couldn't walk around covered with dried mud.

After that he'd go back to the town hall and set a few things in motion.

Finn watched Rixom walk away, then turned to Eddie. 'You shouldn't have done that, lad. It's usually better to behave properly and let *them* show their true colours to the world by behaving badly.'

'I couldn't resist it, Mr Carlisle. I hate that sod.'

'Why?'

'Two years ago he tried to take advantage of my cousin, even though she told him no. He didn't want to come courting, because he already has a wife, just to have a bit on the side. And he had the cheek to offer her money, yes, and then to try to force her. Only a neighbour happened by just in time to stop him raping her. She was only fourteen. What does that make him, eh?'

He glared in the direction Rixom had taken. 'We had to send her away to live with a relative to be sure she was safe. He's like that, takes a fancy to a woman for a while and pesters her. Never one of his own sort, though. He's got a posh wife, one who brought him money. She's a decent soul, they say, but downtrodden, never looks happy.'

Finn shook his head, saddened by this tale. 'There are

some villains around in this world if you poke beneath the surface, there are indeed.'

He'd not interacted this closely with the unemployed men from the village before and had to wonder what else he'd find out. The men seemed to have their own way of linking into gossip and information, just like the women did.

'I'd be grateful if you'd let me know if you hear about Rixom plotting something.'

'Aye. He must be doing that already, or he'd not have bothered to come here today. The only person he represents on that council is himself.'

When he went home that night, Finn shared what he'd found out with Beth, who also seemed to dislike Rixom more than you'd have expected.

'What is it about that man?'

'What Eddie told you. He preys on young girls. Threatens their families if they make a fuss. He's supposed to have crippled one man who upset him, but the man moved away suddenly, so no one's quite sure.'

'I can't believe I'm hearing this for the first time. Who else in the valley is gossiped about?'

She shrugged. 'Half the council. But none of them are as bad as Rixom. They don't have scandals in their personal lives, they just . . . use being on the council for their own financial benefit. That's why I thought *you* should stand for the council. We could do with some honest people on it.'

His heart sank. He'd hoped she would drop the idea. 'I've no experience of that sort of job.'

'No, but you're an honest man, and kind. People would vote for you without needing to be paid or given favours.'

'I'd hate it.'

She shrugged. 'Pity. Now, it's nearly time for tea. And don't forget, you promised to hear Daisy read afterwards. She's coming along so well, loves going to school.'

This was what life was about, Finn thought, family and looking after one another. He was so lucky to have a second chance at it.

21

The following afternoon, Tam got dressed in his best. Cara had to stay at the hostel in case some hikers turned up, and he thought it best that Jinna and little Ned stay with her.

He stopped near the farm, sitting in his van at the edge of the road when he saw that Jeavons was there with another man. They were lifting the coffin into the back of the undertaker's van, so Tam wasn't needed to help with that.

He raised one hand in greeting when Hilda glanced across at him and she gave Frankie a push that sent him walking slowly along the short track from the farm. He had his hands jammed in his pockets and was kicking stones here and there, not attempting to hurry.

Tam opened the car door when the lad showed no sign of getting in. 'You all right?'

Frankie shook his head and kicked another stone, sending it ricocheting against the dry-stone wall. 'Mam says we have to go and live with Uncle James. She doesn't know whether we're going with him straight away after the funeral or whether he'll leave us here for a day or two to clear out the house. We'll have to stay here till we've got rid of the stock, though, won't we, Cousin Tam? Who'll feed them if I'm not here? They can't be left to starve to death.'

'I'm afraid I don't know much about farm animals so I doubt I'd be much good at helping out. Is there someone from the village who could do it for a few days?'

'I don't know. Mam thinks they'll only do it if we pay them, and we haven't got any money, though maybe someone would look after the hens in return for the eggs.'

'Well, we'll no doubt find out what your uncle is planning after the funeral and you can remind him about the stock then. If he's helping your mother to sell up, he won't want the animals to die because they're going to be worth something.'

When Frankie still didn't move, he gestured to the front passenger seat. 'You'd better get in, lad. Looks like the undertaker's nearly ready to leave. We'll wait here for them to lead the way.'

'All right. Thanks for letting me come with you, Cousin Tam.'

When they were in the van, Tam asked, 'How's your mother coping with it all?'

'She's still crying a lot. An' she's hardly eaten a thing. Oh, and she said to tell you Dr Fiske has arranged for a plot in the cheap part of the new cemetery. She said it was comforting to know that Dad would have his own grave an' she's grateful to you for helping with the funeral.'

The undertaker's van came out of the track at that moment and turned down the hill. Tam saw that a big bow of black ribbon had been fastened to the front of the bonnet. Perhaps that was to show that there was a funeral under way. There was certainly nothing else fancy about the makeshift hearse. He set off after them.

As they passed through the village they saw that one or two people had come to stand beside the road and bow their heads as the two vehicles passed.

Nice of them to show respect, Tam thought. Hilda would appreciate that. Eh, she'd miss living here, he was sure. Who wouldn't?

*

When they drew up outside the church, Tam saw a tall, thin man waiting near the main door, looking annoyed. He looked even more annoyed as Hilda got out of the first van and they opened the back to disclose the simple pine coffin.

He moved forward to join Hilda and Tam moved closer to eavesdrop.

'Is this the best you could manage for a coffin, Hilda?'

She drew herself up. 'This one is thanks to Peter's cousin because *I* haven't got one penny left in the world, James, not a single penny.'

'Typical! Your husband always was a poor provider. Who's taking the service?'

She glanced inside the church. 'The curate.'

'I might have known it. All done on the cheap. What are people going to say?'

She ignored that remark. 'Peter's cousin Tam has spent up on the undertaker. You'll have to pay the curate a guinea or it'll look even worse and people will say *you* can't afford it. They already know Tam's paid for the funeral.'

He glared at her, then said sharply, 'Well, I'll have to be repaid from the sale of the farm. It's not *my* responsibility to pay for *your* husband's funeral.'

Disgusted, Tam moved forward to join them. 'Are you all right, Hilda love?'

'I'm managing, thank you. Um, James, this is Peter's cousin Tam. Tam Crawford, this is my brother James Boales.'

James gave him a nod and a sour look.

Some spirit of devilment made Tam say, 'You'll need to help us with the coffin, James, or you'll have to hire another man to do it. There are only three of us.'

'Me carry a coffin?'

'Who else? You're family, aren't you?'

'That wood had better not have splinters. I don't want threads from my best suit catching on it.'

Boales had to be the rudest, most inconsiderate man Tam had ever met. If Hilda went to live with him, her life and Frankie's would be an utter misery. But she seemed resigned to that. Why was she so certain it'd be best for Frankie?

The four men managed the coffin with surprising ease. Peter must have lost a lot of weight because he used to be a big man, Tam thought. Life could treat you so cruelly at the end. He concentrated on keeping his corner of the box steady until they could set it down on the bier.

The curate was standing near the altar waiting for them. He was a stranger but greeted Hilda more kindly than her brother had. He indicated that she and her son should sit in the front row.

James joined them there, so Tam went to the other side of the aisle, also at the front.

The curate came across to whisper to him, 'Are you family?'

'Yes. I'm the dead man's cousin.'

'Oh, right. Only the vicar does like us to follow the usual customs, even at these small funerals. Um, are any other guests expected?'

'I doubt it.'

But to his surprise, Leah and Todd walked in a moment later and sat in the second row behind him, accompanied by Harry Makepeace, the man who lived in the converted train carriage. What a nice gesture to come today! It would mean a lot to Hilda.

After the short service they all drove to the cemetery on the outskirts of Rivenshaw and the men carried the coffin to an area at the rear. Here there were some very small burial plots, one of which had a hole dug in it. This must be thanks to Dr Fiske and his friends.

Of course James Boales turned up his nose at this part of the cemetery, which had no fancy graves and few head-stones, only a few simple wooden markers. Eh, Hilda's brother was one of the sourest people Tam had ever met. The more he watched the man, the more he hated to think of that poor lad living with him. Only there was nothing he could do about it because Frankie's mother had the final say in that.

Tam was glad when the curate didn't waste time and gabbled quickly through a brief version of the interment service. He then led the group in throwing handfuls of earth into the grave, after which he turned to stare expectantly at Boales.

Looking resentful, Hilda's brother fiddled in his pocket and produced some coins, handing them over to the curate one by one, as if it hurt to part with them.

When the curate had gone, everyone else took their leave of Hilda except for Tam, who was expecting to drive Frankie and Hilda home.

However, James beckoned to the lad with one bony finger and said, 'I'll drive you and your mother home. I need to check things at the farm.'

Tam had followed him across and now asked, 'Is there anything I can do to help you, Hilda?'

She was chalk white and swaying as if about to faint. 'I'm sorry. I feel so dizzy I can't think straight.'

'You don't need to think. I'll tell you what to do. Just get into the car. I'm in a hurry,' was all her brother said.

'You've only to send Frankie up to the hostel if you need my help, Hilda,' Tam said.

Boales glared at him. 'They will be coming straight back to Oldham with me.'

'Oh? What are you going to do about the stock?' Tam asked, so that poor Frankie wouldn't have to raise the matter.

'I beg your pardon?'

'The animals will need feeding. They're worth something alive, but they'll be worth nothing dead.'

'Then *there* is something you can deal with for your cousin's wife, Crawford. Feed the stock.'

'I would if I knew anything about animals, but I don't.'

'I could stay and look after them,' Frankie said.

'You're not staying there on your own,' Hilda snapped.

Boales stood for a minute scowling, then said, 'You'd both better stay for a day or two longer while I make the necessary arrangements. I have someone who's going to help me work out how best to dispose of your other possessions, so we can deal with the animals at the same time.'

Tam saw Frankie try to hide a look of relief.

'I'll drive you home now, Hilda, and take a quick look round the house. I'll come back for you in two days. I have a Chamber of Commerce meeting tomorrow that I don't want to miss. Make sure you're packed and ready by ten o'clock the following morning. I don't want to take any more time from my business than I have to.'

Without a word of farewell to Tam, he got into the car, not even opening the door for his sister to join him.

Tam did that while Frankie got into the back.

He watched them go, shaking his head. Those two were headed for an unhappy life, there was no doubt about that.

Back at Skeggs Hill Farm, Frankie watched resentfully as his uncle walked round the house, sneering at their possessions.

When he'd finished his tour, Boales said curtly, 'Pack your clothes and the boy's, Hilda, but nothing else. I've already got someone wanting to buy the rest of your stuff. I'll come back and meet him here for that, so that I can push the prices up. I'll sell the farm for you and use the money it brings towards your keep. I didn't get where I am by letting people take advantage of me.'

Frankie's mother said nothing and had warned her son to keep quiet, but he couldn't help feeling upset and it must have showed because as his uncle passed him, he clouted him across the side of the head, sending him staggering sideways. 'Don't look at me like that, you insolent pup! I'll teach you to behave properly once you get to my house, I promise you.'

After one gasp of shock, his mother shook her head at him, so the boy didn't protest against this injustice, and to his relief, his uncle left soon afterwards.

Frankie confronted his mother then. 'I'm not going to live with him.'

'We have no choice.'

'People go on the tramp all the time. I have the *choice* of doing that.'

'If you run away, I'm the one who'll suffer, the one James will take it out on. He's probably working out how he can use you in his shop, and that'll keep him from being too cruel to you.'

Frankie stared at her and to his dismay, he saw tears running down her cheeks. 'But Mam, he's a *horrible* man.'

'He's a good provider, though. I know it'll be hard but he'll find you a job once you leave school, and there's no other way you can be sure of getting one.' She pulled him to her and hugged him for a moment, a rare thing for her. 'You've seen men who're out of work for years, Frankie. Do you want to spend your life like them?'

When he didn't immediately answer, she shook his shoulder and repeated, 'Do you?'

'No.'

'Then do as I tell you. Put up with James for a year or two. Get a job, learn some skills, as many as you can, and one day you can move away from him. Your whole future depends on it. This is the only chance I can give you, son. It'll be just as bad for me to live with him, you know.'

But Frankie wasn't convinced this was the only way to find

a future for himself. He was good at school work, ought to have gone to the grammar school, because he'd passed the exam. Only, like many others, his parents hadn't been able to afford to pay for his uniform and books, even though his school fees would have been paid by the town council, something it did for a few outstanding pupils each year.

He'd have a talk to his cousin Tam, who was the only person he knew whose advice he trusted. He admired Tam and could ask him about going on the tramp.

Surely there had to be some alternative to living with his Uncle James?

It was all so *hard*.

When Tam got home, Cara came out to greet him and find out how the funeral had gone.

He told her what had happened. 'I'm so worried about that poor lad. He's not only lost his father, he's about to lose his home. And you can bet his uncle will work him like a slave. He's that sort of fellow.'

'There's nothing you can do, love,' Cara said. 'You can't save everyone in the world.'

He gave her a sheepish smile. 'I only want to save everyone in Ellindale.'

She hooked her arm in his. 'No one can do that either, not even Mr Carlisle. Come in and have a nice cup of tea.'

'First tell me truthfully how the children have been. Did they behave themselves?'

'Jinna always behaves herself. When she's worried or puzzled she seems to freeze.'

'And to rub her arm.'

'You've noticed that too.'

'Anyway, they were good as gold today. Jinna got out her pad and drew a picture. It's amazing. It's got all the little creatures we saw on the moors in it.'

'I can't wait to see it.'

'She also asked if she could look at the book we read to them. She treated it very carefully. Ned went to sit with her and stare at it. Tam, she seemed to be reading the words to him, but she must have memorised them. She definitely can't read because I tried her on another book.'

'Like she memorises things she sees. We have to teach her to read. Who knows what she'll do then?'

'I worry that we're pushing her.'

'Doesn't sound like it to me. You didn't ask her to read the book; she did it of her own accord in her own way. I think she'll learn to read and write quickly with her memory.'

When they went inside Ned came running to throw himself at Tam, who picked him up and swung him round and round.

Jinna stood watching them, looking at the way Ned was holding on to Tam's jacket.

It was Cara who came across to them and said, 'Can I cuddle you, Jinna?'

Another long stare followed by a nod.

Cara gave her a long hug, then said, 'You should cuddle me back, Jinna. That's what families do. Everyone cuddles each other.'

'My mother didn't do it.'

'Some people don't. But me and Tam do, and Ned will have a cuddle any time.'

As if on cue the little boy let go of Tam's jacket and flung his arms round his grandma.

Cara set him gently aside and held her arms out to Jinna. 'Let's try it again.'

The girl stepped forward again and imitated the little boy.

'That was nice,' Cara said. 'Now cuddle Tam properly.'

She stared at him and before she could move, Ned chuckled and flung his arms round Tam's waist.

'Good lad,' Tam said and looked at Jinna.

She moved forward and put her arms round him briefly, then stepped back.

'That was nice,' Tam said. 'Good girl.'

When the children went back to their book, Tam cocked one eye at Cara. 'Well done. What about me? Don't I get some cuddling too?' He didn't wait for an answer, but pulled her into his arms.

'I can't wait to get married and find a proper place to live,' he whispered in her ear.

She blushed and smiled at him.

The lovely way his new family had behaved took his mind off his worries about Frankie for a while. But the worries came back when he went to bed.

That poor lad! Tam kept thinking. Eh, life could be cruel.

22

On the Wednesday of that week, two men from the council turned up at Hillam House in the late morning.

'We're here to check this building. There has been a complaint lodged about its dilapidated state by someone worried about the safety of the people using it.'

'I'll fetch Mr Carlisle.' The man who'd opened the door tried to close it.

The council officer put his hand out to stop him. 'We have the right of entry. Let us past at once.'

Other men, who had been listening to the conversation, had moved forward from round the kitchen table to stand solidly behind their companion. There was no way the council officers could push their way through the whole group.

'Let us through!'

Instead, one of the club members put his fingers in his mouth and whistled shrilly. He did this three times. And still, none of the men blocking the entrance made any attempt to move out of the way.

In the attic, Wilf heard the whistles and stood up suddenly. 'There's trouble downstairs, Mr Carlisle.'

'What?'

'Three whistles. We use it in the village when we need help urgently. We've only got one another to rely on most of the time, you see.' He called the last remark over his shoulder because he'd set off down the stairs without waiting for an answer.

Finn followed him, having learned not to be surprised by the way these men looked after one another whenever they could.

In the kitchen the job club members were clustered round the doorway and he could see two men in dark suits standing outside. One of them was brandishing a piece of paper and trying to make himself heard above the noise.

A man at the back of the group realised Finn had arrived and shouted, 'Mr Carlisle is here.' He had to shout it a couple more times before everyone fell silent and then they moved to either side, leaving a way through the group for their leader. The two at the door were still barring the outsiders from entering, however.

There had to be a good reason for this, Finn was sure, because these men in the job club weren't the sort to cause trouble for no reason. He walked to the doorway and as the last two men stood aside to let him through, he stayed on the doorstep, aware of the men moving to stand closely behind him, so that the way in was still blocked. 'Did you want to see me?'

By now the two men working on the garden had joined them and were standing to one side of the council officers, while two women had walked round from the far side of the house to stand at their other side. They'd been whitewashing the laundry and their forearms and ragged pinafores were spattered with white.

None of those outside had spoken but that didn't make them any less threatening. Every line of their bodies radiated anger.

The taller of the officers repeated what he'd already said, for Finn's benefit, saying it word for word as if he'd learned it by heart. 'We're here to check this building. There has been a complaint lodged about its dilapidated state by someone worried about the safety of the people using it.' This time he added, 'Until it's been shown to be safe, it's forbidden for anyone to use the building, so we'll need your keys to secure the doors.'

This caused a deep-throated roar of anger from every person in the group.

'Let me see the letter.' Finn held out his hand and after a moment's hesitation the man gave it to him.

Finn studied it and the signature at the bottom. 'Anyone know this Brian Gratton?'

'He's one of Rixom's cronies,' a voice called from the back of the group.

'I shan't do anything about this until I've consulted my lawyer,' Finn told the visitors. 'And I'm certainly not letting you in or giving you keys. I'll tell your boss what my lawyer says and then we'll all decide what to do, so you might as well go back to your other work.'

The man ran one finger inside his collar as if it felt too tight. 'Begging your pardon, Mr Carlisle, and no offence meant, but you have to do as this letter says from now on.'

Finn read it again, then folded it and put it in his pocket, shaking his head. 'It says this is based on an ordinance from 1875. I don't think one that old can apply to today's buildings, but of course, if my lawyer says it does, I'll obey it. Until then, I'm afraid I must deny you entrance.'

After a brief pause, he added, 'Apart from anything else, I made certain the house was safe before I started using it and I'm quite sure people will come to no harm here.'

'Mr Gratton says if you won't let us in and try to keep council officials out, we're to call in the police to evict you.' He shuffled his feet and didn't meet anyone's eyes as more rumbles of anger ran round the group.

Finn studied him. The poor fellow looked unhappy about having to do this and it wasn't his fault. 'How about I go and phone my lawyer straight away? You two can wait here.'

The second council officer spoke. 'We have to come straight in, Mr Rixom said. He told us we can't allow council rules to be flouted by anyone, let alone having people put in danger.'

Wilf moved forward to join Finn at the door. 'Mr Carlisle is telling the truth. The house is as sound as any other in the village, sounder than some. I'm sure of that because I checked the whole place with him before we started the club.'

'It's the law. You have to do what it says, like everyone else.'

There were more angry and unflattering comments from the men, and one of the two council officers moved a step closer to his companion, looking nervous.

It wasn't till Finn held up one hand and said, 'Shhh!' that the club members quietened. He turned to Wilf and said in a loud voice, 'Can you and the other men keep these chaps outside until I get back from phoning my lawyer?'

Wilf nodded and there were murmurs of assent from those nearby.

'Good thing my home isn't far away. I can phone from there.' He turned to Wilf. 'Make sure there's no violence while I'm gone. I'll be as quick as I can.'

'You go ahead, Mr Carlisle,' one of the women called. 'We're all on your side.'

She edged closer to the second council officer. 'And as for you, Bradley Cooper, you should be ashamed of yourself, coming up here and doing Rixom's bidding. He's not even employed at the council.'

'I've got no choice, Kezzy. Mr Gratton was with him and *he* gave us our orders. If I don't obey them, I'll lose my job.'

'You wait till I tell my Auntie Meg about this. You just see what your mother says!'

'Aw, don't do that, girl. I've no choice, I tell you.'

'You can choose to go back and say Mr Carlisle refused to let you in. You don't need to call in the police.' She glared at her cousin. 'What's more—'

Finn left them arguing and couldn't help smiling when childhood wrongs were quickly brought into play by the two cousins as proof that the other was not to be trusted. Their voices grew louder and shriller and followed him for a while as he strode off up the hill to Heythorpe House.

They were a grand bunch of people up here in Ellindale and he wasn't going to let Rixom spoil the job club for them. The man was only out to make money from this and cheat him out of the ownership of the house, and he didn't care how much distress he caused to people doing it.

Once the minor quarrel between the cousins had ended, the other officer looked pleadingly at Wilf. 'You'd be best to let us in. Even Mr Carlisle has to obey the law.'

'He's my employer so *I* have to do what *he* says. He won't be long. We'll see what his lawyer tells him to do.' After that, he simply folded his arms and waited to see if the officers would try to push their way in.

They didn't, because they were greatly outnumbered by angry people, but they made no attempt to move away from the door, either. As they stood there, the spokesman looked over his shoulder occasionally to see whether Mr Carlisle was coming back.

And all that time anger seemed to hum in the air around them. It might be invisible but it felt tangible. Wilf wouldn't have gone against a group of his neighbours in this mood. It took a lot to rouse these hill folk but they wouldn't back down from a quarrel if they felt to be in the right.

After a while, one of the council officers pulled out his watch, opened the lid and studied it, then showed it to his friend, who spread out his hands in a helpless gesture.

The men in the group stayed where they were, but the two women said they might as well go back to their painting.

The woman who'd been arguing poked her cousin in the arm before she left. 'I'll soon know if them walls were unsafe, our Bradley. Me an' Mary are painting every inch of them an' they built strongly in the old days. Them walls are more solid than those in *your* house, that's for sure! We'll keep our eyes open as we go. *We* won't be taken in by someone at the council telling lies.'

The other woman looked at both the officers. 'As for that Mr Rixom, if *I* had a vote in the council elections, I'd vote for him to be kicked out of the valley. He's never helped anyone up here in Ellindale that I heard tell, for all he's supposed to be our representative on the council.'

Her companion nodded. 'He'll get his comeuppance one day if there's any justice in the world, an' I hope I'm there to see it.'

Finn didn't speed up till he was out of sight of the two men, because that might have given them the impression that he was afraid of the council edict. He strode along quickly, not even noticing two women until he was past them, when he suddenly realised he'd ignored them. He didn't look back. This job club problem was too important.

He burst into the kitchen, calling, 'We've got trouble from the council, damn them!' as he ran straight through it towards the phone.

Beth, who'd been chatting to their cook, followed him but apart from blowing a kiss in her direction, his attention was all on the phone call.

He waited impatiently as the operator put him through to the lawyer in Rivenshaw. He explained the situation rapidly, which told Beth what the crisis was about and made her look at him in shock.

There was silence at the other end, then the lawyer said, 'That's very strange, Mr Carlisle. I'm not even aware of such an ordinance, and I've lived and worked in Rivenshaw for most of my life. I've tried to persuade the council to review and delete various ancient by-laws but failed because they didn't think they mattered since people ignored them. Someone has obviously used one of them to get at you.'

'It must be Rixom, since one of the officers mentioned that he was present when they were given their instructions.'

'That doesn't surprise me. I've had one or two run-ins with the fellow myself. You were right to call me. Will you authorise me to visit the town hall and ask questions on your behalf?'

'Definitely. And could you please do it as quickly as possible, if you don't mind, Mr Lloyd?'

'I shall go there immediately because as we've discussed before, I have my own reservations about some of the things that seem to be going on at the town hall. Shall I phone you at home once I've found out what it's all about?'

Finn hesitated, then shook his head, realised the other man couldn't see that and said, 'Yes, phone here. I have to go back to Hillam House to keep the men out of trouble but my wife will be here to take your message and she's a very capable woman. I trust her judgement absolutely and am happy for her to authorise you to do anything else that's necessary. You can be sure she'll get word to me immediately about whatever you find out.'

'Very well. It may be that I have to come up to see this house for myself, though I'd find it inconvenient to come today because I have a rather important appointment later this afternoon.'

'*You* would be welcome to look through the place at any time. I shall go back there now and stay all day. I'll also post a watch on it overnight as well, just in case.'

'I think that would be wise, given who we're dealing with.'

Finn put the telephone down and looked at Beth. 'Rixom's behind this, of course, but why? Surely his business interests are situated lower down the valley?'

'He probably wants to get his hands on the house for future use, build up stock while things are cheap. It has a bit of land with it, remember, and we've both heard rumours about his ambitions, haven't we? He's a small-scale builder now, but he started out as a bricklayer.'

'Is there anything local people don't know about the village?'

'Not much. They care about their village and the rest of the valley, too. People like Rixom forget that men who're out of work walk around and see many things those at work miss. I've lived round here a lot longer than you have and I've seen what's going on, too, because nobody pays attention to a young woman with children.'

She kissed his cheek. 'Thank you for having confidence in me.'

'You're a very intelligent woman and I trust your judgement absolutely. It's one of the many things I love about you. Oh, look at the time! I've got to go.'

He saw tears of happiness well in her eyes at this compliment and planted a quick kiss on her cheek. Her first husband had been unkind to her and the children. What a way to treat your family!

Finn set off again, his mind now focused on the situation at Hillam House. He was worried that the members of the job club might get into trouble if the council officers made another attempt to get in and they resisted. He didn't want the local folk to lose their refuge.

Henry Lloyd put the phone down and frowned as he considered the situation. He attended the public council meetings occasionally and now he came to think of it, various small changes had been made to regulations and by-laws lately. He hadn't bothered to look into the full implications of some of these, because he was a busy man and had other worries closer to home. But this action had brought his full attention to the situation. He ran through it in his mind and cursed under his breath. It was only too obvious who benefited each time and it wasn't the ratepayers.

These people had made the changes very gradually. Clever, that. Did they think they would get away with placing their own needs and greed above natural justice for all for ever? Or that no one would dare challenge them when people eventually realised what they'd been doing and where it was leading?

Well, if he had any say in it, something would be said and done straight away. This was his town and he knew other people who cared about it being run fairly. It was time to get in touch with them and challenge the corruption that had crept in.

He knew exactly whom he could rely on for support but he would have to tread carefully until he and his friends were ready to strike.

Did he want to get involved?

No, but he couldn't avoid it. He wasn't too old yet to fight dragons once they'd reared their ugly heads. He'd gone into law in the first place because he believed in justice and truth for all.

He summoned his chauffeur, but on the way to the town

hall, he had a sudden thought and asked the man to stop at the police station first. Sergeant Deemer was also very much on the side of law and order, and was not easily fooled. No one would be able to corrupt such an honest servant of the law.

It wouldn't hurt to make Deemer aware of the situation – if he didn't already suspect it.

Henry smiled grimly as he got out of the car and told his driver to wait for him.

Gilbert Deemer looked up as the doorbell sounded, pleased to see Mr Lloyd, who was a very sound gentleman.

'Good afternoon, sir. How may I help you?'

'I think we may be able to help one another – and Mr Carlisle.'

'A very pleasant gentleman, Mr Carlisle. I'm always happy to do him a service.'

Henry explained what he thought was going on and what had happened today.

'If a lawyer like you is worried about the overall situation,' Gilbert said at once, 'it may be useful to put out a few feelers. I know people who would be glad to earn a few pence in return for supplying me with information.'

Henry reached into his pocket. 'Allow me to set up a small fund for this purpose.'

'Thank you, sir. Just a moment.' Deemer went into the back room and came back with an empty jam jar, holding it out for the money.

He would pay whatever was necessary for information, Henry thought as he walked out. This was his town, his valley too, and he cared about how things were done. Depression or no Depression, justice ought still to prevail.

There was no excuse – no excuse at all – for villainy.

It had been a useful discussion, he felt. He had left Deemer sitting at his desk, tapping his pencil in the way he had when thinking deeply.

Getting back into his car, Henry told the chauffeur to drive him straight to the town hall.

First dragon about to be confronted. No, not dragon – weasel.

23

The first person Henry saw at the town hall was that Rixom chap standing in the doorway of the office at the far end of a corridor to the left. He looked as if he was leaving. That was Brian Gratton's office and the two men were laughing about something, seeming to be on extremely good terms.

He went to the front counter and rang the bell for attention, still keeping an eye on the corridor. He noted that Gratton had stopped talking to peer down towards the main entrance and check who had just arrived.

When he saw Henry, Gratton tugged Rixom back inside the office and quickly shut the door. You didn't grab someone like that unless you knew him well. You didn't shut the door so rapidly unless you had something to hide.

The office boy came out to the counter, saw who it was and stopped slouching to gabble off the greeting they'd all been taught to use. 'Good morning, Mr Lloyd. How may I help you?'

'I'd like to see Mr Gratton, please.'

The lad glanced down the corridor. 'His door's closed so he must be busy at the moment, sir. He had a visitor and I haven't seen Mr Rixom leave yet.'

'I saw them both before they closed the door. I want to see Mr Rixom as well, so it's lucky I can catch them at the same time.'

The lad frowned. 'I've been told not to disturb Mr Gratton

when his door's closed, sir. I daren't interrupt, I'm ever so
sorry.'

Just then the mayor came out into the reception area, saying
goodbye to a local shopkeeper. Aha! Fate was smiling on him.
This could give him a much more useful opportunity. Henry
stepped forward. 'Reginald! Just the chap I want to see. Do
you have a moment?'

'For you, always. Come into my office. How about a cup
of tea?'

'Kind offer but another time. I'm in rather a hurry today.'

When they were seated, he told Reginald Kirby about the
attempt to close down the job club, which had the mayor
frowning.

'We haven't begun any slum clearance up in Ellindale. I'd
know if we had. Backshaw Moss is the area that we need to
tackle first. It's an appalling place. What's Gratton thinking
of to upset Carlisle anyway? That job club of his is a damned
good idea.'

Henry didn't allow himself to smile. Anything that pleased
the constituents was a 'damned good idea' in Kirby's opinion.
Especially if it didn't cost the town's ratepayers anything. 'I
was going to ask Gratton about that, but he's closeted with
Rixom and they closed the door the minute they saw me at
the reception desk.' He cocked his head and waited for
Reginald to take this in.

The mayor closed his eyes for a moment or two, then
looked at Henry. 'I'll deny saying this, but I am all too aware
that there are some dodgy things being done around here by
certain people. I've stopped one or two of their fiddles, but
I don't currently have enough support to do much more until
after the coming elections for half our councillors. And sadly,
if more friends of you-know-who get in, I won't be able to
do anything much afterwards, either, because they'll still
control the majority of votes.'

'That bad, is it?'

'Yes. I've seen who's applied to stand for election and the hard times seem to have brought the blood-sucking slugs out from their hidey-holes, ready to take advantage of their fellow men.' He drummed his fingers on his desk, staring into the distance, then looked at Henry. 'I've mentioned it before and you said you weren't interested but I'm saying it again now: I think you should stand for the council in the Rivenshaw East ward. You're well liked, thanks to the way you've helped people pro bono over the years. You'd get elected for sure.'

'That would only bring you one extra vote.'

'I have some other people in mind, including your Mr Carlisle, and I shall be pushing them hard to stand for council.'

Henry sighed. 'I see. I must admit that I don't have any civic ambitions, but since those men need to be stopped, maybe I'll think about getting involved.'

'Do more than think about it: start making plans.' He opened a drawer and pulled out a form. 'Here you are. Fill this in. I really need your help, old boy, or things will go from bad to worse. Some people only stand for council to help make money for themselves. They don't respect the needs of our town or of the poorer people who live here.'

'Oh, very well. You can count on me to seek election, but I'd value your guidance on how best to set about it.' Henry took the piece of paper with a sigh and stared down at it for a few seconds before putting it in his briefcase.

'We'll get together: you, me and a few others I'm going to nudge. What do you think of asking Charlie Willcox to stand for the Birch End ward? He lives there, which is always helpful.'

'He's well liked, but would he want to do it?'

'He won't get much choice when he finds out what's going on: he'll have to stand to make sure his businesses aren't disadvantaged. He's an honest chappie, if a bit pushy, and even though I'm not usually in favour of pawnshops, I'll admit he runs his honestly. And my wife is very pleased with the new electric kettle she bought from him. She's after a refrigerator now. What next? But that's beside the point. What do you think of him as a councillor?'

'Charlie would certainly stir things up. He doesn't mince words when his temper is roused.'

They both chuckled at that thought.

'Now, about this by-law they seem to have dragged out from the dusty depths, I think we need to do something about that straight away. We don't want that job club to be closed down, do we? The voters would go mad about that.'

He hid a smile as Reginald shuddered visibly. 'Can you do anything about it?'

The mayor closed his eyes for a moment, head on one side, then nodded. 'I think so. I'll need you to go up the valley tomorrow and take Deemer with you. Examine the house with him, and I suppose you'd better take those two council officers inside with you as well. Then report directly back to me. But keep those chaps by your side at all times so that they can't claim to have seen something you've missed. Deemer's presence will guarantee that they report back *honestly*.'

'Unfortunately, I can't go tomorrow. I have to be in court and the case may last all week. Monday's the first day I shall definitely be free.'

'Hmm. Pity. I'll have to warn Gratton to do nothing till after Monday, then.'

'You think our going to check the house and report honestly will stop this blatant attempt to take over the whole house and its land?'

'Oh yes. And if *you* have a quiet word with Carlisle first, he'll not make a fuss about letting you in. Do the inspection on Monday, then. That's probably not a bad thing. It'll give me time to authorise everything here at the town hall.'

'What about Gratton and Rixom? Will they stay away from it till then, do you think?'

'They'd better. I'll warn them very strongly to leave this to me from now on. By the end of Monday it'll all be settled, bar a little paperwork, and the job club can continue in the meantime.'

He paused, then added with a wry smile, 'Unless you do find major problems with the building, of course. I could do nothing to help you then.'

'I'm certain we won't because Carlisle has already checked it, and he's nobody's fool.'

'Then we're all set.'

'Are you quite sure you have the power to stop Gratton continuing, Reginald?'

'I don't know whether I am *legally* entitled to do that, but those two rogues won't dare challenge me when I insist on having it done my way. If I tell them the house is in a sound condition and we have your sworn statement about that, together with Deemer's signature on it, plus a report from the council's own officers, that should put a complete stop to their nonsense.'

The mayor shook his head. 'Closing down a job club would be bad enough, but to do it just before an election is foolish in the extreme. I had thought better of Gratton's intelligence.'

'He's under the influence of Rixom.'

'Hmm. And their wives are thick as thieves, always taking tea with one another.'

As Henry turned to leave, the mayor said, 'Would you

mind passing on a message from me to Carlisle? Ask him to tell those two men who've been sent up there that the mayor has sent word that he wishes them to return to Rivenshaw immediately.'

Henry smiled as he walked back to his rooms. The mayor wasn't a close friend of his, but Reginald had reacted exactly as he'd expected to the idea of losing votes through such an unpopular action.

Pity Henry had had to agree to stand for the council to get his support, but there was no getting out of it now. Still, if Charlie Willcox and Finn Carlisle were also elected, he'd have people he trusted on the council with him, so maybe it wouldn't be too bad. Maybe for once, they really could do some good and make progress on that slum clearance.

Reginald Kirby waited until the lawyer had left, watching through his office window until the car had driven away, then sauntered along the corridor to Gratton's office. He didn't bother to knock and the two men inside it jumped in shock at the sight of him.

He forced himself to smile at them as he closed the door, though he would much rather have kicked them out of the building for ever. 'Good morning, gentlemen.' Then he pulled out his watch and pretended to consult it. 'Sorry, it's afternoon now, isn't it?'

They returned his greeting and waited warily.

He let them wait and worry for a minute or two, always a useful tactic, then said slowly, with several long pauses to increase the tension, 'I wanted to let you know – both of you – how glad I am that you're keeping a really close eye on things in Ellindale.'

'Er – which things would you be referring to, Mayor?' Gratton asked.

'Safety of buildings, such as that old house in the village.'

He watched them relax a little, then tugged them to wariness again by adding, 'But sending two minor council employees out is a waste of their time and therefore of our town's resources. So I've stepped in.' Another pause that had Rixom leaning forward as if to listen more carefully. 'I've therefore used my mayoral authority to deal with it more rapidly.'

He watched them exchange worried glances. He didn't say anything further till Rixom asked what he meant.

'I've authorised Henry Lloyd and Sergeant Deemer to supervise a preliminary survey of the old house on Monday. They'll take your two officers with them and will make sure they get them into the house.'

The two men brightened.

'The good sergeant will go round with them and guarantee that it's all done honestly.'

Their smiles faded instantly.

'They'll report back on the state of Hillam House and no one will doubt *their* word. Or their honesty. End of matter.'

He paused and looked from one to the other. 'So unless the house really is in a bad state, we won't need to waste any more of your valuable time, will we, Rixom? I'm sure you have a living to earn as well as your civic duties to perform.'

'Yes, of course.'

With a nod, Reginald left the office. He'd enjoyed doing that.

Gratton nipped out from behind his desk to close the door again, leaning against it as if exhausted.

'What's he up to?' Rixom asked.

'Don't ask me. I never know how to take him. He's very

popular in the valley, bound to get elected again. Um – is that house really in bad condition?'

Rixom shrugged. 'Who knows? I haven't been able to get inside it. And if the two officers are working under Deemer and Lloyd, they won't dare do anything but give us an honest report.'

'Well, at least we'll know . . . for future reference.'

'I would have preferred for us to act now, while prices are at rock bottom.'

'I can't go against the mayor,' Gratton protested. 'It's as much as my job here is worth. We'll have to let that one go.'

'It'll cost us a lot more to buy it in future, once times improve.'

'Well, Carlisle might not be willing to sell.'

Rixom thumped one hand down on the desk. 'I'll find a way to force him. You just see if I don't. *Damn* the fellow!'

'I think the mayor is more concerned about Backshaw Moss at this stage. It's an eyesore and a public health menace. People are complaining about it regularly. I've seen some of the letters myself. He doesn't like complaints.'

'And clearing it up will win him a lot of support in future from those qualified to vote, whereas closing down the job club, unless there's a very good reason, will be extremely unpopular. Damn the fellow.' Then Rixom suddenly snapped his fingers. 'They're not going to inspect it till Monday and—' He paused, nodding slowly.

'And?'

'And the job club won't be open at the weekend. Sunday observance and all that. I wonder if we should . . . No, too risky.'

'Surely you're not thinking of—'

'Shh. Not another word.' He glanced at the wall clock. 'If I stay any longer it'll look as though we're plotting something.

You'd better pop round to my place tonight after dark and we'll see what we can come up with. Use the back entrance. I'll give the maid the evening off, send her to the cinema. Make certain no one sees you.'

Gratton shook his head. 'I really don't think we'd better risk—'

'Leave the thinking to me. You'll not regret it financially. You haven't before.'

When she saw the mayor go into Gratton's office, Helen slipped out of the building and round to the rear. Hidden behind the bushes, she listened to the conversation between the three men.

After the mayor left she was about to leave when she heard the other two making plans.

She didn't have any power to stop what they were doing, not officially, but she'd written anonymous letters before.

Would Mr Carlisle take heed of a warning from 'a well wisher'?

She could only try.

Her office seemed to grow smaller every day.

She pulled a piece of headed notepaper towards her, transferred her pen to her left hand and began to write.

She posted the letter on the way home, giving it a quick kiss for luck before she put it into the slot in the post office wall.

As Finn strode from his gardens into the road, he met Leah Willcox strolling down the hill with a basket on her arm. However much of a hurry he was in, it would be rude not to stop and say hello. He'd normally have enjoyed a chat, because he liked his neighbour, but at the moment he was too worried about the council's actions to enjoy anything.

After only a couple of remarks, however, she said abruptly,

'I think something's wrong, Finn. Is it the job club? Is there anything I can do to help?'

'There is something wrong, but I'm afraid there's nothing you can do at the moment. I'll walk with you into the village and tell you what's going on.'

They stood outside the shop while he finished his tale.

By now she was looking angry. 'Why do people do things like this?'

'Greed. Lack of morals. Who knows? Doesn't matter where you are, what you're doing, there always seem to be a few villains popping up to try to dip their fingers in your pockets. They can't get away with as much in small villages like Ellindale, but the bigger the town, the more invisible they feel and the worse their behaviour. Well, that's what it seems like to me.'

'I agree. I hope you know that Todd and I will be happy to help if we can do anything. Never hesitate to ask.'

'Thank you.'

He started to tip his hat to her, then remembered he wasn't wearing one. Nor was she. They'd both have felt the need to wear them in Rivenshaw. The unwritten rules of respectable society amused him at times, irritated him at others. His mother wouldn't even have nipped across the street to the corner shop without putting on a hat or headscarf.

And what was he doing thinking of manners and customs when he had men waiting to hear from him? Not that he had any news for them yet.

The only thing he was sure of at the moment was that he wasn't letting those two men from the council into the old house unless his lawyer said there was no getting out of it.

The people Finn had left at Hillam House were still hanging around near the rear door, keeping the council officials out.

Had they moved at all while he was away? He ran his eyes over the group. The women had left, probably gone back to their painting of walls, and there seemed to be fewer men protecting the doorway.

He stopped just short of the two officials. 'My lawyer is going to the town hall straight away to find out what's caused all this and where we stand legally.'

They looked tired and worried, and it was out before he could think. 'Would you like a cup of tea while we wait? We're just about to make one.'

The leader gaped at him for a moment, then said, 'We'd love one, sir. If it's not putting you to too much trouble. It won't make any difference to what we have to do, though. It's our jobs, you see, Mr Carlisle. We don't want to lose them.'

'Who would in times like these? Someone will bring you out a mug of tea each when it's ready.' He nodded to Wilf to join him, and two other men from the village took over at the door.

As he and Wilf walked inside, Finn murmured, 'We'll have to keep a careful watch on this place from now on.'

Wilf nodded, then, as they stopped near the kitchen table, he said, 'Going a bit soft, aren't you, offering them officials cups of tea?'

'Never hurts to treat people decently. And these are only minor clerks. It's not their choice to come and cause trouble here, is it?'

'I suppose not. I was at school with the elder brother of the younger one. He left the valley for a job in the south but Bradley stayed behind because he had a job with the council.'

'We don't even divide neatly into villains and honest folk, do we, in Ellindale?'

'I suppose not.'

*

It was an hour or so before one of the men who'd gone back to working in the garden called out, 'Your wife is coming down the path, Mr Carlisle.'

Finn went out to meet her.

'Mr Lloyd phoned.' She explained what had been arranged. 'He says the mayor wants us to tell the two officials to go back to the town hall.'

'My pleasure!'

They walked down to the kitchen door and he passed on the message, then waited till the men had left to say to Wilf, 'Do you think the place will be safe tonight?'

'Not a chance of it.'

'What? You're that certain?'

'I am, yes. Gratton isn't to be trusted and as for Rixom, I'd like to push him over the nearest cliff. He's made his money by nasty tricks and hasn't hesitated to use violence. How he got elected to the council, I'll never understand.'

Beth nudged Finn. 'We have to find someone to oppose Rixom as councillor for Ellindale. Who else is there?'

After a moment or two she said thoughtfully, 'Women are allowed to stand, aren't they?'

'Yes, but they don't usually get as many votes.'

'Unless they're very well thought of. How about Leah? She's done a lot of good in the village.'

He smiled. 'Do you think she'd do it?'

'Let me have a word with her.'

'I wonder what Todd will think about the idea. He's very protective of her.'

Beth waved one hand dismissively. 'She's a strong woman. Look at how she runs a business. I envy her that!'

'Let's both ask her,' he said thoughtfully, 'and if she agrees to do it, I'll volunteer to help her campaign. There are some farmers outside the village who will need to be spoken to about voting for a woman. I have no trouble speaking to people casually. It's formal situations that make me freeze up inside.'

'You do that. And there are some women qualified to vote, aren't there? Surely they'll vote for her. I'll find out who they are and see what they think. This is going to be very interesting.'

'You're not to overdo it, Beth.'

She gave him a mock salute and a cheeky grin. 'No, sir.'

The following day a letter arrived on council notepaper. Finn ripped it open, stared at its contents in surprise.

KEEP A WATCH ON HILLAM HOUSE. THEY'RE PLANNING TO DESTROY IT.

A WELL WISHER

He screwed it up and threw it in the wastepaper basket.

A few minutes later he pulled it out again, smoothed it carefully and re-read it, before going to show it to Beth.

'Do you think this is genuine?'

She read it and let out a puff of surprise. 'Might be. Doesn't say who "they" are, does it?'

'No, but I couldn't get it out of my mind after the events of yesterday. I think it is genuine and I'm pretty sure I know who sent it.'

'Why?'

'Because I saw her print the name on a file in capitals and she wrote the E with that little curl to the middle bar.'

'That's rather a long shot.'

'I know. But still, it *might* be genuine and that only adds weight to my feeling that Rixom and Gratton may try to damage Hillam House.'

'Surely not, now that the mayor has intervened.'

'The land could be worth a lot of money when times improve. Builders have to think a long way ahead.'

'What are you going to do?'

'Talk to Wilf and make sure we keep a very careful watch on the house every single hour of the weekend, especially the nights.'

'It never hurts to be careful.'

24

On the morning Boales was due to come and collect his sister and nephew, Tam went down to Skeggs Hill Farm to say his farewells.

Early as it was, he found them ready, with a shabby old trunk and a big bundle wrapped in a sheet standing by the door. He stopped and stared at these. 'Surely that's not all you're taking with you, Hilda?'

'James said just our clothes.'

'Not even a favourite ornament or two?'

She shook her head and said in a voice thickened with tears, 'I shan't mind leaving this place, because I don't like farm life, especially without Peter. But I shall mind losing all my bits and pieces. And my books. James thinks books are a waste of time. He won't have them in the house.'

'That's shameful. What's going to happen to the farm animals?'

'Who knows? James will have worked something out, I suppose. He won't miss a chance to make money.' She frowned. 'He's grown so much worse that I hardly recognise him. He wasn't as bad as this before.'

'You're still letting him sell your house and pocket the money?'

She spread her arms wide in a helpless gesture. 'I don't have much choice. He says he'll give me the ten pounds I'd have got and keep any more if he gets it. The other money will go towards our keep. I am sure he won't let us starve, out of sheer pride.'

'The mean devil!'

Frankie had been standing to one side listening and he joined in the conversation. 'Whatever Mam says, I'm not staying with him if he knocks me around. He hit me after you left us last time.'

'What on earth for?'

'Looking at him cheekily.'

'Hit you for *looking*? But—'

Hilda intervened hastily. 'It was just a quick backhander.'

Tam didn't let himself comment further, but he didn't like bullies who hit children for no reason. 'I can understand you're upset, but you're too young to go on the tramp, Frankie lad. There are dangers on the road you haven't even thought of.'

She nudged her son. 'There! You listen to Cousin Tam. He's been travelling round England for years. He knows what it's like.'

But Frankie only shook his head again, an obstinate expression on his face that reminded Tam of the lad's father. The Kerkhams had always been known in the family for being pig-headed when they decided to do something. Looked like the son was determined about this. The lad had grown up fast as he watched his father sicken and die, and had taken over most of the farm work. He was well on the way to being an adult physically and mentally.

And to hit a grieving lad for nothing, well, it was shameful.

Tam looked at the fire and realised what had been puzzling him. 'You haven't lit the fire. How did you make a cup of tea this morning?'

'We haven't got any wood left and besides, it wouldn't have been worth lighting the fire, because we had no tea leaves, either. We had a drink of water. It's lovely, the water from our spring is. I shall miss that.'

'How about I treat you to a pot of tea at the shop as a

farewell present? They're set up for summer visitors wanting refreshments now, got their wooden tables outside.'

She hesitated, then looked at the clock. 'James won't be here yet. Thank you, Tam. You're very kind.'

They all walked along to the shop and Tam made sure Frankie got a good breakfast inside him while they were at it.

Hilda nibbled at a piece of toast but didn't seem hungry. She was trying to hide how upset she was, Tam could tell. But though she was set on giving Frankie the chance of eating regularly and finding a job, he wasn't so sure that Boales would bother to train the lad in anything worthwhile, nephew or not. He'd probably use him as a general dogsbody and work him half to death on poor rations. Tam had seen other employers take advantage of people like that on his travels.

Eh, he didn't know when he'd taken such a dislike to a fellow!

When Hilda and Frankie went home again, Tam got into conversation with Harry Makepeace from next door to them.

'Any news about what's going to happen to the farm after Hilda leaves?' Harry asked.

'No. I don't really know what's going to happen to her and the lad, either, only that Boales is supposed to be looking after them. I'm that worried about it all.'

Harry looked at him sympathetically.

Tam had a sudden thought. 'I think I'll buy myself another pot of tea from Lily and wait here. I shan't sit outside, because I don't want Boales to see me, but I'll be able to see him arrive and perhaps see what happens from one of the tables inside the shop.'

But an hour passed and nothing happened, so in the end, he went home.

Had Boales changed his mind about looking after his sister?

No. That'd mean changing his mind about making money out of her.

At the youth hostel Cara listened to Tam's worries and agreed that Hilda and her son were heading for an unhappy life. After they'd sat down to an early dinner at midday, she took his hand and patted it. 'Go back and keep an eye on them. You'll just sit and worry if you stay here.'

'Well, it is strange that her brother hasn't arrived yet.'

'Very.'

'He's up to something.'

'Seems like it.'

He picked up her hand. 'You won't mind me leaving you here with the kids?'

She didn't pull away. 'Of course not. It's such a lovely day, I think we'll get a few hikers wanting beds. I shall probably be quite busy. Leah warned me about that when I spoke to her. So I daren't leave.'

'Well, all right. I will go and see how they are. I might even buy them something else to eat if Boales doesn't arrive soon. I wonder what's keeping him?'

When he thought about it, Tam decided not to call on Hilda, just to keep watch from the café again, because Boales would probably object to his presence at the farm and take it out on her.

It was one o'clock before a ramshackle old truck Tam didn't recognise chugged up the hill, followed by Boales' motor car. To his surprise another car followed them and drew up on the main road behind the other two vehicles. He recognised it as Rixom's. What was *he* doing here?

People in the village had come to their doors to stare, not used to seeing three motor vehicles arrive at once and wanting to find out what was happening to the Kerkhams.

Boales got out of the first car and waited for the driver of the second car to emerge.

Rixom looked so smug, Tam groaned aloud. The man was up to something, you could tell from his expression. It didn't bode at all well for Hilda if those two were in cahoots.

They seemed to be on excellent terms. Rixom stopped to speak to the driver of the truck, who had stayed in his vehicle. Boales waited for him and they stopped near the entrance to the narrow track, gesticulating and talking as they looked at the farm.

Tam was surprised that they stood there for several minutes. Why were they studying the place so carefully? What were they pointing out to one another in the field at the back? Something was definitely going on between Boales and Rixom, which said a lot about what sort of fellow Boales was.

Frankie ran into the house and warned his mother that her brother had arrived. 'He's got Mr Rixom with him. And there's a truck stopped out on the road as well.'

'That'll be to take our furniture and things away. He's probably sold them.' She went to the front door to watch her brother but though she was sure he saw her, he made no attempt to wave a greeting as she'd done. That was James for you, concentrating absolutely on what he considered important. But he hadn't been so rude in the past. And why was Rixom there? Her Peter had loathed the man.

Eventually they came along the track on foot, pausing twice on the way to point to something else, still taking no notice of her.

When they got to the house, Rixom nodded to her and James greeted her with, 'Don't stand there all day blocking the doorway, Hilda. Put the kettle on while I show Mr Rixom round the house and outbuildings.'

'I don't have any wood for a fire, or any tea leaves either.'

'I might have known.' He glanced at his companion. 'See how they've been left, absolutely penniless.'

Hilda felt her face heat up and was so embarrassed she didn't know what to say or do.

'We could send for a pot of tea from the shop. They're used to catering for visitors to the village. The lad could go and fetch it,' Rixom said.

'Good idea.' He turned to Frankie. 'Well, what are you waiting for? Go and ask them to send us a big pot of tea for two and some cakes or scones. We'll pay when we leave. And make sure you don't spill anything on the way back.'

'You'll have to give him the money now,' Hilda said. 'Lily doesn't give credit to anyone.'

Scowling, James fumbled in his pocket and slapped a couple of coins down on Frankie's outstretched hand.

'It isn't enough,' the boy said.

'What? How much can two cups of tea cost? You weren't expecting me to buy one for you, surely? *You* won't have missed your midday meal like I have, sorting out this business.' He waved one hand around to indicate the farm.

'It still isn't enough.'

Another coin was slapped into his hand.

'Do as he says, Frankie,' Hilda put in quietly.

When the boy had run off, James turned to his sister. 'Go and feed the chickens or whatever needs doing outside. And check for eggs. Someone's coming to buy those hens later but we might as well take the eggs till then. And don't come back into the house till I tell you. You wouldn't understand what we're talking about and I don't want you interrupting.'

She stood gaping at him for a moment, shocked to the core by the way he was treating her in front of Rixom.

He gave her a shove. 'Go on! Move, woman!'

She told herself to pay no attention to his rudeness as she went outside. She was providing for her son, that was what mattered. But it hurt that her brother was treating her like a slave, a nothing. And unless she'd been very much mistaken, he'd enjoyed upsetting her, showing off his power over her in front of his friend.

She didn't cry. She was beyond tears. But though she went outside, she couldn't move for a while, she felt so upset.

Rixom had smiled and looked at her as if she was a worm. No wonder no one in the village liked him.

Feeling suddenly sick to her soul, she plumped down on the bench near the door, folding her arms across her chest and rocking to and fro. How was she going to bear this sort of behaviour? It was far worse than she'd expected. Not even respect for her grief, let alone him treating her as a close relative.

Had she made a mistake?

Inside the house Rixom looked at Boales. 'You were certainly blunt with your sister.'

'She's only my half-sister, and she's as stupid as they come. But she's strong and a hard worker so she'll earn her keep, and I shan't have to pay her any wages. Never mind her, let's look round the house and see what there is to sell.'

They spent a pleasant half-hour going round and haggling over what Rixom was prepared to pay for various larger items, interrupted only by the return of Frankie carrying a tray with a teapot on it.

'Is there no change?' Boales snapped.

'No.'

'They're cheating you. Go and wait outside with your mother. And you'd better learn to move quickly when I tell you.' He gave the lad a sudden clout round the ear that sent him staggering on his way. He laughed as Frankie bumped into the door frame and let out an involuntary yelp.

He turned back to Rixom.

'Come and have a cup of tea. We need to discuss the price of the farm. Your offer is too low. You're not getting it for nothing. There will be others who want to buy it, if you don't improve what you're prepared to pay.'

Rixom shrugged. 'I'm sure we can come to some arrangement, but I'm not paying you a fortune for it, because it'll be a long time before I get my money back.'

Frankie shut the door, but the catch was faulty and it swung slightly open again. He couldn't be bothered to close it properly and stood for a moment or two listening to the two men arguing about the price of the farm.

Then he looked sideways at his mother. She was looking terrible! Her face was chalk white and she had her arms folded across her chest, as if to protect herself. Worst of all, she was rocking to and fro just like one of the old women in the village did, only *she* had lost her wits while his mother was usually sharp-witted.

In the end he went to stand in front of her and put one hand on her shoulder to stop her rocking. 'Mam? Mam, what's wrong?'

She looked at him, then blinked in surprise and looked at him more carefully. 'What's happened to your cheek?'

'My uncle clouted me again and I crashed into the door frame. And no, I didn't do anything to deserve it. I just took him in the tray of tea from the shop. An' I'd carried it really carefully, hadn't spilt any of it. It wasn't *fair* to hit me.'

'Come and sit down with me a minute, Frankie love.'

He shook his head and picked up his bundle of clothes. 'I'd rather stand so that I can run away if he comes out. That's decided it. I'm not going with him, Mam. You can live with him an' let him hurt you, but I'm *not* putting up with it. That's twice he's hit me before we've even left here. What'll he be like in his own home?' He shook his head again.

'We've nowhere else to go, no way of making a living.'

'Uncle Tam offered to buy the farm an' *he* was going to give you a fair price. That'd give us some money for a new start.'

'And what would happen when the money ran out? You've two years before you can leave school, and when you do, there's hardly any work to be found. Even if *I* find a job, they pay women less than men, so it'd not be enough to manage on. And there are the council rates to pay every year, remember. Besides, I'd already promised to sell the farm to my brother. He said he'd give me ten pounds. I don't go back on my word.'

'Sell it for ten pounds! It's worth more than that, and he knows it. He's cheating you, then selling it to Mr Rixom for a lot more money, so he'll be making a profit straight away.'

She looked at him in puzzlement. 'Why do you say that? I thought Mr Rixom was here to buy the contents of the house for his junk yard and market stall. That's his yard man waiting out by the truck.'

'He's buying the furniture too. They've been looking round the house and they were bickering about prices as I went in. Now they're arguing about the price of the farm.' Frankie hesitated and when she said nothing, he took a step backwards. 'I'm sorry, Mam, but I daren't hang around any longer. I'm *not* going to live with him.' He turned and ran off along the track.

She jerked to her feet, one arm outstretched, then let it drop. She didn't shout after him because she didn't want to attract James's attention.

When Frankie reached the end of the track, he turned up the hill and she sighed in relief. He was going to Cousin Tam's, she'd bet her life on it. They'd have to pick him up before they left. They couldn't impose on her husband's cousin, who had a family of his own to look after.

She wished she hadn't promised James the farm. But it was done now, and at least they'd have a roof over their heads and food in their bellies when they lived with him. Many people didn't even have that.

She had to put up with the unkindness, for the boy's sake. Maybe James would be kinder when he saw how hard she and Frankie both worked. Surely he would?

The voices inside the house grew louder as the two men came downstairs again. She heard them joke about squeezing hard to get another cup each out of the teapot from the village shop. Then they started laughing about how much money James was making from his sister's stupidity.

Hilda moved closer to the door and this time she really listened to what they were saying instead of listening to her own sad thoughts.

Frankie ran up the hill as fast as he could, the bundle bumping against his right leg, terrified his uncle would come after him. His parents had never thumped him for no reason but he could see in his uncle's face that he enjoyed hurting people.

There was a lad at school whose father beat him and he had a fresh bruise every few days. Frankie wasn't going to put up with that.

He skidded to a halt as he saw Tam in the café. He didn't hesitate, he was so afraid of being pursued, just shoved the door open and ran inside. When Tam turned to see who it was, Frankie flung himself into his cousin's arms. 'Don't let him take me. Please, please don't let him take me.'

He burst into tears, something he hadn't expected to do, because men didn't cry. His father had been telling him that for years. But he was so afraid, he couldn't stop sobbing. He just couldn't.

He sobbed against the warmth of his cousin's chest and

no one shouted at him. Gradually he started to calm down, soothed by the patting and gentle murmurs. To his relief, there was no one else in the shop. Maybe Tam would help him. Maybe he would manage to escape.

When Cara saw the state Frankie was in, she took Jinna and Ned into the bedroom. The girl was very upset by Frankie's distress.

'He's crying,' Jinna kept saying. 'That boy's crying. He's hurt.'

Ned looked from one to the other, bottom lip quivering.

So Cara sat on the bed with a child on either side and tried to explain that something had upset Frankie, and yes, people did cry when they were very upset. 'It's all right to cry,' she ended up. 'He'll stop soon.'

But Jinna was rubbing her arm in the way she had when she was nervous and clutching the umbrella, while Ned was clutching his grandmother and looking ready to cry himself.

Cara stood up. 'You stay here and I'll just see how things are going. I'll be back in a minute. Look after Ned, Jinna. Hold his hand.'

She peeped through the doorway into the other room. Frankie seemed to be calming down and it was lovely the way Tam was holding him and patting his back. She went back to sit down on the bed and hugged each child in turn.

'Frankie's getting better now. Listen! He's not crying as loudly. We'll have to be kind to him, make him feel better.'

Jinna frowned as if she didn't understand this.

'We cuddle people who're upset,' Cara explained. 'Like this.' She gave Jinna a hug, then Ned. Ned hugged her back enthusiastically, being used to displays of affection from his grandmother. As before, Jinna sat stiffly in her embrace.

Hilda had an idea. 'Come and see.' When she opened the door to let them peep into the kitchen area, they saw Tam hugging Frankie. She whispered, 'See. He's making Frankie feel better.'

She watched Jinna give the scene one of her long, hard stares.

Ned ran into the kitchen before she could stop him. He put his little arms round Frankie's waist and hugged him, shouting, 'Make you better, Frankie, make you better.' Trust Ned to join in.

Cara led Jinna out to join them and somehow they were all hugging one another. It felt good, so very good, to be part of a family again, Cara thought, even in an unhappy moment.

Then she made a pot of tea and as she was putting out some biscuits to go with it, Tam came across to help her and whispered, 'Could we look after another child, do you think?'

She didn't hesitate. 'Of course we could. Frankie's a good kid.'

'I'm not letting that poor lad go to live with that brute, if I have to hide him till they've left the valley. Or even if we have to move away to keep him out of the hands of that nasty sod. I'll just tell him that, if you're sure. It'll make him feel a lot better.'

'Of course I'm sure. It'll make a perfect family.'

He smiled into her eyes. 'Eh, you're a grand lass.'

When they turned round, they saw all three children sitting close together. Frankie had stopped crying and they looked like a family group.

Cara watched Tam go across and crouch in front of Frankie, saying gently, 'Would you like to live with us from now on, lad?'

Frankie stared at him wide-eyed. 'Really?'

'Really and truly.'

'Where would we live? I don't want to be anywhere near my uncle.'

'I don't know yet. But I'll keep him away from you, whatever it takes.'

'Thank you.' The words were more like gulps and the boy was crying silently now, tears of relief.

Cara felt tears well in her own eyes, it was all so lovely. Oh, she did love this man, already she did! How could you not?

She watched Tam pat the boy on the shoulder. 'You stay here with Cara and the kids, and I'll go down to the farm and talk to your mother.'

Frankie grabbed his sleeve. 'Tell her if she drags me back, I'll only run away again. Make sure she understands that I won't put up with it, not if he kills me, I won't.'

'I'll do that.'

'And watch out for *him*. He might try to thump *you*. There's something wrong with him.' He tapped his own forehead suggestively.

Tam had to agree. Something very wrong.

Cara went out to the gate to watch him walk down the hill and give herself time to calm down after all the emotion.

Would Tam manage to persuade Hilda not to drag the boy to a miserable life? Oh, she did hope he would.

25

Hilda sat very still on the wooden bench, unable at first to believe what she was hearing from inside the farm. James was again calling her a stupid fool who deserved what she got, and she knew she wasn't stupid. No stupid woman could have managed to make ends meet for so long on such a poor farm.

She sat listening, really listening for another few moments after Frankie had run up the hill. She felt numb and helpless, wondering how to deal with this.

It was a good thing she had stayed there quietly, because what she overheard next made up her mind for her about what to do and brought her right out of her daze.

'I wonder what your dear little sister will do with her ten pounds,' Rixom asked, laughing loudly. 'Oh my, it's a good story, that one. What a nice fat profit you'll make out of her stupidity. You're a man after my own heart, Boales.'

'You don't think I'm going to give any of that ten pounds to *her*, do you? Or even spend it on her? I just told her that to make her come quietly. She'll earn every bite of food in my house and I'll replace her clothes only when necessary. Same for the lad.'

'Won't she be a bit upset about that?'

'Hanged if I care whether she's upset or not. She's too dopey to sell the place herself and too terrified of her lad not getting enough to eat to try to manage on her own. Well, I'll soon have her working so hard she'll be exhausted and then she won't have the energy to worry about that soft creature she's brought up. Cheeky brat, isn't he?'

'They all are at that age.'

'My kids aren't. They don't open their mouths in my presence unless I give them permission to speak and I'll beat good manners into him as well.'

Rixom's voice was hesitant. 'You seemed to enjoy beating him.'

Hilda heard James let out a harsh caw of laughter and his words sickened her.

'I did. I really enjoy training people to do as I tell them. You never saw such an obedient wife as mine. A few good thumps soon train women to toe the line.'

'That lad might resist as he grows older. He's twelve and going to be a big chap like his father. He might hit you back one day.'

James laughed again. 'By the time he grows up, he'll be as obedient as the rest of them. And while he's growing up, as long as he goes to school for a day or two each week, I can use him in the shop the rest of the time without needing to pay him wages. He'll more than earn his keep and he'll not learn enough at school to turn him into a smart aleck.'

Hilda stuffed one hand in her mouth to stop herself from crying out.

What had she done?

She'd been so lost in her grief, she had been stupid, but she'd signed nothing and she wasn't going to now she'd come to her senses. She wouldn't let James treat her lad like that. Or herself.

Her brother had turned into a monster. Where had he got such an attitude from? Their father hadn't been a bully and his second wife, James's mother, had been a nice woman, good to Hilda.

Slowly determination ran through her and she stood up, straightening her skirt and pushing her hair out of her eyes. As she was taking a deep breath and bracing herself to confront her brother, her eyes fell on an old axe handle that had been kept under the bench for years because it came in useful for all sorts of little jobs.

Feeling as if she was just waking from a deep sleep, she picked it up and held it behind her in her right hand as she went into the kitchen, just in case she had to defend herself. James wasn't as big as her Peter had been, but he was a strong man and was bound to be angry with her.

She also left the door open behind her in case she had to run to the shop for help.

Tam hadn't felt this angry since he'd had to rescue Jinna from those bullying lads. No, he was more than angry this time; he was absolutely furious. He strode down the hill in best route march style and stood to one side for a car to pass him. It braked suddenly and Todd Selby poked his head out of the window, then got out and grabbed Tam's arm as he tried to walk on.

'What's wrong?'

'What do you mean? Let go of me.' He tried to shake off Selby's hand but the other man wouldn't let go.

'I've seen chaps with that expression on their faces murder people during the war, so I'm not letting you go till you've told me what's thrown you into such a rage.'

'That brother of Hilda's has been thumping the lad again, hard enough to bruise him – for *looking at him cheekily*. Frankie's run away from the farm and we've got him with us at the hostel. I'm going to tell Hilda and that Boales sod that the lad is going to live with us from now on. And if Boales ever tries to lay one finger on him again, he'll answer to me.'

'There were three cars parked outside the farm. You'll be outnumbered. Rixom is there too.'

'I'm not surprised. He's a rotten sod as well.'

'I think I'd better come with you, Crawford. There will be two, and perhaps three of them against one, otherwise.'

'They're not going to attack me, though they may shout a bit!'

'They might attack you. And anyway, three against one isn't good odds for an argument.'

'I don't care whether you come or stay. Let me get on my way.'

Selby went back to slam his car door shut and then ran after Crawford.

When Hilda went into the house she stayed near the door and the two men turned round to scowl at her.

'I said not to come in till I told you to,' her brother snapped.

'It's still my house, so I can come and go as I please. And I've changed my mind about selling it to you, so I want you to leave.'

He looked shocked and studied her as if trying to work out what had made her speak to him like this after her former meekness.

'She must have overheard us,' Rixom said. 'We should have been more careful.'

'She needs her first lesson in obedience, then.' James got up and walked across to her, raising his hand to slap her.

Hilda brought out the old axe handle as the hand came down at her and hit out at James with it. She took him by surprise, hitting his arm just above the wrist and knocking it away. She hit it good and hard with all the force of her anger at him for hurting her son.

James yelled and took a step backwards, rubbing the arm. 'You bitch!'

Rixom stood up. 'I'll help you take it off her.'

James gestured to him to stay back and picked up a heavy wooden stool. 'I don't need help to tame one woman.' He took Hilda by surprise, not using the stool to protect himself, but hurling it at her. It hit one side of her body hard and she dropped the axe handle involuntarily as part of the stool thumped into her arm.

Before she could do anything, James grabbed her and hurled her across the room with such force she stumbled and hit her head on the edge of the sink. She screamed in pain and tumbled to the floor.

She screamed again when he followed that up by kicking her body with his heavy boots.

'You'll sign the bill of sale to me now,' he growled, standing over her and threatening her with his fist. 'Or I'll keep on *persuading* you.'

'Never.' She cowered back as he lifted his foot.

'In that case—' He kicked her even harder and she screamed as the boot connected.

Rixom stood to one side, frowning. 'Watch out, Boales. You don't want to kill her.'

'I'd rather kill her than let her defy me. In fact, why don't I do that? We can say she fell and hit her head. It'd make things a lot easier to manage.'

'Hey, I'm not getting involved in murder. That's enough. Stop kicking her.'

Another kick was his answer. 'She'll learn to do as I tell her or pay the price.'

Rixom looked at his companion's expression, which had gone from anger to mindless rage. This was so different from the earlier smiles and there was a madness in Boales' face. He didn't like how the situation was developing and feared what would happen next. Making money was one thing; committing murder was a step too far.

He moved so quickly that Boales didn't manage to stop him getting to the door. But he chased after him and grabbed Rixom's jacket, trying to prevent him from going outside.

For a few moments the two men struggled, but the material gave way and Boales cursed as his hand slipped. Rixom seized his chance, leaped through the doorway and set off running down the narrow track, heading towards his car.

Boales stood watching him, cursing, then turned back. 'Now, you stupid woman—'

'What the hell is going on?' Tam exclaimed as they saw Rixom burst out of the house and start running down the track towards them. He kept looking over his shoulder and didn't notice them until they grabbed him.

He yelled in shock, then shouted, 'Let me go!' struggling frantically in their grasp.

'I'll let you go as soon as you tell me what's happening inside the farmhouse.'

'Boales has gone mad. I think he's going to kill his sister. I knew he was a violent man, but not that he was a lunatic. *Will* you let me go!'

Tam shoved him away and set off running towards the farmhouse, with Selby following.

Rixom didn't waste time watching them but told his yard man they weren't buying anything after all, and to drive straight back to the warehouse. He then got into his own car and drove off down the hill, shuddering at what he'd seen.

Tam burst into the house, to find Boales about to smash a stool down on Hilda. She was curled up against one wall, trying in vain to protect herself. He ran across the room in time to yank Boales backwards by the collar.

The stool fell to the ground and with Selby's help, Tam wrestled Boales down on the ground. The man was yelling and shouting incoherently, seeming only half aware of his surroundings, all his attention focused on attacking his sister.

Rixom was right: Boales had gone completely mad.

Tam was relieved to see Hilda struggle to her feet and shouted, 'Quick! Have you got a clothes line?'

'Hanging behind the door.'

Boales was hard to hold down and they were having difficulty restraining him. He was utterly incoherent with rage.

'Fetch it quickly.'

Hilda limped across the room, unfurling the rope clothes line as she brought it back and obeying Tam's instructions to tie it round one of her brother's wrists, then leave it to them. She moved out of the way of his flailing limbs, not objecting when Tam managed to tie his hands together and cut her one and only clothes line. He used another piece of it on his captive's ankles, then fastened him to the chair with the rest.

When they stepped back, Boales began rocking to and fro, trying to get away, but they jammed the chair between the table and the wall, then they stepped back again, keeping a wary eye on him.

He struggled in vain for a few moments, then seemed to calm down as it got him nowhere. Panting, he glared at them, muttering to himself.

'What the hell did you think you were doing?' Tam demanded. 'Were you trying to kill her?'

The look Boales threw at his sister was vicious, but he spoke more calmly. 'Of course not. But she deserved a beating and I was making sure she got it.'

'Why did she deserve a beating?'

'Saying she'd sell to me, then changing her mind.' Another glare in Hilda's direction and more words burst out, this time with a shrill edge to them. 'Above all, for being disobedient. I *will not* have members of my household disobeying me.'

'You're mad.'

As Tam helped Hilda to a chair on the far side of the room, Boales yelled at the top of his voice, a wordless sound that still managed to sound threatening. He began to struggle vainly against his bonds once again.

Tam beckoned to Selby and said in a low voice, 'I don't think there's any doubt that he's run mad.'

'I agree. There's a strange look to his eyes, like a feral animal. I've never seen fury take a man like that.'

'He's safely tied up, so could you go to the shop and phone the police station? Tell Deemer what's happened and ask him to come up here and bring Dr Fiske. We can't turn Boales loose in case he hurts someone else.'

'Or comes back to attack your cousin Hilda once she's alone again. Yes. I'll go straight away.'

They checked the ropes fastening Boales to the chair, ignoring his cursing and threats, then Selby hurried off to the shop.

Tam went to see if he could help Hilda, who must be in pain from such a beating. She was badly bruised on one side of her face and he hated to think what her body would look like.

Well, Boales wouldn't be able to claim that he hadn't hit her, Tam thought, because two witnesses had seen him do it more than once.

'Can I help you in any way?' he asked Hilda.

She shook her head, so he kept an eye on her as she tidied her clothing and combed her hair. She was shaking and so pale, he was afraid she'd faint.

When she'd finished, she surprised him by asking quietly, 'Do you still want to buy this farm, Tam?'

'Yes. Twenty-five pounds all right?'

'Fine. It's yours.'

Boales had been listening and now yelled, 'She can't do that. She's promised in writing to sell it to me. Me, me!'

'When people see what you've done to her, you damned brute, they'll not take your side.'

He blinked and spoke more sensibly. 'We'll see what the law says. You can untie me. I'm not going near the stupid bitch again. I'll leave it to the lawyers to sort out.'

'I can't risk untying you till my friend comes back in case you run mad again.'

Another wordless jumble of loud shouting greeted that remark.

Tam turned to Hilda. 'Come and get a breath of fresh air.' He stayed in the doorway to keep an eye on her brother while he told her that Selby was phoning for the policeman to bring a doctor to check Boales and see whether he was certifiably mad.

She shuddered. 'I'm sure he is. I truly believed he was going to kill me.' She leaned against the door frame.

'Do you want to stay out here while we wait for the doctor?'

'If you don't mind. I don't want to be in the same room as my brother, not ever again.' She looked at Tam, distress on her face. 'When he started trying to kill me, Rixom ran away. He didn't even try to help me.'

'Yes. We'll catch up with him later.' He raised his voice. 'I think I'd better go back inside and get something to hit him with if he tries to escape.'

Once in the big room, he unhooked a blackened old frying pan from the wall and banged it on the table, making Boales jump in shock.

'Just try to escape,' he said softly. 'I'd love to hit you over the head with this.'

Boales froze, so Tam emphasised the point by thumping the frying pan down again, then he went back to the doorway so that he could watch for Selby coming back from the shop and keep an eye on Hilda as well. But he kept hold of the frying pan.

After a couple of minutes he saw Selby striding towards them.

'He's coming back.'

Hilda looked up and managed a near smile, though she'd winced when she moved and her face was badly bruised.

Selby was carrying a plate of sandwiches and a bucket with cups and saucers in it. He was accompanied by a lad carrying a large enamel teapot wrapped in a tea towel.

Tam gestured to them to go inside and set the things down on the table.

The lad goggled at the sight of Boales tied to a chair. When the man glared at him fiercely, he backed hastily out of the room, thanking Selby for the threepenny bit he slipped him.

Tam went outside to Hilda. 'Shall I bring you a cup of tea, love?'

'I'd die for one.'

'And a sandwich?'

'I couldn't eat a mouthful.'

Before Tam could go inside again, Selby joined them outside, saying in a low voice, 'Deemer's coming straight away and bringing Dr Fiske with him. I told him this was a serious emergency.'

'It is. Boales is as mad as a hatter, if you ask me.'

When they were all supplied with warm drinks, Tam tried again to persuade Hilda to eat something as well, but she shook her head.

Tam crouched in front of her. 'You really should eat something, love.'

'I can't face eating anything now, Tam, I just can't. But the tea is just what I need, and if there's another cup, I'll have it.'

'I'll get it for you once you've finished that one. There's plenty left.'

Selby also stayed near the doorway, keeping watch on their prisoner, who was now quiet and watchful.

Tam looked at him. What was Boales plotting now?

26

For all the urgency of the situation, it was nearly an hour before Deemer and Dr Fiske arrived. They looked horrified when they saw Hilda's badly bruised face.

'What happened?' Deemer peered through the doorway but didn't go inside, turning back to the three people waiting.

Tam quickly explained and Boales must have been able to hear him as well because he suddenly shouted from inside the house, 'He's lying. Come in and set me free.'

When no one went to him, he yelled, 'Don't listen to them. This is a plot to stop my sister selling me the farm.'

Deemer looked through the doorway again. 'I'd better go in to him. Will you come with me, doctor?'

'Yes, of course.'

'Don't untie him. He turns into a madman when he gets upset. It took two of us to subdue him and stop him killing his sister.' Selby rolled up his sleeve to show a big bruise on his own arm.

The doctor whistled softly. 'We'll be careful.'

The two men watched them from the doorway while Hilda sat staring down at the ground. Tam felt increasingly outraged as Boales told lie after fluent lie, insisting it was a conspiracy and he'd been set upon purely so that Tam could buy the farm.

Selby muttered angrily a couple of times.

The doctor came out again. 'Mr Boales doesn't seem mad, just extremely angry.'

'Wait till you see the rest of Mrs Kerkham's bruises. That'll convince you he's mad. No sane person would beat a woman like that.'

'Hmm. Can I examine you somewhere private, Mrs Kerkham?'

She got up, wincing as she moved. 'I don't want to go past James. Can't you take a quick look at my side here? I can unbutton my blouse if Tam and Mr Selby will turn away.'

The doctor looked surprised but that turned to shock at what he found. He asked her to lift her skirt and found more bruising on one of her legs. 'This is dreadful. You must be in considerable pain. Why did he do this to you?'

'I told him I wouldn't sell the farm to him and that made him furious. He said he'd teach me to be obedient, threw me across the room and began kicking me as I lay there. When I wouldn't obey him, he said it'd be easier to kill me.'

'He actually said that?'

'Yes. And he meant it, too, doctor. You won't let him loose again, will you? If you do, he'll come after me, I know he will.'

Dr Fiske sighed. 'I'm afraid I can't simply commit him to the asylum on your word. Boales seems angry but he's not showing any signs of madness. He answered my questions and Sergeant Deemer's in a way that made sense.'

'If it weren't for the fact that he was telling bare-faced lies,' Tam put in grimly. 'Well, I saw him kicking Hilda several times and so did Selby.'

'He could be charged with assault, then. May I bring Sergeant Deemer to look at your injuries?' the doctor asked.

She nodded, clearly beyond caring about modesty.

When the policeman had seen how badly bruised her body was, he went back to ask Boales why he'd done that, but the man denied inflicting the injuries, insisting that Crawford had done it to make her sell him the farm.

Deemer came back to her, his expression full of pity. 'Someone has beaten you severely, Mrs Kerkham. For the record, can you please tell me who did this? Doctor, will you please witness this conversation?'

'Of course.'

'Mrs Kerkham?'

'I *told* you already: it was my brother who did it. Tam and Mr Selby will bear me out on that. They saved me.'

'Unfortunately, as your brother pointed out, Tam is an interested party, and your brother's accusing him of doing it.'

'Mr Selby isn't involved in buying the farm and *he* had to help Tam to rescue me.'

The doctor joined in. 'We aren't going to get anywhere tossing accusations about and we can't leave Boales tied up for much longer. I think we'd better take him down to the police station and bring in another doctor to give a second opinion. Could you two gentlemen and Mrs Kerkham come too and make statements about what you say occurred?'

Tam said suddenly, 'You could ask Rixom about Boales as well. When we arrived, he was running out of here, looking terrified of being pursued.'

'Ah. Another witness would be very useful. He must have seen something.'

'If Rixom tells the truth,' Tam said. 'He couldn't lie straight in bed, that one.'

Deemer didn't comment on that remark. 'Can you two help me to get Boales into the back of my car? We'll need to undo the rope round his ankles and I'll have to tie his hands in front of his body, so that he can sit safely in the back. I have a bar fitted there to which I can attach ropes or handcuffs to secure him. I don't often have to use it, but it works well and allows me to drive without interruption.'

'Of course we can help you, then I'll nip back to the hostel for my van and bring Hilda to the police station. She won't want to get in your car with him, even if he is tied up.'

Deemer looked at Selby. 'You'll come too, of course.'

'Yes. I'll come in my own car. It's just up the road.'

'Very well. I'd better start the engine before I bring Boales out.' Deemer grimaced. 'I'm afraid the police car has been behaving temperamentally lately and sometimes it's hard to keep the engine running till it's fully warmed up. I really must get it looked at.'

This time, however, the car started without trouble.

But as Deemer undid the rope from Boales' hands and began to edge him into the back seat of the car, Selby called, 'Watch out! She's going to faint!'

He moved to support Hilda and Tam hurried to help him.

As Deemer turned to look at them, Boales seized the opportunity to kick out with both feet from where he was sitting on the edge of the car seat. He did it so hard, he sent Deemer spinning away from the vehicle to land in the shallow ditch that ran down the side of the road.

Boales at once leaped into the front seat and undid the handbrake, accelerating hard even as he was closing the driver's door, but leaving the back door swinging to and fro.

By the time Deemer got up again, the car was twenty yards away and moving faster every second. He'd have no chance of catching it on foot and could only stand and watch indignantly as the car gathered speed.

'Damn him! Can we use your car to chase him, Mr Selby?'

But before they could make a move, Selby said, 'He's going far too fast for that bend. He'll run off the road if he doesn't slow down.'

They watched in horror as another car came round the bend towards them at that very moment. Boales swerved to avoid it, but he was going so fast he lost control and couldn't slow down enough to avoid running into the solid dry-stone wall that edged the road.

Loud sound filled the air as the car crumpled against the heavy stones. Metal screamed a protest and shards of glass flew everywhere as car windows smashed. The car body was battered into a wreck within seconds. Black smoke billowed from the engine but there was no movement from inside the vehicle.

The sudden silence seemed to echo around them. It was as if everything nearby had paused.

The oncoming car had managed to run off the road at the inner edge and stop. The engine cut off abruptly and they could see the occupant moving.

Normal sounds built up again gradually, with people running out of houses, calling to one another, and footsteps on rough ground as some ran to help.

There had still been no movement from the crashed vehicle.

'Oh, hell!' Deemer set off running down the road, followed by the other men, leaving Hilda leaning against Selby's car, watching in horror.

The driver of the other vehicle involved in the accident got out of his car and vomited by the side of the road, then leaned against his car, shaking visibly.

The doctor reached the crashed vehicle and pushed his way through a group of younger men who'd got to the wreck first.

'He's dead,' one of them called. 'Look at him. He looks as if he's snarling but you can tell he's dead.'

'There's a lot of blood,' another said. 'He must have bashed his head good and hard.'

A third turned away, shuddering at what he'd seen.

Dr Fiske confirmed this diagnosis almost immediately and one of the men helped him pull the body out of the car.

They moved some distance away, afraid the engine would burst into flames because it was still pouring out smoke.

Hilda had heard what they said and now muttered, 'He's dead.' The words seemed to repeat inside her head till she could think of nothing else. *Dead. James is dead. He's dead.*

One of her neighbours put her arms round Hilda, startling her. 'Don't faint on us, love. Let's sit you down on this low bit of wall, eh?'

For a while she let them do what they wanted with her. She was desperately trying to work out whether the accident was her fault, to think what she could have done to avoid all this horror.

It wasn't her fault, surely it couldn't be?

The other women moved back as Tam came to stand next to them, leaving Selby to stay with Deemer and the doctor.

Tam seemed to read Hilda's mind and laid one hand on her shoulder, looking earnestly into her eyes. 'It wasn't your fault, love. Boales had run mad, yes, but it was an accident. The other car coming round the bend was what made it happen, and that was sheer accident, nothing to do with you. Your brother was in such a wild state, he'd probably have run off the road anyway, but not in such a bad way.'

'Are you sure?'

'Yes, love. I promise you none of it was your fault. Definitely not your fault.' He waited a few seconds and said again, *'Not – your – fault.'*

The repetition made these words gradually sink in and Hilda nodded, feeling a burden lift slowly from her mind. She realised then that she only wanted two things for certain at the moment and it felt important that she make plain what these were.

'I definitely want to sell the farm to you, Tam, and I don't want to come back to Ellindale again. *Not ever.*' She shivered.

'We'll find you and Frankie somewhere else to live, then.'

She looked at him, thinking hard, grateful that he waited for her to speak.

'Thank you, Tam, but I'll find somewhere for myself. I need to make a new life.' She gulped, fighting for control over her emotions before continuing, and again he waited for her. 'Will *you* take Frankie in? My boy deserves a normal life with a family, and he'd not thrive in a town. He's a born farmer. I can't give him that.'

'You're sure?'

'Yes. Very sure.'

'Then of course I'll take him in. You could lodge with us at the youth hostel for a day or two as well, if that would help, though you'd have to sleep in the dormitory. Or you could stay on at the farm. I could—'

'Stay here! Never. It'll not only remind me of Peter now, but of James and the way he tried to kill me. My own brother! And as soon as I came outside I'd see the part of the road where James died.' She shuddered and hugged her arms round herself. 'I have to get away, Tam, have to.'

'Are you sure you want to leave your son?'

'Frankie needs a man's influence if he's to become a good person. I have nothing left in me to give him. You'd make a marvellous father. Please, Tam.'

He didn't tell her he'd already offered Frankie a home. It was better that she think it her own idea.

'You'll come back to visit?'

'If— no, *when* I have recovered. It's been a long hard year, Tam. Very hard. I have to . . . sort things out in my head, make a new life . . . recover.'

She was right. She was in no state to look after her son. They could always change their arrangements later. 'Well, if you're sure, Hilda love, I'll look after Frankie for you and do my best by him. But remember: you'll always be welcome to visit us and see him. Or even to come back and live with us.'

'I can't think that far ahead, Tam. I'll have to force myself to go back into the house – just once more – to pack some more of my things in the suitcase. I'll leave the rest of my personal things at the house for the moment, if you don't mind. Put them in one of the sheds. What's in the house is yours.'

Again, they could give them back to her if she needed them, so he just said yes. 'Where will you stay, then, Hilda?'

'I can find lodgings in Rivenshaw tonight if you'll advance me some money from the sale.'

'Of course I will, love. But don't leave town till we've made the sale legal and I've paid the rest of the money. I don't carry that much around with me.'

'Oh, yes. Of course. Right.'

'I'll come into the house with you, shall I?'

'Yes, please.'

He could see how close to a breakdown she was still.

What a horrible, horrible thing to happen! And just after she'd lost her husband.

Eh, that poor boy! Frankie would need a lot of loving to get over this, and they'd make sure he got it.

And Hilda – well, he could only hope she'd get better gradually. Surely she would?

It didn't take Hilda long to sort out her clothes, and once she was ready Tam went to bring his van down the hill. 'I'll take you back up to the hostel first to see your son, shall I?'

She hesitated, rubbing her forehead as if it ached. 'I was going to do that tomorrow.'

'I think he needs to see you today, love. And Selby has offered to drive you down to Rivenshaw afterwards to find lodgings because he's going home there anyway. Will that be all right? I think I need to stay here with Frankie. He's very upset.'

She nodded. 'Don't tell him how badly I'm hurt.'

'He'll see the bruises on your face and how you wince when you move.'

'But he won't know how bad it is.'

Tam carried on talking because it seemed to soothe her. 'I'll come down to Rivenshaw and see you in the morning once the banks are open, then I can draw out the rest of the money for you and we can register the sale officially. You won't run away, will you?'

'No.'

When she'd packed her suitcase, she sat down on the bench. 'I'll wait for you here, Tam. The fresh air will do me good.'

But he could see what a huge effort everything was taking and how much pain she was in. Such a brave woman!

But a person can only take so much and she'd reached her limit.

When he came back, she looked a bit more composed. 'You're right, Tam. I have to speak to Frankie before I leave.'

He picked up her suitcase, stealing a quick sideways glance at the farm. *His* farm from tomorrow on.

He wouldn't attempt to do anything about the place that night. There was no need even to lock doors in this village.

He was upset, too, and like Hilda, he needed time to pull himself together. Time and his family around him. It wasn't every day you were forced to watch a madman kill himself.

Hilda didn't look back as they drove away.

As they arrived at the hostel, Frankie ran out and stopped dead at the sight of his mother's face. 'What did he do to you?'

'Hit me.'

'Cara says to come inside.'

Hilda accepted a seat at the table and Tam took his family outside to leave her alone with her son so that she could tell him what had happened.

Frankie listened, then said, 'I'm glad he's dead. Don't expect me to be sorry.'

'No, I won't. I'm not sorry either. He was mad, I think.' She tried to work out how to tell him she was leaving him here.

'What will we do now, Mam?'

'I'm selling the farm to Cousin Tam and he says you can live with them. I can't stay there, son, I just can't.'

'Can't I come with you?'

She shook her head. 'I've no home to offer you and besides, you love that farm. The animals will need you, too, because Tam doesn't know how to care for them.'

'But you're my mother! I'll *miss* you.'

'I'll miss you, too. But I'm all muddled in my head, and I think I'll be able to straighten myself out better if I'm on my own for a while. It'll take time to get over what happened today and even more time to build a new life.'

She'd worked out what to do first while she was sitting waiting for Tam to pick her up.

'I'm going to visit my cousin Nellie, the one who lives near Wolverhampton. I haven't seen her for years, but we've kept in touch by letter, remember?'

'Oh. Yes.'

'I'll write to you every week.'

'But how will you manage?'

'Thanks to Cousin Tam, I'll have the money from selling the farm, and I'll see if I can find myself a job and lodgings. Once I've settled down somewhere, maybe you can come and visit me, eh?'

He looked at her pleadingly, and she wanted to help him, oh, she did! Only she had nothing left in her to give.

'I have to go now, Frankie love. I need to find somewhere to stay for the night. I need to lie down and be quiet.'

But as she got up, he put his arms round her and hid his face in her shoulder.

They hugged for a long time, then she stepped back, brushed his hair from his forehead. 'You'll be happier with Tam. I know that for sure.' She tapped her forehead. 'It's the one thing I'm not muddled about. I'd not leave you else.'

Tam had come to the door and Hilda said, 'I'm ready to leave now.'

When they went outside, Cara put an arm round Frankie's shoulders as he watched his mother get into Mr Selby's car. That embrace surprised him and he was even more surprised when Cara dropped a kiss on his cheek. He could feel the imprint of it, cool and damp on his skin, such a comfort.

Ned came to stand on his other side and smiled up at him. What a lovely little boy he was! Something eased inside Frankie's chest. Just a little.

He saw Jinna hover uncertainly beside the group for a moment or two, then she went to stand on her adopted mother's other side.

When Cara put her other arm round the girl, Jinna leaned against her briefly.

These were loving people, he thought. Maybe he'd be all right here.

But would his mother be all right?

Cara waited to speak till the newest member of their family pulled away and gave her a half-smile. 'Let's go and have one of those Nice biscuits I bought, then we'll have to bring in a mattress from the dormitory for you to sleep on, Frankie love. We'll be a bit squashed tonight, because there's only one bedroom and you and Tam will have to sleep in the kitchen, but we can maybe move to the farm in a day or two. You'll have to show us round it tomorrow. Will you do that?'

He nodded, so pale and quiet and obedient, she was worried about him.

'I'm sure you'll see your mother again soon.'

He spoke very quietly and slowly, as if having to dig deep for the words. 'It won't be the same, though, will it? Can't be.'

'Life never stays the same, Frankie love. You have to expect changes, whether you're old or young.' She tousled his hair. 'Come on! Let's find you a mattress.'

'I'll have to go and feed the chickens afterwards.'

'I'll come with you,' Tam said at once. 'There may be some eggs. Nothing like a fresh egg for breakfast.'

When they got back with three eggs in a bowl, there was a meal waiting for them, but Frankie didn't eat much and no one urged him to.

He remained quiet as the evening passed and they got ready for bed. It was Ned who seemed to cheer him up most, so Cara let her grandson stay up later than usual.

Jinna had got out her sketch pad and when the evening ended, Tam asked if he could see her new drawing.

The girl nodded and held out the pad to him.

'Why, that's wonderful. You are so clever, Jinna.' He held the sketch out to Frankie, who stared at it in amazement. 'It's very like you, isn't it?'

The lad nodded. 'You're very good at drawing, Jinna. I didn't realise how good.'

He got a solemn nod from her.

It took a lot to make that girl smile, Tam thought. Jinna seemed so wary of any new situation. Would that ever change? He hoped so.

'She's done one of Ned too. Can you show that one to Frankie, Jinna?'

More thinking, then she went into the bedroom to get it and held it out.

'That's exactly how he looks at you,' Frankie said. 'It's lovely.'

She took it back from him and went to put it carefully away with the other drawings.

'I thought she was slow-witted,' Frankie whispered to Tam.

'No. She definitely isn't. But her mother kept her shut up in one room most of her life, so Jinna hasn't had much to do with other people. She's still exploring the world and she gets very nervous in new situations. You'll have to help us build up her confidence.' He smiled wryly. 'And help us keep an eye on Ned. He's a right little love, but sometimes he gets into mischief.'

Frankie nodded, then said thoughtfully, 'You're all trying to help one another, aren't you? I like that.'

'It's what a family is for. And as long as you're living with us, you're part of the family, lad. Don't forget that. One of us.'

Frankie swallowed hard and Tam saw that his eyes were bright with tears, so he changed the subject.

Then it was time to go to bed. When the other three had gone into the bedroom, Tam helped the lad to make room for his mattress on the floor and the two of them lay down at opposite sides of the table.

After a few minutes he heard Frankie crying but trying to muffle it in his pillow. He pretended he was asleep. The poor lad's world had turned upside down today. It would take a while for him to settle down again. Let him have his cry.

But if Tam had any say in it, they'd make a happy family life for them all at that farm. Eh, fancy a whole house to live in! He couldn't wait to get proper sleeping quarters again and wondered how soon Leah could replace Cara to run the youth hostel so that they could all move to the farm.

He couldn't wait to get married, too. It wouldn't be long before that happened. He prayed nothing would go wrong with their arrangements. He liked and respected Cara more every day.

She was a handsome woman, too, and affectionate. It'd be wonderful to share a bed with her and equally wonderful to have three children to care for.

He was such a lucky man.

All was peaceful that night at Hillam House. Most people in the village had either seen the crash happen or gone to see the battered wreck of the police car, so the lights went out in their houses later than usual.

Eventually, all was quiet and two men slipped into the old house to stay there overnight, ready to sound a warning if anyone attempted to break in. They were very careful, taking it in turns to sleep, not showing any lights, keeping quiet.

But nothing happened.

Wilf was the first there on the Friday morning, bringing half a pound of butter and a loaf from the village shop for their breakfast. He greeted them with, 'Good thing they deliver the first batch of bread from the Rivenshaw bakery early, eh?'

One of them raised his nose to inhale deeply. 'By, that smells good!'

'Tuck in. You've earned it.'

'You know, I don't think they'll dare try anything,' one of the men said when they'd finished eating. 'There are too many of us living nearby.'

'You could be right. Perhaps we're being too careful.'

Wilf didn't contradict him because Finn had told him about the anonymous letter. He'd had an idea about the defence of this house and their job club. He waited till Finn arrived and seized the first opportunity to have a private word with him.

'Look, if someone is planning to break in here and they know any locals, they'll have heard that we're keeping watch. You know how word gets around.'

Finn nodded slowly. 'Yes. We should have thought of that.'

'What if we tell people that we're locking it up carefully, because the job club's closed for the weekend? We should only tell one or two of the men about keeping watch and whoever is doing it should go into the house secretly after dark. Do you think that'll tempt Rixom's men into the open if they're planning anything?'

'It might very well do. It's worth a try, anyway. You choose a couple of men you trust and set it all up for them to sneak back after everyone has gone home tonight. I'll pay them watchman's fees again.'

'I'll stay with them, if you don't mind. I don't want them to be targets for violence, so I'm going to make sure I can call for help.'

'How?'

Wilf grinned. 'I've got a cracked old gong in my shed. I'll take that into the house openly during the day and we'll use it to call everyone to dinner. It still makes a very loud noise if you bash it with a hammer, so it'd be perfect to summon people from the village. Our kids loved playing with it but it nearly drove me and Enid mad, so we locked it away.'

'Is there anything you haven't got in that shed of yours?'

Wilf shrugged. 'I like to collect things. It's surprising what comes in useful. And of course I have the pieces of wood I find for my carvings.' He flushed slightly and added, 'The animal carvings are still selling now and then at the market. My friend takes ten per cent and the extra money comes in useful to us both. It's saved me and Enid going without food quite a few times.'

'You should be famous. Those carvings are beautiful and lifelike.'

Wilf's flush deepened. 'I enjoy carving but it's building things that I love most. I've really enjoyed repairing Hillàm House, making it right.' He moved his hands as if putting objects together.

Finn had seen him 'build' imaginary items before when describing something and had a great respect for his companion's abilities when it came to constructing or mending things. If he'd come from a family with even a little money, Wilf might have been an architect by now, and a good one, too. It was sad how lack of money placed so many restrictions on people's lives, and it was even worse for women than men.

If his child turned out to be a girl, Finn intended to make sure she had every opportunity she needed to make a success of her life.

27

On the Friday morning, after planning the security precautions at the old house with Wilf, Finn went up to Spring Cottage to speak to Leah, as he'd promised Henry Lloyd he would. He wasn't sure she'd agree to stand for council, but if she did, he'd do whatever he could to help her get elected.

She was just coming out of the fizzy drinks factory, a bottle in her hand, and waited for him to park his car.

'Come into the house and try out the new drink one of the women in the factory has concocted from a recipe of her grandmother's. I think we're going to use it. I doubt any of the big manufacturers will have anything like it.'

He stopped in the kitchen to smile at her little son, who was sitting in a high chair in the kitchen, banging a rattle on his wooden tray under the watchful eyes of Ginny and Betty. Leah poured small glasses of the drink for the two maids to try, then they went to the sitting room for their chat.

But first Finn accepted a glass of the pink liquid, interested to see what it would taste like. It was lightly fizzy, very refreshing and not too sweet. 'That's delicious. What's in it?'

Smiling at the sound of a crow of laughter from her son in the next room, Leah leaned back in her chair. 'The recipe is a very big secret, I'm afraid. I'm glad you like it, though. Now, tell me what you wanted to see me about, Finn.'

'I've been asked to speak to you about standing for council in the coming elections.'

'Oh, you must do it. I'll certainly vote for you.'

He held up one hand. 'No, no! I mean *you* standing for council.'

Her mouth fell open and she didn't seem able to string two words together, so he took the opportunity to tell her about the group of people who were trying to get enough votes on the council to put a stop to some of the selfish and corrupt activities of the present group.

'But surely *you* would be a better candidate than me!'

'I try to help people, but not in that way. Besides, I've got the job club and the coming baby to think about.'

'That's no excuse. I'm rather busy myself, with young Jonty to care for, a business to run, my sister to raise, not to mention being about to get married.'

He wriggled uncomfortably. 'I know. And I might have agreed to do it if it weren't that . . . Oh dear, I'll have to tell you my secret: I absolutely hate making speeches when it's in a formal situation. I suffer from nerves and it makes me stutter. Stupid, isn't it? I can fight for my country and stand up against individuals, but I go to pieces if I have to make a formal speech in front of even a small crowd. I can talk to a group informally, but not – you know, when it's something official. You'd do the job far better than me. I've heard you speak to groups of people in the village and you seem able to say just the right thing to touch their hearts.'

She looked at him incredulously. '*You* are that nervous of public speaking? You're kidding me.'

'Actually, I'm not. Cross my heart.' He performed the appropriate action and looked at her pleadingly.

'Who'd have thought it?'

'We all have our weak points. Please don't tell anyone.'

'Of course not.'

'Anyway, it'll be good for the valley to have another woman on the council, one who isn't a doormat this time, like that Mawson woman. Beth agrees with me about that.'

Leah sat very still, frowning slightly, then said, 'I must admit I've been worried about what Rixom's doing, or rather not doing, for Ellindale, and about one or two other things that Charlie's told me about. I detest dishonesty. Does Mr Lloyd really think I'd get in?'

'Yes. And I do too. You've done so much for the village, people are bound to vote for you.'

'The trouble is, I'm not sure I can do it well enough.'

'Don't doubt yourself, Leah. You're a very intelligent woman and the world is changing. We need women to play their part in public life – as they did during the war.'

'Jonah used to say that. He thought we were behind the times in the valley. He'd have agreed with you about me standing.'

'Does that mean you'll do it?'

'I'll think about it, speak to Todd, see if he minds.'

'No. Don't think, dive in.' Finn smiled at her conspiratorially. 'I'll tell you a secret: Henry Lloyd is going to approach Todd to suggest the same thing to him. The Rivenshaw West ward needs an honest councillor to represent it.'

When she still didn't speak, he added, 'Surely you're not going to let Rixom get elected again? As a councillor, he's done nothing for Ellindale, only for himself.'

She stared at him for so long he thought he'd failed and she was still going to refuse, then she exhaled and said, 'All right. I'll try.'

'I couldn't be happier. I know you'll do better than I ever could. I'll help you in any way I can, I promise – except for making speeches.'

'I don't have a clue how to start.'

'Don't worry. There's going to be a meeting with the mayor

at Henry's and he'll tell you all you need to know. I'll be attending too, as a behind-the-scenes helper.'

'Thank goodness.'

As he walked home, Finn grinned, wishing he could be a fly on the wall when Henry tackled Todd about the same thing.

Finn phoned Henry to tell him Leah had agreed to stand and Henry said he'd go round to see Todd straight away.

When Todd answered the door, he asked, 'Got a problem with the car? Just a minute while I finish my sandwich and I'll see what I can do.'

Lloyd shook his head. 'No, it's not that. I need to speak to you about something else, something much more important than my car. May I come in?'

'Of course. Would you like a cup of tea?'

'No, thank you. I just want you to listen to what I have to tell you and then say yes.' Lloyd explained the situation, then cocked his head at his host. 'So . . . will you stand for the local council in the coming elections?'

Todd gaped at him. 'Why me?'

'Because you're an honest chap, who served our country in the Great War. Voters still respect that. The present councillor for Rivenshaw West managed to get an exemption in the war and there was considerable doubt as to whether he was telling the truth about his medical condition. Some people might have given him the benefit of the doubt, but he hasn't made himself popular since, especially with women because of the patronising way he treats them. It's very marked. Stupid of him, eh? Not to mention the mistress he keeps in the better part of Backshaw Moss. That's known about, too.'

'But I . . . I wouldn't know how to start.'

'I'm standing for Rivenshaw East and there are others you

know who'll be joining our group to try to clean up the council. Reginald Kirby is a popular mayor and this is his idea, so he'll guide us. We're going to hold a secret meeting at my house in a day or two. There isn't much time before the closing date for nominations.'

'Surely there are better people than me for the job?'

'Your wife-to-be has agreed to stand for Ellindale.'

'*What?*'

'Why not make it a family affair?'

'Are you sure she's agreed? Leah hasn't said anything to me about it.'

'Finn phoned me a short time ago. He'd only just spoken to her.'

Todd smiled ruefully. 'And I no sooner finish helping Tam to capture a madman then you come and dump this on me. I'd say no, only I've had my doubts about council decisions too. Rivenshaw isn't as quiet and peaceful as it looks, is it?'

'There are always currents flowing beneath the surface in any town, but the corruption at the town hall here has increased steadily over the past few years. I don't really want to stand for the council, but enough is enough. Someone has to stop it. Or do you want your children to grow up in a town controlled by corrupt people?'

'I don't have any children.'

'Yet.'

Todd ran one hand through his hair, then flung his arms wide. 'I must be mad but all right. I'll do it.'

'Good man.'

As soon as he'd shut the door on Lloyd, Todd picked up the telephone and rang Leah. Like him, she didn't know whether to be annoyed or amused about this. But at least they'd be doing it together. *If* they got elected.

He'd travelled the world after the horrors of the war, but

this valley was his heart's home. He'd be proud to help look after how it was run.

Tam had to go down to Rivenshaw on the Friday morning to draw money out of the bank and pay Hilda. Frankie hovered nearby while he got ready, clearly wanting to come with him.

In the end, Tam said bluntly, 'I know you want to see your mother again, lad, but it'll only make her feel worse. Let's leave it this time, eh? She's not leaving you because she doesn't love you, but because she's very fragile at the moment. You go and feed those animals. You're the only one who knows how to run a farm.'

Feeling terrible at leaving the lad behind, Tam drove off but for once he didn't weaken. He really did think it was for the best for Hilda not to go through any more agonising farewells.

He went to the bank and drew out the money to buy the farm, plus a bit extra because he didn't know what he'd find there. He'd only been in the kitchen and the downstairs room that Peter had died in, after all. Fancy buying a house when you hadn't even seen it all! Crazy Tam again!

Afterwards he called in on Selby as they'd arranged, to find out where Hilda was staying. To his surprise he found her waiting for him there.

'I stayed here last night,' she said. 'The lodging house was full and Mr Selby had a spare bedroom.'

'You don't look as if you slept well, and have you got hold of some arnica for those bruises?'

'No. It doesn't matter. I just want to get things settled.'

'How about I nip to the chemist's and get some arnica for you while you're sorting out registration of the sale?' Selby offered.

'Thank you.'

Tam counted out the money and wrote out a simple bill of sale, which Selby witnessed, then Hilda put it in her handbag and the two of them went to the town hall to register it.

The man at the counter looked at them in shock. 'Are you sure this is legal?'

'What do you mean?'

'Well—' He hesitated, looking shifty.

'You thought Rixom was buying that farm, didn't you?' Tam finished off for him, noting the name on the man's desk for future reference. 'Well, Mrs Kerkham decided to sell it to me instead because I was paying her a fairer price. What problem can there possibly be about that?'

'Um, no problem, none at all. I thought the sale had already been settled, but I must have heard wrongly.'

'If it had already been settled, they would have registered it.'

'Um, yes.'

'So get on with it, man!'

The new ownership of the farm was duly recorded, then the two of them went to the Yorkshire Penny Bank, which had branches nearly everywhere in the country, and Hilda opened a savings account. She had felt nervous carrying so much money around with her.

When they came out she said in wonderment, 'I've never had so much money to fall back on in my whole life. It makes me feel . . . safer, as if a weight's been taken off my shoulders.'

'Good. And you've got us to fall back on, if you need somewhere to stay. Any time, lass. Any time. Just turn up.'

She nodded and gave him a tremulous smile. 'I've never been on my own before. There was always Peter, right from when I was sixteen and still living at home.'

Anna Jacobs

'You'll manage. You're not a stupid woman. Now, let's get on with it. What time's your train, Hilda?'

'Midday. I change trains at Manchester and I'll be in Wolverhampton by early evening. Todd helped me send a telegram to my cousin this morning as soon as the post office opened, to let her know I was coming.'

'You're sure she'll help you?'

'Yes, definitely. Nellie's a widow too, you see, and she's the only relative I really care about. We were like sisters when we were younger.' She paused and stared into the distance. 'Eh, it seems so long ago, but it's only seventeen years since I got married and left home. Nellie came to my wedding and the following year she met her husband and moved to the Midlands. I didn't get to her wedding because I was expecting Frankie, and anyway, we didn't have the money to spare.'

He kept her going with nods and murmurs, wanting to send her off in a positive frame of mind.

'Her husband died last year. TB. But they had a corner shop and he had life insurance, so she was left all right. She's still running it and living in the flat upstairs. They never had any children, sadly.'

They went back to Selby's house to get her suitcase and he gave her the arnica, then Tam drove her to the station. He watched her walk into it, the only person travelling on her own today, and felt sad for her. But she was a capable woman and he was sure she'd find a way to make a new life. At least she wouldn't be completely on her own in Wolverhampton.

His spirits lifted as he drove back up the hill to Ellindale and he slowed down to look sideways at Skeggs Hill Farm, *his* farm now, but he didn't turn off the road, just drove past, because he was determined that they should all go there for the first time as a family.

He'd let Frankie show them round. It was bound to be upsetting for the lad to have new people take over the only home he'd ever known.

It would be the only proper home Tam had had for many years. He couldn't wait to move in

Cara was waiting for him at the hostel, looking as excited as he felt. After assuring Frankie that his mother had got off safely, Tam turned to her. 'Has something happened? You look full of yourself, my lass.'

'Mrs Willcox has found someone else to take over here. She asked me to stay till Monday, when this new woman will arrive, because weekends are the busy time. It's a relative of Ginny's and the poor woman's been recently widowed. So . . . we can all move to the farm on Monday. Ooh, I'm dying to see it properly, Tam.'

'Eh, that's good news. Let's have a quick sandwich, then we'll all go to the farm and Frankie can show us round. We'll buy some tea-making stuff and biscuits at the shop on the way and leave them there. Hilda left us all the crockery and household stuff.'

He turned to the boy. 'Were the chickens all right this morning?'

'Yes. I brought the eggs back here. There are more of them than we need at this time of year, you see, but we can still sell the others to the shop if we don't use them.'

'If you'll take charge of the chickens, lad, *you* can sell them to the shop for us and keep half the money they bring.'

Frankie gaped at him.

'It won't hurt for you to have some money of your own from now on and learn to manage it carefully. You'll want to start saving for when you're grown up and setting up a family yourself.' He gave in to temptation and hugged the lad good and hard. 'Don't look so surprised. We won't be scratching for every farthing, because I've not only got some money left in the bank, I've got the van, too. I'm going to set up as a carrier cum taxi with it, so we'll have to get a phone put in. Eh, I've got so many plans fizzing in my mind.'

Ned broke the tension by joining in the hug, which made them all laugh.

'I think we ought to put that lad on the stage when he grows up,' Tam said. 'He's good at making folk laugh. Or maybe he can become a doctor and make them better when they're ill.' He didn't know how people became doctors but if *he* could own a house of his own, he was quite sure that anyone could do anything. He'd woken in the night to marvel at his good fortune and lain smiling in the darkness for a long time.

After they'd had a quick meal, Tam couldn't bear to wait any longer and stood up. 'Come on, everyone. We'll stack the dishes in the sink and wash them later. I'm dying to go to the farm.'

He turned to the sad-faced lad. 'Will you show us round, Frankie? We're going to be relying on you to help us settle in.'

Which made Frankie stand a little straighter, but the sadness was still lingering in his eyes, Tam could see. Well, that was only natural, wasn't it? No life was without sadness.

They walked down the hill, with Ned holding Jinna's hand and Jinna clutching her umbrella. Tam offered Cara his arm and when he looked sideways, her face was lit up with excitement. Even the weather was on their side, because the sun had come out.

When they purchased their supplies they told Lily that Tam had bought the farm, sure that she'd mention it to everyone from the village who came in from then onwards.

After crossing the road, they stopped at the entrance to

the short track that led into the farm to stare at their new home as if they'd never seen it before.

'It's a pretty building,' Cara said. 'Such a nice balanced shape.'

'Needs doing up a bit, and painting,' Tam said. 'But we can work on that gradually.'

The chickens clucked and ran around their pen as the group passed them, as if wanting to say hello to their new owners.

'They're nearly as good as watchdogs in the daytime,' Frankie said. 'We used to have a dog but it died and Dad was getting sick so he didn't want to train another.'

'We could get one again,' Tam said. 'There are always pups needing homes.'

'You need a special sort of dog on a farm. Ones with a bit of collie in them are good. If you asked around, you'd soon get one from another farm.'

Tam exchanged glances with Cara and they nodded at one another. The idea of having a dog seemed to have brightened up the lad's face a bit.

'Once we've settled in, we'll look into that,' he promised rashly. 'Now, show us round the house, lad.'

The kitchen was a huge room and still bore the marks of the struggle with Boales. Cara eyed it proprietorially. 'I'll soon get this place sorted out.'

'We'll all muck in,' Tam said firmly. 'I'm good with my hands. You wait. You won't recognise the place once I've finished with it. Eh, it's a fine big room, isn't it?'

'Dad always said the house was over two hundred years old, but his family only came here a hundred years ago.'

Only a hundred years! Tam marvelled at the thought of one family living in a place for so long. Then it occurred to him that they might be his ancestors too, since he was a cousin of Peter's. 'We'll have to bring it up to date. You can help me, Frankie. Carry on now and show us the rest of the rooms.'

To the back right, there was a big scullery, where the water from their very own spring had been piped in to a big, old-fashioned tap. Beyond it was a laundry with a big copper boiler. A corridor on the left led to the other end of the back area, and the bedroom where Peter had spent his last days.

On the way they passed the stairs and a huge cupboard, part of which was used for linen, and the rest for miscellaneous crockery and household items.

'I can't believe I'll have all this space,' Cara said softly and tried to wipe tears of sheer happiness from her eyes without being seen.

But Tam laughed gently. 'You obviously cry when you're happy, my lass.'

'Yes. I do.' She turned to the boy. 'Frankie, I can see what a clean house your mother kept. She must be a very good housewife.'

He nodded and swallowed hard.

'Let's go upstairs now,' Tam said. He'd been keeping an eye on Jinna, who hadn't said anything and who was looking round nervously and staying close to Cara.

'We're coming to live here soon, Jinna,' he said to her.

'Remember what I told you this morning,' Cara said and gave the girl one of her quick hugs. 'You'll have a bedroom of your own here.'

This time Jinna didn't wince away. But she didn't say anything, either, and she still looked nervous.

The upstairs took Cara's breath away. 'Four bedrooms,' she murmured. 'Four. Just the right number. It's a palace. Which is yours, Frankie?'

He indicated one at the back, which looked out across the moors.

'May we go in and have a look?'

He seemed faintly surprised to be asked that but nodded.

The room was as tidy as the rest of the house, with the bed made. There was a big wardrobe with carved wooden panels on the doors and a chest of drawers. The window seat looked well used and the lad went across to it as if that was his usual practice.

Jinna was still looking uneasy and Frankie had been told by Cara that it helped to comfort or distract her in new situations. He beckoned to her now. 'Come and look out of the window, Jinna. You can see for a long way.'

She moved across slowly but when she got there, her whole body relaxed. 'Oh! That's lovely. I'll draw it.'

She still spoke rather quietly, but he felt proud to have got her to talk to him.

'Is there another bedroom with a view?' Tam asked.

'The other one at the back.' Frankie led the way to it. There was a wooden bed frame with metal springs, though no mattress or bedding, plus one old wooden chair, a rickety wardrobe and a chest of drawers. The view was very similar to his own.

Tam looked at Cara and at her nod, he said, 'Would you like to sleep in this bedroom when we move here, Jinna? We'll get you a proper mattress and bedcovers, and I'll make a desk for you to use for drawing.'

He stopped talking, realising too much information would confuse her.

'This is Jinna's room,' Ned announced and went to clamber up on the window seat and stare out.

'My room,' the girl said, turning slowly round on the spot, then going across to the window.

Tam would have bet she'd already memorised everything in the room.

'Let's find a bedroom for you now, Ned love.' Cara held out her hand.

He ran back to take his grandma's hand and they went to the front two bedrooms.

The bigger one was obviously meant for the master of the house. Cara beamed at the old-fashioned bed and faded curtains. She'd make it really nice, the sort of bedroom you saw in magazines and dreamed about.

Then Ned tugged her impatiently, so she set aside her own longing to examine every inch of that room and went into his room first.

'Is this for me?' he asked.

'Yes, darling. Your very own room.'

'There's no bed.'

'We'll get proper beds for you and Jinna.'

He went to stand on tiptoe by the window. 'I can see the chickens. Look!' That seemed to please him greatly.

Finally, they went up to the attic. Most attics had lots of old stuff in them and there were a couple of battered-looking trunks here, but there was no collection of old furniture here. Had it all been sold?

Tam went to lift the lids of the trunks. 'Old clothes. Papers. Ah, books! We'll go through them later. We'll have to buy a bed frame for Ned and mattresses for them both. That's the important thing.'

'Can we afford it?' Cara looked at him.

'Yes, definitely.'

She let out a sigh of relief.

Two dormer windows and a skylight let light into the attic but there were no electric lights. Tam went downstairs and there were none there, either. He hadn't realised till now that the house wasn't connected to the electricity service. And when he checked there was no gas in the kitchen either.

'Didn't your parents want gas and electricity?' he asked Frankie.

The lad shrugged. 'They couldn't afford it.'

'Well, I'll have to get them both installed quickly. I'm not having my Cara slaving over an old-fashioned kitchen range and doing the washing the hard way. Wilf will know who to contact.'

'I can manage,' Cara insisted.

'You don't have to. Well, except for the first week or two.'

They exchanged fond glances, then he asked Frankie where the wood was kept.

'We hadn't got any left.'

'Well, I'm thirsty now and if there's no way of making a cup of tea here, we'll have to go home for it. You'll have to tell me who delivers wood and I'll order some.'

He stood for a minute or two longer looking round. 'It's a nice big house, isn't it?'

'It's lovely!' Cara said. 'I never dreamed I could live somewhere like this.' She turned to Jinna. 'Do you like this house, love?'

The girl nodded. 'I like looking out of the window. I like my bedroom.'

Cara turned to the boy. 'Frankie? Will you be all right with us living here?'

The lad shrugged and Tam moved his hand slightly to warn her not to pursue that, then led the way outside. This time he locked the door carefully, because the house now felt as if it truly belonged to him.

'You lot go home. I'll call in to see Wilf and get things started. He always seems to know how to get things done. He's a clever chap, that one. Save me a cup of tea, Cara.'

He parted company with them at the main road and stood watching them walk up the hill till they vanished from sight. His family. A perfect family. All of them needing to be loved. And a house to live in with them. You couldn't ask much more from life.

He had to blow his nose a couple of times to get rid of

the tears of joy that were filling his eyes to overflowing. He hadn't realised how lonely he'd been, had just soldiered on, doing what he had to, scratching a living any way he could.

He'd tell Cara exactly how much money he had in the bank that very night. It'd set her mind at rest about the necessary expenses of settling into Skeggs Hill Farm.

28

Wilf was delighted to help Tam, quickly working out in his head how to get the various jobs done as soon as possible, as well as how best to fit them in with the other jobs he was organising. He could do some of them himself, but not all of them.

He didn't say it, but he thought it. He could see why they called this man Crazy Tam. Look how he was diving head first into modernising the old farm. You couldn't do that for nothing. How would he find the money?

He had to ask that. 'You're sure you can afford this?'

'Yes. I can't do everything I want to but I've got some savings and I can afford to get the basic services put in.'

Tam must have more money tucked away than people realised. How could he have managed that? Wilf wished he had money tucked away. He'd felt trapped for years by the sheer hard work of scraping a living for himself and his family, and it had become an even heavier responsibility since they'd adopted the two kids – though of course he wouldn't be without them, not for a fortune.

Anyway, helping to make the farm into a real home again, instead of a bleak place where every aspect of living was hard work, would be really satisfying, and bring in more money.

No one wanted to be without electric light once they'd experienced how bright it made the evenings. And who wanted to go back to daily chopping and hauling wood when they could turn a switch on the gas cooker and get an instant flame?

Wilf sometimes liked to speculate about where all these inventions would lead. To an easier and more interesting life for ordinary people, he hoped.

He smiled. Recently work had started coming to find him and he hoped, oh, he hoped desperately, that this would continue, because he had a few secret ambitions. A smaller one was perhaps near to being achieved. He wanted a proper modern radio so that he and his family could listen to clear broadcasts of any kind: concerts, talks, news. They listened now, but with a lot of crackling and hissing because like many people round here, he only had a home-made crystal set that he'd cobbled together years ago.

Dare he trust that he'd continue to earn money? Dare he spend some on a real radio? Better wait just a while longer, to be absolutely sure. But with the jobs he was getting now, it wouldn't hurt to look around for a second-hand one. If he found a bargain, he'd snap it up. It'd make such a difference to their evenings to hear the concerts and plays clearly.

His biggest ambition of all was a long way from being achieved: to have his own van, a bigger one than Tam's, so that he could do building work. And by heck, once he did get a vehicle, he wouldn't just use it for work, he'd take his family out on trips at weekends, show them more of Lancashire at least. He didn't hanker to be rich, had never run after money for money's sake, like that greedy Rixom fellow, but he did hunger for a more interesting life.

Enid nudged him. 'Stop daydreaming, Wilf Pollard. You need to come and eat your tea, then have a bit of a rest if you're going to keep watch on Hillam House tonight.'

He surprised her by pulling her towards him and kissing her lovely soft mouth.

'What's that for?'

'Because I wanted to.'

She gave him a shove. 'Get on with you. What will the children think?'

'They're getting used to us being affectionate now.' He grabbed her again as she turned away, plonking a kiss on each of her cheeks and sending her to get tea with a flushed face and a happy expression.

He had to calm down after that, because there might be a night full of trouble ahead. However much you disliked fighting, sometimes you couldn't avoid it. But at least he knew what he was fighting for: home and family. They were more important than anything else.

Wilf waited till the last light had gone out in the houses round the village green before creeping out of his own house the back way. Taking advantage of every patch of shadow, he made his way slowly and carefully round the green to Hillam House. The moon had risen and gave enough light once your eyes were used to the semi-darkness.

There was no sign of anyone else out at this hour until he got to the rear of the house, where he found Stan waiting for him, leaning against the wall in a corner, which was out of sight unless someone came close to the house. He'd chosen this young man because he was noted for being physically strong but with a calm approach to life. Wilf didn't want any hotheads involved if there was going to be trouble. He put one finger to his lips and Stan nodded. Unlocking the back door, Wilf led the way inside and again put one finger to his lips.

Shortly afterwards, another man came round the back to join them. Wilf let him in and shut the door quietly, locking it this time. Donald was older, not noted for saying much but again, a strong chap.

He beckoned to them to come closer, speaking in a very low voice so that they had to lean forward to hear him. 'We'll take it in turns to have a nap, as we planned. You go and keep watch on the front entrance from upstairs, Stan. Donald, you see if you can get some sleep. I'll wake you in a couple of hours, or sooner if any intruders turn up.'

Time passed slowly and the three men used Wilf's watch, and an old one borrowed from Finn, to tell the time and organise their spells of rest.

Just after one o'clock in the morning there was the sound of faint footsteps outside the back. They'd already planned what to do if this happened. Wilf went to the foot of the stairs and made a faint hissing sound. Donald, who had been taking his turn to keep watch above, tiptoed down to join him. They hid in shadowed areas of the big kitchen, where they couldn't be seen from outside but could keep an eye on the windows and door, in case someone tried to force an entry.

If Stan woke and heard them, he was to stay where he was unless they called up to him. The big gong was upstairs, and if necessary he was to fling a window open and bang it good and hard. It'd be heard by anyone close to the village green and the men who knew what was going on would come running to help.

The three of them waited . . . and waited . . . to see what the intruders would do. Whoever was creeping around was moving very slowly indeed. Eventually, he came right up to the windows and peered in, going from one to another, but making no attempt to break in. It wasn't possible to recognise him because he had a scarf round his face.

After a while the fellow went away again and once the faint sound of footsteps had receded, Stan came down to say he'd only been napping lightly and had been woken up by Wilf's hissing, so he'd kept watch upstairs, which was on the same level as the village green.

He'd not heard anything outside but had seen a man run off across the green and another figure join him at the far side. Both had turned down the road towards Rivenshaw.

'I think they came here tonight to check whether anyone was keeping watch or not,' Donald said.

Stan pursed his lips. 'They're planning this very carefully.'

'My guess is they'll be back tomorrow with others to wreck the house.' Wilf hesitated, but it had to be asked. 'Do you think any of the club members could be telling them what we're doing? If we make plans for tomorrow, we don't want anyone betraying us.'

All three stood thinking, then Donald shook his head. 'No. Ellindale folk have allus stuck together, except for them dratted Judsons, and they've left the village now, one way or another.'

'How about the women in the job club?' Wilf wondered aloud, because he didn't know them as well as the men. 'Might they betray it by mistake?'

'No. Them two lasses are all right. I know them and their families. As for the other women in the village, they want the club because it keeps their menfolk happier to have something to do, *and* they get fed a meal here. That means a lot when you're short of food.'

'Then I think we'll get more of the lads here tomorrow night and surprise any unwanted visitors,' Wilf said. 'I'll tell Mr Carlisle about it.'

Tam and his family spent a happy Saturday morning shopping in Rivenshaw for basic essentials while Ginny kept her eyes open for hikers. They'd promised to be back at the hostel by dinner time because Saturday afternoon was the busiest time of the week.

Jinna was getting more used to being with the others and didn't seem as anxious until she saw her former tormenters in a side street, then she shrank back with a little moan.

Tam grabbed her arm as she turned to flee. 'I won't let them hurt you. Stay next to me. You'll be all right.' But he kept hold of her arm.

'I know them,' Frankie said. 'Lazy, they are. I'm here, too, Jinna and I'll help Tam to look after you.'

She hesitated, looking from one to the other, then she stopped trying to run away, but stayed close to them.

To Tam's relief the boys didn't come any closer, though one shouted a rude remark at Jinna, who winced. But a bystander cuffed the lad and told him to mind his manners in public, then the lads ran off, presumably to create more mischief elsewhere.

Tam drove back up the valley with a loaded van: two mattresses, one bed frame, bedding and the sort of food supplies you couldn't get from the village shop.

Cara had to stay in the hostel that afternoon to book people in, but Tam took Frankie down to the house, to set up the furniture in the bedrooms. Cara was still giving him instructions as he prepared to leave.

'I wish I was free to come to the farm as well,' she said wistfully as he moved towards the door.

'You'll be free come Monday, love.' He hesitated, then gave her a quick hug and a kiss on the cheek. She pulled him back to kiss him properly and Ned crowed in delight, put up his arms and shouted, 'Kiss me! Kiss me too.'

They parted with everyone laughing, even Jinna.

★

That night, eight village men made their way after dark to Hillam House. Once inside they tied white handkerchiefs round their upper arms so that they could tell friend from enemy in the moonlit darkness, and found places to wait for the possible attack.

'We'll look right fools if nothing happens,' Donald said.

Wilf scowled. 'I personally will be glad if we don't have to fight.'

Three other men were posted in the back room of the pub, to capture anyone else who might have come up the hill to keep watch from the road like last time. Wilf was taking no chances on anyone involved in the attack on the old house escaping.

'I hope that Rixom sod comes to watch and we catch him,' Micky said. 'He threw my cousin's family out of their house when her husband fell ill and they couldn't pay the rent. If I could just land a few good punches on him, I'd be a happy man.'

'You keep your punches to yourself,' Wilf said, even though he sympathised with Mick.

A little later, a man keeping watch on the green from upstairs, where they'd left the window open at the top, said, 'Shh! What's that?'

There was the sound of a motor, faint and not coming right up to the village. He called down softly to let the people in the kitchen at the rear know something was going on. Cars didn't usually come to Ellindale in the middle of the night, let alone stop on a stretch of road without houses.

Wilf made a scoffing sound. 'Ha! That's their second mistake.'

'What was the first?'

'Planning to attack us at all.'

There was a ripple of low laughter, then silence fell and

everyone waited for the trouble to start, hidden behind cupboards or in the scullery. Because there would be trouble, that seemed clear now.

The same man called from upstairs, 'They're coming across the green now. About half a dozen of them, and they're all carrying something, tools they look like. There are two men still standing near the road, watching.'

The intruders moved round to the back of the house, and there was the sound of someone trying to jemmy the door open. Still Wilf didn't give the signal to take action.

Even when the door crashed inwards, the waiting men did nothing until every intruder seemed to have come inside. By that time a couple of them had gone up the stairs, acting as if they knew their way.

'Now!' Wilf roared suddenly, and the man nearest to the back door slammed it shut and shot the bolt, as had been planned, then stood in front of it.

Defenders slipped out of the pantry and scullery, trapping the intruders who were left in the kitchen.

Upstairs other job club members confronted those who'd gone up there.

As the fighting began, Wilf felt so furiously angry he didn't even feel the blows the intruders landed on him. The attack must have been carefully planned because these fellows were carrying the sort of tools they could use to smash things up: sledge hammers and mallets and crowbars. Only they didn't get much chance to use them.

In the mayhem that followed, the white handkerchiefs worn by the defenders showed clearly who was friend and who was foe.

The fighting was fierce but there were more angry men defending their territory than intruders and only one of the outsiders managed to escape.

*

The three men in the inn had crept out of their hiding place after the group of silent attackers had passed, but they managed to get to the nook on the upper edge of the green where old Simeon often sat without being seen. They stood close together in the shadows waiting, within earshot of the men keeping watch near the road.

When the sound of fighting sounded from Hillam House, one of the watchers said, 'Damn! There must have been someone keeping watch, after all. I ordered you to check that.'

'There was no one there last night. I made damned sure of that.'

When the gong sounded, lights went on in some nearby houses.

A man ran round from the back of the old house, yelling, 'They've caught the others, Mr Rixom. Get away!'

A voice the three village men hiding nearby recognised called out, 'Back to the truck, now! I can't afford to be seen here.' The outsider turned and began running.

At that point the three village men burst out of hiding, all three young and noted for their ability to run fast. One tripped up the man who'd escaped from Hillam House, another tackled Rixom as if it was a game of rugby and the third yelled for help at the top of his voice as he ran further on to grab the driver.

From the house the gong continued to sound loudly and two women raced across from one house to help hold the intruders. Both men and women followed from the other houses, some going to Hillam House.

It didn't take long to subdue all the outsiders, by which time Finn had run down from Heythorpe House to join them.

'Let me go at once!' Rixom ordered. 'I shall sue you for assault. I was doing nothing wrong.'

For answer Mick punched him in the face so hard he went flying backwards. 'That's for my cousin.'

Another man waited for Rixom to stand up again. 'You won't sue anybody because you'll be under arrest.'

'I've done nothing. You can't arrest a man for watching. I was about to call for help.'

Wilf came across the green to join them. 'Someone go and phone the police from the shop. We're doing this properly, sticking to the law.'

'In that case, you'd better tell them to let me go,' Rixom said loudly.

'The man who escaped from our ambush called your name. Why would he do that when he hadn't even got close to you?'

'How should I know?'

'Rixom was one of them and we overheard him saying he'd organised this,' one of the village men said.

'You're sure?' Finn asked, joining in for the first time.

'All three of us overheard him, Mr Carlisle. Sounds carry further than you'd expect them to on a still night like this.' He smiled triumphantly at Rixom and managed to stamp on his hat, which had been knocked off. 'Oops!'

'You're lying! Carlisle, surely you will uphold the law. I've done nothing wrong.'

They all heard Rixom's voice wobble.

'I'm not lying,' the same man said. 'We all heard you.'

It was half an hour before Deemer arrived and then a further two hours till he'd roused the officer in charge of the area and arranged transport of the men into custody. There were far too many to fit in the tiny Rivenshaw lock-up.

When the last vehicle had driven away, Deemer called loudly, 'Well done, lads. You resisted the temptation to take matters into your own hands and left it to the law to punish these villains.'

'Rixom won't agree with you. He managed to get in the way of a fist.'

There was general laughter.

'Just one little accident, only to be expected. Very commendable restraint.'

Once Deemer's car had driven away, Mick grinned and said in a low voice to his friend, 'I got my punch in, though. And oh, dear, I'm afraid someone also damaged his hat.'

'Shh! Don't go round telling people that or you will land in trouble.'

With a shrug and a smile Mick walked home, where he waltzed his surprised wife up and down the hall before yawning and going up to bed.

'That showed him!' he muttered as he fell asleep with a smile lingering on his face.

Finn and Wilf were the last two left and stood talking for a few moments.

'Well done!' Finn said. 'You're a good organiser and men follow you.'

'They're good lads, those.'

'I doubt Rixom will wriggle out of this.'

'He'd grown overconfident, hadn't he?' Wilf said. 'That was his downfall.'

'Indeed he had. I'm sure Mrs Willcox will make a much better councillor representing our village.'

'She'll have a lot on her plate. She's getting married soon, isn't she?'

'Yes, on the same day as Tam and Cara.' Finn yawned. 'If there's nothing else, I'll get home to bed.'

'Not much of the night left now.'

'I'll get a bit of sleep though.'

Wilf watched him walk away. Mr Carlisle's compliment meant a lot to him. The evening had gone well, and somehow he'd known how to organise the men and make sure they behaved properly. Well, all except for that one punch that no one would ever admit to having seen.

He grinned. He'd enjoyed seeing it, too. Rixom was a scoundrel and a cheat.

29

The next few days were busy as the authorities charged all the men and witnesses were called. People in Ellindale talked of little else but what had happened, and the members of the job club re-hashed their triumph many times and joked about 'the great battle'.

Tam wished he had been involved, but Cara said she was glad he hadn't. She didn't want a bridegroom with bruises all over his face.

'We've just got time to move into Skeggs Hill Farm before we get married,' she said.

On the Monday, Tam and his family got up early to pack their final things in the van, then Frankie went ahead to feed the chickens.

They waited impatiently for Cara to feed the last two hikers their breakfast.

'I'm glad they wanted to leave early,' she said as she washed up the final dishes and Jinna dried them.

The van was quite full so Tam decided the two children could walk down to the farm. Cara was a bit nervous about leaving Ned in Jinna's care, but Tam shushed her when she opened her mouth to protest.

'You have to give her the chance to live normally,' he said quietly. 'She understands perfectly well what's going on. We'll send them off first, then pass them on our way, if it makes you feel better.'

'Only a little. She's so vulnerable.'

'Not here in Ellindale, she isn't. It's her home now and people are starting to understand her better.'

At the farm, Frankie came out to join them and they waited for the other two to arrive.

'There,' Tam said when Jinna and Ned came into sight. 'They look like a real brother and sister, don't they?'

He put an arm round Frankie's shoulders and added, 'I hope you'll come to think of them as your brother and sister too.'

Frankie looked at him, then gave a hesitant smile. 'Is that what you really want?'

'Yes. Very much. With you, we've got a perfect family.'

'*Perfect* family?' He sounded surprised.

'Yes. Two people acting as parents and three children looking after one another. Not too big a family, just right, don't you think?'

'I've always been an only one, always wanted brothers and sisters,' Frankie confided.

'Well, now you've got them.'

The lad gave them a broad smile and ran to meet the other two children, waving his arms and saying 'Welcome to your new home!'

Ned at once started jumping up and down, yelling, 'Welcome! Welcome! New home.'

Jinna stood still for a moment, then smiled and said, 'New home.'

Cara realised that for the first time Jinna wasn't clutching her umbrella. Had she forgotten it or had she decided she didn't need its comfort any *more*? It felt like a big step forward, either way.

'Come on, you three!' she called. 'We've a lot to do. It's Easter on Friday and I want us all to go to church together as a family.'

★

The week passed quickly with men going down to Rivenshaw to give statements about what they'd heard on the night of the attack.

Rixom had been let out on bail, but he wasn't going to escape from this scot free, and might even be sent to jail. He'd resigned as a councillor and hadn't been out of his house ever since he was freed.

At Easter, Finn and Beth put on a meal for everyone in the village at the pub, something they'd done before.

Leah agreed to go and was presented there as a candidate to be their next councillor. Beth did that.

Finn had said he could do it, because he knew all the people in the village, but she smiled and said, 'You'll still get horribly nervous, won't you?'

He nodded.

'How did you hide it from everyone for so long?'

'With difficulty and quite a few sleepless nights. I don't feel I need to hide my weaknesses now.'

'We all have them.'

The two weddings from the village were booked for the same day: Thursday 5 April.

Leah and Todd got married in the morning, with the small family ceremony they wanted. But then Charlie tricked them into returning to his house in Birch End and they found themselves facing a large gathering of neighbours and friends from all over the valley.

'I'll pay you back for this one day, Charlie Willcox,' Leah threatened, pretending to be angry.

'You can try, Mrs Selby. Goodness, it's going to take me a while to remember your new married name.'

'Why not stick to Leah?'

So he kissed her cheek. 'I wish you happy, Leah.'

Then people elbowed him aside and told him to stop monopolising the bride and let everyone else kiss her.

Tam and Cara had a much quieter wedding, with just the three children and their one witness from outside the family: Phyllis, who had brought them together in the first place. Frankie was the other witness and the registrar didn't approve of someone so young doing that job, but Tam managed to persuade him that Frankie was a mature and sensible lad. Which he was.

As they left the town hall, Phyllis said she had to get home and Tam gave her a present, an envelope with a ten-shilling note in it.

'I should be giving you something,' she protested.

'You have. You've given us each other. Best gift I ever had.'

When she'd left he said to Cara, 'I know you said you could cook tea, but not on your wedding day. I've asked Lily to put together a meal for us and leave it in the house, something that doesn't need cooking. I'd have taken us out for a meal but I don't think Jinna could have coped with that. And I've got in some bottles of ginger beer to drink everyone's health with.'

It took them a while to get back to the car because Tam had to stop and tell everyone they met that he knew about them getting married.

Cara shook her head fondly. That was her man for you! Sometimes he bounced about like a big rubber ball.

When they at last got near the car, they bumped into Vi from the pawnshop.

'You're all looking very smart.'

Cara nudged Frankie, who grinned at her and mouthed the words as Tam said yet again, 'Me and Cara have just been getting married.'

'Oh, congratulations. The same day as Leah and Todd.

Look, I'll only delay you for a moment, but is Jinna able to do that sketch of my nephews for me yet? I want it for my sister's birthday.'

He turned to his adopted daughter. 'Jinna love, Vi would like you to draw a picture of her nephews and she'll pay you money to do it. Will you do that for her?'

'How many nephews?'

'Two.'

'I'll need a bigger piece of paper.'

'I'll buy you some big pieces to practise on,' Vi offered.

Jinna frowned. 'I don't need to practise. I know how to draw.'

'She gets it right first time,' Tam said proudly.

'That's wonderful.'

'I'll call in at the shop and arrange it next week. For the moment, we want to go home and celebrate.' He tipped his hat in farewell.

The farm seemed to welcome them, and the house felt happier inside than before, Cara decided.

Food was set out on the table: crusty new loaves, ham, a jar of chutney and another of pickled onions. For dessert there were tins of peaches and Carnation milk. And there were three bottles of ginger beer to drink.

Finally, there was a small package wrapped in newspaper.

Tam opened it with a flourish. 'Lily wasn't sure she could get these.'

They looked at the little packets inside the wrapping paper and then looked at him in puzzlement.

'I don't know what they are,' Cara said at last.

'I don't, either,' said Frankie.

Jinna watched them carefully.

'They're a new thing, called potato crisps,' Tam said. 'Fried potatoes, cut very thin. They're delicious.' He opened one packet at the top and took out a little screw of blue paper. 'This is salt, so that you can sprinkle a bit on the crisps.' He did that. 'Not all of it. That's too salty.'

He handed out the packets and they each examined them, then Frankie opened one. Jinna imitated his movements exactly, and Cara helped Ned.

Very carefully all of them sprinkled salt, then the other two children looked at Frankie. He picked out a crisp, sniffed it and said, 'It smells delicious.' Putting it in his mouth, he chewed and swallowed, closely watched by the others. Then he beamed at them. 'It *is* delicious. Try one.'

It seemed very exciting to eat something new and special, setting the seal on the day. When they'd finished, they looked at the food waiting for them on the table.

'It's a real feast!' Cara exclaimed. 'Shouldn't we save some for tomorrow?'

Tam put his arms round her. 'No, love. Today we're celebrating in style because I'm so happy to have married you.'

Tears filled her eyes. 'You say the nicest things, Tam Crawford.'

He looked at the children. Jinna was looking a bit anxious. 'Cara cries like this, just a little bit, see, when she's happy. These are happy tears. See, she's smiling.'

Jinna stared, then looked relieved.

When Tam sat down he poured them all a glass of ginger beer each. Frankie stood up.

'I know what to do now.' He raised his glass and the other children followed suit. 'I'd like to wish you both very happy.' He clinked his glass against Jinna's, then Ned's, hissing at Jinna, 'Say it now!'

She stood beside him and said, 'I wish you very happy, too.'

Ned pushed between them. 'Wish you happy.' Then he looked at Frankie.

'You can drink now.'

It was Tam who was crying for happiness now. 'Oh, Cara love, it's what I said: this is an absolutely *perfect* family.'

Epilogue

The votes were in, and Finn and Sergeant Deemer had taken charge of the counting. They'd foiled an attempt to push a false ballot box in with the others and kept strict control over who was to do the counting.

Now, the good sergeant went up on to the stage and the people waiting in the town hall quietened down and looked at him expectantly.

He started announcing the candidates who'd been elected to the Rivenshaw Town Council in a loud, clear voice. 'These people have been duly elected. Ellindale: Mrs Leah Selby.'

Loud cheers rang out.

'Rivenshaw East: Mr Henry Lloyd.'

The cheers were more subdued.

'Rivenshaw West: Mr Todd Selby.'

Polite clapping and a few cheers.

'Birch End: Charlie, I mean Mr Charles Willcox.'

Very loud cheers and whistles.

When the other two successful candidates had been announced, the mayor stood up and made a short speech, welcoming the new members to his council and promising that they would all serve the valley faithfully and honestly. He repeated the last word very emphatically and there were scattered hurrahs among the audience.

'And the first thing we're going to do, fellow citizens, is clear away the worst slum in the valley. Backshaw Moss must go and we'll need to build new houses there. These will be owned by the council and used for people in need of houses. This will be partly funded by government grants and will provide employment for a good many men.'

The loudest cheers of all rang out at this last piece of news. Work was the thing the people of the valley craved most.

'Look at them,' Charlie whispered to Leah. 'We've given them hope.'

'It's wonderful to see.'

'I knew you were a good woman, but I never thought you'd do this well when I suggested you marry my brother. You made the last years of his life very happy, started the fizzy drinks factory to give some people employment, and now you've got another good, hard-working husband to walk by your side. Who knows what the two of you will achieve?'

She smiled as he blew his nose loudly, because in spite of being a clever businessman, Charlie was a sentimental fellow at heart and it upset him still to talk of the brother who'd died slowly from the effects of being gassed during the Great War.

Todd came to join them, putting an arm round his wife's shoulders and lightening the mood. 'I wonder what the next few years will bring. Some exciting improvements in people's lives, I hope.'

'Most of all, we need work for the people of our valley,' she said. 'And I dare to hope for happiness in our own families.'

The two men nodded at that, and they all stood quietly for a minute or two, wishing hard, because most people shared those same wishes.

Then Charlie blew his nose again and stepped away from them. 'Time for me to go home and leave you newly-weds to bill and coo.'

Leah smiled. 'Bill and coo, indeed.'

Todd put his arm round her. 'I don't mind billing and

cooing, in fact I'm getting quite used to it. We still need a bit of practice, though.'

His words brought a flush to her cheeks and a happy light into her eyes. She said softly, 'I'm very willing to practise it, Todd love. Very willing indeed.'

'Let's collect your sister and go home, then. Jonty will be asleep and once Ginny's gone home, we can practise some more.'

The story of the valley continues in the Birch End series, the first book of which, A Daughter's Journey, *is available now.*

This is a photo of my parents' wedding – taken just after the period in which the book is set – but boy, the women's hats are the same. This is not my favourite era for women's hats! In the front row, we have my Auntie Con, aged fourteen, my father (twenty) and my mother (eighteen). Behind my aunt is my paternal grandmother and behind(between my father and mother is my maternal grandmother. I have no idea where my grandfathers are.

My parents got married very young because of the war, of course, and then my father was sent away when I was about six months old – and I didn't meet him till I was nearly five. So there are no more photos of me with him till much later.

Dive straight into Anna Jacobs' brand new series, set just down the road from Ellindale.

A DAUGHTER'S JOURNEY

Birch End Book 1

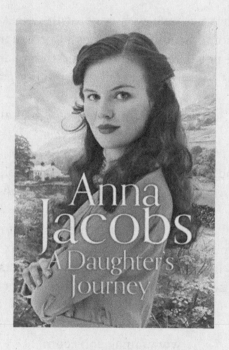

Available now

HODDER & STOUGHTON

CONTACT ANNA

Anna is always delighted to hear from readers and can be contacted via the Internet.

Anna has her own web page, with details of her books, some behind-the-scenes information that is available nowhere else and the first chapters of her books to try out, as well as a picture gallery.

Anna can be contacted by email at
anna@annajacobs.com

You can also find Anna on Facebook at
www.facebook.com/AnnaJacobsBooks

If you'd like to receive an email newsletter about Anna and her books every month or two, you are cordially invited to join her announcements list. Just email her and ask to be added to the list, or follow the link from her web page.

www.annajacobs.com